the coven's secret

COLLEGE OF WITCHCRAFT BOOK ONE

ALICIA RADES

To Megan.

This book features characters with the following medical conditions. The information included is meant to educate readers on disabilities featured within the College of Witchcraft series.

LUPUS

Lupus is an autoimmune disease that affects approximately five million people world-wide. Symptoms may include chronic pain and fatigue, sun sensitivity, and rashes, among other complex symptoms. Lupus affects each patient differently, and symptoms can come and go throughout the course of the disease.

TYPE 1 DIABETES

Type 1 diabetes affects insulin-producing cells in the pancreas. Insulin is the hormone responsible for allowing sugar into the body's cells. Patients require insulin injections to regulate their blood sugar levels. Without treatment, symptoms may include fatigue, blurred vision, and—over time—life-threatening complications such as nerve damage, kidney damage, and eye damage.

DEPRESSION & SUICIDE

Depression is one of the most common mental disorders in America, and affects over 264 million people world-wide. Symptoms may include fatigue, insomnia, and suicidal thoughts or actions. Suicide is the tenth leading cause of death in the United States and affects people across race, age, and gender identity.

ONE

Several Months Earlier

The coven claimed the town cemetery was haunted, which made it the perfect place to sneak into tonight. See, when I was a kid, I lost a bet to my buddy Grant. Loser had to go through with their Evoking Ceremony in the darkest, creepiest place we could find. Nothing beat the abandoned mausoleum on the far side of the cemetery.

"Let's speed it up, losers!" Chloe called from ahead of us. "The witching hour is approaching."

It was the end of November and freezing out. Snow dusted the ground, and the wind bit at my face. Tall trees rose up on either side of us, and the narrow dirt road ahead was so dark that I couldn't see the end of it. Above us, the moon was half full, and the stars didn't do much to illuminate the Connecticut landscape. The darkness didn't bother me, though. I was used to it.

Grant leaned over to me. He wore a thick dark winter coat that matched the color of his eyes. His black hair was gelled to stand on end in a trendy way that seemed like too much work. He looked a lot like his mom and had inherited most of her Latin American features.

Grant spoke in a low whisper. "Lucas, remind me again why we invited her."

I shrugged and glanced ahead at Chloe, who wore a dark jacket over a black dress and thick tights. She carried a black leather bag and walked with a skip in her step. I swore, that girl thrived off the energy of the moon or something.

The truth was, I didn't know why I'd invited Chloe. We weren't dating, and she could be kind of a bitch sometimes. But when she asked to come see what an Evoking Ceremony was like, I couldn't refuse. I'd watched my brother's and Grant's ceremonies, and they'd helped me prepare for tonight. She hadn't had a chance to take part in one yet, so I figured I could at least prepare her for her own.

"We're coming, princess," Grant called up to her.

She tossed her raven hair over her shoulder and stopped in the middle of the path to wait for us. "Get to know me a little more and you won't be calling me princess."

She winked at him, and he shot me a curious glance. The two didn't know each other well. Chloe and I met in high school. She still had a year left, while Grant and I were in our first year at Miriam College of Witchcraft. He'd moved away from Octavia Falls when we were kids after his parents split, and he'd only just moved back for school.

"What am I *supposed* to call you?" Grant asked.

"Wicked," I joked, cutting in.

Chloe cackled for show. "You know it. Now come *on*, Lucas."

She grabbed me by the arm when we reached her and started pulling me down the road. She squeezed so tight I thought I might lose feeling in my hand.

"Where's Eric, by the way?" Grant asked. "Is he meeting us there?"

"Dunno," I said.

I was staying home for the weekend and had checked his room before I left, but it was empty. It wasn't unusual. My older brother didn't sleep well and often went for midnight walks to clear his mind—to quiet the voices in his head. I shouldn't have taken it personally, but I really wanted him here with me tonight. I already knew my parents wouldn't be. Dad didn't care, and Mom was dealing with enough already.

"Forget Eric," Chloe said, clearly not reading my fallen expression. "We're here."

Where the thick forest ended, a towering iron gate began. On the other side stretched an endless graveyard, with headstones large and small reaching up toward the night sky.

"You're up," Chloe said, clapping Grant on the back.

Grant stepped forward and wrapped his hands around the lock that secured the gate shut. He'd gone through with his Evoking Ceremony last month and was the only one of us three who had magic. He was an Alchemist—and had the cauldron mark on the back of his arm to prove it.

Grant muttered an incantation under his breath. *"We seek to step upon this grass. Unlock this gate and let us pass."*

A green glow lit up his hands. Tendrils of magic swirled out of his palms and twisted around the gate. Then came a soft *click*, and the gate swung open.

Grant smiled proudly and stepped inside the cemetery, holding the gate open for Chloe and me. "Easy peasy."

Chloe snorted. "I don't know why they even bother locking this place up."

I shrugged. "To deter people, I guess?"

"Well, nothing's going to deter us," Chloe stated confidently.

"Come on." I cocked my head in the direction of the mausoleum. "It's this way."

They followed me through an endless maze of gravestones, until we reached a line of trees. We left the graveyard and stepped into an overgrown forest. Prickly berry brush, fallen logs, and sharp rocks lined the forest floor, but I walked right over them and continued on my way.

"Are you sure this is the right spot, Lucas?" Grant struggled through the brush as it caught on his clothes.

"For sure," I replied. "It's just up here."

Just as I said it, the mausoleum came into view. The bricks were covered in moss and had weathered over time, and the roof had long ago caved in. The building had to be as old as our town itself.

Apparently, the bodies had been removed and buried elsewhere, but rumors said some of the skeletons remained. According to legend, certain spirits wanted their bodies to stay in the mausoleum, so they hounded a group of Seers until they gave in and moved their corpses back to their proper resting place. The rumors had never been confirmed, of course, but Grant said he hoped to see a skeleton tonight. I told him he wouldn't be able to handle it, considering he'd screamed when he saw the plastic hand we'd put in the punch bowl at Halloween.

Chloe looked amazed. After a few moments, she picked her jaw up off the ground and said, "Well, what are we waiting for?"

She rushed ahead. I stepped over broken bricks and shattered beer bottles to follow her. It was kind of creepy inside, with a small bit of moonlight illuminating the shadows. The room wasn't very big, barely the size of my bedroom. Most of the grave markers had been smashed, leaving behind large holes in the walls that could fit a casket. Others were intact. I wondered about those, but I wasn't curious enough to investigate. The ground was flat concrete, but it was covered in dirt, dust, and broken bits of building.

Chloe kicked rocks and other debris aside, making room for the ceremony. She set her bag down and pulled out five candles—one to represent each of the five Casts within our coven. Tonight, our goddess, Mother Miriam, would awaken my magical powers and assign me to one of the Casts. I was pretty sure I'd get Mentalist like my parents—the Cast known for their telepathic and telekinetic abilities—but it was hard to say. We all thought Eric would be a Mentalist, and he'd been gifted the powers of a Seer.

Chloe placed the candles in a wide circle, then pointed to the center. "Lie down, loser."

Grant frowned at her choice of words, but I didn't care. Like I'd told him before, it was Chloe's term of endearment.

I sat on the cold ground, propping my elbows on my knees. "Well, Grant. Take it away."

"Okay, if you're ready." Grant plopped himself cross-legged in front of me on the other side of the candles.

Chloe used a lighter to light each of the five candles, then found a seat on a huge rock, watching intently. The light cast flickering shadows across the walls of the mausoleum. My heart started to pound heavily in my chest, but I didn't let it show.

"We're not to the witching hour yet, so allow me to say a few words before we begin." Grant snapped his fingers, and a small leather-bound book materialized out of nowhere. He opened it to the first page.

"Aw, man," I complained. "Do you have to?"

Knowing Grant, it was something stupid, like a collection of roasts to rile me up before the ceremony.

"Yes, I have to," he deadpanned. He cleared his throat before he began reading. "Evoking Ceremony... what is it?"

Chloe groaned. "We know all this."

Grant frowned up at her. "Humor me, would ya?"

Chloe didn't say another word as Grant returned his attention to the book.

"As I was saying…" He made a show of reading the passage like it was a scary story. *"On the eve of a witch or warlock's nineteenth birthday, at the witching hour, they become eligible to contact Mother Miriam through a sacred ritual called the Evoking Ceremony. This ritual can be performed only once, and only on the night of eligibility."*

He broke character to add, "So don't screw it up, okay?"

"I'm not going to screw it up," I huffed.

Grant turned back to the book and continued. *"Through this ceremony, the witch or warlock will be tested by Mother Miriam. If she judges you a fit for the coven, your powers will be awakened, and you will bear the mark of one of the five Casts within the Miriamic Coven. Should you fail Mother Miriam's test, you shall be banished from the coven for all eternity."*

His voice fell dramatically at the last three words.

I raised an eyebrow. "All eternity?"

Grant shrugged. "That's what it says here."

I rolled my eyes, but inside, I was quivering. I didn't know what would happen during the ceremony or how Mother Miriam would test me, since the trials were different for everyone. But I knew one thing. I couldn't be banished from the coven. This was my home. These were my people.

Grant continued reading. *"The ceremony requires at least one witch or warlock who has already undergone their Evoking Ceremony. Place five candles in a circle"*—he gestured to the candles we'd already set up—*"and repeat the following incantation."*

He paused for a moment, and Chloe eagerly asked, "What's the incantation?"

"That's for me to know and you to find out," Grant said. "Lucas, you're going to need to lie on your back. Says so here."

"Okay." I did as I was told and stretched out across the cold floor. My gaze turned up through the gaping hole in the roof—if you could call it a roof anymore, since there was almost nothing of it left. I stared at the stars, trying to force my pulse to slow. I shouldn't be afraid of what was to come, so why was my body freaking out?

Grant checked his phone. "We have one minute until midnight. Are you ready, Lucas?"

I took a deep breath. "Ready as I'll ever be."

"Good," Grant said. "Let us know if there's anything we can do to help you feel more comfortable."

"Conjure a space heater?" I joked.

Grant nudged my foot with his. "Shut up and relax, smartass."

I gave him a salute, and he chuckled.

He stared down at his phone a few seconds longer. It felt like an eternity. Finally, he took a breath and set his phone aside. "The witching hour is upon us. We can begin."

I heard Chloe shift on her rock, but she stayed silent, which was actually kind of shocking. The girl never shut her mouth.

Grant began to mutter the spell beneath his breath. *"The clock has struck the witching hour. It's time to wake this warlock's power. We call our goddess down to earth. To bear witness to this new rebirth. A series of tests he shall partake. And join the coven before day breaks."*

My body began to rise from the concrete as Grant repeated the incantation. I knew this would happen, as I'd seen it in ceremonies before, but the sensation was stranger than I imagined. I felt as if I could fall at any moment, but I tried to push the fear from my mind. I trusted Mother Miriam and the rituals she'd put in place for the coven. She wouldn't have us do this if it could hurt us. So I closed my eyes and relaxed.

Grant's voice continued as he repeated the incantation over and over again. The words started to fade together as I let the magical feeling of floating in mid-air overtake me. Warmth entered my bones, which was weird because of how cold it was outside. A little warmth was all I needed to know that this was working, that I could take whatever Mother Miriam threw at me. I belonged in the coven, and no trial was going to change that.

Suddenly, the sensation of falling jolted throughout my body. My eyes shot open as my body slammed into the ground, knocking the wind out of me. I sprang upright to a sitting position, my heart pounding against the walls of my chest. Shit. Something had gone wrong.

As my pulse slowed, I glanced around. It was so dark that all I saw were shadows. For a second, I forgot where I was. It took me a moment to make sense of my surroundings. The crumbled bricks of the abandoned mausoleum were scattered all around me, and the candles Chloe had set up were still there, but they'd been blown out. My friends were nowhere to be seen.

Concern whipped through me. I reached into my jacket pocket to pull out my phone to use as a light, but it wasn't there. I checked the other pocket, then my pants, but it was gone.

Fucking Chloe. I should've known she'd pull some stunt like this. I was fuming.

I got to my feet and called out into the forest. "Really, guys?"

There was no reply, except for the sound of the wind whistling through a hole in the wall. A chill traveled down my spine, and my breath turned to ice in the air.

"It's not funny!" I shouted. "This isn't the time for some stupid prank."

All that met me was silence—until I heard the sound of a stick breaking in the distance. I stepped out of the mausoleum and started making my way through the brush toward the noise. Thick fog blanketed the forest floor, so much that I could barely see the underbrush beneath my feet. The moon was all I had to light my way.

"Grant?" I yelled into the trees. I couldn't believe he'd agreed to go along with this!

By now, he was probably crouched somewhere with his hand over his mouth, trying not to give his location away. Any second now, he'd burst into laughter he couldn't hold back.

Except the laughter never came.

I slowed my step and listened closely. It was eerily silent—so much that the hair on the back of my neck stood. That was never a good sign.

"Guys, you need to come out right now!" I demanded sternly. I wasn't screwing around. This whole thing was starting to freak me out.

I opened my mouth to shout again, but before I could get anything out, a groan met my ears. It was a pained groan that sent my stomach plummeting to my toes—the kind you couldn't fake. I immediately started racing in the direction it came from as worry slammed into me. The groan came again, louder this time. I only ran faster, dodging around thick tree trunks and jumping over thick brush.

And then I saw him. A figure lay on the ground in the fog, curled up in the fetal position and shivering.

I came to an immediate halt, but I couldn't make out what was happening in the darkness. I took a cautious step forward, my heart racing. "Grant?"

If this was all an elaborate plan of Chloe's, I was going to curse the bitch the second I got my magic.

The figure let out another pained cry, and I nearly shit myself. The voice was familiar, but it wasn't Grant's. All the blood drained from my face—though it felt as if it was being sucked out of my entire body. My knees went weak, and my hands shook at my sides.

"Eric?" I stepped closer, until I could make out his features in the shadows.

Eric lay in the middle of the forest next to a thick oak tree, clutching his stomach. A dark substance coated his hands—

Holy shit! It was blood! And it was everywhere. It was so thick that it dripped out of his hands and soaked into the forest floor. It looked like he was trying to hold his guts inside himself.

I dropped to my brother's side in an instant. "Eric! What are you doing here!?"

Eric's face had paled until it was entirely void of color. A thick sheen of sweat coated his skin—even though it was ice cold out and all he wore was a t-shirt and jeans. Beside him lay a black cloth bag with its contents spilled out all over the forest floor. All I could process was a few potions vials, a deck of tarot cards, and a bloody dagger.

The dagger caught my attention, but only briefly. It didn't cross my mind whether the person who'd done this was still lurking around. I was less concerned about finding out what had happened to him and more concerned about getting him somewhere safe. I didn't know how much time we had before he'd lost too much blood. Eric gave an involuntary shudder.

I quickly stripped my jacket off and tossed it over him. "Tell me how bad it is. Eric! Eric!"

He opened his mouth, but nothing came out. Forcing my quivering hands to steady, I cupped his face in my hands and slapped him a little to get his attention.

"Eric, look at me," I demanded, staring him dead in the eye. "We have to get help."

I grasped at the first thought that came to mind. Headmistress Verla's house was right on the edge of the cemetery. She was an Alchemist, one of the best in all the coven. At the very least, she'd be able to whip up something for the pain and stop the bleeding before the paramedics arrived.

I glanced in the direction of her house, though I couldn't see it from here. I quickly calculated how long it might take me to run there, get help, and come back. I didn't know if we had time for that. If Eric was going to make it, I had to get him to Headmistress Verla's the quickest way possible.

I rolled my jacket up until it resembled a long, thick rope.

"Eric, I'm going to need you to let me look at this," I said, tugging his hands away from the wound.

I expected him to protest, but he didn't. He must've been in too much shock. His hands fell away from his stomach, and blood poured faster out of the wound. I placed my rolled-up jacket over the wound and shoved the end between his back and the ground, wrapping it around his body. Then I twisted the two ends together and secured them tightly, creating a makeshift bandage to help slow the bleeding.

"Okay, Eric," I said, resituating myself. "I'm going to need you to—"

Eric looked at me with a blank expression, then his eyes rolled back into his skull.

Shit. Shit. Shit! We didn't have long.

I gave it everything I had. Taking one of Eric's limp arms, I wrapped it over my shoulder, then hoisted his body up onto my back. He was heavy, but it didn't matter. I'd carry him until he crushed me if I had to.

I knew I might regret this later—I was pretty sure it was the exact *opposite* of what they told you to do in emergencies like this—but it was the only option that made sense to me.

A small groan escaped my brother's lips as I began to carry him through the forest toward the gate at the front of the cemetery. The sound should've made me want to vomit, but it gave me hope. My brother was still alive. I could still save him.

We broke out of the trees to the wide expanse of the graveyard lawn. I almost stumbled over the nearest gravestone when I spotted a dark cloaked figure staring our way. Was it a reaper, here to take my brother's soul to the afterlife? No, that was silly. If it was, I wouldn't be able to see them.

When the dark figure began making their way toward us, I got the strangest feeling that they were not to be feared—that they were there to help. Was it perhaps the cemetery groundskeeper?

The figure reached me, then spoke before I could. "Lucas Taylor."

I didn't know why, but I was surprised to hear a woman's voice come from under the dark hood. Her voice was so melodic that it sounded like a song.

"Yes," I said quickly. "My brother. He's hurt. Can you help?"

The woman nodded once, then brushed her hand through the air. I felt the weight of my brother's body vanish. I whirled around, expecting him to be floating there behind me—I figured this witch was a Mentalist with telekinetic magic—but what I faced was entirely different.

Eric's features had been stamped into the fog like he was a ghost. Just as I caught a glimpse of ghost-Eric, his image washed away, like a cloud in the wind. Anger and fear coursed through me all at once. I spun on the woman in a flash, my nostrils flaring.

"What did you do!?" I cried. "What happened to my brother?"

"Relax, Lucas," she said kindly, like my harsh tone didn't bother her at all. "Your brother is fine for now."

For now? I wanted to ask, but she didn't give me the chance.

"You've impressed me," she said softly.

"I… what?" I asked. The anger had melted from my tone, replaced by confusion. What the hell was going on here?

She reached up to her hood. "It's me, child."

Her velvet hood fell to her shoulders, revealing her face. I'd never seen anyone so beautiful before. Her features were perfectly symmetrical, and her pale skin was so smooth that it looked airbrushed. She had dark eyelashes and red lips, though she wore no makeup. Her dark brown hair fell in loose waves around her shoulders.

My knees buckled beneath me, and I fell to the ground. I hadn't meant to do it, but I was so shocked I couldn't stop myself. I leaned forward to bow, because it seemed like the proper thing to do in the sight of a goddess.

"Mother Miriam," I said breathlessly, my eyes pointed toward the ground. "It's an honor."

"Lucas, my child." She bent to one knee. "There is no need to bow to me."

"But you're—you're…" I looked up to see she was smiling down at me. It was a truly loving gaze—the gaze of a mother. It was stupid of me to think I could argue with her. She reached out and helped me to my feet.

I straightened. "Is this real? Or is it part of my test?"

"It is in your mind," she said.

I sighed in relief. Eric wasn't in any danger. He'd only been an illusion.

"What happens now?" I asked our goddess. "What's my next test?"

She shook her head and smiled. "You only needed one, Lucas."

"Only one?" I asked breathlessly. Most people went through at least three or more.

"Walk with me," Mother Miriam said, offering her hand.

When I took it, the fog around the graveyard dissipated, and a warmth spread over me. The cool wind completely died down, and it felt like a warm spring night.

"In this test, there were many different choices you could've made," Mother Miriam explained. "Among the coven's Casts, the Mentalist would've made Eric comfortable and gone to find help. The Alchemist would've looked through the potions to see if there were any that could help. The Seer would've reached for the cards first—though most would never use them in such a dire situation, but whether they use them or not is not the important part."

"And Mortana?" I asked, looking over to her. *The Death Cast.*

"Most Mortana would've considered the dagger as a means to a merciful death," she said. "But you, my child, took a route most would not. You carried your brother's burden on your back. It's clear where you belong, Lucas."

"Where?" I asked, not understanding what she was saying. There was only one other Cast she hadn't mentioned—one that had died out years ago. But I didn't see how my choices would put me there. Could I be the first Curse Breaker of my generation?

"Where do you *want* to be put?" she asked.

I contemplated the question. No one had ever told me Mother Miriam offered a choice. I'd never really thought about it before. I always figured it didn't matter; I'd accept whatever gift she gave me, because I knew she'd choose the right one for me.

"I will do whatever you ask of me," I told her honestly.

I barely noticed that we had returned to the trees near the site of the mausoleum. I was too entranced by being in the presence of a goddess. This was a once in a lifetime opportunity. I couldn't take my eyes off her.

"*Anything* I ask, Lucas?" she asked.

I nodded. I couldn't think of anything she could ask that I wouldn't do. Her teachings were simple. *Protect the coven.* I'd do anything to protect the ones I loved.

"Anything," I confirmed confidently.

Mother Miriam led me up the rocks to the entrance of the mausoleum. Nothing had changed since I left.

She stopped and guided me around to stand in front of her. "I'm so glad you feel that way, Lucas. I know you'll make me proud."

When she said that, it felt like I was floating in the air again. My parents never said they were proud of me—not even Mom, though I knew she loved me. This was our goddess, the very deity we worshiped, and she thought *I* could make her proud.

"I'll do my best," I promised her. "Which Cast will I be placed in?"

"Shh..." She held an index finger to her lips. "You will find out soon enough. Have faith, my child, for I am always with you."

She shoved me hard in the chest, and my heart leapt up to my throat. The chill air returned, whipping by me as I tumbled backward. My body slammed hard against the concrete, sending an ache shooting through my body. My skull throbbed from where it impacted with the ground.

"Lucas! Lucas!" I heard Grant's voice, but it sounded like it was coming from a mile away.

Chloe's voice came a second later. "Here, let me try."

A small, cold hand slapped against the side of my face. My cheek stung as I shot upright. Grant was so close that we nearly knocked heads. He quickly jumped out of the way.

"Holy shit!" I cried, cradling my cheek. My friends were inside the burning candle circle now. "That was one helluva swing, Chloe."

She smiled proudly. "Told you I could wake him."

"Fuck," I groaned. "What happened?"

"You were floating there, and then your body just slammed to the ground," Grant said, sounding worried.

"That's normal, dipshit," I said, shoving him. "It signals the end of the ceremony. You didn't need to get the Wicked Witch of the West here to make me lose feeling in my face."

I made a show of moving the muscles in my face to test them out. Chloe didn't look concerned at all. She just beamed at the Wicked Witch comment, like she wore it as a badge of honor.

"So, which Cast were you assigned to?" she asked eagerly.

"I don't know," I admitted, turning my hands over for any sign of a mark. "Mother Miriam didn't say."

"What was it like meeting her?" Chloe asked. "Was she as beautiful as they say?"

"Slow down," Grant insisted. "Let's figure out which Cast he's in first."

I stripped off my jacket and tossed it aside, looking up and down my arms. The mark would appear as a tattoo, as if I'd just come fresh from the tattoo shop. I checked the back of my bicep, where Grant's mark was, but there was nothing there. It could be anywhere.

Chloe nudged me. "Take your shirt off."

I sighed and stood, then tugged my shirt over my head. I hoped I didn't have to strip down all the way to find the mark. It was cold as shit out, and I sure as hell wasn't giving Chloe a strip tease. She'd enjoy it a little too much.

"There it is!" she cried, pointing to my lower back. Her hand slapped over her mouth, and she stifled a giggle.

"What?" I asked, turning to try to get a good look. "What's wrong? Why are you laughing?"

"You have a tramp stamp!" Chloe cried, reeling back in uncontrollable laughter.

"Aw, fuck," I muttered. "I'm never going to live that down, am I?"

Even Grant had joined in on the laughter. "No, bro. You're not."

"Would you just tell me what it is?" I demanded. I hated being the last to know. "I can't see it."

"It's a skull," Grant said. "Here, let me get a picture."

He lifted his phone and took a flash photo of my backside.

"Let me see," I begged, and he handed the phone over.

I half expected him to be lying to me, but Grant sucked at lying. It was there clear as day, a skull mark tattooed along my spine just above my waistline.

"Mortana," I said breathlessly. I was a Death Warlock.

I backed up and steadied myself against the rock Chloe had been sitting on earlier. Being Mortana wasn't inherently a bad thing, but their magic was definitely seen as darker. Death magic was the touchiest of all. When it went wrong, it went *wrong*. Like, shit hits the fan wrong. Mortana were the kind of witches and warlocks who could reanimate the dead, kill with the touch of their hand, or see how people were going to die. I even knew one who could read the auras of a room and tell if a death had occurred there—and how bad it'd been.

The mark only told me my Cast, not which type of magic I'd inherited within that Cast. It could be days or weeks before I knew my specialty.

"You okay, bro?" Grant asked, rising to his feet and stopping beside me. He held out my shirt and jacket.

"Yeah," I said, shaking off the sinking feeling in my gut. I put my clothes back on, contemplating what this meant.

I didn't want to be the kind of guy who had magic everyone feared. But I'd been telling the truth when I told Mother Miriam I'd take whichever Cast she assigned me. Whatever my gift was, it was important to her.

I straightened. "I'm fine. It'll be great. Maybe I'm a necromancer. I'll raise an army of cat skeletons."

"That'd be badass," Chloe said.

I barely heard her as another voice cut through the silence. It came as if he was standing next to me, just beside Grant.

"I made a mistake. I don't want to die."

Every muscle in my body froze as my brother's voice invaded my mind. It took me a second to realize he wasn't here—that he hadn't just shown up out of the blue and spoken those soul-chilling words for all of us to hear. My friends stared back with a blank expression. They hadn't heard him.

It hit me so hard and fast that I suddenly became nauseous.

No! No, no, no... please don't let this be what I think it is.

I took off running before I could explain. I tore through the forest to the cemetery, then hurdled over gravestones as I sprinted toward the front gates. Chloe and Grant called from behind me, but I could barely process the sound of my own name.

Please, Mother Miriam, let this be a hallucination or something.

My feet carried me as fast as they could blocks away. My lungs were starting to burn by the time I reached home. I ran up the front steps so fast that I skipped several on my way. The door slammed into the wall when I flung it open. I pounded upstairs to my brother's bedroom. Commotion came from my parents' room as they were awakened by my loud entrance.

I skidded to a halt in the darkness of my brother's doorway. My heart race, and it only quickened when I saw that his bed was still empty.

"Lucas, what in the bloody hell is—?" my father started, but I didn't have time for questions.

I whirled around in the hall and shoved him out of the way. On any normal day, I wouldn't get close enough for him to touch me, but right now, I wasn't scared of him. I was terrified for my brother.

"Where's Eric?" I asked Mom, who had stumbled out of their bedroom behind my father, looking only half awake.

"He's not in his room?" she asked.

"No," I barked. "Something's wrong."

Eric should've been back by now. He didn't stay at school—since his professor of Seer Studies suggested it was best if he took the semester off —so he didn't have anywhere else to go.

I checked my bedroom, then ran back downstairs to check the kitchen, living room, and bathroom. Each room was as empty as the last. My parents followed behind me, trying to get an answer out of me, but I couldn't bring myself to tell them, not until I knew for sure what it meant.

I reached the door to the garage and flung it open. And that was when I knew...

I hadn't imagined a damn thing. Those words I'd heard in the mausoleum were real—and they were meant for me.

I stopped dead in my tracks as my blood ran cold. Every inch of my body shook as I took in the sight before me. Dad stumbled in the doorway, catching himself on the door frame.

"My boy!" he cried, his voice wavering in genuine agony. I'd never heard him use that tone before.

"What's going—?" Mom started, but I quickly cut her off.

"Don't look!" I spun around as she came closer. I threw my arms out and cradled her face to my chest. She didn't resist.

While I held my mother and let her tears soak into my jacket, my father rushed into the garage, like he could save Eric. But I already knew he couldn't. I couldn't explain it, but I could *feel* the void in the room. It wasn't just the gaping hole opening in my chest, either. It was a supernatural force telling me Eric's life was over. It was part of the gift I knew now with certainty I had.

Only one member of the coven inherited this power per generation. Mother Miriam chose me to carry the burden of the dead—to take their last thoughts to the other side with me when I died, where I'd become a reaper for the coven. I suddenly realized what a huge mistake I'd made promising her anything. I was now the Reaper's Apprentice.

And the first thought I'd carry was my brother's. It was the last thing that went through his head before he killed himself.

Mother Miriam thought I would make her proud.

She was wrong.

nadine

TWO

Two weeks ago, a darkness took over my life. Grammy promised things would get better as time went on, but so far they'd only gotten worse. My bedroom didn't even feel like my own. The walls were bare, and the sheets removed from the bed. All that was left were a few of my most prized possessions.

I ran my hand over the cover of the Agatha Christie novel Mom and Dad had given me for my birthday last year. The cover was already worn, and the corners tattered. I sat on my bed and opened the cover.

To Nadine, who always loved a good mystery. - Mom and Dad

A lump rose to my throat, but I forced it down. My parents liked to write me letters, but looking at their handwriting was a terrible reminder of what had happened. I quickly flipped the page. A small piece of paper fell out of the pages and fluttered to the ground. I leaned down to pick it up.

A ticket. I'd forgotten I used it as a bookmark the last time I read the book. It'd come from my ticket book that was filled with discounts to mysterious New England attractions. This particular ticket had been used when Mom and I drove five hours to Baltimore to visit the *Ripley's Believe It or Not!* Museum.

I placed the ticket back inside the pages and added the book to my last box on top of my *Clue* board game. The edges of the box were tattered and worn from the years Dad and I spent playing it every Sunday night.

I moved slowly, deliberately, because I wasn't ready to leave yet. Leaving only meant I had to admit I was never coming back. I couldn't move much faster anyway—not with the way my joints ached. I hadn't felt this awful in years.

I reached for a photograph propped up on my nightstand. It showed me and my best friends, Carly and Jessica, on the deck of a riverboat, each wearing a Sherlock Holmes hat. It'd been the night of the murder mystery riverboat tour we took last summer.

Tears pricked at my eyes as I thought of my friends. I'd already said goodbye to them at the funeral, because I couldn't stand to see anyone right now. I'd never forget our last fun night together, because it was the night I got the call—the one telling me my parents had died.

My life with Carly and Jessica was over. They were headed off to college together, and I knew the weekend sleepovers and Friday night bowling excursions had to end sometime.

I was *supposed* to be headed to the police academy. My goal had been to work the homicide division one day, but those dreams had been crushed when I'd been rejected from the academy last-minute. They told me there'd been an error in processing my paperwork, but I knew the truth. They didn't want me because of my *condition*. They were afraid I was more of a liability than I was worth.

Screw them.

After everything that happened—getting the letter from the police academy, only to lose my parents in a car accident days later—moving in with Grammy was my last option.

She'd made a pretty compelling argument when she invited me to come live with her. Mainly, offering to pay my college tuition—even though I was still undecided on my major. I didn't exactly have the money to live on my own right now, so I couldn't really refuse. I didn't *want* to live alone, either. Besides, I loved Grammy. Living with her would be great.

I just had one last thing to add to the boxes. My stomach twisted as I reached for the small wooden box on my nightstand. I hadn't had the guts to open it yet. If I did—if I looked at what was inside—all I'd think about was how my parents were gone. And though I knew what had happened was real, I couldn't face it yet. I couldn't truly say goodbye.

I shoved the wooden box deep within the packing box, covering it up with a few things inside so I wouldn't get tempted to open it. I couldn't deal with that right now.

A light knock came at my door, and Grammy stepped inside. Her footsteps seemed louder than they should in the empty room. Grammy was in her sixties, with short white hair, age lines, and the kindest smile I'd ever known. Like every day, she wore a long floral skirt that fell to the floor. She'd come to stay with me while we worked out the funeral arrangements and listing the house.

"Are you ready, Nadine?" she asked gently.

I closed my eyes and took a deep breath. It took me a moment to compose myself, but I finally lifted my head and nodded. "Yeah, Grammy. I think I'm ready to go."

I stood with my box and followed Grammy down the hall. The house didn't feel right, now that all the pictures had been removed as we prepared to sell. It didn't even smell right, as the scent of lemon cleanser masked the usual smell of baked goods and clean linens. Everything just felt… empty. Which was how I felt without my parents.

Sometimes, I forgot they were gone. I swore I could hear my dad working in the garage or smell my mom cooking in the kitchen. And then it all came crashing down on me again. I was glad I was moving in with Grammy. It was the fresh start I needed.

I loaded my last box in the front seat of my car. The back seat was packed to the brim, as was Grammy's vehicle. There was just so much I didn't want to leave behind.

"If you're not ready, Nadine, we don't have to leave yet," Grammy offered.

I took one last look at the white two-story house I grew up in. I knew this day would come eventually, but I didn't think it'd come like this. I couldn't keep dragging this out. "Let's go."

Grammy drove in front of me as I followed behind her in my car, where the music was on full-blast to drown out my thoughts. The drive wasn't long, only about an hour and a half, but it seemed longer.

I could tell we were getting close because the road narrowed and became more twisted as we drove through the foothills of the Appalachian Mountains. Tall trees rose on either side of the road, and the forest was bright green with summer foliage.

The road took another twist to the left, and I got my first view of the town in the valley below as we crested the hill. It was bigger than I expected, considering Grammy had always talked about the small, tight-knit community she came from. I was excited to see it was large enough to have at least a mall and a movie theatre.

The road twisted to the right, and the town disappeared from view as we dipped back into the trees. The forest seemed to close in on us, but in a comforting, warm-hug kind of way. We reached the base of the valley, and the trees slowly parted. A huge black sign read *Welcome to Octavia Falls*. Below that were various smaller signs advertising attractions like corn mazes, hayrides, and ghost tours.

Count me in on the ghost tours.

I took a deep breath as I slowed the car to match the speed limit. Tall maples and oaks lined the streets. My jaw dropped as we passed by beautiful homes. Each one was bigger than the last, and they all had a unique gothic charm to them. My favorite house had dark red siding with black trim and a tall turret. I turned the music off so I could take it all in.

I passed over a narrow bridge, and the beautiful houses gave way to four-story buildings. The lower levels were all small businesses, selling things like maple syrup and honey, as well as a cute coffee shop and a candy store.

The further we drove, the more crowded the streets became. It wasn't until the buildings parted and I spotted an expansive parking lot that I saw why. The lot was filled with canopies and people milling from one booth to the next like a farmer's market. I spotted vendors selling herbs, candles, and crystals—along with a booth advertising palm readings. The middle of the lot had been set up with a stage, where a woman sang a haunting melody and a group danced around her in a slow, beautiful display.

I barely caught a glimpse of it all before it was out of sight. We drove past more businesses, and I tried to get a feel for what was here in case I wanted to go shopping later, but it all passed by quickly. I noticed a few clothing stores, whose display outfits totally looked my style—dark top, skinny jeans, and my signature leather jacket. We passed by an apothecary and a metaphysical store before we came upon the industrial portion of Octavia Falls.

This part of town had every kind of drink manufacturer you could imagine—breweries, wineries, distilleries, and a cider mill. Grammy had told me about the orchards around here, and I was eager to check them out sometime.

I understood now why Grammy called this a small town. Despite the population in the tens of thousands, it had that quaint small-town charm to it.

I'd slowed to a crawl to take in the beauty of Octavia Falls, and I nearly missed Grammy take a turn ahead of me. Snapping back to attention, I picked up speed and followed behind her.

I expected the architecture to change as we moved into a new neighborhood, but it didn't. Every house looked like it should be hosting a Halloween party or something. I absolutely loved it.

Grammy slowed at the end of a street near a cluster of trees and a sign that read *Octavia Falls Park*. She pulled into the driveaway of the last house.

My eyes went wide. For eighteen years, we'd lived an hour and a half from my grandmother, and I'd never visited her. If someone had told me this was where she lived, I would've begged to visit sooner. Her house was huge, with pale yellow siding and white trim. A large porch wrapped around the front of the house, and a rounded turret reached three stories high. It already felt like it was calling me home.

I parked behind Grammy and opened my car door. My muscles ached from sitting so long, and my joints protested as I forced myself to step out of the car.

"Grammy!" I scolded as she made her way over to me. I still couldn't take my eyes off the house. "You didn't tell me you lived in a castle."

She chuckled. "Don't be silly, Nadine. It's just a house."

"A mansion," I corrected her. "When do I get the grand tour?"

"Now, if you'd like," she offered. "We can move your stuff in later."

I swung my purse over my shoulder and grabbed the box on the front seat. It was filled with odds and ends and pretty light.

"Here, let me take that," Grammy said quickly, stealing it from my hands.

I wanted to take it back and tell her I had it handled, but she turned quickly before I could. I knew what Grammy was doing. She was *coddling* me, because she knew how easily I got fatigued.

I didn't like being coddled. I could manage on my own.

I followed behind Grammy. My gaze traveled over the elaborate woodwork on the porch railing and the beautiful carvings in the front door. I seriously couldn't believe Grammy lived here. I'd kind of always wondered if Grammy was keeping a secret, since she'd come visit us on birthdays and holidays but we never came here. Plus, what was with a woman of her age having a cauldron tattooed on the inside of her wrist? Mom had the same one on her ankle. It kind of made me wonder if Grammy was part of a cult and that's why Mom never wanted to come back or something.

My imagination was getting away on me.

Grammy led me inside to a wide hallway. A sleek black cat ran down the stairs, then rubbed itself up against Grammy's leg, purring.

"This is Cornelius," Grammy introduced. "He's very friendly."

"Well hello, Cornelius," I said, bending to scratch him behind the ears. "You're just the prettiest kitty, aren't you?"

Cornelius tilted his head into my hand, showing his affection. I petted him a while longer, then stood to take in the rest of the house. To the right was a large living room with a beautiful brick fireplace and a welcoming, homey feel. On my left was a dining room with a display cabinet that stretched across the far wall. Inside sat endless vials of colored liquid. I had no idea what they were, but they shimmered beautifully in the light.

Grammy led me into a large kitchen. Back home, Mom was always in the kitchen, brewing up some sort of concoction that usually turned out better than the last. I knew she got the skills from Grammy, because my grandma couldn't come over for a holiday without a feast packed in her car—and it was always the *best* food. Her brisket was to die for.

Her kitchen just proved what kind of a cook she was. It was clean, but obviously used. Pans hung from a rack above the kitchen island, along with herbs that'd been tied upside down to dry. Her stove looked like it belonged in a restaurant, since it had six burners instead of the usual four. Plus, she had two of those built-in ovens on the wall, one on top of the other, and the fridge was big enough for a family of fifteen.

"Holy crap, Grammy," I said, trying to take it all in. "How many people do you feed?"

She waved her hand, like it was nothing. "Oh, I run a cooking business out of the home."

What the heck? Why didn't I know that? I was starting to sense there was a lot I didn't know about her.

"If you think this is impressive, you should see my garden." Grammy gestured to the back window, and I took a step closer to get a good look. Her yard stretched far back to a line of trees and over to the edge of the park. Almost half of the lawn was covered in a well-cared for garden. I recognized some of the plants, like lavender and sage, but others were more obscure. One of the bushes had big yellow flowers that looked like they were growing tentacles, and another had purple fruits that reminded me of radishes.

"You take care of all that yourself?" I asked.

She shrugged. "It keeps me busy. Do you want to see your room?"

"Yeah, of course."

Grammy pointed me down another hall and into the guest room. The walls were pale yellow like the outside of the house, and she'd made the bed with a light blue comforter. It was *so* not my style, but I was just glad to be here with her.

I stepped into the room, and my eyes caught a photograph of my mom on the nightstand. My heart sank. It looked like an old school photo, and reminded me a little of myself. Mom and I shared the same chocolate eyes, dark brown hair, and full lips. My guts twisted just thinking about her.

And how she was gone, along with my dad.

"I know you won't be here much, with college starting up soon," Grammy said, pulling me from my thoughts. She set my box on the bed. "But I want you to feel at home. Feel free to move things around."

I turned to her, picking at my nails. "Thanks, Grammy. About college, though. It's already the end of August. Isn't it a little late to enroll?"

I really didn't want to take the semester off. I was afraid if I did I'd fall into a deep, dark hole I couldn't pull myself out of. I needed something to distract me from my parents' death.

Grammy placed a gentle hand on mine. "It's all taken care of, Nadine."

I swallowed the lump in my throat, relaxing a bit.

The doorbell rang, stealing Grammy's attention. "Why don't you get settled in a little, then we'll talk about it? We have a lot to discuss."

I nodded, and the doorbell rang again.

"I have to get that," Grammy said. "Let me know if you need anything."

"I will," I said, then Grammy hurried off to answer the door.

I set my purse down, then sank onto the bed. I didn't lie down, because I knew that if I did I'd fall asleep for hours, and it was too late in the day for a nap. I started picking through my box instead. The first thing I pulled out was my yoga mat, which was rolled up on top. I hadn't used it in weeks, which was probably why my joints were so achy lately. That and the stress.

I closed my eyes and clutched the silver star necklace around my neck. My parents had given it to me when I was fifteen, on the day of my lupus diagnosis. When I started getting down on myself, I used it as a reminder of how far I'd come from that day. I was a completely different person from the "problem child" I used to be.

There was a saying we had in the lupus community. "I have lupus, but lupus doesn't have me." My mantra was more along the lines of, "Lupus can kiss my ass."

I repeated the phrase in my head until I started to relax. I told myself I'd get the yoga mat out before bed. Doing yoga before bed helped with the stiffness in the morning.

That was one of the drawbacks of having an autoimmune disease. My own freaking body couldn't help but attack its own healthy tissues. It was like my body couldn't help but destroy itself in every way it could for no good reason. Lupus liked to torture every patient differently, and my own brand of shit meant that I got joint pain every time I got a little stressed or spent too much time in the sun.

Check mark on the stress lately.

I sighed and pulled my journal from the box, then stood to place it on the dresser. As I crossed the room, movement outside caught my eye.

I stepped closer to the window and pushed aside the thin curtains. I became alert when I spotted a guy in a dark grey zip-up hoodie bent over Grammy's garden. His hood was up, concealing his features, but I could tell he was around my age, with long legs and broad shoulders. Every muscle in my body froze as I watched him, sensing he was nothing but trouble. What the hell was he doing out there?

He stood, and I noticed a collection of green leaves in his hands. When it hit me, a wave of heat washed over me, and my hands turned to fists. He was stealing from Grammy!

I quickly reached for the window and flung it open. "Hey, jackass!" I shouted across the lawn.

He turned and started walking toward the park.

"Hey!" I yelled again, louder this time. He just kept on walking, ignoring me.

Excuse me!? No one stole from my grandmother and got away with it!

I quickly turned from the window and ran out of the room, hurrying toward the back door in the kitchen. Grammy was still at the front of the house, talking to whomever was at the door, but I didn't hear what they were saying.

By the time I got outside, the guy was almost to the trees. The sky had darkened as storm clouds rolled in for the night.

"Stop!" I called to him. "What do you think you're doing?"

I knew I should've turned back and just let it go. I mean, it was only a couple of leaves, right? But I was curious to a fault and wasn't the kind of girl who avoided confrontation. I'd set anyone straight if they needed an ass whooping.

Besides, this was Grammy's livelihood. You couldn't just walk into someone's yard and compromise the health of their crop.

My breath grew hot, and my chest started to burn as I ran across the lawn. Screw the pain. This asshole wasn't going to get away with this.

I hurried into the trees behind him, but once I stepped inside the forest, it was like he'd vanished. I glanced around, looking for any sign of movement, but the forest was still. All I heard was the rustle of wind through the trees and the distant sound of an owl.

It was the time of day between sunset and nightfall, which left the forest cast in a dull light. The air felt chilly, and goosebumps broke out across my arms. It was class-A spooky-movie creepy. Most girls would turn around and run back home, but I wasn't most girls.

I continued forward, staying on high alert. My pulse thumped loudly in my ears, as if warning me to turn back—which only made me want to push on.

The narrow dirt pathway took me deep into the forest and past a steep ravine. And then I heard it—the sound of sticks breaking in the distance, like a pair of footsteps traveling off the path. The crunch of leaves came then, picking up in pace and intensity. I quickly realized I was listening to more than one set of footsteps.

I threw myself behind a thick tree as the footsteps came closer. One guy I could deal with. A whole group of them? Probably not.

I peeked around the tree to see four girls walking my way. They all looked my age, but they seemed anything but the kind of girls who would be walking in the woods after sunset. The vibe they gave off suggested they frequented the mall more than the outdoors.

The first girl was gorgeous, with sleek black hair and rich red lips. She wore a skin-tight black dress and low-cut boots with a heel to them. In her hands, she held what looked like a mini witch's cauldron the size of a softball. She had this look her face that said *get out of my way, bitch*, even though she faced nothing but trees. She was definitely the leader of the pack.

To her right walked a girl with porcelain skin, ruby red lips, and long white curls. Her legs went on for miles. The girl on her left had full lips and stick-straight dark hair cut just above her shoulders. It shimmered a deep red and had clearly been done at the salon.

The three of them looked like they could be Instagram models. They were enviously beautiful, with perfect hair and thin bodies. I was pretty sure if I got close enough, I'd see that their nails were done to perfection, too.

"Amy, get up here," the first girl snapped.

The final girl hurried forward. She looked the most down-to-earth of all of them. She was pretty, but in a different way than the Instagram-model chicks. She had jet-black hair and almond-shaped eyes, but she dressed more casually in jeans and a burgundy top.

"Sorry, Chloe," she said quickly, not meeting the main bitch's eyes. "I was just—"

"Shut up and grab the toad," Chloe snapped. "It's right there, or are you too blind to see it?"

Amy's eyes went wide for a second at Chloe's insult, but she quickly followed her instructions and bent to catch a toad I couldn't see from here.

It was clear Amy didn't fit in with these girls. She seemed timid around them, while they held up their noses at her. I wanted to cut in and rescue her, but I was too curious to break things up now. What the heck was going on? Was this some kind of hazing ritual, where they made the sorority pledge eat a live toad or something?

Amy caught the toad, and Chloe held out her mini cauldron. She nodded toward it impatiently. "Well…?"

Amy hesitated. "We really shouldn't be doing this."

Chloe rolled her eyes. "It's harmless. It'll wear off in twenty-four hours."

I furrowed my brow. What would wear off?

Amy bit her lower lip. "Yeah, but it's complicated. What if something goes wrong?"

"Will it?" Chloe asked, making it sound like a threat—like if something went wrong, Amy would be the one to blame. "Remember what we're doing here for you, Amy. You do this for us, and we'll help you find your cat."

The way she said it suggested Chloe knew *exactly* what happened to Amy's cat.

Amy looked torn. She glanced to the cauldron but held the toad close to her chest, like she was protecting it.

I watched curiously. What exactly was it they were asking her to do?

"It's not like we're going to hurt Mandy," the blonde girl said, though I didn't sense honesty in her tone.

"Gwen's right," the third girl added. "We just want to teach Mandy a lesson."

Amy swallowed hard. "What… what did she do to you?"

Yeah, I'd like to know that, too. It was like I was watching a drama TV show. I couldn't tear my gaze away.

Chloe pursed her lips, looking angry at the mention of this Mandy chick. "She's dating Ryan. This is her one and only warning."

"I thought you and Ryan broke up," Amy said.

Chloe took a swift step forward so she was up in Amy's face within an instant. Amy breathed heavily, like she was a little scared, but she held Chloe's gaze.

"You're not here to ask questions, Amy," Chloe snarled. "You're here to do the spell. I have eight months until my ceremony, so until I get my powers, you're going to help me. Now *finish it.*"

Hold up. Did she just say *spell*?

Amy took a step back and straightened a little. "No. I won't help you do this to her."

Chloe's featured hardened by the second. "You wouldn't want Mittens to… meet an untimely end."

"That's not her name," Amy mumbled, but Chloe ignored her.

"Besides, it's not like we're turning Mandy into a toad *forever*," Chloe said. "It's not permanent."

Turn someone into a toad? Was she serious?

Amy's jaw clenched. "You're a real bitch, you know that?"

Chloe tilted her head and sighed. "You say that like it's supposed to hurt my feelings."

Amy rolled her eyes. "Fine. I'll do it. But just know that I'm not here to be your on-call Alchemist."

Huh? Spells? Alchemy? Maybe I wasn't so far off with that cult idea. That, or these bitches were straight-up bat-shit crazy.

Amy gently placed the toad in the cauldron, then took it from Chloe's hands. She started mumbling words under her breath that I couldn't hear. I didn't know what to think at first, until I saw a dark blue light swirl out of Amy's hands, lighting up the cauldron. The tendrils of light swirled around it like some CGI shit, until they reached the open top and sank into the contents inside.

My eyes widened as I stumbled back from my tree. What in the living hell did I just see? A trick of the light? A hallucination? Swirling light didn't just come out of people's hands like that!

The girls hadn't noticed me, but I knew it was time to hightail it out of there regardless. What kind of crazy ass shit was going on here?

I ran away so fast that I lost track of the trail. I glanced behind myself to see if they were following, but they weren't. When I turned back around, my heart shot up into my throat as I stumbled over a rock. My body flew forward, and I went tumbling head over heels down the side of the ravine.

"Whoa!" I cried as I tried to catch myself, but my momentum didn't slow until I hit the bottom.

I lay on the ground, aching from the bruises I'd accumulated on the way down. The trees swayed in the wind above me, but I didn't move right away. I was half cursing myself for not watching where I was going and half just waiting for the initial shock to pass.

Finally, I pushed myself to my elbows—only to find a tall shadow standing over me, holding out a hand. He came as a beacon of safety. I didn't know what possessed me to take the stranger's hand, but I found myself reaching up to him. He pulled me to my feet, and I finally got a glance at his face.

Time seemed to slow when I looked into his mesmerizing green eyes. The sounds in the forest disappeared, and it felt like the world was spinning around me. For just the briefest of moments, my heart seemed like it was floating in my chest. It was a welcome change to the heavy weight I'd been carrying around lately.

It was *him*, the guy in the gray hoodie who'd been stealing from my grandmother's garden. He was hella attractive, with dark hair and cupid's bow lips, but his eyes were hooded in a darkness that both terrified and intrigued me.

I took a breath, and the world became normal again as time once again sped up. The weight on my chest returned, and the whistling of the wind became audible again.

I cleared my throat. "Um, thanks."

Above us, the sound of hurried footsteps rustled the leaves on the ground. He brought his index finger to his lips, signaling for me to be quiet.

"Follow me," he whispered. His voice was smooth, like a beautiful song.

Since he was still holding my hand, he kind of dragged me behind him. We ducked behind a large boulder that was big enough to conceal us both. We crouched low, our bodies almost touching. My hand tingled from where he held it. I could feel the heat coming off him in waves, and my heart pounded so hard I could feel it.

"What is it, Chloe?" I heard one of the girls ask—the one with the short brown hair.

The footsteps stopped at the top of the ravine. "Shut up, Camille," Chloe snapped. "I'm trying to listen."

"Listen to what?" Gwen asked.

"Didn't you hear it?" Chloe growled. "Someone's out here."

"Well, whoever it was is gone now," Camille said.

Chloe huffed. "I swear to our goddess, if Mandy is following us, I'll—"

"She wouldn't do that," Amy cut in.

"Whatever," Chloe said dramatically. "We got what we came out here for. Let's go."

Their footsteps faded as they distanced themselves from us. I didn't move until I could no longer hear them—and even then, I remained put for nearly a minute longer.

Finally, I relaxed, as did the stranger beside me. It wasn't until he helped me to my feet that I finally let go of his hand.

I crossed my arms and faced him. "Care to explain to me what's going on?"

He eyed me curiously, and I felt a blush rise to my cheeks. "What do you want to know?"

"Who were those girls? And why were you stealing from my grandma's garden?" I pursed my lips, waiting for his answer.

"You're Helena Tucker's granddaughter?" he asked, sounding a bit surprised.

"Yeah, I am. So tell me why you were stealing from us."

He crossed his arms and leaned his backside up against the boulder. "I wasn't *stealing*. Your grandma said I could take some leaves from her matus shrub whenever I wanted."

"Matus shrub?" I asked skeptically. I'd never heard of such a thing.

"You chew on the leaves to help relieve anxiety," he explained. "Anyway, will you be staying long?"

I hesitated, reluctant to give him too much personal information. "As long as I have to."

He pushed himself off the rock, then started for the edge of the ravine. I followed and climbed behind him.

"In that case, you'll want to steer clear of the Lucky Three," he said.

"What's the Lucky Three?" I asked.

He reached the top and held out a hand again. I almost didn't take it, because he seemed to be acting a little *too* helpful, but the ravine was super steep, and I didn't want to embarrass myself by falling down it again. He helped me onto level ground and quickly found the trail. We fell into step side by side as darkness began to envelop the forest.

He shoved his hands into his pockets, and I noticed a pair of earbuds hanging out of one. That must've been why he hadn't heard me earlier. "The Lucky Three are those girls you just had the pleasure of meeting."

"Seriously?" I asked. "Their gang has a name?"

He shrugged. "It was a nickname they got in high school that stuck. They always got lucky when it came to the popular vote. You know, student council, prom court, that kind of thing."

They got lucky, or they cheated. Something told me they were the kind of girls who'd stuff the ballot box.

"Are they, like, in some sort of cult or something?" I asked him.

He chuckled lightly and looked a little surprised. "A cult? What makes you say that?"

"They used some pretty cult-ish sounding words," I explained. "They were talking about spells and alchemy. And Main Bitch talked about *our goddess*."

He sputtered, like he was choking on air. "*Main Bitch*. I'm going to have to remember that one. It's a pretty accurate description of Chloe."

I smiled proudly.

We reached the edge of the trees. Grammy's house stood in front of us with the lights inside illuminating the garden.

"Anyway," he said, turning to me. "You should probably ask your grandma about the rest of it."

Way to stiff me on the details. I couldn't just leave my curiosity unchecked.

"Well, you're a big help," I said sarcastically.

He shrugged. "What can I say? It's a blessing."

I rolled my eyes at him. Fine. If he thought I should talk to Grammy, that's exactly what I'd do. I started across the lawn toward the house. "See you around."

"Wait," he called.

I stopped in my tracks and turned to him. I was once again taken off guard by the enchantment in his eyes. I didn't get it. I mean, yeah, he was a total hottie. But like, he was just *standing* there. What made *him* so special?

It was a rhetorical question, but a little voice inside my head told me I was going to find out eventually.

"What's your name?" he asked curiously.

I placed a hand on my hip. "Yours first."

"Lucas," he told me without hesitation. I half expected him to play back and demand mine first. *He's no fun.*

"I'm Nadine," I said.

An emotion I couldn't quite read crossed his eyes when I told him my name. I almost thought it was surprise, but there was a sense of familiarity there, too. I must've been reading him wrong, because it didn't make any sense.

"Anyway…" I broke the silence and gestured to my grandma's house. "I've gotta go. It was nice meeting you."

He nodded. "Yeah, you too. Stay safe, Nadine."

I laughed. "No promises."

I wasn't really the *stay safe* kind of girl. I was the *run into danger* kind. Life was more fun that way.

When I got back inside, I found Grammy standing at the kitchen window, looking out over the back lawn. Cornelius sat in her arms, purring. She raised a curious eyebrow that made me want to crawl into a hole.

"I see you've met Lucas Taylor," she said lightly, obviously teasing me.

I shrugged. "I guess."

"And…?" she pressed.

"And what?" I asked innocently. "He was fine."

"He's a nice boy," Grammy said. "Just be careful."

"Careful how?" I sensed there was more she wanted to say.

She shrugged, like she didn't have a real answer.

If she was trying to drive me away from him, she was doing it wrong. I liked a little mystery.

She sighed. "You look really tired. Why don't you turn in for the night and we'll move in everything in the morning?"

She was right. I was absolutely exhausted and wanted to crawl into bed and sleep for three days. But at the same time, I had questions that needed answering.

"Didn't you have something you wanted to talk to me about?" I asked. "Besides, I'm curious about a few things, and Lucas told me to talk to you."

Grammy waved her hand. "It can wait."

"But Grammy—"

"I'm not taking no for an answer, Nadine. You need to take care of yourself."

I really didn't need a babysitter, but Grammy was a little overprotective. Even though I tried to protest, she insisted I needed my rest.

I crawled into bed that night with a hundred burning questions on my mind. One thing, however, was very clear. There was something weird going on in this town.

And I intended to figure out what.

THREE

Her name was a warm light within my cold, dark world. *Nadine.* Of all the thoughts I'd collected over these past few months, there was one that stuck out. *Stay safe, Nadine. I love you.* There was more to it than that, but that was the part that hit me the strongest.

I didn't know who had died and why they mattered to her, but somehow I instinctively knew—there was no other Nadine. This was the girl who someone had dedicated their dying thought to.

And that was something special. There was this glow to Nadine that I bet she couldn't see. It was in the way she walked and the way she held herself. It was how she had this sarcastic, playful thing going on that I half wanted to be a part of. I had a hard time letting that side of me out.

I thought about her all night and into morning. I admit, I didn't have to cut through the park for what I had to do today, but I did anyway—if just for a chance to catch a glimpse of her. I watched her grandmother's house as I passed by, hoping I'd see her, but at the same time praying I wouldn't.

It wasn't until I was almost to the trees that I heard the sound of the back door slamming and her voice carrying over the lawn. My heart lifted, despite every warning bell going off that told me to leave this girl alone. She'd only get hurt getting involved with a guy like me. I couldn't taint the light within her with my own darkness. Besides, she was a curious soul—that, I could already tell. And there were things she would want to know that I could never tell her. It was best if I kept my distance, but apparently I'd decided that too late, because she was already crossing the lawn toward me.

"Lucas!" she called.

I put on my stone-cold expression so she couldn't read me. It was easier to keep my secrets that way. "Nad."

I didn't know why I called her that. Half her name slipped out, and the other half just didn't. She didn't seem to notice or care.

Nadine's eyes lit up when I turned to her, but the sparkle quickly faded as she took me in. "Wake up on the wrong side of the bed this morning?"

"No," I said. I hadn't even woken up in a bed, but I didn't tell her that. I'd been crashing at Grant's dad's place over the summer and sleeping on their couch, since the dorms were closed and I didn't want to live at home. I couldn't wait for school to start back up and be back in my old dorm room.

"Then I guess you won't mind if I tag along," she said brightly, swinging her arms and bouncing on her toes like she had no care in the world.

"Um, I kind of do." Or so I claimed. I wasn't exactly stopping her when I started down the path and continued on my way. Of course, she followed, which I was starting to sense was a Nadine thing.

Yesterday, I thought she'd come after me because she knew who I was —because she wanted to use me for my gift. It wasn't unusual. People came to me all the time to ask what their loved ones' last thoughts were. They tended to be brutal—regrets, secrets, and mixed emotions—but I liked to make shit up and tell people what they wanted to hear. It gave me less to deal with that way.

Nadine wasn't like that, though.

"Did you talk to your grandma?" I asked.

She waved her hand. "Nah, she blew me off last night and is still sleeping."

Nadine looked wide awake, like she'd been up for hours. She was the kind of girl who had a natural beauty and didn't have to wear a ton of makeup to impress a guy—the total opposite of Chloe. It only made her that much more appealing. She had big curls in her hair that seemed light and bouncy. I wanted to run my fingers through them to see how soft they were.

Okay, I was officially a creep.

"Anyway, I saw you and thought..." she started, before she trailed off.

"You thought?" I asked.

She shrugged. "I thought maybe we could hang out."

Girls and guys didn't just *hang out*. Not in my experience, anyway. Why would Nadine want to hang out with *me*?

I raised an eyebrow. "By *hang out*, you mean I can tell you things your grandma didn't."

She sighed dramatically. "Oh, come on! The suspense is killing me."

It was clear she didn't know about the coven, which her grandmother should've told her by now. Big mistake. But Nadine wasn't going to take no for an answer.

So what do I do? The stupidest thing I can think of, because apparently I'm an idiot.

"How about I show you?"

Nadine's face lit up, and for a brief moment, I felt like I'd made the right choice.

"What's in the bag?" she asked, gesturing to the backpack I was carrying.

I smirked. "You'll have to wait and see."

She squirmed. I was kind of enjoying how easy she was to toy with.

I led Nadine to the other side of the park. We stopped in front of an old house with paint so worn I could hardly tell what color it had originally been.

Nadine had been surprisingly quiet the last few minutes, but she looked skeptical as she stared up at the run-down house. "Is this where you take all your girls on the first date?"

I snorted—and immediately wanted to turn invisible. "Is this a date?"

She ignored the question and said, "You're not denying bringing other girls here."

A foreign feeling tugged at the corner of my lips, and I decided to play along as I started up the walkway. "Maybe I do. Does that scare you?"

Nadine hurried ahead and took the porch steps two at a time, until she was standing right in front of me, our bodies nearly touching.

"*Nothing* scares me, you hear?" She hesitated, then quickly added, "Even though this reeks of a kidnap scenario."

She narrowed her eyes at me, as if trying to judge whether I was going to tie her up in the cellar or not.

"Okay, then." I gestured to the door. "Ladies first."

I figured this could go one of two ways. One, she was fascinated by what she saw inside, or two, she'd be so freaked out she never asked to hang out with me again. Option two was probably best, because we could *not* be friends. She'd only get hurt.

I had enough on my plate already. It's why I was here. Professor Warren suggested I try to find some good in my gift. Okay, *suggested* wasn't the right word. He was pushing me—and pushing me hard. He said if I didn't find the good in my gift, things would just get harder from here on out. The sooner I found the light, the better. I feared I'd eventually cave to the pressure, and I was terrified of that. I wasn't ready to give up, not like Eric had. So I had to find some way to deal.

To do that, I was paying a visit to the recently deceased. I didn't know the guy; I'd only heard of him. Everyone in town called him Old Man Keller, and I knew he was a Mentalist with telekinetic powers. I never thought much of him until I heard his thoughts come to me. Since then, I'd heard rumors he hadn't moved on. He just blatantly refused to go with the reaper who'd come for him. Which meant he had some unfinished business. Maybe my gift was enough to help him resolve it and move on.

The door was unlocked, which I was a little disappointed about. I bet my magic would've impressed Nadine. It wasn't unusual to leave doors unlocked around here, though.

We stepped inside. If there ever was a haunted house, this was it. Even though it was early morning, it was dark inside. The curtains were all closed, and the whole place was in disarray, since someone had been moving things around to get the house ready to sell. A thin layer of dust covered everything, and the floorboards creaked under our weight. I swore the temperature dropped a few degrees, too. I wasn't a Seer, but I could feel the shift in energy as we entered the house. He was already here.

Nadine glanced around, peeking into the bathroom and then up the stairs.

"In here," I said quietly, like I might frighten the ghost.

Nadine followed me into the living room, and I plopped down right on the hardwood floor, even though there was a sofa nearby. The energy seemed stronger in here than it had in the entrance.

Nadine sat across from me. "What are we doing?"

I unzipped my bag and pulled out a Ouija board. It folded in half, which was the only way I managed to fit it into my bag. It was dangerous to use, since I could summon a demon by accident, but the chances were slim. I knew the ghost would be here, which meant he'd connect to the board before any demon could get his hands on it.

Nadine's eyes widened when she saw the board, but it wasn't like she was afraid. It was more like she was excited.

"You really know how to woo the ladies," she joked.

"Is that what I'm doing?" I asked. "Wooing you?"

Nadine smirked, but simply said, "You know I don't believe in Ouija boards, right?"

A smile tugged at the corner of my lips. "We'll see about that when we're done here."

I placed the board between us, then set the planchette on top. Nadine looked skeptical, but she placed her fingers next to mine anyway.

"Who are we contacting?" she asked.

"Everyone calls him Old Man Keller," I explained, pretending like she believed me. "I don't know a lot about him, other than I saw him walking the Black Circle every now and then."

"The Black Circle?" She made it sound like a biker gang or something.

I sighed. "Seriously, you need to talk to your grandma about this town the minute you get home. Anyway, the Black Circle is the trail that circles town. It's fifteen miles long, and Old Man Keller walked parts of it every day with his cat."

Nadine's eyebrows shot up. "His cat? Don't people normally walk dogs?"

"Pretty much everyone in Octavia Falls has a cat," I said. "Anyway, what I heard was that he was on the Black Circle Trail when he tripped and hit his head on a rock. No one found him until it was too late."

Nadine furrowed her brow. "And what happened to the cat?"

Good Goddess, was she serious? I just told her a man died, and she was wondering what happened to his *cat*?

"I don't know," I admitted. "Probably given to the family."

"Okay." She seemed satisfied with the answer. "Let's get started, then."

I took a deep breath, then called out to the dark room. "Old Man Keller? My name is Lucas Taylor. I'm here to talk to you about why you're here. I'm hoping I can help. Are you here with us now?"

The planchette began to move across the board. I could feel the spiritual energy pushing it and knew it was Old Man Keller's ghost, but Nadine looked shocked.

"You're doing that," she accused.

I just shook my head and focused on the board. The planchette stopped over the word *yes*.

Relaxing a little, I asked, "Do you remember how you died?"

The planchette wiggled a little, but it didn't move off the word *yes*.

"How can I help you?" I asked.

The planchette began to move again, stopping on the letter F, then moving on to the letter I. Nadine read the letters out loud until they started to form a sentence. I gritted my teeth as it began to spell out the word *find*.

Not this again.

For some reason, Old Man Keller held on to his last thought, and that's why he couldn't move on. If only he could say something—anything —else. But that's how ghosts were. They were confused and had a hard time communicating. Even a Seer couldn't help us now, not if he couldn't get anything out besides this nonsense.

That's all it was, really. Nonsense.

Find the crystal cave. Whatever that meant. It was the last thought I'd heard from him and exactly what he was spelling out now.

Nadine noticed my fallen face. "What do you think it means?"

It was almost like she kind of believed Old Man Keller was communicating with us. But I could still see the skepticism in her eyes.

I shook my head. "I don't know. Ghosts don't often make sense."

"Mm…" Nadine thought for a moment, then asked, "Are you confused about your death?"

The planchette moved again and stopped over the word *no*.

I furrowed my brow. "He's probably confused about that, too."

"Maybe it's a name," Nadine suggested.

"A name?"

"Yeah, like a woman. Crystal Cave."

"Then why say *the* crystal cave," I pointed out. "If it were a woman, he'd say *Find Crystal Cave.*"

Heat flared throughout my veins. I thought I could help him, but there was nothing I could do if I didn't understand his message. I wasn't a freaking interpreter. This whole thing had been a bust.

I snatched up the planchette and folded the board, then shoved both of them back in my bag.

"What's wrong?" Nadine asked.

Clearly, she thought we were just goofing off. But this was serious to me. My gift was fucking useless.

"Lucas," Nadine pressed as I got to my feet and started for the door. She stood but didn't move to join me.

I stopped and pressed my fingers to my eyes, then turned to her. "Look, Nad. I'm sorry I brought you here."

There I went again, calling her by half her name.

"We should just go—" I started.

Nadine cut me off with a terrified scream. I whirled around to where she was looking, only to come face to face with a ghostly figure. I couldn't make out his face. All I saw was a dark fuzzy outline of a body, like the shadowed imprint of a soul. The temperature in the room plummeted as he took shape.

"Find... the... crystal... cave..." His shaky voice filled the room.

I rushed over to Nadine, who was frozen in shock. She couldn't take her eyes off him.

I took her by the shoulders and shook her a little. "Calm down, Nadine. Ghosts can sense your fear. It might set him off."

"It's a... a..." She couldn't get the words out.

"Nad, look at me!" I demanded.

She did, but it was already too late. Old Man Keller let out a hauntingly high-pitched scream, then charged. I threw myself in front of Nadine, but his spirit swept straight through me like I was nothing but air. It chilled me to the bone, and I could feel the buzz of my magic wane as he stole a portion of my energy.

I whirled around just in time to see the ghost's figure slam into Nadine's chest. His hands solidified, and he shoved her. She went stumbling back. I tried to reach her, but I didn't have time. Her head slammed into the edge of the coffee table, knocking her out.

"Nad!" I cried.

I was at her side in an instant, cradling her head in my lap. Her whole body was limp in my arms. My chest twisted into knots.

"Nadine!" I slapped her face a little, until she moaned, but her eyes didn't open.

I quickly glanced around for signs of Old Man Keller, but he must've used all his energy up, because he was nowhere to be seen.

"I'm so sorry, Nad," I said, even though she probably couldn't hear me. "I didn't mean for you to get hurt."

I cradled Nadine in my arms and carried her out of the house, back through the park towards her grandmother's. The whole time, I couldn't stop staring down at her, thinking about how this was all my fault—because I'd gone searching for the good in my gift.

Right now, I hated being the Reaper's Apprentice more than ever.

nadine

FOUR

Lucas's scent surrounded me. He smelled like spiced apple and pumpkin, and I felt a warmth and comfort in the scent. Someone moaned, and it took me a second to realize it was me. I tried to open my eyes, but they felt heavy.

"It's okay," Lucas said. "We're almost back."

Where? Everything that happened this morning came rushing back. Did I seriously just get attacked by a *ghost*?

"What happened?" a stern voice demanded. I thought it was Grammy, but I was still so out of it I could hardly tell.

"Haunted house," Lucas said coolly, like it was an everyday thing. "She hit her head."

"Set her right here," Grammy instructed. "I'll get some ice."

I felt my body being placed on a soft surface. My head pounded like a bass drum. Grammy placed an ice pack under my head, then I felt her part my lips and pour something down my throat. "Drink up, Nadine."

I barely processed the words. I didn't know what the liquid was, but it tasted sweet, so I drank it.

"What is that?" Lucas asked.

"A potion to cure the concussion," Grammy told him.

I was barely in my right mind, but did I just hear *potion*?

That was the last thing I heard before I slipped off into a dark oblivion.

Whatever Grammy had given me must've knocked me out for hours, because I woke up that afternoon in my own bed. I didn't know how I'd gotten there, but it just confirmed that everything that happened had been some wild, vivid dream—

Until I heard the sound of Lucas's voice coming from the kitchen. I touched the back of my head, where it was still tender. How could that be? What had *really* happened?

I wanted to jump out of bed and demand answers, but my joints protested as I slowly pushed myself to a sitting position. It took me ten minutes to drag myself out of bed. The world seemed to stay put instead of spin around me, so that was a good sign. I tried to listen to what Lucas and Grammy were saying, but they spoke so quietly that I couldn't make out their words.

I made my way to the end of the hall and stood in the doorway to the kitchen. Neither of them noticed me.

"It's almost done." Grammy stood over a huge pot that bubbled over a burner on the kitchen island. No, not a pot—a *cauldron*. What the hell?

Grammy stirred the solution. Small glass containers filled with herbs lined the counter beside her. "We'll tell her as soon as she wakes."

Lucas glanced over his shoulder in the direction of my room. His eyes brightened when he saw me standing there. He straightened from where he sat on a stool beside the island.

"Nadine," he said breathlessly. "You're awake."

"Am I?" I replied in a groggy tone. "What are you still doing here?"

The fact that he was still there sent a warm sensation to settle in my gut. It was like he *cared*. Which was stupid, because he didn't even know me.

Lucas stood. He looked like he was about to approach me, but he caught himself at the last second and stayed put. "I wanted to make sure you were all right."

Okay, I guess he did care. Cool.

"My head is better," I admitted, "but I'm going to need some answers."

"And that's exactly what I intend to give you." Grammy gestured for me to sit.

I took the stool beside Lucas, and he sat back down, so close that we were almost touching. I could feel the heat of his body, which made mine turn to mush.

I tried to ignore that. "What happened? Did I pass out?"

That had to be it. I hadn't passed out in years, but with my lupus in flare-up, it wouldn't surprise me.

Grammy set her stirring spoon aside on the counter. She looked at me with a grave expression. "No, honey. You fell and hit your head."

"I—I think I remember," I said cautiously. But no way was I remembering everything right. I must've imagined that ghost part when I'd hit my head. "What is it you need to tell me?"

Grammy took a deep breath, but she didn't speak right away.

"It's time, Helena," Lucas pressed.

Grammy shifted her weight between her feet. "I wanted you to rest first, since this might take a long time, but…" She sighed. "You'll find out one way or another, and I'd rather you heard it from me."

"What, Grammy?" I demanded, sitting up a little straighter. "Tell me what's going on."

Grammy gave me that look—the one Mom always had when she needed to talk over something serious. I half expected her to give me the sex talk right then and there.

Sorry, Grammy. Mom beat you to it.

The seconds ticked by at a snail's pace as I waited for Grammy's big reveal. She was obviously a woman of many secrets, but what could be so serious that she was looking at me like that?

"There's no easy way to say this, Nadine," Grammy started slowly. "You're a witch."

I lightly scoffed and said, "Yeah, okay."

In the back of my mind, I was freaking out. I mean, I grew up reading about sparkling vampires and binge-watching supernatural shows on Netflix. The paranormal wasn't a completely foreign concept to me. But it wasn't *real*.

"Nadine," Grammy scolded. "I'm being serious. This town, Octavia Falls, has a secret. We're all members of the Miriamic Coven, and so are you."

She spoke with such honesty that it was starting to scare me. Did she seriously think she had magical powers? I looked to Lucas to see what he thought of this, but he wore the same serious look as Grammy did.

Holy shit. They weren't playing games.

"So, you're all Wiccans?" I asked, trying to make sense of what she was saying.

Grammy shook her head. "No. Wicca is a completely different religion from ours."

"So, what are you saying?"

"Octavia Falls is home to a coven of four different classes of witches and warlocks," Grammy explained.

"Five, technically," Lucas muttered.

"Yes," Grammy agreed, "but only four left. We can do magic, and so will you."

Now it was time for me to give *my* look. I scrunched up my brow and gazed at her sideways. Was my grandmother suffering from some sort of dementia episode? I didn't even know she *had* dementia.

Lucas caught my expression and said, "Your grandma's telling the truth."

"Oh, really?" I raised a challenging eyebrow. "Then prove it."

Lucas smirked proudly, accepting the challenge. "Okay."

He held his hand out, and a glowing white orb formed in it from out of nowhere. I recoiled, nearly falling out of my stool.

Holy shit! How did he do that?

I couldn't do anything but stare. Lucas tossed the orb into the air, and it burst into a hundred smaller orbs. They floated above our heads like lightning bugs, all orbiting in a uniform circle.

"What the…?" I was so entranced that I couldn't finish my sentence.

He watched the lights beside me. "It's a simple spell. Any witch or warlock can create orbs."

One of the lights floated in front of me. I reached out to touch it, but pulled back at the last second.

"Go ahead," Grammy encouraged. "It's not going to hurt you."

After a moment of hesitation, I reached out for the orb. It was warm, but it didn't hurt as my fingers went right through it.

"What is it?" I asked in wonder, still trying to convince myself what I was seeing was real and not just a trick of the light.

"They're magical lights," Grammy explained.

Lucas twisted his fingers, and the rotation of the orbs shifted to his command. They swirled around the room, weaving in and out of one another in a beautiful lights display. They blinked on and off, then joined and split like a kaleidoscope. I'd never seen anything so beautiful in my life.

Lucas waved his hands again, and the orbs floated toward me, surrounding my body but not touching me. I gazed at them, completely starstruck by what he could do. He closed his palm, and the orbs disappeared from where they hovered mid-air. He wore the slightest of smiles, like he enjoyed watching me view magic for the first time.

It took me a moment to find my voice. "Show me something else."

Grammy cleared her throat and held out her hand. In the blink of an eye, a box of chocolates appeared in her palm.

I nearly shit myself. "Grammy! What the hell? You can make chocolate appear out of nowhere?"

She chuckled. "Kind of. It's another ability all members of the coven have—conjuration. You'll learn all about it in school."

"School?" I balked, nearly choking on my words. I was still trying to wrap my head around the whole *my grandmother is a witch* thing! "There's a school?"

Lucas nodded. "Miriam College of Witchcraft. I'll be a sophomore this year."

"No," I said firmly, shaking my head. "This is insane."

Except I just saw my grandma materialize a box of chocolates from out of nowhere. And now she was eating them.

"Want one?" she asked, holding the box out toward me.

I eyed it skeptically. "Not really. What does magic chocolate do to you?"

Grammy laughed. "It's not magic chocolate, Nadine. It's normal chocolate. All I did was conjure it."

"Oh," I said flatly, because I didn't know what else to say.

The crazy thing was, I didn't just *believe* them. I *wanted* to. I mean, this was *magic*. If there was even the slightest chance they were telling the truth—which I still wasn't sure of, even though they'd just shown me things beyond explanation—I wanted to be a part of it.

"So, um... what else can you do?" I asked.

Grammy seemed pleased to see I was warming up to the idea. "We can all perform simple incantations and defensive magic, as well as use Ouija boards, read tarot cards, summon demons—"

"Summon demons!?" I cried. That sounded scary—and dangerous.

"Yes, but I *highly* advise against it," Grammy said firmly.

"What about séances?" I tapped my fingers against the counter, and my heart pitter-pattered as I eagerly awaited an answer.

Grammy's lips pressed into a thin line. "I know what you're thinking, Nadine, and the answer is no."

"But Lucas and I did one earlier!" I cried.

"And you got hurt," Grammy reminded me.

I raised a challenging eyebrow. "They're not going to hurt me."

She knew who I was talking about, but I was purposely vague since Lucas was sitting right there.

Grammy sighed and gazed at me with a soft expression. "We'll talk about this later, Nadine. Anyway, back to our discussion. Each Cast has a unique set of abilities."

She knew she could distract me by piquing my curiosity.

"What kind?" I asked.

Grammy cleared her throat, then picked up one of the bottles of herbs. She grabbed a pinch of dried leaves, then tossed them into the cauldron. The thick, milky solution bubbled more, then a puff of smoke rose into the air and swirled into the shape of a cauldron. It hovered in the air like a hologram.

"I'm an Alchemist." Grammy pointed to the tattoo on her wrist. "That's what my cauldron tattoo means. Alchemists infuse magic into potions to create things like magical medicine or love potions."

Ooh, love potions!

"Alchemists also grow their own magical herbs," Grammy explained.

My jaw dropped. "That's why you garden."

Grammy nodded proudly.

"So… Mom has that same tattoo," I pointed out. "Does that mean she was…?"

"An Alchemist, like me," Grammy confirmed.

I was so shocked I could hardly move. My mom… a witch?

"What other Casts are there?" I asked, eager to know more about all this.

Grammy tossed the herbs in again, and the smoke shifted into the shape of a skull.

Lucas leaned in closer, his elbows on the counter. He looked from the skull to me, then gave me this look I couldn't read. All I knew was it made my insides dance. "Mortana are known as the Death Cast. Their abilities vary, but they all have to do with death."

"Like necromancers?" I asked brightly. That'd be badass.

Grammy nodded. "Yes, some Mortana can reanimate the dead. Others might see how a person is going to die, or can read the auras of a location to tell if death has occurred there."

"And the other Casts?"

This time when Grammy tossed the herbs in the mixture, an eye took shape in the smoke.

"Seers are the Psychic Cast," Grammy explained. "Like Mortana, their abilities vary. Seers can get visions of the past, present, or future, talk to spirits, read auras, or get feelings through touch. It's the broadest Cast of them all."

She added more herbs, and the smoke turned into the shape of a tree. Grammy looked to Lucas, inviting him to finish the story.

"The last Cast is Mentalists," Lucas told me. "They can do anything relating to the mind."

"Like, read minds?" I asked. That'd be a cool ability to have, but I didn't want anyone else reading my mind. There were some dark and dirty thoughts there that I never wanted to escape.

"Yes, but it's rare," Lucas said. "Most Mentalists have telekinesis."

My jaw dropped. "Shut up! They can move things with their minds?"

Grammy and Lucas both nodded. I glanced to Lucas's wrist, trying to see which mark he had, but he wore that gray hoodie and his wrists were covered. I didn't see a mark anywhere else on him.

I shook my head. This was all too insane and fantastical. But I had just seen Lucas create light from nothing and Grammy conjure chocolate from out of nowhere.

My next question came out slowly as I calculated each word. "So, I'm going to have some of these powers?"

"Yes," Grammy said, tossing more herbs into the cauldron. The smoke transformed into tiny human figures. One of them lay down with five candles placed around them in a circle, while the other stood outside of the circle. The figures were so detailed that they were nothing less than a work of art. I was so entranced that I couldn't take my eyes off the scene playing out before me.

"On the eve of your nineteenth birthday, you will undergo an Evoking

Ceremony. You will contact our goddess, Mother Miriam, and she will assign you to the Cast best fit for you." Grammy waved her hands, and the figure in the candle circle began to levitate. "She will awaken your powers, and you will receive your tattoo indicating your Cast."

"Receive your tattoo?" I asked. "How?"

She made it sound like you didn't just walk into a tattoo parlor for it.

"It appears once your ceremony is complete," Lucas explained.

Interesting… but I had so many other questions.

"So your goddess… she gives you magic?" I asked. "Can anyone get magic from her?"

"Yes, but it becomes a bit complicated," Grammy answered. "You must marry into the coven, and then you become eligible to join on the first anniversary of your marriage. You would be welcomed as a full member of the coven, but without Miriam's blood in your veins, your powers would be limited. Even so, you'd be eligible to live with Mother Miriam and our ancestors in Alora."

"Alora?"

"Our afterlife," Lucas clarified. "Think of it like our version of heaven."

I paused for a moment, absorbing everything they were saying. "So, if you don't marry into the coven, how do you join?"

Grammy brightened, like it was a good question. "You're born into it. All witches and warlocks born into our coven are descended from Mother Miriam. We are born with magic in our blood, which has the potential to become any type of magic—like a stem cell. But it's suppressed until your Evoking Ceremony. After that, it's up to you to exercise it. Like a muscle, it can be strengthened and improved upon."

"Are you the only coven with magic?" I was eager to know what else was out there—if anything. Witches had been mentioned all throughout history, even as far back as biblical times. What if there were others?

"There are many different magical societies around the world, each with their own gods and their own types of magic," Grammy told me. "We all remain secret, as exposing ourselves could lead to very dangerous consequences."

Lucas scoffed. "Yeah. Just look at the witch trials."

My eyebrows shot up. "Your coven was part of the Salem Witch Trials?"

"Those weren't the only ones," Lucas pointed out. "Our coven dates back before the Burning Times in Europe. And Salem's just one of the trials here in the states. The first execution for witchcraft in America took place right here in Connecticut. Fifty years later, and eleven people in our state alone were killed for witchcraft."

"All from your coven?" I balked.

"No," Grammy said firmly. "That's one of the reasons why we came together and formed Octavia Falls, and surrounded it with a protection spell. Just our mere existence caused fear and chaos. Innocent people were being hurt in our name. So… we went into hiding."

I went breathless for a moment. It was hard to wrap my head around everything. "I'm sorry you all feel like you have to hide."

Grammy waved her hand, like it wasn't a big deal. "Don't worry about it. We have two rules within the coven. One, do whatever pleases the Goddess. And two, protect the coven. If you follow those two rules in this life, you will be rewarded in the next. It's no inconvenience at all to protect our own people."

She sounded so noble when she said that.

Silence settled for a few seconds. I was still taking it all in, and they were waiting for my next question. I couldn't believe I was born a witch and would get magical powers in just a few months. It was like a fantasy I'd dreamed of my whole life, minus the sexy vampires. That said, I was sure this town had plenty of sexy warlocks—namely, the one sitting beside me.

"I just have two more questions," I said.

Grammy leaned in, looking eager to answer them.

"Why did Mom leave the coven?"

Grammy's spine straightened, and I didn't miss the fallen look on her face. She stilled for only a moment before quickly relaxing. "She met your father, and the rest is history."

There was a thickness in the air that left me feeling a little uncomfortable.

"What do you mean?" I asked, sensing there was something she wasn't telling me. "Couldn't Dad have stayed here with her?"

"They didn't want to. That's all," she assured me. "Your mother fell in love and followed him."

I guess it made sense. My parents weighed every decision carefully. They must've thought our family would be happier outside the coven.

"What's your other question?" she asked.

"This school… Miriam College of Witchcraft." I could hardly believe I was entertaining the idea that it was a real place. "That's the college you enrolled me in?"

A smile formed across Grammy's face. "Yes. The college was formed to ensure all Miriamic people have control over their magic and know how to use it, so we can avoid magical accidents. All students begin studying the year their magic will awaken, to prepare them beforehand and then teach them after."

"I can't believe I'm going to be studying magic." Even as I said the words, it felt like some make-believe role-playing game, not reality. But it was. I couldn't tell myself otherwise. It was like somewhere deep inside of me, I always knew I was a witch. It just made sense.

"It's nothing to be afraid of," Grammy assured me. "Besides, Lucas will be there to show you around. Won't you, Lucas?"

He looked shocked for a moment, but he quickly relaxed. "Yeah, sure. I'll show her around."

"Well…" Grammy spoke in a brighter tone as she turned the burner off. The cauldron stopped bubbling, and the smoky figures disappeared. "It's past lunch time. Are you hungry, Nadine?"

"Famished," I said quickly.

Lucas stood. "I think I'm going to go."

"Nonsense," Grammy insisted. "Sit down and eat something, Lucas."

He took a step away from the counter. "No, really. I'm not hungry. I should be getting home anyway."

Grammy frowned, but she didn't protest further.

"I'll see you two around." Lucas waved as he headed down the hall.

I hesitated a moment. There were still things I wanted to ask him. He reached the front door. If I was going to catch him, it was now or never. I scrambled out of my seat and down the hall.

"Lucas!" I called when I got outside.

He'd already started down the street. He turned to me with an expectant look on his face. "Yeah, Nad?"

No one had ever called me Nad before, but for whatever reason, it sounded good coming out of his mouth.

I stopped on the sidewalk in front of him. "How do you know my grandma? You two seem to like you're close."

They were on a first-name basis after all. The last thing I needed was for him to be my second-cousin or something.

Lucas shoved his hands into his pockets and glanced toward the house. "I guess you could call her my therapist."

Therapist? Was this guy hiding a deep, dark past or something? Not that I had any right to ask.

"Therapist? Is that what my grandma does?" I asked.

"She's more of a… magical pharmacist," he admitted. "She makes some of the best magical medicines in town."

"Right," I realized. "Because she's an Alchemist."

He nodded.

An awkward silence settled between us, but I wasn't ready to leave yet.

"So, you're going to be a sophomore," I said lamely. "That makes you a year older than me. Have you gone through your Evoking Ceremony?"

"Yeah, I have."

"What is it, exactly?" I asked.

He took a long breath. "It's a test from Mother Miriam. It's different for everyone, but you're going to have to prepare for it."

"Prepare how? If I can't even do magic yet?"

"Mentally and spiritually."

Wow. Less than four months to prepare for the biggest mental test of my life. That didn't sound like enough time.

I swallowed. "What happens if I don't pass this test?"

"If Mother Miriam doesn't find you fit…" He paused. I couldn't stand the suspense. "You'll be banished from the coven."

My blood ran cold at his words. Grammy was the last family I had left, and I couldn't be separated from her. Which meant I had to do everything in my power to pass.

Come hell or high water, I was joining this coven.

FIVE

The look Nadine gave me when I showed her the orbs stuck with me over the next few days. She had such wonder in her eyes that I'd never seen before. To her, magic wasn't an everyday thing like I'd grown up with. It was this beautiful new journey she had yet to discover—and I got to introduce her to that. It was like, for the first time in my life, someone actually appreciated that part of me.

Move-in day arrived on Saturday, and it was the first time in months that I woke up feeling positive.

"Rise and shine." I burst into Grant's room that morning and pulled open the shades. I had to be careful where I stepped, since his room was a complete disaster.

He shielded his eyes as sunlight streamed onto his face. "Dude, can't a guy get a little privacy?"

He pulled the blanket up over himself, since he was sleeping in nothing but his boxers.

"Not today," I told him.

He dropped his arm from his face and eyed me curiously. "You seem in an unusually happy mood."

I shrugged. "I get to sleep in a real bed tonight."

Grant suddenly seemed more alert. He propped himself up on his elbows and wiggled his eyebrows. "And you get to see that girl again, huh?"

"Shut up." I threw a pile of clothes at him from the foot of his bed and turned away so he couldn't see my face.

Yeah, I was excited. So sue me. If Nadine thought my light display was something, she was going to freak when she saw the mansion, and I wanted to be there when she did.

"I just want to move in before the rush," I told him.

I threw his clothes into a pile and waved my hands over them. *"Eye of frog and witch's brew, make these clothes as good as new."*

My magic glowed a dark purple as it intermingled with the threads. I lifted the shirt on top and smelled it. It had a fresh, clean linen scent to it, and all the dirt had disappeared. I tossed the shirt to Grant. "Your clothes are clean. Time to pack."

Grant sniffed the shirt. "Thanks, but seriously? *Eye of frog?* In what universe is that a cleansing spell?"

I shrugged. "Worked, didn't it?"

Grant rolled his eyes. "Yeah, I guess."

"Okay, then let's go."

Grant groaned as he rolled out of bed. "Give me a few minutes to wake up, dude. I need some breakfast before we leave."

Unlike me, who often forgot to eat, Grant needed to eat every two to three hours.

"Right," I said. "Well, let me know how I can help."

After a shower, breakfast, and three hours of packing—since Grant was *that* slow—we made it to campus. Miriam College of Witchcraft was situated on the edge of town in a mansion that, from the outside, looked ten times the size of the house I grew up in. It had sharp peaks, pointed roofs, and the gothic architecture shared with the rest of the town. Miriam Mansion was easily the coolest building in town.

Stepping inside was like coming home. It wasn't just the magic inside —like how it'd been enchanted to be bigger on the inside than the outside so it could house more dorms, a fitness center, and an Olympic-sized pool. It was the entire feel, like it was the one place I could be myself without fear of backlash.

At the same time, entering the foyer didn't bring the thrill and excitement as my first semester. Things were darker and more sinister. I was supposed to be here to learn about my gift, and so far, I was struggling with it. These wide, expansive halls were just a reminder of the endless nights I'd spent roaming them, trying to walk away my insomnia. The classrooms held memories of the magic I had yet to embrace.

Maybe I'd been wrong. Maybe this wasn't home. But it sure as hell was the closest I'd come, and I was going to have to live with that.

The school was already buzzing with activity. The foyer was crowded with students and parents. All around us, people were chatting away. One sophomore girl bragged to her friends about the Mentalist powers she'd gotten over summer break. She showed off by making her luggage float behind her up the grand staircase. The three other girls, who all bore the mark of an Alchemist, looked intrigued. At the top of the stairs, the Mentalist girl nearly bumped into a guy who looked to be in a heated conversation with someone I couldn't see. I caught a glimpse of an eye tattoo on his arm and knew he must've been a medium. Some ghost must've been asking for his help.

In the corner at a seating area, a group of freshman sat in a circle reading tarot cards. Beside them, two junior girls were changing their makeup at will and giving each other their opinions.

Grant and I walked across the foyer to the registration table, where we picked up our dorm keys and our class schedules. We climbed the stairs and took a left. There were so many people that we had to weave in and out of them, even though the hall was a good eight feet wide.

Our room was the same one as last semester, and not much had changed when we stepped inside. It was bigger than a normal college dorm, more like the size of a hotel room. There were two beds, two dressers, and two desks, with a couch between them facing a TV. Like the rest of the mansion, everything was decorated in dark tones.

Grant plopped onto the bed farthest from the door. "Dibs."

I shrugged. "Fine by me."

I conjured my bag and set it next to my bed, then turned around.

"Where are you going?" Grant asked. "Aren't you going to unpack?"

"Later," I told him. "I'm going to explore and find out where my classes are."

"Okay. I'll text you when I'm ready to hit the pool." In his next life, Grant was coming back as a fish, considering how much time he spent at the pool.

I stepped out of the room, glad he hadn't questioned me further. I hadn't exactly lied to him, but the truth was that I was only going to explore in hopes of running into Nadine.

I headed back down to the Main Foyer, but I didn't see her at registration, so I continued down the hall. I passed by endless classrooms, until I reached the Lounge. It was a huge room separated into different areas, with everything a student could ask for when they weren't in class—couches to sit on, big-screen TVs to watch, and games like pool and darts. There was even an arcade section and four bowling lanes, along with a restaurant. It was like the entertainment district all crammed into one room. Everything was cast in dim lighting, like a club but without the booze and pounding music.

I walked straight past the restaurant to the sitting area, then stopped dead in my tracks when I spotted a group of five guys in leather jackets gathered around the pool table. I tried to step away slowly before they noticed me, but Prime Asshole lifted his head and caught sight of me before I could make my exit.

"Well, if it isn't Lucas Taylor," he practically sang in the most condescending manner he could.

"Ryan." I nodded my head toward him.

The five of them stepped closer to me. Ryan came in close and wrapped an arm tightly around my shoulder so that even if I wanted to run, I'd have to put up a fight to do it.

"How you doing, *old pal?*" His hand tightened on my shoulder until it hurt.

I didn't let the pain show. These guys might have had the rest of the school fooled, but I wasn't scared of them. They were a gang of Mentalists, and despite their sophomore status, they had everyone else convinced they ruled the school. They called themselves the Treacherous Tarantulas, like they were some badass gang—and had a tarantula emblem on the back of their jackets like it proved something. It was a dumb name, and I was allowed to say that, since I was the one who came up with it.

"We're back to old pal now?" I asked casually. "Last time we talked, you called me a traitor."

"That's because you are," Ryan snarled.

He came in so close to me that I could smell the stench of his breath. I seriously didn't get why girls swooned over him. Sure, he had that tall, muscular, star-quarterback look going on, but underneath all that was garbage. My only guess was they liked him for his dick, but it couldn't be *that* big. I didn't care if it was two feet long; nothing could make up for his rotten personality.

"First, you leave the Tarantulas—"

"You stole Grant's insulin," I snapped.

The Tarantulas had never been a great group of guys. I should know. I used to be one of them.

I'd been thinking about leaving them for a long time, after some shit went down the summer before college. The final straw was when they decided to sneak into my dorm without my consent and take Grant's entire insulin supply in what they called a "harmless prank." I lost it. I traded in my leather jacket for this hoodie a year ago next week, and it'd been one of the best decisions of my life.

"And then you started fooling around with my girlfriend," Ryan continued, like he hadn't even heard me.

I resisted the urge to roll my eyes. "Seriously? We're back to that? How many times do I have to tell you that nothing ever happened between Chloe and me?"

I didn't find out until months later that the only reason Chloe asked to attend my Evoking Ceremony was to make Ryan jealous and get him to pay more attention to her. It worked for a while, I guess, but not before I was dragged into the middle of their relationship.

"You can tell me that all you want," Ryan sneered. "I'm still not going to believe you."

"What do you care, anyway?" I demanded. "You and Chloe broke up."

"Doesn't change the fact that you betrayed us." Ryan narrowed his eyes at me. "I don't want to see you coming around the Lounge anymore, you hear?"

"I pay my tuition, same as you," I said. It wasn't *exactly* true, since I was here on scholarship due to my parents' lack of funds. But Ryan didn't have to know that. "I'm free to use the Lounge as I please."

Ryan finally dropped his hand from my shoulder. "Do as you please, Lucas, but there will be consequences."

"Oh? Like what?" I knew Ryan was all talk and no action. He thrived on fear, and as long as I didn't give in to that, he couldn't touch me.

"Like this." Ryan flicked his wrist, and the cue ball flew off the table at full-speed toward my nose.

I flinched and ducked, but Ryan shot his hand out and caught the ball before it reached me. His posse laughed. I wasn't amused.

"Funny," I said flatly, straightening up. "Now if you'll excuse me, I have an appointment to get to."

I didn't give them a chance to respond. I turned and hurried out of the Lounge, the sound of their laughter echoing behind me. The truth was, I didn't want to get into it with those guys. As much as Ryan didn't scare me, if I swung, he'd swing back.

I *did* have an appointment, but it wasn't official. Professor Warren told me to stop into his office whenever I got settled in my room. It was on the way back to the foyer, so I figured it wouldn't hurt to swing by now.

Professor Warren's office was through his classroom. The door was open when I arrived. He sat behind his desk, his hand hovering over a dead mouse that lay in front of him. The mouse twitched, but it didn't get up and move like I'd seen Professor Warren do to creatures before.

I cleared my throat.

He jumped a little, then relaxed when he saw it was just me. "Lucas. Good to see you. Come in."

I stepped inside his office. It wasn't a very big room, but it was comfortable. One wall was made up completely of bookcases, while the other was decorated with various things that didn't seem to fit together at all—empty potion vials, an oil lamp, and several ships in a bottle. He even had a skeleton of a cat, which I found kind of creepy.

"Everything okay?" I asked, gesturing to the rodent corpse.

"Fine," he said quickly. "Just a little weak today is all. Take a seat."

I furrowed my brow, but I sat anyway.

Professor Warren stood to close the door, then returned to his chair. He was in his forties, with dark hair and a bit of stubble I guess the ladies liked or something. He was a widower and never had kids. He told me once his students were enough, though I wasn't sure I believed him. He seemed like a lonely guy.

"How was your summer?" he asked.

I shrugged. "Good, I guess."

Total lie. Honestly, I couldn't remember half the summer. I'd slept through most of it. The only parts I really remembered were disc golfing at Octavia Falls Park with Grant.

"And the task I gave you?" He gave me a curious look.

Professor Warren was a necromancer who taught Mortana studies. As my mentor, it was his job to help me understand my gift. The only problem? I was his first Reaper's Apprentice student. The last Apprentice in the coven died just days before my Evoking Ceremony. Rumor had it, he'd lived to be over a hundred. Professor Warren didn't exactly have a lot of experience in this area, and as much as I respected him, I wasn't sure he could really help me.

"I'm trying to find the good in my gift," I assured him. "But…"

"But what, Lucas?" he pressed.

I turned my gaze away from him and looked out the window, which was lined in red drapes. Not far from the window was a dark forest.

"I can't help you unless you talk to me," Professor Warren said.

I shook my head. "I tried to help Old Man Keller cross over, but it was a total bust."

"Oh?" He straightened in his chair. "I'd very much like to hear about that. What happened?"

I summarized the best I could. "By the end of it, the new girl got a concussion, and I'm not any closer to helping Old Man Keller," I concluded with.

Professor Warren didn't respond right away. He leaned back in his chair with his lips pressed together, like he was deep in thought.

"What?" I asked.

"You say your gift is nothing but a curse, but this girl…"

"Nadine," I said quickly.

He nodded. "Nadine. You sound fond of her."

"What?" I scoffed, my cheeks heating. Where'd he get that idea? "I don't even know her."

"Nonetheless, your gift brought you two together, correct?" Professor Warren raised a curious eyebrow.

"Um, I mean, not really."

If we were going to stretch it that far, I guess I could say my anxiety led me to Nadine, since I wouldn't have met her if I hadn't been picking her grandmother's matus shrub leaves. But we would've met at college anyway, so I couldn't say this was exactly a perk of my gift.

"If that's what you choose to believe, Lucas, that's up to you," Professor Warren said. "But I see no harm in taking this experience as a positive. Perhaps it's worth adding to your journal."

Professor Warren had given me a journal after my Evoking Ceremony when he started mentoring me. So far, I hadn't added anything to it. He only wanted me to add the *positive* about my gift. I told him it would be faster if I filled it with the negatives. He didn't like that.

"Yeah, I guess it'd be nice to finally add something to the journal," I stated flatly. "But what good is meeting a girl? She could become the Reaper's Shadow. I can't put that kind of burden on her."

He raised a curious eyebrow. "You realize you have complete control over the Reaper's Shadow situation, don't you?"

I sank further in my chair. "Things could get out of hand."

He frowned at my tone. "Lucas, I can't help you if you don't want to be helped."

A lump rose to my throat at the accusation. The bright mood I'd woken up in that morning suddenly seemed to darken. My lips tightened. "I *do* want help."

Professor Warren sighed. "I don't have a magic bullet. I can guide you, but you're the only one who can change your attitude."

"This isn't an attitude problem," I snapped. "This is a matter of circumstance. A fact. My gift sucks."

"That's your *perspective*," Professor Warren tried to convince me. I wasn't buying it.

"Would you think that if you were put in my place?" I challenged.

He shook his head and dropped his gaze. "Lucas, I can't say what I would feel in your situation. The only thing I can do is offer my support. If we don't sort this thing out, your powers are going to consume you."

He didn't say it explicitly, but I knew what he meant. If things kept going the way they were, Professor Warren worried I'd throw in the towel and off myself like Eric did. I wouldn't lie and say I hadn't thought about it more than once, but if he really thought I was going to do it, he didn't know me at all.

I crossed my arms. "That's not going to happen."

"It is happening, though," he pointed out. "You've cut yourself off from people. You've stopped doing the things you used to love."

I was quick to retort. "I cut myself off from people who are toxic. That has nothing to do with my gift. And the things I used to love? It's because my brother and I used to do them together."

Rock climbing, paintballing, kayaking—those were all mine and Eric's things, our means of escape when Dad got in one of his moods. The only reason I stuck with disc golfing was because it was the only thing I was comfortable doing on my own.

"I know you're still grieving," Professor Warren said.

I pressed my fingers to my eyes. "Can we not do this again? How many times are we going to have this conversation?"

Professor Warren paused for a moment, and a look of regret crossed his features. "I'm sorry, Lucas."

"I'm fine." If I said it enough times, maybe I'd start believing it.

"Okay, then." He nodded, accepting my claim, even if he didn't believe it. "I'll see you in two weeks."

I started to get up, but he stopped me.

"And Lucas." He gave me a pointed expression. "I want to see that journal."

"Right." The word felt dry in my mouth. "See you."

I left the room before I heard his goodbye. As soon as I stepped into the hall, a wave of nausea slammed into me. It was so strong that I stopped dead in my tracks. I resisted the urge to double over, because I knew nothing would come from trying to heave. This kind of thing happened to me daily now. I leaned up against the wall as sweat broke out across my body. I forced myself to control my breathing as the nausea worsened.

"I should've told her about the affair," a voice said in my mind.

It sounded like an old man's. Just another regret—a secret—for me to carry around for the dead. Not like I had a fucking choice.

The nausea passed as soon as the voice faded. I glanced around, wondering if anyone had seen, but there weren't very many people in the hall, and those who were here didn't look at me.

I breathed a sigh of relief, knowing the episode was over. I summoned an old leather-bound notebook—the kind used for recording spells and incantations. I wrote down the thought beneath the others. Professor

Warren didn't know about *this* journal, the one where I kept track of everything I heard. I kept it just in case one day I needed to shove it in his face as proof of the shit I carried. Next week, I'd check the paper for the obituaries and try to match each thought with whoever had passed.

Maybe Professor Warren was right. Maybe I *was* focusing too much on the negative.

At least now I had one positive thing in my life. *Nadine*. I guess it was time to finally add an entry to the positivity journal.

nadine

SIX

Most mornings, I woke with a headache and stiff joints. Today was no exception. It took me over half an hour to get out of bed. While I waited for my joints to relax, I wrote my symptoms down in my journal.

Feel like shit. Joints ache. Another day in Paradise.

I'd been doing this since I was thirteen, so I could track my triggers. I knew most of them by now, but I figured it was still good to keep track. I poked at my phone for a while, then finally got out of bed to run myself an Epsom salt bath. After soaking in the tub, I finally felt like I could move.

Grammy knocked on the bathroom door while I was getting dressed. "How's it coming?"

"I fell in," I joked through the door.

She chuckled. "Do you need me to come in and rescue you?"

"Nah, I'll be fine."

"You sure?" she asked playfully. "I'll break down this door."

"I'd like to see that," I teased.

Grammy laughed. "Let me know when you're ready. Your ride will be here soon."

"My ride?" I asked through the door. "I thought you were taking me."

"I'll meet you there," she replied. "You don't want to miss the limo. It's a special opportunity for First Year students. Everyone looks forward to it."

I liked the sound of a limo, so I hurried up and got dressed. Twenty minutes later, Grammy stood at the front door with me. She picked a cat hair off my shoulder, then looked at me like she was proud.

"You're going to love college," Grammy assured me. "I just know it."

"I hope so," I said nervously. "This whole magic thing is really new to me."

"Pft," Grammy said, waving her hand. "You'll get used to it in no time."

"So… about that séance?" I said slowly.

Grammy's shoulders fell. "I know how hard this is for you, Nadine, but contacting your parents will be nothing short of emotional torture. I went through it with your grandpa, and believe me when I say contacting the dead makes it *much* harder to move on. I need you to trust me on this."

"I do trust you," I told her. I just wasn't sure I trusted her on *this*. It wasn't fair I never got to say goodbye to them. That was all I wanted.

Grammy glanced out the front window, and her eyes lit up. "Your ride's here. Now, remember, I'll meet you at the school to help you unpack. Have fun in the limo, and make lots of friends."

I chuckled lightly. "I'll try."

I gave Grammy a hug, and she squeezed me back tightly. I was glad she was meeting up with me later, because I didn't want to go through with this day on my own. I didn't take my bags with me, as Grammy would be coming with those later.

I stepped outside and walked to the end of the sidewalk, where a sleek black limo was parked. An old man dressed in a suit and cap bowed his head to me. "Miss Evers?"

I fiddled with the strap on my purse. "That's me."

He smiled kindly. "Welcome to The Hearse."

He reached out a white gloved hand and opened the door. I ducked inside and was shocked at what I found. I expected a few rows of seating and a couple other students, but there must've been a *hundred* people my age in there.

Holy crap! Inside, the limo was as big as a train! The ceiling was high enough for me to stand, and the red velvet seats stretched so far back I couldn't see the back window. It should've been impossible, since the limo only looked a dozen feet long from the outside.

The floor of the limo was all black carpet, and the seats ran the length of the windows. I could see houses passing by us outside, but the ride was so smooth I could barely tell we were moving. Every couple feet was a small table, and there were various counters with baristas behind them, serving up coffee and snacks. An *Evanescence* song played softly from the speakers. Students laughed and chatted with each other. Several people were stroking cats on their laps, or flinging strings around so the cats would chase them.

I noticed the Lucky Three a few seats down. They were surrounded by a big group of people and laughing like they were the life of the party.

No one noticed my arrival, except a girl with dark skin and black hair sitting closest to me. She was dressed in a trendy black skater dress, with red tights and high-heeled boots. She kind of reminded me of a gothic Princess Jasmine. Her nails were painted red, and her hair was twisted into braids. She obviously had a good sense of fashion, and there was this friendly, approachable air about her. She was all alone, and she smiled sweetly when my eyes met hers.

"Need a seat?" she asked kindly.

"Sure," I agreed. I sat beside her and glanced around.

"You've never been in The Hearse before, have you?" she asked.

I crinkled my nose. "That obvious?"

She chuckled. "A little."

"I'm told I'm a witch, but I'm a total magic virgin," I admitted.

She waved a hand and sat up straighter. "Don't worry about it. You'll catch on quickly. I'm Mandy, by the way."

Mandy? Could she be the girl I'd heard the Lucky Three talking about?

"Nadine," I introduced.

Mandy shook my hand, but she didn't let go right away. She turned my palm in her direction and looked down at it. "Wow, I love your hands."

I furrowed my brow. Was she hitting on me?

Mandy noticed my expression. "Oh, sorry. I just mean… I'm studying palm reading. I notice people's hands. Yours are really soft."

She ran her fingers over my palm. I should've found it creepy, but she came across as really friendly.

I laughed. "I'm flattered."

"Can I read it?" she asked.

My heart fluttered. I'd always wanted to get my palm read. "Sure."

Mandy inspected my palm closely. "Judging by the shape of your hands, you're really curious and have a lot of ideas, but you tend to worry a lot and are prone to stress."

My eyebrows shot up. "You're psychic, then?"

Mandy smirked, obviously proud that she'd hit it on the nose. "Nope. My ceremony's not until next semester. I just know my palms. The good thing about your hand shape is it means you're a good communicator, though you don't always share your feelings."

If she weren't a First Year, I wouldn't have believed she wasn't psychic.

Mandy ran her finger across one of the creases in my hand. "Your heart line suggests you fall in love easily, but your heart also breaks easily. If I'm reading your head line right, you're creative and spontaneous, and you love adventure. Now for the fun one..."

Mandy wiggled her eyebrows, but I was starting to get a little creeped out. So far, she was spot on.

Mandy touched the longest line on my hand. "This is your life line. Yours shows that you're tired a lot, but you're really strong. But—oh, no."

A shadow fell across Mandy's face.

"What?" I asked urgently.

Mandy sucked a breath between her teeth. "There's a circle on your life line," she said, and I sensed that was really bad.

I shifted in my seat. "What does it mean?"

Mandy's face fell. "It means you're either going to suffer a severe injury or be hospitalized."

I laughed, because it felt really ironic.

She furrowed her brow. "You don't believe me?"

"No, I believe you," I assured her. "It's just creepy how accurate you are."

Mandy looked uncomfortable, like she wanted to ask about my hospitalization, but she didn't. "Well, at least there are no surprises. Um... one more thing."

"What?" I asked.

Mandy cleared her throat. "I noticed your fate line is really prominent."

"What does that mean?"

"It means your life is controlled by destiny," she told me.

I tilted my head to the side. "You believe everyone has a destiny?"

Mandy shook her head. "Not everyone. But yours, Nadine… it seems pretty important."

We both went silent. Something about what Mandy said seemed really ominous. Mandy looked just as uncomfortable as I was, so she changed the subject.

"Since you're a magic virgin, it's my obligation to tell you to check out The Hearse for breakfast, lunch, and dinner," Mandy said. "And *definitely* visit after midnight."

"Why?" I asked.

She gestured around us. "In the morning, it's a coffee shop. At lunch, it becomes a café, and at dinner it's a fancy restaurant. It's at the witching hour that things get fun, though."

I leaned in, intrigued. "What happens at the witching hour?"

Mandy grinned. "The Hearse turns into a nightclub."

I bounced in my seat. "Ooh, sounds fun."

"Don't get me wrong," Mandy said. "The coffee shop is great, too. Come on, let's order something. Everything's free today on our ride to school."

Mandy and I stood and walked up to the barista. My eyes caught a vine plant wiggling on the countertop.

"Is that… alive?" I asked Mandy.

She chuckled. "All plants are alive, Nadine."

I scoffed. "Well, yeah. You know what I meant."

Mandy shrugged. "It's just a vitamort plant. Makes wonderful tea, but be careful. If you eat the leaves raw, it'll kill you."

I took a step away from it. "That sounds… dangerous."

Mandy shrugged. "Only if you eat it raw. What do you want?"

"Mm…" I continued to eye the menu. "A hazelnut cappuccino sounds good."

Mandy leaned against the counter and laughed. "Do you *want* to be awake for three days straight?"

"No," I replied.

"These aren't normal cappuccinos, Nadine," she told me. "They're made by Alchemists and infused with magical properties. You should try the vitamort tea."

"Didn't you just say it could kill me?" I asked warily.

"Not if you prepare it right," she said. "It's really good for nerves."

I couldn't deny that I was really nervous about today, so I went with Mandy's recommendation and got the vitamort tea. It was really sweet and had a hint of lemon to it. I finished it quickly and could already feel my nerves calming.

Mandy glanced out the window and inhaled a sharp breath. "We're here!"

Miriam College of Witchcraft was on the edge of town. I glanced out the window, and my jaw dropped when the campus came into view. A huge gothic structure stood towering three stories high. It was the kind of place that should be cast in a dark sky and a full moon, with the howl of a werewolf in the distance. Just one look, and I was already eager to get inside.

A large iron gate surrounded the property, with a thick forest behind the school. Inside the gates was an expansive lawn where groups of students were lounging under oak trees or playing Frisbee in the grass. A couple of girls sat on the sidelines and giggled as the Frisbee was sent off course. The guys started arguing about using their Mentalist powers unfairly, when it was clear from this perspective the girls were messing with them.

I was surprised to see how many cats were on campus—nearly one for every two or three students. If I had known we were allowed to bring pets, I would've considered adopting one.

The Hearse pulled up to the front of the school. When I stepped out, Grammy was already waiting for me with my bags at the front doors.

"Thanks for letting me sit by you," I told Mandy. "And for reading my palm."

Mandy waved her hand, like it wasn't a big deal. "No problem. Hopefully we'll run into each other soon."

"See you around." I waved to Mandy, then hurried over to Grammy.

"Did you have fun?" she asked when I approached.

"Yeah," I told her. "The Hearse was pretty cool."

Grammy smiled. "Told you."

"Come on, we're going to end up in the back of the line." I grabbed one of my bags and rolled it behind me. I could hardly get inside fast enough.

I stepped through massive double doors into a huge foyer two-stories high. Deep red carpet spanned the giant room and met up with a grand staircase painted in a black, glossy finish. Above our heads hung a black iron chandelier with burning candles on it. The walls were made of a dark wood and lined with beautiful sconces or elaborate mirrors. Everything was either red or black, and the lighting was dim, but I didn't mind. It was like we'd stepped into a vampire's lair, and I was down for that.

All around the crowded room were various plush sofas and chairs where students sat and chatted. One corner even had a huge fireplace, where a painting taller than me hung above the mantle. It depicted a beautiful woman wearing a corset dress. She had long flowing brown hair and beautiful bright eyes. Her skin was impeccably smooth, and her expression warm and welcoming. She was the kind of woman who you could go up and hug even though she was a stranger.

Grammy caught me staring. "That's Mother Miriam."

"Oh?" I asked, unable to take my eyes of the artwork. "She looks lovely."

I finally tore my gaze off the painting to look at the students. They performed magic out in the open like it was nothing. I witnessed someone conjure their class schedule and overheard one girl telling another her aura was off today. At the fireplace, a group of Alchemy students were cooking something sweet-smelling over the coals.

"This way, Nadine." Grammy led me over to a line behind the registration table. She stared straight ahead, like all of this beauty was an everyday thing. Meanwhile, I was still trying to take it all in.

"Is something wrong?" she asked.

I shook my head. "No, it's just that this foyer's so big. I'm wondering how much of the mansion is left."

Grammy smiled sweetly. "There's no shortage of room in this mansion. It was enchanted long ago with a space-bending spell to make room for new students. There's much more to this campus than meets the eye."

"Which Cast can do that kind of magic—the spacial thing?" I asked.

"All of them… and none of them," Grammy answered.

I furrowed my brow. "What do you mean?"

"When members of different Casts gets together, they're capable of extraordinary things—things we can't do on our own," Grammy said.

For the first time in weeks, I felt relaxed. "I can't wait to start classes to learn more about magic."

At the registration desk, they gave me a folder filled with information about my room, my schedule, and a map of campus. I also got a beautiful beaded bracelet that Grammy informed me was enchanted. It unlocked my dorm and acted like a credit card as long as I was wearing it. Every time I bought food on campus, the total would be deducted from my meal plan, which like my tuition, Grammy was paying for. Count me in on the magic credit card!

I groaned a little when I saw my first class was at 9:00 a.m. I wasn't exactly what you'd call a morning person. At least the classes sounded cool: Miriamic History, Demonology, Introduction to Tarot, and Conjuring Basics.

Looking at the map, I saw that Grammy was right. This place was *way* bigger on the inside than it looked on the outside. It was like an endless maze, one I wasn't sure I'd ever manage to learn. Great. The new girl was going to get lost on her first day.

"Come on, Nadine." Grammy cocked her head, and I followed her up the grand staircase, lugging one of my bags behind me. Grammy carried the rest of my luggage.

At the top, a huge, ornate window looked out over the forest. I glanced to the left, then to the right. Each hallway was identical to the other. They seemed to go on forever, as if someone had set up two mirrors facing each other. The same red carpet and dark walls from downstairs spanned in front of us. The walls were lined with beautiful sconces every few feet.

"The second floor is the dormitories," Grammy explained as she led me down the hall to the right. We weaved between other parents and students. Even though the hall was wide, there was so much foot traffic that it was a little crowded. "The first floor is where you'll find all your classrooms."

"Okay." I nodded along, but I kept my eyes on the doors as we passed by. Each was marked with a number, with the even numbers on the right and the odd numbers on the left. They started at 100. I was relieved to see that my number was 112. I didn't have long to walk.

When we reached my door, it was propped open. A haunting but upbeat melody played from somewhere inside. The beautiful noise spilled out into the hallway. I stepped up to the door and peeked inside. The room was bigger than I expected, with a huge closet and a bathroom right up front. A set of beds stood beyond that, with a couch between them. The furniture was all dark wood and smooth curves. Red drapes hung in front of the window and matched the bedding. I was pleased to see the bathroom had a tub, as I'd need that for my Epsom salt soaks.

A white cat lay curled up on the bed furthest from the door. In the far corner, a petite girl with brown hair, blue eyes, and smooth skin sat at a keyboard, playing the song. I noticed she didn't have sheet music in front of her, as if she was playing from memory. She looked up and stopped playing when she noticed Grammy and me in the doorway.

She cleared her throat, and her voice came out soft and a little higher than mine. "Oh, hello. You must be Nadine."

"Don't stop playing," I said quickly. "It sounded great."

She blushed a little and stood. "I was just practicing. I'm Talia, your new roommate." She walked over to the bed and picked up her cat. He stirred a little and blinked as she held him up. "And this is Gus."

I stepped further into the room. "Aw. He's precious."

I set my bags at the end of my bed and reached out to pet Gus. He nuzzled his head against my hand and purred.

"He likes you!" Talia said sweetly. She glanced behind me, as if searching for something. "Where's yours?"

"My cat?" I asked. "I, um, don't have one. Am I supposed to?"

"No, dear," Grammy replied. She set my largest suitcase on the bed and started arranging my clothes in the nearest dresser. "Cats are common in the coven, but not required. We believe them to be reincarnations of those who have passed on. Cornelius is actually your Grampy."

"Shut up," I told her. "He is not."

Then again, I just found out magic was real. Reincarnation wasn't totally out of the realm of possibility.

Talia furrowed her brow. "You don't know?"

I shrugged. "I'm new."

"Ah." She nodded. "That explains it."

"Explains what?"

"Why I didn't recognize your name. I know everyone in my class from high school. I figured you must've skipped a grade or something."

I shook my head. "Nope. Just new."

Talia's eyes brightened. "Oh my Goddess! You're going to love it here.

First things first, we have to visit the Lounge. The restaurant there carries Barry's Enchanted Muffins. They're made by an Alchemist in town and can turn your hair purple or make you burp bubbles!"

I laughed. She seemed really excited to have a new person to show around. "That sounds amazing. Where's that at?"

"Downstairs," Talia said in excitement.

"I'd love to check it out after we unpack," I said. I noticed her bags were still full.

She glanced to them. "Yeah, I only got as far as the keyboard. I was going to unpack after my parents left, but the music was calling me."

"You're really good," I said as I started lining books up along the top of my dresser. "How long have you been playing?"

"Um, about thirteen years." She looked like she was trying to calculate it in her head.

"Wow." I'd never stuck with anything that long.

Talia shrugged. "It's always been a comfort to me. Ever since I was a kid, I struggled with reading because I'm dyslexic, but music makes sense. I can *feel* it. I don't have to worry about reading the notes."

"Wait," I said, glancing back at her piano. "You do all that without ever looking at sheet music?"

Talia offered a shy smile.

"Do you want this hung in the closet?" Grammy interrupted, holding up a slim black dress I'd never worn. I kept it just in case I ever happened to get invited out on a hot date—which would probably be never. She stopped in her tracks when she realized how short it was. "Good Goddess! You call this a dress? You'll bend over and everyone will see your cooch!"

"Grammy!" I exclaimed, covering my ears for show. Talia burst into laughter. "Don't ever let me hear you say that word again."

"Which word?" Grammy asked innocently. "Cooch?"

"*Grammy!*"

"Okay, okay," she sighed as he headed toward the closet to hang it up.

"I'll wear leggings under it," I promised.

It took another hour of moving around the room and giving introductions before we'd finished unpacking. Even though I'd paced myself, I was exhausted by the end of it.

Grammy picked up her purse and took a deep breath. "Well, I guess I'll leave you to it."

"Thanks for all your help, Grammy." I reached out to pull her into a hug. "I'll see you this weekend."

"I look forward to it. Bye, Nadine." She gave me one last squeeze, then turned to the open doorway.

"Oh!" Grammy whirled back to me like she'd forgotten something. "I meant to give you these."

She reached into her purse and pushed a pile of foil packets into my hands. I took them, not realizing what they were. She reached in for another handful and shoved them into my other hand, until they started falling onto the floor. When it hit me, I wanted to crawl into a hole.

"Grammy!" I cried, shooting a quick glance to Talia, who sat on her piano bench. She slapped her hand over her mouth and was trying not to laugh. She wasn't succeeding.

I turned beet red and hissed at my grandma. "Condoms!?"

Grammy shrugged, like it was no big deal. "You're in college. I want you to be safe."

"Grammy, I—I—" I couldn't find the words. It was too awkward.

"What?" she asked innocently. "You *are* going to be having sex, aren't you?"

"Oh my God," I groaned. Of course I was going to lose my virginity eventually—and probably in college—but couldn't she be a normal grandma and pretend I never would?

Grammy huffed. "Well, if you don't want them, give them back."

She reached for the pile of condoms, but I jerked away from her. Grammy raised a curious eyebrow. Talia could no longer contain her laughter. She doubled over, trying to catch her breath.

"I'll keep them," I told Grammy. "You know, just in case."

"That a girl," Grammy said proudly. "I'll see you girls later. It was nice to meet you, Talia."

"You too!" Talia called as my grandma left the room.

As soon as she was out of sight, Talia and I exchanged a wide-eyed look, then we both broke into a fit of laughter. I had to sit down on the bed, I was laughing so hard.

"Oh my God," I cried between laughs. "I can't believe she just did that."

"She's just looking out for you," Talia giggled, eyeing the pile in my hand.

"What?" I held them out to her. "You need one?"

She smirked. "Tell you what. We'll start a condom box."

"A condom box?" I asked.

She stood and bounced over to her dresser. She grabbed a jewelry box that opened from the top and turned to me. "We'll keep it stocked, and if anyone needs one, there will always be one handy."

I placed the condoms into the jewelry box, then leaned over to pick up the others that had fallen out of my hands. "Thanks, Talia. It's a good idea, considering you'll probably use most of them."

"Me?" she balked. "Uh, no…"

I snickered. "Then this condom box is going to last us a while."

She looked curious as she closed the box. "Wait. So you haven't…?"

I shook my head and quickly added, "Not that I don't *want* to. I've just never been in that situation."

"Shut up," she said with an eye-roll. "You're banging hot, Nadine."

I smiled. "Thanks, but I didn't have many options. I dated this guy in high school for two years, which kept me out of the dating pool. But it was just kind of puppy love, you know?"

For him, at least. I'd always wanted more, which made the break-up that much worse.

"Oh, I *know*," Talia said, like she'd had her fair share of crushes.

"Anyway, it didn't end well. He told me he was saving himself for marriage, but I guess he forgot about that when he fucked the head cheerleader."

Talia's jaw dropped. "He did not!"

My gut sank at the memory. Brandon made me believe he was saving himself for *me*. Nope. Just waiting for someone hotter to show up, I guess.

"Whatever." I brushed it off. We'd broken up months ago. I was over it. "I'm glad I never slept with him."

"Totally. I hope you whooped his ass," Talia said.

I chuckled. "I made a scene, all right."

In front of the whole lunch room, too. I dumped my entire milk carton over his head. Jackass.

I would've done a lot more had my friends not held me back. They had to remind me how much I'd regret it. I'd buried my dark side long ago. I wasn't the crazy bitch who started fist fights on the playground anymore.

Talia set the condom box on my nightstand and sat on the couch, leaning over the arm to face me. "I want my first time to be special, but like, I'm not the kind of girl who needs a ring first."

I laughed. "Me neither. Give me a loyal boyfriend, and I'll be good to go."

Talia made a crude motion with her hand and her tongue. I threw my head back in laughter.

"Oh, good." She gave a sigh of relief. "I was afraid my roommate would be a prude."

"Girl, you can make dick jokes all day long and it's not going to bother me."

"In that case…" Talia made another motion with her hands. I couldn't stop laughing.

A knock came at the door, which was still open. I leaned forward on my bed to peek around the bathroom at the door. A woman I didn't recognize stood in the doorway. She was at least my parents' age, with dark brown hair and hazel eyes. She wore a pantsuit and looked like she was someone important. A fat black cat followed at her heels.

"Excuse me?" she said kindly.

Talia shot to her feet and nodded politely. "Headmistress Verla."

Since I didn't know the proper protocol, I stood beside Talia.

Headmistress Verla smiled at the two of us. "Do you mind if I come in?"

"No, not at all," Talia said.

Headmistress Verla stepped into the room and extended her hand out to me. "Hi, Nadine. I'm Headmistress Verla, and this is Odin." She gestured down to her cat. "It's a pleasure to meet you."

I furrowed my brow. "How do you know my name?"

"I know all my students." She turned to Talia and said, "Talia Murphy."

Talia looked like she was going to pass out as she took Headmistress Verla's hand. You'd think she was meeting her pop star idol or something.

"To what do we owe the pleasure?" I asked. I glanced down to Odin, who was sniffing Gus curiously. Gus's hair stood on end, like he didn't like the other cat in his territory.

"I've come to welcome you to the school," Headmistress Verla said kindly. "I don't know if you're aware, Nadine, but I was friends with your mom. I know how hard things must be for you right now, especially after what happened."

Her expression turned sad. There was a genuine sorrow behind her voice that suggested she and my mom were very close, though I'd never met her. "I just want you to know that if you ever need anything, you can come to me. It's the least I can do."

"Thank you, Headmistress Verla," I said genuinely.

"Oh, please," she replied. "Call me Clarice."

Hold the phone. *This* was Clarice!? The friend from high school my mom always talked to on the phone? I'd heard so much about her.

She must've noticed the shocked look in my eyes, because she said, "I take it your mom has mentioned me?"

"Yeah," I said breathlessly, unable to believe I was finally meeting her. "She talks about you all the time."

It hit me that I'd said *talks*, like I still thought about my mother in the present tense. It was a hard habit to break.

Headmistress Verla gave me a smile, but it didn't quite reach her eyes. I bet she was thinking about how my mom was gone. I knew I was, and it was killing me inside.

Finally, she cleared her throat, and her eyes focused on me again. "I'm so glad to hear that. Well, I'll let you get back to things. I just wanted to come and introduce myself. It's great to meet you, Nadine."

"You, too," I said, feeling relieved that she didn't say anything more about my parents.

When she and Odin left the room, I turned to Talia. "She seems really nice."

Talia frowned. "Yeah. All the students love her. I just feel so bad for her."

"Bad?"

Talia dropped her gaze. "She's had it really rough these last few years. First she lost her sister. Then just a few weeks ago she gave birth to a stillborn."

"Seriously?" I asked, my heart breaking for her. I couldn't imagine. "She seems a little old for a baby, doesn't she?"

Talia shrugged. "I don't think it was planned. She's not married."

"That's still gotta be hard, though," I said. My guts twisted at the thought. She'd lost so many important people in her life in such a small amount of time. I couldn't imagine adding any more people I loved to the list of those I'd already lost.

"She said something happened to your parents?" Talia asked softly. It didn't sound like she was trying to prod, but rather make sense of what Headmistress Verla had said.

A heavy weight settled on my chest at the mention of my parents, so I sat on the bed to ease it. "Yeah. It was a car accident. That's why I came here."

Talia's frown deepened. "I'm so sorry, Nadine."

My breath wavered. "I don't really want to talk about it."

Talia's expression was soft, like she understood. "I could cheer you up."

I looked up to her and cracked a smile. I was glad my roommate was so nice. "You can try."

Talia sat on her piano bench and positioned her hands over the keys. Gus hopped onto the bench beside her and watched as her fingers began to move expertly, creating a soft, beautiful melody. I lay back in the bed, relaxing as I let the beautiful sound wash over me.

"This is the only way I know how to cheer people up," Talia admitted without missing a note.

"It's working," I told her.

"That's good."

She continued playing while I took deep breaths. My mind was on my parents now, which meant it could be hours until I stopped thinking about them. I loved them with all my heart, but sometimes it was easier to forget that they were gone. When I brought up their memory, a huge hole opened up in my abdomen, and it felt like it was trying to suck the rest of my body inside of it.

My head started to hurt, and my bottom lip quivered.

Suddenly, the music stopped.

"Can I help you?" Talia said.

My eyes shot open, and I pushed myself up in bed to see who she was talking to. I didn't get a look at the door before the voice came.

"I'm looking for Nadine."

That hole inside my stomach seemed to slam shut, and the tension in my head eased instantly. In fact, my whole body felt lighter as a fluttering sensation overtook my insides. Was that *Lucas* standing in my doorway?

I got to my feet and walked around the side of the bed where he could see me. His eyes seemed to light up, and the weight melted off my shoulders.

"Well, you found me," I told him. "Come in."

Lucas stepped into the room, followed by another guy I didn't know. Lucas must've noticed me eyeing him, because he quickly introduced us. "Nadine, this is my roommate, Grant. Grant, this is Nadine."

"Hey," Grant said, but his eyes remained locked on Talia.

Talia didn't seem to notice him, as she'd turned back to her piano and kept on playing. Grant smirked and stepped forward, leaning against the wall next to her.

"Well, *hello* beautiful," he said.

Talia didn't miss a beat on the piano. "Really? That's the pick-up line you go with?"

Grant stood straight up, looking shocked. "I'm sorry. Did it not work? Let me try again."

He leaned back against the wall and cleared his throat. "Did it hurt when you fell from heaven?"

Talia kept her eyes on her moving fingers. "Try again."

Beside me, Lucas chuckled. "Good Goddess, he's making a fool of himself."

"Really? I find it a little entertaining," I admitted.

Grant tugged at the collar of his shirt. "Is it hot in here, or is it just you?"

"Again," Talia said flatly.

Grant took a deep breath, like he was about to go in for the kill. "If I told you that you had a beautiful body, would you hold it against me?"

"No," she deadpanned. "Try again."

Grant groaned. "You're killing me."

Talia shrugged, but continued playing. "I'm going to make you do it again until you get it right."

Damn it. I loved this girl already.

Grant sighed, then stood up straight and spoke softly. "Hey, I'm Grant."

"I'm Talia," she introduced.

"Talia," he repeated, sounding pleased. "I couldn't help but notice that you're really talented. Is that *Dark Midnight* by the Wicked Warlocks?"

Talia glanced up at him with half a smile. "It is. You've heard of them?"

Grant beamed, pleased that she was responding. "Oh, yeah. I watched them play live last year."

Lucas leaned over to me and whispered, "The Wicked Warlocks are a local band."

"I figured," I whispered back.

"Have you seen them play?" Grant asked.

Talia's smile widened. "Considering my brother is their lead singer and I write half their songs, I'd have to say yes."

Grant's jaw dropped so low it was comical. "Shut up! Your brother is Tyler Murphy?"

"The one and only," Talia said.

"What would you think he'd say if I asked his little sister out on a date?" Grant asked.

"Smooth," Lucas mumbled.

Talia stopped playing, then looked up to Grant. "He'd probably castrate you for asking."

Grant's eyes went wide.

Talia snickered. "Good thing you don't have to ask him, seeing as I can speak for myself."

Grant relaxed and beamed at her. "So, what would you say to a date?"

Talia looked thrilled, but she was having too much fun. "How about we hang out with some friends first?"

Grant narrowed his eyes. "But, like, as a date?"

Talia laughed. "Let's start with this and maybe it'll turn into a date."

Grant shrugged. "I'll take it."

"Perfect." Talia stood and bounced over to her bed to grab her purse. "Nadine and I were talking about heading down to the Lounge to order some of Barry's Enchanted Muffins. She's never had them before."

"Sounds good," Grant said. He looked to Lucas for confirmation.

Lucas hesitated. "Oh, uh. I was just there and..."

He trailed off and looked to me. I was already reaching for my purse, excited about these magic muffins.

Lucas cleared his throat. "Never mind. Let's go."

We stepped out into the hall, and Grant took a right while Lucas went left. I followed behind Lucas, who kept walking without looking back. "This way, bro."

Grant whirled around and scrambled to catch up with us. "I swear to the Goddess, I'm never going to figure out this campus's layout."

"Is there anything that way, anyway?" I asked. "I mean, besides other dorm rooms?"

"No," Lucas said. "Unless you want to play Russian Roulette with the East staircase."

I tilted my head to the side. "What do you mean?"

"We call it the Vanishing Stairwell. There used to be a stairwell at the end of each hall, as well as the grand staircase in the middle," Lucas explained. "A few years ago, some girls in the room at the end of the hall wanted to expand their dorm, so they tried a space-bending spell. It clashed with the current spell and spread to the stairwell. Now it just kind of comes and goes."

"Huh. That's weird," I remarked. "What happens if it vanishes while you're inside?"

"Believe me," Grant said. "It's best to avoid it all together. Someone once got stuck in there for a month, and he starved to death. Rumor has it, he still haunts the staircase—when it appears, that is."

My eyebrows were raised so high I could feel the tension in my face. "Wow. Okay. Use the main staircase. Roger that."

The Main Foyer was quieter now that most students had been through registration. Lucas led us down the stairs and to a wide hall behind the staircase. He slowed as a pair of double doors came into view.

"Ladies, let me introduce you to the Lounge." He gestured to the doors and let Talia and me step inside ahead of him.

The Lounge was huge, with various walls sectioning off different areas. I couldn't see it all. The restaurant was straight up front, so I started for that first. Like the rest of the school, the lighting was dim, and there were various chandeliers that hung over the tables. It reminded me of an upscale bar, but without the liquor behind the counter.

There weren't very many people here. A large menu was hung above the main counter, so I assumed that was where we ordered. I couldn't take in the entire menu. There was a section of regular meals, then a menu of all different desserts that seemed to have magical powers—things like Glamour Gelato, Yodeling Yogurt, Slimming Sundae, and literal Humble Pie.

A girl with curly red hair who looked older than me stepped out of the back and up to the counter. I noticed the cauldron tattoo on her collarbone. Her name tag read *Darcy*. "Let me know when you're ready to order."

"Thanks," Lucas said. "We'll just be a minute."

"Is that Slimming Sundae for real?" I asked. Who wouldn't love to eat a sundae and lose a few pounds?

Talia crinkled up her nose, like it wasn't that great. "It only lasts for a few hours."

"In that case, let's stick with the muffins," I said.

Lucas stepped up to the counter. "We'll take a dozen of Barry's Enchanted Muffins. It's on me, guys."

"A dozen muffins?" I balked.

He shrugged. "They're pretty small."

The red-head girl turned to a rack behind the counter, where there were stacks of pre-packaged muffins. She handed the box to Lucas, who promptly turned and headed to an empty table. She never told him his total or gave him a receipt. It was like our bracelet-slash-credit-cards knew how much to charge to our account based on our order.

The four of us sat around a table next to a beautiful painting of a cat. Lucas sat across from me and opened the box. The muffins were bite-sized and all different colors. I didn't know which one to choose first.

"Try this one." Talia picked up one that looked like chocolate and slid it over to me.

"Talia, no," Lucas warned. "Maybe something a little tamer."

"What does it do?" I was intrigued.

Talia smirked. "Just try it."

I picked up the muffin and began peeling off the paper cup. I'd try anything once.

Lucas sighed. "Don't say I didn't warn you."

I popped the muffin in my mouth. A rich, chocolate taste filled my mouth, but it was better than regular chocolate, like I could taste the magic infused into it. Almost instantly, I felt this tingling in my chest. I looked down, then *bam!* My boobs were the size of watermelons. They almost ripped my shirt to pieces! My bra stretched tightly across the massive things.

"Talia!" I screamed, throwing my hands over my chest and ducking my giant boobs beneath the table. It barely did anything to hide them. If anything, leaning over just made my cleavage that much more obvious to the two guys across the table.

Talia burst into a fit of laughter. Across from her, Grant's eyes were glued to my chest, and he had his hand over his mouth as he tried not to laugh.

"My eyes are up here, buddy," I snapped at him, but it was all in jest.

Even Lucas cracked a smile. At least he was being decent and wasn't staring, though I caught him glance downward a few times.

"How long do these things last?" I asked. "I can't walk around like this all day!"

"They'll be gone in a minute," Talia assured me.

I relaxed a little. "Okay. Let's see what yours does."

Talia ate a muffin that looked like lemon-poppy-seed. Within seconds, her eyebrows started growing, until they formed into a single long, bushy unibrow. She leaned forward on one elbow and gave Grant a suggestive look while she wiggled her eyebrows. "Still want that date, sweetheart?"

He beamed. "Hell yeah."

She looked a little surprised and sat up straighter. "Well, let's see yours first."

Grant ate a banana muffin. I waited for something to happen, but several seconds ticked by and nothing changed.

"What does that one do?" I asked.

"I don't know," Grant said, but it wasn't in his own voice. It was at least an octave higher and sounded like he'd inhaled helium. His eyes went wide at the sound. "Dude, that is freaky!"

"Sing something," I encouraged.

"I don't sing," he replied in the comical high-pitched voice.

"Come *on*," Talia begged.

"Okay," he caved, then launched into a silly version of *Twinkle, Twinkle Little Star*.

Lucas rolled his eyes. By the time we got to him, my boobs had shrunk to their normal size and fit into my bra again.

"Your turn," I said, nudging him with my foot under the table. I didn't expect my foot to tingle at the contact, but it did. And then he looked at me, and my whole body was done for. It turned to mush. It was like he had this magic around him that did that every time we touched.

Lucas held up a red muffin like it was a shot and said, "Here goes nothing."

Except it never got to his mouth. He froze in place as his eyes locked on something behind me. I turned to see what he was looking at and found myself staring at three perfect girls strolling into the Lounge. They were the same girls I'd seen a few days ago—the Lucky Three. There was main bitch Chloe in front, followed by Gwen and Camille.

Talia frowned when she spotted them. "Not these bitches."

"You know them?" I asked.

"Yeah, we're in the same year," she said. "They were queen bees of our high school."

"Doesn't look like they've realized that doesn't make them king shit at the college," Grant whispered under his breath.

He was right. They walked in here like they owned the place.

Chloe didn't see us right away, as she had her eyes fixed to the front counter. But something must've caught her attention out of the corner of her eye, because she did a double take and looked straight at us.

Lucas groaned, but he'd already been spotted. Chloe changed course and started making her way over to us.

"Hey, Lucas," she practically sang, almost like the two had a thing. Judging by the way Lucas looked at her with disdain, whatever it was must've been one-sided.

"Chloe," he said politely.

"Why don't you introduce us to your friends?" The way she said it suggested that was the only reason she came over here.

Talia looked up to her with a raised eyebrow, which was back to normal now. "I'm Talia Murphy. You know me."

Chloe furrowed her brow and spoke with fake politeness. "Do I?"

Talia stared at her in disbelief. "Yes. We've been in class together since the first grade. I live on your street."

"Hmm…" Chloe mused. "I guess you just have one of those faces. You know, it blends in with all the others."

"On the contrary, I think she's beautiful and stands out," Grant growled.

Chloe looked down at him with a sneer. "Yeah, you would."

Whatever that meant.

Chloe turned her gaze on me. "I haven't seen you around before. And I know *everybody*."

"Apparently not," Talia mumbled under her breath, but Chloe ignored her.

"I'm new," I said.

"Huh. We don't get many new kids," Chloe shrugged.

"Well, we exist," I replied.

She glanced to Grant and turned up her nose. "Yeah, I can see that. I'm Chloe Olson, by the way."

"Mm…" I pretended to think. "Never heard of you."

She squirmed a little, like that bothered her. "And you are?"

"Nadine Evers," I told her, not really caring if she knew or not.

"Nadine Evers?" she repeated under her breath. "Why does that sound —wait! Are you Helena Tucker's granddaughter?"

"The one and only," I answered proudly.

Chloe's nostrils flared, like I'd just said something to seriously offend her. She slapped her palms flat on the table and leaned down to get right up in my face. She punctuated each word and spoke very clearly. "What the fuck are you doing in Octavia Falls?"

I leaned back in my chair, totally taken off guard. It was like she had something against me. I hadn't even done anything to piss her off yet… unless she'd seen me spying on her the other day.

Lucas shot to his feet and put a hand on Chloe's shoulder. "Back off, Chloe."

She slapped his hand away and whirled on him. "Don't tell me what to do."

She turned back to me, unadulterated hatred marring her features. I seriously had no idea what I'd done wrong. "You don't belong in Octavia Falls. You never should've come here."

I scoffed and crossed my arms. "Ominous, much?"

"I'm serious," she warned. "If you want to stay here, you won't go through with your Evoking Ceremony."

I rolled my eyes. All these basic bitches were the same. I'd handled them in the past. I could handle her. "Yeah, okay. I'll keep that in mind."

Chloe narrowed her eyes toward me, like she was trying to curse me with them. Lucas threw himself between us. "Seriously, Chloe, you need to leave."

She didn't take her eyes off me, but she started backing away. "This is far from over."

She whirled around, and her girl squad followed without a word.

I turned back to my friends. "Holy crap. What was that about?"

Talia shot a scowl at Chloe's retreating form. "No idea."

"She's just like that," Grant said. "I bet she's trying to scare you because you're new. She did the same thing when I first met her. She called me Hispanic scum."

I frowned. "I'm sorry."

Lucas sat back down, but he didn't take his eyes off Chloe, as if watching her for potential threats.

"Thanks, by the way," I told him. "She looked like she was about to curse my ass."

Lucas chuckled lightly. "No problem. She can't, though, because she hasn't gone through with her Evoking Ceremony yet. And if she did curse you, she'd get in trouble."

Something told me she'd find a way to talk herself out of repercussions.

"She's just threatened by you," Lucas assured me.

I gave him a skeptical look. "Threatened by me?"

He shrugged. "Yeah, because your grandma is such a powerful witch. Her family's powerful, too. Chloe's slated to be one of the best witches of her class. She doesn't want to lose her spot at the top."

I rolled my eyes. Like I said, all these basic bitches were the same. "Whatever. She has nothing to worry about."

Talia smiled. "Well, you already made the top of *my* list."

I reached for another muffin. "Good to know. I'll be sure to steer clear of Chloe from now on."

"A good idea," Lucas confirmed.

"Is this one any fun?" I asked, holding up a chocolate chip muffin.

Lucas smirked from across the table. "Will you still eat it if I told you no?"

I nodded firmly. "Absolutely."

I popped the muffin in my mouth, and my hair instantly changed to an I-don't-give-a-fuck bright blue.

"Ah," I said. "The perfect muffin to fit my mood."

C·

CLASSES STARTED ON TUESDAY, the day after Labor Day. Luckily, Talia and I had explored campus the day before, so we knew where our classrooms were. We had Miriamic History together, which I was grateful for, since I didn't want to attend my first class on my own.

The classroom was huge and set up like a movie theater, with big comfy chairs lined in rows. There must've been at least a hundred First Year students here. I noticed the Lucky Three up in front, but they didn't see us as we took our seats in the middle of the room.

"I'm totally going to fail this class," I groaned as I pulled out my laptop to take notes.

Talia scoffed. "You are not. What makes you say that?"

"Because everyone here knows all this history. It's brand new to me," I explained.

"You'll catch up in no time," Talia promised.

Our professor entered the room. He looked really old, like the history he'd be teaching would be told first-hand. His white hair was in stark contrast to his dark skin. He wore all black, including a silk black tie over a black button-down shirt. Though he looked ancient, he moved with grace down the main aisle until he came to the front of the room. The entire class quieted as all eyes turned to our professor.

"Good morning, students," he said kindly. "I'm Professor Richards, and this is Miriamic History. Welcome to your first semester at Miriam College of Witchcraft. Today, we will be studying the basics of our history. Later this week, we'll jump into more in-depth topics. There is no textbook in this class, so I suggest you don't skip my class, as you'll find it very difficult to pass your exams."

Professor Richards jumped into the lecture immediately. I rushed to start taking notes. "We're all familiar with Mother Miriam. She is the mother of all witches and warlocks within our coven, the very woman we are all descended from. The beginning of our coven starts with her story."

Professor Richards pointed his palms to the high ceiling. Small orbs the size of marbles floated up from his hands. They started out bright, then dimmed to various shades as he arranged them above himself in an intricate pattern. The orbs came together to form the image of a woman. Her face was identical to the painting that hung above the mantle in the foyer. It was clear he was a talented artist as well as a historian.

"Mother Miriam lived as a handmaiden in Europe during the fourteenth century," Professor Richard lectured. As he spoke, the orbs began to move to create a scene. The image of Mother Miriam began walking through thin air, performing chores like we were watching a play. "Her master was very mean to her. If she didn't do exactly as he asked, he'd lock her in the cellar for days without food or water. If she asked questions, he beat her."

The image of a whip came out of nowhere and slashed across her back. The orbs shifted quickly to make it look as if she was crying out in pain.

"You don't want to know some of the terrible things he did to her," Professor Richards said sadly. He took a deep breath and continued. "One day, she accidentally spilled a pail of water while doing her chores. He punished her by making her stand in the hot coals of the fire. The flesh burned clean off her feet."

Shudder.

"That night, she crawled from the house and fell to her knees, praying for someone to help her escape these terrible conditions."

The image depicted a woman on her knees with her hands folded in front of herself, looking toward the skies. My guts twisted as he told the story.

"She'd spent many nights praying to the gods, but they never answered her prayers," Professor Richards continued. "So instead, she summoned a demon to beg for retribution against her master. She was willing to do anything to escape his tyranny, including selling her own soul to a devil."

Silence settled over the room for a moment as we all took in the heavy weight of the story.

"A demonic god by the name of Santos appeared. As you all know, he is the father of all Miriamic people." More orbs floated up out of Professor Richards's palms and formed a second figure beside Mother Miriam. He seemed to look down upon her with mercy.

Professor Richards continued. "As he listened to her story, he became enraged. He traveled to the house of her master and killed him. It was after he sliced her master's head clean off his shoulders that he spoke his famous quote, *Even a demon would not be so heartless.*"

First of all, decapitation? Gross! Second, if this master guy was pissing off *demons*, there was a lot more about his treatment of Miriam that Professor Richard wasn't telling us. Part of me was curious to know, and the other part was grateful he'd spared us the gory details.

"In exchange for what he did, Mother Miriam pledged her soul to Santos, but he would not take it, for he felt she'd already given up enough to her master, that she didn't deserve an eternity in the Abyss," Professor Richards said. "To protect her, Santos remained on earth with Miriam, where they lived out the rest of their lives together. It was during that time that she taught him how to love, and they had five children together."

I gasped and leaned over to Talia. "Does that mean we're all part demon?"

She nodded.

Holy shit. Why hadn't Grammy mentioned this earlier? I had demon blood running through my veins!

"Each of these children had a different power," Professor Richards said. "With each child born, so was a new Cast. When Miriam died, Santos gifted her the power of the gods, and she became a goddess herself. Together, they formed Alora, our afterlife, and Mother Miriam became the sole judge of our people. Follow her, and you will be welcomed to Alora with open arms. Defy her, and you will be cast into the Abyss."

"The Abyss?" I whispered to Talia.

"It's basically hell," she whispered back.

"You have hell?" I asked.

She looked a little shocked by the question. "Well, yeah. Don't all religions?"

Touché.

Professor Richards went on to discuss the importance of Miriam's relationship with Santos and how together they had changed demonic principles that had been in place since basically the beginning of time.

"No demon, be it a demonic god or a lesser spirit, had ever created a utopia before," he continued. "It was the compassion Santos felt for Miriam that changed him, and her undying gratitude thereafter that helped them grow together. It was only because of their love for one another that they could create Alora in the first place."

By the time class ended, I had so much information to process.

"What is it?" Talia asked as we walked out of the lecture hall.

I shook my head. "I just can't imagine that kind of love—so strong and passionate that you can create an entire afterlife out of it. Can people really change like that?"

Talia cringed. "Don't let anyone else hear you say that. Santos's story is a beacon of hope for us. We believe in forgiveness and second chances."

I furrowed my brow. "But can't Mother Miriam kick you out of the coven as she pleases?"

"Yes," Talia confirmed. "But not without giving you a second chance."

I didn't know what a second chance entailed, but worry knotted in my gut as I wondered if that'd be enough—or if being an outsider had already doomed me for failure.

SEVEN

The first week of classes passed by before I realized it. After Necromancy Safety on Friday, I waited until everyone else left the room before approaching Professor Warren.

"Lucas," he said brightly. "What can I do for you?"

I looked down to the positivity journal I clutched in my hands. My heart beat rapidly, though I couldn't explain why. This journal was *private*, and it felt like handing over a part of myself. I didn't like being vulnerable, but Professor Warren was my mentor. He'd said it more than once that he couldn't help me if I didn't help myself.

"I, um, wrote down a few things, if you wanted to take a look," I said.

He stood straighter, looking somewhat surprised. "Sure."

I handed over the journal. Professor Warren glanced at the first page, then flipped to the next to see if there was more. I hadn't even filled the first page yet, but at least I had a start.

Professor Warren didn't look at the journal long enough to read what I'd written. He closed it and handed it back to me, and I felt a weight lift off my shoulders. It eased my nerves to know he wasn't reading every entry. He probably wouldn't have made sense of what it all meant, either.

My gift led me to Nadine.

Muffins in the Lounge.

We met Talia.

Grant seems happy.

It wasn't sure if half that stuff counted. Technically, Grant meeting Talia had nothing to do with my gift, but if Professor Warren thought my gift led to Nadine—and meeting Nadine led to meeting Talia—then I guess it counted. Grant couldn't shut up about her since they day they met. He kept asking me when we were going to hang out with *the girls* again. I told him he had to give her time or he was going to suffocate the poor girl.

"I'm glad to see you taking this seriously," Professor Warren said. "I hope it's helping."

I shrugged. "I think so. I'm not sure yet."

"Well, we've only started," Professor Warren pointed out. "I want to see the next page filled by our next meeting."

I nodded. "I'll try."

It'd been like pulling teeth. I'd sat there for hours trying to think of one other thing besides meeting Nadine that my gift had done for me. It was only when I started playing off meeting her that the other ideas came to me. If I could tie everything back to that, I could probably have a page filled by next week—assuming things went well tonight.

"How have you been, Professor?" I asked.

He tilted his head in question. "I'm fine. Why do you ask?"

"You said you weren't feeling well the last time we talked," I reminded him.

"Ah, yes. I'm quite well now, thanks for asking. Whatever it was wasn't long lived."

"That's good to hear," I said. "I have to get to Afterlife Studies, but I wanted to keep you updated on my assignment."

Professor Warren nodded. "I appreciate that, Lucas. Keep up the good work."

I left the classroom feeling proud. None of my professors had called anything I did *good work*. In fact, I barely passed last semester at all.

Afterlife Studies was pretty easy so far. We were studying the many ways ghosts could communicate with us. We'd covered how ghosts speak to mediums, and we were moving on to Ouija boards next week. Later in the semester, we were supposed to conduct our own séance and write a paper about it.

After class, I went looking for Nadine, since I wanted to talk to her about tonight. I stuck my head into the Lounge, but she wasn't there. I considered visiting her room, but I didn't want to look overly eager, so I checked all the other common areas, like the pool and the foyer. Eventually, I headed outside. I swear to the Goddess my heart stopped when I saw her.

Nadine sat below a huge maple tree on the front lawn. Her back was leaned against the trunk while she typed on her laptop. She was wearing a black floppy hat with a wide brim that should've looked comical on her but was actually kind of hot, along with a dark long-sleeve shirt and matching skinny jeans. I thought she looked really good in all black. A gray tabby cat came up to her and started rubbing against her foot. She stopped typing to scratch it behind the ears.

I walked up to her casually, pretending as if I'd just been passing by. "Hey."

She glanced up, and a smile spread across her face. "Hey, Lucas. What's up?"

I shrugged. "I couldn't help but notice you were sitting alone. Did you want company, or were you busy?"

"No! Not busy at all." She shut her laptop and quickly gathered her books, then gestured beside herself in the grass. "Sit."

I took her offer and sat beside her in the shade. It was a beautiful day, and the lawn was crowded with people. "What's with the hat?"

She lifted her hand to touch it lightly, like she forgot she'd been wearing it. "Oh, uh, a fashion statement?"

I eyed her. She sounded unsure of herself, which was weird. I didn't know Nadine well, but she didn't seem like the kind of person who did things without a purpose. "A fashion statement?"

She wrinkled her nose, like she'd been caught in a lie. I found it kind of cute. "Okay, truth is, I don't like the sun."

I raised an eyebrow.

"I mean, I'm sensitive to it," she quickly added. "It's not a big deal."

She seemed like she didn't want to talk about it, so I changed the subject. "What are you studying?"

"Miriamic History," she said with a sigh. "It's a lot to take in."

I smirked. "Yeah, I can see that, if you didn't grow up with it."

Nadine groaned. "I told Talia I'd never be able to keep up, but she didn't believe me."

I chucked. "Who do you have?"

"Professor Richards," she said. "He's a great storyteller, but he moves so fast."

"Well, there's a lot to cover," I pointed out. "If you need help, I can slow things down for you."

Nadine's spine straightened. She was so excited that she grabbed my arm. "Really?"

"Yeah, why not? It's like, the one subject I'm actually good at."

"Shut up," she said lightly. "Are you serious? Because I have so many questions and I need to be caught up by next week."

"Absolutely," I replied. "Whenever you want."

"Are you free now?" she asked with bright eyes.

She had so much energy radiating off of her that I actually found myself smiling. I could tell I'd just made her whole day.

"Yeah, my classes are done for the day. I have a few hours until this party I'm going to tonight. But hey, why don't we study until then and you can come with me?"

Okay, I officially deserved some sort of award for slipping in that invitation so casually. I expected it to go a lot differently, mainly involving stumbling over my own words and fucking up the invitation.

Instead, Nadine smiled. "Yeah, that sounds great."

Score one for Lucas.

"So, what are you stuck on?" I asked.

"Just about everything," she joked. "Okay, so I get that the demon Santos saved Miriam and all that, but like, I don't get why he did it. He was a demonic god, so that makes him evil, right? How could he have any compassion for her?"

It was obvious Nadine was digging into things she didn't need to know for her exams, but it was a valid question.

"Demons aren't inherently evil," I explained.

Nadine tilted her head to the side. Damn it, she was so cute. "Then what makes a demon a demon?"

"Demon is a term for someone who lives in the Abyss," I told her. "There are a lot of reasons someone might end up there. Usually, they've either rejected their god or have been rejected *by* their god. Once cast to the Abyss, they usually band up with a demonic god and are gifted a set of powers to do that god's bidding. They make people do horrible things and turn them away from their religion so more people will join them in the afterlife."

Nadine furrowed her brow. "But Santos *was* a god."

"Right, but the other gods rejected him," I said. "All the demonic gods are outcasts."

"How'd he become a god?" she asked.

I was a little taken aback by the question.

She seemed to notice. "I mean, Santos made Mother Miriam into a god. Who made him?"

"There's more than one way to become a god," I explained. "You're either born a god or made into one by another god. Santos was a god at birth."

She looked more and more confused as I explained. "How many are there? Gods, I mean."

I shrugged. "I don't think anyone knows."

"So what makes a demon different from anyone else?" she asked.

"It depends on who they follow," I said. "Think of the afterlife like a big city, with endless gated communities. Each of these communities have rules in order to enter. If you don't pass or you leave, there's only one place left to go."

"The slums," Nadine said with a frown. "The Abyss."

"Right," I confirmed. "It's where the worst of the worst go. But it's just chaos—a constant war zone. Trust me, you don't want to end up there."

"Well, why don't all these demonic gods just go create their own communities?" Nadine asked.

I shrugged, wishing I had all the answers. "A lot of reasons, I guess. Some don't have the followers for it. Others want complete control and aren't willing to step aside and focus on their own people. Some are fighting their own wars with other gods. The whole thing is a mess, really. Anyway, back to your original question. You're right to assume demons are evil, because most of them are. But they're still capable of the same emotions we are. They just have to get past the bad first."

Nadine nodded, looking deep in thought. "I guess I can understand that. It must be hard for them, after being rejected and outcast like that."

Spoken like a true witch. No one else would show compassion for a demon.

"So, when people say we have demon blood, what does that mean?" she asked. "If Santos changed, does that mean he's no longer a demon?"

I shrugged. "Once a demon, always a demon, I guess."

Nadine glanced down to her textbook. "So, what happened after Miriam died? Like, to the coven, I mean? So far we've only talked about how she got her powers from Santos and they went on to create Alora."

I opened my mouth to explain, but I suddenly came up with a better idea. "Why don't I show you?"

Nadine's eyes widened in intrigue. "Show me what?"

I stood and reached out my hand to her. "It's a surprise."

She eyed my hand curiously, then took it and let me help her to her feet. She placed a hand on her hip and narrowed her eyes at me. "Just don't kidnap me, okay?"

I chuckled and pressed my hand to my heart. "Nad, I'm offended. I would never."

"Liar." She poked me in the side. It was the smallest of touches, but it made my insides flip. I swore to the Goddess, if she got any closer to me, my dick was going to give away just how I felt about her.

Shit. I shouldn't be thinking about that.

"Okay, okay," I teased back. "You caught me. I'm here to kidnap you. Are you going to put up a fight?"

She pretended to think about it. "Nah, I'll let you kidnap me just this once."

"Perfect. Let's go."

I helped Nadine gather her books, then led her outside the gates of Miriam College.

She hiked her backpack up a little. "Is it a long walk?"

I shrugged. "Not far. Less than a mile."

"Oh," she said flatly, but she kept her eyes forward and tightened her grip on the strap of her bag.

"Do you want me to carry those?" I asked.

"My books? No, I've got them," she assured me. "Tell me more about the coven's history."

"I told you," I reminded her. "I have to show you."

"Right," she said. "Then tell me more about you."

My body tensed. I didn't often talk about myself. There were a lot of things she probably didn't want to know.

"Like what?" I asked.

She shrugged. "I don't know. What do you like to do in your spare time?"

"Um, not much." Seriously, I didn't even know what I did with myself these days. Most times, I just felt like a shell of a human being. I'd rather sleep than anything, but Grant usually forced me out of bed and made me go outside. "I like nature, I guess," I admitted. "I like walking the Black Circle trail. Speaking of which…"

I gestured ahead of us to the trailhead that crossed the road to campus. "We'll be taking it to get where we're going."

"Cool." Nadine turned onto the trail. Her eyes went skyward, and she took in all the trees hanging over the path. It was really pretty out here, but I personally couldn't keep my eyes off her.

"There's a disc golf course close by that I like to play at," I told her.

"Oh, that sounds fun," she remarked. "I've never been."

"It's fun. You might like it." I didn't know why I said that, since I hardly knew her. "What do you like to do?"

She reached up to touch a leaf on a low-hanging branch. I noticed her pace slowed when she did it, and it never picked back up. I slowed my steps to walk alongside her. We were so close that we could've been holding hands. It was the first time I noticed that she smelled like roses, which I really liked.

"I like to read and binge watch TV, if those count," she said.

"No, they don't," I deadpanned.

Nadine shot me a look, and I couldn't hold in my laugh.

"I'm joking," I said. "They totally count."

"I do yoga, too, but not since…" Nadine trailed off.

"Not since what?" I asked curiously.

She sighed. "Not since I moved here. I really need to get back into it."

"Yeah, it sounds relaxing."

We walked for another ten minutes before we took another path and finally arrived. A small clearing spanned in front of us, where a massive, twisted oak tree sat in the center. Nadine's head tipped so far back that she had to hold her hat to keep it on. She stared at the tree in wonder.

The tree was huge and took five people hugging the base to reach all the way around. It reached up so high that you couldn't see the top when you were standing beneath it. The gnarly, twisted branches spanned so wide that the small clearing was completely shaded. The branches were heavy and hung low enough to climb onto them, though it was considered disrespectful among the coven to climb the tree. Huge leaves bigger than my hand fluttered gently in the breeze, and an assortment of acorns littered the ground. Several park benches were placed around the clearing. In the fall, the tree turned a rich, beautiful orange. It was the most beautiful tree in all of Octavia Falls.

"Wow." Nadine finally looked to me, and her expression was incredible. It was like I'd just given her the best gift in the whole world. "I've never seen anything like it."

"Come on," I said. "Let's sit."

Nadine seemed relieved as we took a spot on one of the park benches. She took her hat off and set it beside herself. The park was completely empty at this time of day, so we were alone.

"This is the Protection Tree," I told her, gazing up to its twisted branches. "It holds the power that fuels the protection spell around the town, which keeps out anyone who's not of Miriamic descent or preapproved into the coven."

"That's why it let me in," she guessed. "Because I have Miriamic blood."

I nodded. "So it sounds like Professor Richards left off with Mother Miriam's death?"

"Yeah, that's all I know so far."

"After she died, Mother Miriam's descendants spread across Europe," I told her. "A lot of them were accused of witchcraft, which led to mass hysteria and marked the beginning of the Burning Times."

"The witch trials?" Nadine asked.

"Right," I confirmed. "It lasted hundreds of years, and a lot of innocent people were burned or hanged for witchcraft."

Nadine dropped her gaze to her hands. She looked sad.

"The Miriamic people came to the States around 1600 to escape the trials," I continued. "But the trials only continued here. To protect themselves from further persecution, her descendants banded together and formed Octavia Falls in the early 1700s."

"Was that when the tree was planted and the protection spell made?" she guessed.

"The tree wasn't really *planted*," I clarified.

She tilted her head in question. "What do you mean?"

"The tree wasn't grown from seed," I told her.

Her eyes sparkled with intrigue.

"Ever wonder why we call our town Octavia Falls?" I asked her.

"I thought about it," she admitted. "Where exactly *are* the falls?"

I shook my head. "It's not *falls*, as in waterfalls. It's *falls*, as in a verb. Years ago when the town was formed, five priestesses came to this very clearing to perform the protection spell. But it was a very complicated spell, one that required the magic of four priestesses to flow through the fifth— the Curse Breaker. Her name was Octavia Barrows. The spell required more magic than she could give, and so she gave it all. Octavia fell right here in this clearing. The earth claimed her body, and out of her grave grew the Protection Tree, which activated the spell. She died to protect the coven."

"Wow," Nadine breathed. She looked back to the tree, and complete wonder crossed her eyes.

I noticed her shift a little. "What's wrong?"

She took a deep breath. "I'm still trying to wrap my head around all this. Some days I wake up and forget that magic exists."

I smiled. "Yeah, it's pretty cool, isn't it?"

Nadine looked up to me with those bright eyes, and I knew I was done for. I just wanted to reach out and touch her.

No. Yes.

Do it!

I didn't know what possessed me to do it. It just happened. I reached out and tucked a strand of hair behind her ear. As I pulled my hand back, I conjured a quarter, then held it up to her.

Nadine placed her hand over her mouth and snickered at me. She was obviously amused. "Oh my God. You're a real magician."

I rolled my eyes. "Warlock, but yeah."

Nadine seemed to relax as she dropped her hand from her mouth. "Thanks, Lucas."

I furrowed my brow. "For what?"

"For telling me about our history. It all makes more sense now. I just have one more question."

"What's that?" I asked.

A grin slowly spread across her face. "What should I wear to this party?"

☽

IT WAS TEN O'CLOCK, and I still hadn't spotted Nadine. The party was down at the lake, and the beach was packed, so I could've just missed her. But believe me, I'd been keeping an eye out. Grant and I sat in camp chairs close to the bonfire, and I'd been keeping watch for everyone who came and went from the parking lot. Music boomed across the beach, and the moonlight glistened across the water.

"Dude, you have to chill," Grant insisted, leaning back in his chair and taking a sip of beer. "They'll make it eventually."

I rolled my eyes at him. "Says the guy who just asked me for the third time in ten minutes if I'd spotted Talia."

We were both obsessed. Might as well admit it.

"I just hope they show up—" I started to say, but my words halted in their tracks when I saw her.

I'd told Nadine to wear a dress, since most of the other girls would, but I didn't expect her to come looking like *that*. My dick was practically trying to tear its way out of my jeans.

Fucking virgin, I chastised myself.

Nadine walked down the hill from the parking lot in a tiny black number that left very little to the imagination. It hugged her curves and showed so much skin—boobs, legs, and everything. There were even slits in the sides covered by see-through black fabric that showed the smooth skin along her torso. She wore her brown hair down in waves and fancy black sandals.

Grant stood. "Wow, she looks amazing, doesn't she?"

I was almost drooling. I swear I wasn't trying to objectify Nadine, but my dick kind of had other plans. It would *not* calm down.

"Yeah," I said breathlessly, rising to my feet beside him. "Nadine's really hot."

Grant elbowed me in the side. "Not her, lover boy. Talia."

I'd been so enamored by Nadine that I didn't even realize Talia was walking beside her. She was all dressed up and had on a dark pink dress, but she couldn't compare to Nadine.

"Hey, guys!" Talia called. She waved as they approached, then stopped in front of us. "Uh, Grant. You have a little something… there."

Talia touched the corner of her lip. Grant snapped his jaw shut and wiped the drool off his face.

I cleared my throat as Nadine met my eyes. "Glad you could make it."

"We're glad you invited us," she said, tugging at the bottom of her dress. She looked a little uncomfortable. I noticed Talia elbow her in the side. It was obvious Talia had made her wear the dress.

Out of respect, I forced myself not to look downward at her cleavage, which was fucking hard because her boobs looked amazing in that dress.

"Do you want something to drink?" I asked.

"Uh, no. I'm fine," Nadine said.

"Sure!" Talia answered at the same time.

Grant led Talia over to the coolers to get a drink, while I pulled up two chairs for the girls.

"Have a seat," I said. "The fire's nice."

Nadine took my invitation and sat. She crossed her legs, then uncrossed them, looking like she didn't know what to do with them. I quickly stripped off my hoodie and handed it to her. "Your legs look cold."

She blushed a little and took it. "Thanks."

Nadine draped the hoodie over her knees. I could tell she was only using it for modesty. I didn't want her feeling uncomfortable—ever.

Nadine relaxed into her chair and turned to me. "So, what are we cele-brating?"

I took a sip of my drink and shrugged. I hated beer, so I'd mixed some vodka with soda. It wasn't very strong, though. "Do we have to celebrate something to have a party?"

Nadine smirked. I wanted to kiss the smirk off those lips.

Good Goddess, where had that come from? I wasn't even drunk yet. And I could *not* kiss her.

"Usually," she teased.

"I don't know," I said. "We're celebrating the first week of school, I guess. Ask Cody White. His parents are mega rich, and he hosts one of these parties almost every weekend."

She raised an eyebrow. "And no one gets caught? I mean, most everyone here is under age, aren't they?" She glanced around to take in the crowd.

I shrugged. "Everyone just kind of looks the other way, I guess. We won't get in trouble. Is that why you don't want a drink?"

"Oh, no," she said with a wave of her hand. "I just… don't drink."

I tilted my head a little to the side. "A witch who doesn't drink? That's a new one."

Nadine perked up as a new song came on over the speakers. Her eyes went a little wide at the upbeat tune. "Hey, I actually know this one."

I listened for a few seconds and realized what it was. I groaned. "Seriously? They play this at every party. It's getting kind of old."

Nadine poked me in the shoulder. "*Love Potion Number Nine* is a classic."

"You can't even dance to it," I argued. "And it's basically an insult to actual love potions."

"Oh, come *on*," Nadine said. "It's fun. And you *can* dance to it."

I raised a challenging eyebrow and leaned closer to whisper. "Then prove it."

Nadine pressed her lips together, contemplating my challenge. Finally, she grabbed my hoodie from her lap and handed it to me as she stood. And holy fuck, I was glad she did. I needed something to hide the boner that was quickly forming. When Nadine danced, it was like magic of its own. She held her arms in the air and got lost in the music as she swayed her hips from side to side. Her hands traveled down her body and landed on the side of her hips on the beat. She slowed her hips to make a circle as the song rang out its signature line.

Nadine winked at me as the song transitioned into the next verse. She moved in a slow circle. When her back was to me, she threw her arms out on the beat, then shoved them into her hair in the sexiest display I'd ever seen while she shimmied her ass in my direction.

Was she trying to turn me on? Because it was working.

Nadine glanced back to assess my reaction, and she totally lost it. She went into a laughing fit.

"Woohoo!" Talia called as she and Grant returned. "Shake that thang, girl!"

Nadine's face turned beet red, but she shook her butt one last time for show. She clammed up when she noticed she'd started drawing some eyes. She quickly returned to her seat.

"Hey, don't stop for us," Grant teased. "Some of us were enjoying the show."

"Well, it wasn't meant for you," Nadine shot back playfully.

Grant held up a hand in surrender. "Hey, I didn't say *I* was the one enjoying it."

I kicked him hard, though the girls didn't notice. I mean, he didn't have to blurt out my crush on Nadine and scare her away.

Though, maybe that was best.

"Forget it," Nadine said. "The song's almost over anyway—"

"What are *you* doing here?" a female voice sneered from behind us, cutting Nadine off.

The four of us turned to see Chloe standing a few feet away, though she wasn't talking to us. Camille and Gwen stood on either side of her, each of them wearing a matching look of disgust. Chloe was dressed in her usual attire—a dark dress and heels—and she was staring down a girl I didn't know. The girl had light brown skin with red undertones, stick-straight black hair, and dark brown eyes. She seemed to cower under the weight of Chloe's stare.

"I, um, I..." the girl stuttered.

"I thought I told you not to come, you slut," Chloe growled.

Nadine's jaw dropped from beside me. Even I was a little shocked. Chloe was mean, but she usually kept her bitchiness in check around other people.

"You can leave me alone now," the girl said timidly, not meeting Chloe in the eye. "Ryan and I broke up."

"I don't care, Mandy," Chloe sneered. "It doesn't change that you slept with him."

Mandy's lips tightened. It was obvious she hated Chloe but was having a hard time standing up to her. "Yeah, well, that was his choice, not yours."

Chloe's hands curled into fists. She looked like she was about to start a girl fight. "Leave now."

Mandy's whole body shook, but she stood her ground. She lifted her head and looked Chloe straight in the eye. "Or what?"

Chloe didn't give second warnings. She raised her hands and shoved Mandy so hard that she stumbled backward and landed on the ground. Chloe reached down and grabbed Mandy by the ankle and started dragging her through the sand. "Then I'll make you!"

"Ow! Let go of me!" Mandy cried.

I leapt to my feet, but Nadine was faster than me. She rounded her chair so fast that it fell over, and sprinted over to Chloe, where she shoved her away from Mandy. I was only halfway there before Chloe was tumbling to the ground, kicking up sand.

"Leave her alone!" Nadine shouted.

At the same time, someone else had rushed over. She must've been one of Mandy's friends, because she helped Mandy to her feet like they knew each other.

Camille and Gwen turned their wicked gazes on Nadine. They looked like they were about to jump her. I threw myself in front of her, and they quickly backed down.

Chloe immediately recovered and pushed herself to her elbows. Shock crossed her face when she realized who'd tackled her. She pointed a manicured finger at Nadine as she got to her feet, like she willed a curse upon her or something. "You need to take a fucking seat, because this isn't about you."

Tons of people had stopped to look. Even though the music continued to play over the beach, and the bonfire crackled, all chatter had died down.

Nadine shoved her way past me to get up in Chloe's face. I wasn't going to lie, it kind of turned me on.

"Look at my face." Nadine's voice remained calm and steady as she pointed to her expression. "Does it look like I care? No. Because rule number one of the coven, we protect each other. So when I see someone being pushed around, I'm going to take a stand. That's what witches do. So maybe *you* need to take a damn seat and think about that for a minute."

Chloe's nostrils flared, and her lips tightened. It looked like the only reason she hadn't already punched Nadine was because so many people were watching. She held her head up high and said, "Bitch, this isn't even your coven. You're an outsider, and everyone knows it."

Nadine narrowed her eyes. "Oh, really? We'll see who the coven accepts when I'm the one standing up for them instead of beating them down."

"Okay," I said quickly, reaching for Nadine's arm. "That's enough."

I pulled Nadine away and stepped in front of her, creating a barrier between her and Chloe. "Chloe, this beach is big enough for everyone. Chill."

She narrowed her eyes at me. "Nobody asked you."

"Yeah, well, they didn't have to," I snapped.

By now, Grant was by my side, and Talia was right behind him.

Camille stepped forward and grabbed Chloe's elbow. "Let's go. This party's lame anyway."

Chloe didn't move for several seconds. She eyed me up and down, then shot daggers at Nadine. "You're not going to make it far in this coven. Sooner or later, everyone will see you for what you truly are."

"Fine with me," Nadine shot back.

Chloe turned on her heel and walked away. Camille and Gwen followed closely behind.

As soon as Chloe was gone, Nadine whirled around and went to Mandy's side. Mandy was standing beside her friend, looking relieved.

"Are you okay?" Nadine asked.

Mandy pushed her dark bangs out of her eyes. "I am now. Thank you."

Nadine offered a friendly smile. "It was no problem."

Mandy turned to the girl beside her. "Amy, this is Nadine. We met in The Hearse."

"Hi," Amy said with a wave.

"It's nice to meet you," Nadine replied. "Why don't you come sit by us?"

The girls glanced at each other and shrugged. "Yeah, why not?" Amy answered.

We found two more chairs for the girls and formed a circle not far from the fire.

"So, what's the deal?" Nadine asked boldly. "With Chloe, I mean?"

Talia leaned in a little closer to hear the gossip.

Mandy sighed. "It's dumb, really. I started dating her ex over the summer, and she's had it out for me ever since. We broke up because..." Mandy trailed off and looked to Amy.

Amy chuckled. "Because Chloe tried to turn her into a toad."

Grant's eyebrows shot up. "Did she really? How'd that go, considering she doesn't even have magic yet?"

Amy rolled her eyes. "She wanted *me* to do it, since I'm a Second Year. But I went to warn Mandy before Chloe could slip her the potion. It's how we met."

Mandy nudged her. "Yeah, and now you're not going anywhere. You're my soul sister."

"True," Amy replied with a smile.

"Anyway," Mandy said, "when I told Ryan, he laughed and said it would've been funny. So I broke up with him on the spot."

"That a girl!" Talia cheered, lifting her drink in celebration.

The other three girls joined in.

After about an hour, the girls were all getting a little tipsy, except for Nadine. But when Talia insisted they dance, Nadine joined them. The girls crowded around each other as they swayed their hips to the music. I just sat back and watched, because I wasn't much of a dancer. Plus, Nadine looked really nice.

"You gonna get in there?" Grant asked without taking his eyes off Talia.

"Nah," I said, sinking a little further into my seat. "You know how I feel about dancing."

"Bro, you need to get out and live a little," he insisted. "I want to see you smile for once."

"I *do* smile," I argued.

Grant looked at me sideways and spoke flatly. "Really?"

I suddenly realized how tense I was and that my arms were crossed. I dropped them to the armrests of my chair and sat up a little straighter. "Totally. See?"

I forced my lips into a smile, but it kind of ruined the mood. Forcing smiles was the worst. I'd been practicing it for almost a year now. You'd think I was a pro. But no. I hated it. But it kept people off my back.

"There you go." Grant clapped me on the shoulder. "Even though I can tell it's totally fake."

I shrugged. "Yeah, well, I wasn't trying very hard."

Grant looked back to the girls. Mandy and Amy were grinding on each other, and Talia was shaking her butt in Nadine's direction. Nadine threw her head back in laughter, then slapped Talia playfully on the ass.

"If you're not going to get in there, I am," Grant said eagerly. "See ya."

He gave me a salute, then stood and rushed over to the girls. Talia lit up when she saw him, then reached out for his hand. He spun her around, then caught her as she stumbled.

Fuck. I wanted to spin Nadine around like that. But I was a really, really bad dancer. I'd probably drop her rather than catch her.

Nadine shot a glance my way. I almost thought she was going to ask me to come join them, but she didn't. She smiled a little, then turned back to her friends. But that smile was enough. It warmed my heart in ways I didn't think possible.

I should just tell her I like her already.

The thought slipped into my mind before I could stop it.

No. I shot down the idea as soon as it came.

Friends was as far as we went. I shouldn't even be enabling that, but I just couldn't stay away from her.

I noticed Nadine's dancing slowed as the minutes ticked by. Her eyes kept darting over in my direction. I hoped she wasn't getting self-conscious because I was watching. Was I making it *that* obvious?

Eventually, she broke off from the group and came to sit beside me. She looked exhausted as she plopped down.

"Party pooper," she teased.

"I'm not a party pooper," I defended. "I just…"

She raised a curious eyebrow. "You're just…?"

My shoulders fell. "Fine. I'm a party pooper."

"I know," she chuckled. "But there's so much I *don't* know about you, Lucas."

"Like what?" I asked. "I'm an open book."

Mostly.

"What's your Cast?" she asked, like she was trying to figure me out.

It wasn't a secret. Everyone else already knew. But I liked the way she looked at me, like she was hungry for answers. So I decided to play with her.

"Guess," I said.

"Lucas!" She swatted my shoulder, but it was so light I barely felt it. "Unfair."

I shrugged. "You asked."

She eyed me up and down, like she was looking for my tattoo. Too bad she wasn't going to find it unless she wanted to strip me down.

Now that was something I wouldn't object to.

"Alchemist?" she asked slowly, like she was unsure of herself.

"No," I replied.

She pressed her lips together. "Seer?"

"You only get one guess."

"Hey! That wasn't part of the deal." She stuck her bottom lip out into a mock pout.

My gaze flickered down to her lips, and I started laughing. Damn, it felt so good to laugh. "You should've read the contract first."

She narrowed her eyes playfully. "Is this a sell-my-soul-to-the-devil kind of contract?"

"Do I look like the devil to you?" I teased.

"I don't know. You're all… mysterious."

I chuckled. "I'm not mysterious."

"You are! I still don't know your Cast." She paused for a second. "Or is that rude to ask?"

I shook my head. "Not rude. I just like watching you squirm."

Nadine squirmed in her seat for show, then said, "Seen enough?"

I smirked as my gaze flickered down to her cleavage. Damn it! I hadn't meant to do that. Not that I didn't want to, because Nadine was smoking hot. But I didn't want to be *that* guy.

"Not yet," I said.

Nadine went in to swat me again, but I grabbed her hand to stop her. Electricity sizzled between us when we touched. For a second, we both just sat there in silence, staring at each other. Her eyes were so soft, and she looked at me like she felt it, too. My stomach flipped in my abdomen.

Just friends, I reminded myself.

I dropped her hand before I let my feelings get away from me. Nadine cleared her throat and sat a little straighter in her seat. I noticed she was starting to look a little pale. She pressed her hand to the side of her face.

"Are you okay?" I asked, suddenly concerned.

"Yeah, it's nothing," she said softly. Her demeanor had quickly changed. "I'm just getting really tired."

It sounded like an excuse, but I didn't press her. "I guess it's getting kinda late. Do you want me to take you home? Back to school, I mean."

"What about Talia?" Nadine asked, glancing toward her.

"If she wants to stay, I'm sure Grant will get her home safely," I said.

"Yeah, okay," Nadine replied. "Let me go talk to her."

Nadine stood, though it looked like her knees were shaking. I didn't know why, since she hadn't drank anything all night. She made her way over to Talia and said a few things I couldn't hear, then returned.

"Grant's going to take Talia home in his car. Do you mind driving mine?" she asked.

"Not at all." I got to my feet and took Nadine's hand. My whole body lit up with nerves when I did. I didn't even know where it came from. It just seemed natural.

I was about to pull away and apologize, but Nadine leaned into me, like she was okay with it.

"Walk with me," she said.

I strolled alongside Nadine toward the parking lot. She pointed out which car was hers, then gave me the keys when I was in the driver's seat.

"Are you sure you don't mind leaving?" she asked. "I don't want to ruin any of your fun."

She had no idea I'd rather be right here in this car alone with her than anywhere else right now.

"You're not ruining any of my fun," I assured her as I shifted into drive. "I was ready to go anyway."

Nadine leaned against the door and stared out the window. "That's good to hear. You should wear your seatbelt, though."

I glanced to her for a moment, before turning my eyes back on the road. "We're just driving through town."

Nadine rolled her eyes. "You still need your seatbelt. It's like you have a death wish or something."

My whole body froze, and my hands tightened on the steering wheel. "I don't."

I said it harsher than I intended. She must've noticed, because she didn't say anything all the way back to the school.

"Lucas," she finally said after I'd parked. "Will you walk me to my dorm?"

"Yeah, of course," I answered before I could stop myself.

It was only when Nadine took my hand again that it struck me this might be some sort of invitation. How many times did I have to tell myself I couldn't get involved with her before I stepped away?

Too many, apparently.

But when we got to her room, she opened the door without inviting me inside. I was half relieved, but the other half of me really wanted to see what would've happened.

Nadine stood in the open doorway with her hand on the frame. "Thanks for making sure I got back safe, Lucas."

"Yeah, of course," I said. "I had fun tonight."

"Me too." She ducked her head and blushed a little. She paused for a few seconds, as if waiting for me to say something. Before I could come up with something clever, she said, "I'll see you later."

Disappointment washed over me. All I wanted was one more minute with her.

But instead, I said, "Bye, Nad."

And just like that, the door shut behind her and she was gone. My shoulders fell. It was like I could still feel her presence there, and I didn't want to let that feeling fade.

But eventually, I had to get back to my room. What would Grant and Talia think if I was still standing there pining after Nadine when they got back? Talia would tell Nadine for sure, and then she'd think I was a creep.

As I turned away from her door and headed down the hall, one thing became very clear. No matter how much I told myself I couldn't be with Nadine, my heart still wanted her.

I wasn't sure how long we had before I caved.

EIGHT

The party took a lot out of me. I loved to dance, and it was a lot of fun while it lasted, but I couldn't keep up the bright appearance forever. Eventually, I had to cave to my body's demands and admit it was time to call it a night. Lucas was like a blessing from Mother Miriam herself. He held my hand and supported me across the parking lot when I was getting too fatigued to walk on my own, and then he'd made sure I got home all right. I mean, he could've at least *tried* to kiss me at my door, but it was probably best he didn't. I might've passed out right there in his arms.

I didn't know why I didn't tell Lucas about my lupus. I guess I didn't want him to think less of me, like I was some burden who needed constant observation. Because I wasn't. I could handle myself. It was just nice to have someone around at times. And I was glad it'd been Lucas.

All I wanted to do Saturday was sleep, since I was totally wiped. Social outings did that to me. They were draining beyond belief, and it usually took a couple of days to recover. I lay in bed that morning, eyeing my yoga mat that was wedged between my bed and the nightstand. I thought about using it, but I couldn't find the energy. Gus was snuggled up next to me, and I didn't even want to lift my hand to pet him.

Across the room, Talia was picking out her clothes for the day. She glanced toward me and noticed I was awake. Her brow furrowed as she eyed me. "You okay, Nadine?"

"Fine," I lied. It was my go-to response, because it was easier than having people worry about me all the time. I still hadn't told Talia about my lupus either—not because I was hiding it from her, but it'd just never come up.

"Are you sure?" she asked. "I drank more than you, and I feel fine."

I took a deep breath. "It's not that."

Talia set her clothes aside and crossed the room to sit on the couch. She leaned over the armrest to look at me. "Did something happen last night? Between you and Lucas?"

"What?" I squeaked. "No. What about you and Grant?"

She shrugged. "Nothing happened, but I'm not so sure about Grant."

"What do you mean?" I asked. "He's nice."

"I don't know. He seems like he tries too hard. I don't really feel like I know the authentic him yet."

"I think that *is* the authentic Grant," I teased.

"I guess we'll see eventually," she said, before changing the subject. "Do you want to get some coffee or something?"

"No. I'm fine." I repeated my usual phrase without realizing it.

She narrowed her eyes at me. "You sure, Nadine? You seem tired all the time. Maybe you should see a doctor about it."

The comment was like a slap to the face. I knew Talia meant well, but she had no idea what I'd been through with doctors these past few years. It was like she thought I wasn't taking care of myself—and I was doing the best I could.

"I have," I snapped. I didn't mean to be so harsh. I quickly softened my tone. "I'm actually meeting my new primary care physician today."

Talia's eyes widened, and she sat straighter on the couch. "Nadine, I'm sorry. I didn't mean—"

"It's okay," I quickly assured her. "You didn't know."

She relaxed. "So, um..."

"It's called lupus," I told her.

My gut sank at the word, like it was some sort of curse. I always hated telling people about it, because they all got the same look on their face. The corners of their lips fell into a frown, and their eyes glistened. It was like they were watching a puppy being tortured or something.

Talia was shooting me the same look just now. I could see the moment her entire impression of me shifted. One moment, I was just Nadine, a regular girl with a thing for long baths and Netflix marathons. The next, I was this completely different person, a fragile girl you had to tiptoe around because if you made the wrong move, she'd crumble into a million tiny pieces.

"It's an autoimmune disease," I explained. "My body attacks itself. It makes me really fatigued all the time."

"I'm sorry," she said softly, like it was somehow her fault. "I didn't realize."

"Well, I didn't tell you," I said simply.

"Is there anything I can do to help?" she asked.

"No," I replied, before quickly adding, "I don't want you to think any different of me because of it."

Her shoulders fell. "Of course not, Nadine. What do you say I go down to the cafeteria and bring back some breakfast, then we watch a few episodes of that sexy vampire show you've been watching?"

A genuine smile crossed my face. "I'd love that, but there's something else I've been meaning to ask you about."

She tilted her head to the side. "What's that?"

I fiddled with a loose thread on the corner of my blanket. "What do you know about séances?"

Talia shrugged. "I come from a family of Seers, so I've done a couple. They're pretty easy."

"So you can do it before you get your magic?" I asked.

"It's like, the only thing we can do. Why do you—? Oh." Talia's face fell. She realized what I was asking before she finished the question.

"I just want to say goodbye to my parents," I said.

Talia took a deep breath, like the suggestion weighed on her. "This is up to you, Nadine, but… are you sure? We're always told not to contact loved ones unless it's an emergency."

I furrowed my brow. "Why not? If you have the power to do it, shouldn't you take advantage of that?"

Talia dropped her gaze. "Yes and no. Contacting someone once is one thing, but contacting your loved ones can become… addictive. It's not recommended as part of the healing process. It's taxing on you and on the spirits."

I couldn't believe the coven had this sort of power and didn't use it.

"That's the problem, Talia. I'm *not* healing. I just want to see them one more time."

"It's more than that," she said. "Messages from the dead are ambiguous. You can't just call up the dead and talk to them."

"What do Seers do then?" I asked. "Don't they see and talk to ghosts?"

"Yeah, but they can't always choose who they see or who gives them visions," Talia explained. "When you do a séance, you're opening yourself to talk to anyone."

"Is it a problem if someone else shows up?"

"It can be," she said. "It's hard for spirits to communicate through words. More often than not, it's through signs and visions. Even Seers, who get messages more clearly, can't always make sense of them. Séances can be fun, but they're dangerous, too. It's like calling someone up on a shared phoneline. Anyone can answer. They could pose as your loved ones and use your grief to manipulate you."

My heart dropped. "I guess I see your point. But I still want to try."

Talia frowned. She looked deeply contemplative, like she wanted to help me but wasn't sure if she should.

Finally, she let out a breath she'd been holding. "I'll help you, but on one condition."

"Anything," I told her.

"We only do this once," she stated. "This is going to be really emotional, and I won't stand by and watch my friend hurt herself over and over. Do you understand?"

I nodded firmly. "I get it. Once and done. That's all I ask."

Talia's shoulders relaxed. "Okay. When do you want to do this?"

"The sooner the better," I told her.

She looked uncertain, but she walked over to the window and shut the curtains anyway, casting the room in darkness. "Let's get started then."

Talia had me gather my parents' belongings. I pulled a box out from under my bed, where I'd kept the things I hadn't been able to part with. I sat across from her on the floor and placed a photograph of my parents between us. For my mom, I chose her signature apron; for my dad, an old collector's license plate that came off the last car he and my grandpa restored together.

Gus curled into Talia's lap while she lit the candles. A chill traveled down my spine, and I swore I already felt an energy in the air that wasn't there before.

"Take my hands," Talia said softly. "Remind me of your parents' names?"

"Faith and Nathan Evers," I told her.

"You focus on them, while I call out their names," she instructed. "Deal?"

I nodded.

"Faith? Nathan? Your daughter wants to speak to you," Talia called out to the darkness.

I did my best to relax, but the more I thought about them, the heavier the weight in my gut became. I still couldn't admit they were gone.

But they weren't gone for good. At least, that's what I kept telling myself. I was going to see them soon. This *had* to work.

Talia continued to call out their names. The temperature in the room dropped, but nothing else seemed to change. I glanced around hopefully, expecting a spirit to be lurking nearby, but I saw nothing.

"Are they here?" I asked Talia.

She kept her eyes closed but pressed her lips together. "It feels like… like their energy is blocked or something."

My pulse quickened. I could practically taste their presence.

"Mom? Dad?" I called out to the quiet room. "Are you there?"

No response came.

I squeezed Talia's hands tighter, and the lump in my throat grew. I tried to picture my parents actually being here, and it tore a hole straight through me. "Dad, what do you say we play a game of *Clue*? Or maybe we can work on the Corvette this afternoon? Mom, how about a batch of cookies? We could head to the flea market and see if they have any of those old lamps you've been talking about."

Talia must've noticed the pained look on my face, because she said, "Maybe we should stop."

"No," I insisted. "We have to keep trying. Dad, if you're out there, please just let me know. Give me a sign."

Still, nothing came. My stomach twisted, and pain flared in my joints. I was starting to get a tension headache.

"Please?" I begged.

Then I heard it—the sound of my name. It was distant and distorted, but I swore it was a male voice.

I glanced around the room. "Dad?"

Talia's eyes darted every which way, but neither of us saw anything. She looked like she was holding her breath.

"Nadine…" Energy sizzled in the air like static electricity, and I heard a distant hum that seemed to distort the voice.

"I'm here, Dad!" I called out.

Talia gasped, and my gaze snapped to my right where she was looking. My heart lurched. A ghostly figure hovered in the air, but it looked like nothing more than a transparent smoky mass. I wanted it so badly to be my parents, but truth be told, I couldn't tell.

"Mom? Dad?" I asked carefully. "Is that you?"

"Don't… careful…"

The voice came in and out like we were tuning in to a distant radio station. I couldn't make out what they were trying to say.

"You're almost there!" I cried. "I'm right here."

The smoke swirled and started to dissipate. My stomach dropped to the floor.

"No!" I screamed, my voice cracking. "Come back!"

"Sorry… go…"

My heart felt like it was breaking into a million tiny pieces. That couldn't be it! My parents couldn't leave me yet!

"Don't go! Please!" I begged. My hands shook in Talia's. "I need more time—"

My breath stalled as the smoke disappeared and the room returned to its normal temperature.

"No," I sobbed. I turned to face Talia. "Bring them back! Please, bring them back! I didn't get to say anything I wanted to."

Talia's eyes shimmered, and she wore a look of sorrow. "I'm sorry, Nadine. I don't think I can."

I gaped at her. "That's it? That was all the time I got? I didn't say goodbye."

"I know, but we gave it our best shot," she said regrettably. "We actually got further than I thought we would."

"But we don't know if it was my dad." I let go of her hands and started gathering my parents things. "We'll try again. We'll get it right next time."

Talia shook her head. "We did nothing wrong, Nadine."

"We don't really know what we're doing," I insisted.

Talia sighed and wore a true expression of apology. "You agreed to do this once, remember? You'll always find another reason to contact them. Nadine, I really am sorry."

I blinked away the tears and wouldn't look her in the eye. I placed my parents' things back in the box and slid it under my bed. I wiped at my eyes. "I don't blame you. I just… I just want to be alone."

"I'm not leaving you alone," Talia promised. She helped me back into bed, then pulled the blanket up to my chin. "Let me know if you need anything."

I lay there curled in a ball. I stared at where the smoky mass had hovered during the séance, as if expecting it to return.

"I will," I rasped.

Talia left my side and went into the bathroom. I knew it was her way of giving me privacy without really leaving me.

I felt horribly sick that the séance didn't go well. It was as if a black hole had opened up beneath me and I was clawing tooth and nail just to hold on.

I suddenly knew what my grandmother meant by torturing myself. And the sad part was, I didn't know how to stop.

☾

GETTING to the doctor's office was hell. After the séance, I didn't want to go, but I forced myself to anyway. At least I didn't have to wait long in the waiting room.

"Nadine Evers," the nurse called, butchering my last name by pronouncing the *e* with a short vowel sound.

I stood and followed her into a long hallway with a bunch of identical exam rooms. She led me to the one on the end and gestured me inside. After taking my vitals and asking me a few questions, she told me the doctor would be in shortly.

I pulled out my phone to scroll through while I waited. It was usually a good fifteen to twenty minutes before the doctor came in. Which was why I was surprised when a knock came at the door less than a minute later.

The door swung open, and a man in his late forties stepped inside. He was good looking, with dark hair and a kind smile. He didn't wear scrubs like the nurse, but instead had on nice slacks and a black sweater. He reached out a hand to me. "Hello, Nadine. I'm Dr. Yonker. It's a pleasure to meet you."

"Hi," I said, shaking his hand. My grip felt weak, and it wasn't just from the flare-up. I was a little nervous about this whole appointment. Maybe as an Alchemist, Dr. Yonker had insight my other doctors didn't.

He sat in his chair in front of the computer and turned to me. "How are you feeling today?"

I shrugged. "Could be better."

My doctors were the only ones I didn't lie to about how I felt, because they might actually be able to help. The only thing anyone else could offer was sympathy, and I didn't need it. Plus, Dr. Yonker had this friendly thing going on that made me feel like I could trust him.

"Well, we're going to see what we can do about that," he said. "So, I heard you just moved here."

I shifted a little in my chair. I didn't want to explain everything, but he was my doctor, so he had to know. "Yeah. My parents passed away recently, and I came to live with my grandma. She helped me enroll in Miriam College. I've been having a lupus flare-up from the stress."

Dr. Yonker nodded in understanding. "I assume one of your parents is Miriamic, while the other is not?"

I furrowed my brow. "Yeah. How'd you know?"

He sat a little straighter in his chair. "Autoimmune diseases like lupus are very common among mixed children, though they don't all react in the same way. Some don't get ill at all."

Well, now it made sense why Mom pushed the doctors so hard toward an autoimmune diagnosis. She knew there was a chance I'd have it.

"When you're born, your magic is within you, but dormant," Dr. Yonker explained. "Your human side recognizes that magic as foreign and realizes something's not quite right. It triggers your immune system, usually in late childhood or early teens. However, since magic isn't a physical substance, your immune system can't find it, so it starts attacking your body."

"Do other magical races react the same way?" I asked curiously.

"Every society's magic is a little different," he said. "Their bodies react differently than ours."

So, witches were the only ones who had to deal with this shit? Good to know I'd been born into the wrong magical society and it was trying to kill me. But at least the coven had to have a cure.

"What can we do about it?" I asked hopefully.

Dr. Yonker sighed. "Well, we have a couple options—immunosuppressants, steroids, anti-inflammatories."

So basically everything I'd already tried. A wave of heat washed over me, and I held back from snapping at the doctor. Seriously? He had magic and was going to use the same drugs I could get anywhere?

"You mean, there's no potion that can help?" I asked in a small voice.

Dr. Yonker shook his head regrettably. "Magical healing works by enhancing the body's natural abilities inside of you so that you can heal yourself. Since your condition is a side effect of your magic, it will never balance out. Magical healing, however, is something the Miriamic Coven possesses in only small doses. Very few magical races have the power to heal on such a drastic level."

Great. What was the point of having magic if it couldn't heal me? Heck, it was *because* I had magic that I was sick in the first place. I was so frustrated that a heavy weight settled on my chest. I couldn't believe I'd gotten my hopes up for nothing.

Dr. Yonker's face fell. "I'm sorry, Nadine. There's nothing we can do until your magic awakens but keep you on the same medications."

"What happens when my magic awakens?"

He took a deep breath. Great. Sympathy. From my own fucking doctor. Could no one just treat me like a normal person? Was I walking around with LUPUS stamped to my forehead? *Hello, everyone! I'm hella sick. Feel bad for me!*

"In the Miriamic Coven, diseases like this often go into remission the more you use your magic," he explained. "You can train your body to recognize your magic as native."

I forced the lump down my throat, feeling my body lighten a bit. "So, once I have magic, it will act like a treatment?"

Dr. Yonker nodded. "In a way, yes. Symptoms will worsen at first, because your body will see the magic as foreign. Within a year or two, you'll be able to train your body to accept it. At that point, symptoms should go away completely."

"No more flare-ups?" I asked.

If that was the case, count me back in on the magic train.

"Most likely," Dr. Yonker said.

Relief washed through me. Dr. Yonker wasn't giving me a sure thing. There was no cure. And yet no doctor had ever given me so much hope in my life. I was always left hanging with, "We'll see what happens." To hear there was a treatment that could reduce my flare-ups was such a relief. I never thought it'd happen.

"In that case, I'll do whatever I have to do with my magic to get rid of these symptoms," I said.

Dr. Yonker gave a friendly smile. "I'm glad to hear that."

We spent the next half hour talking about my medical history. The weight gradually lifted off my chest as I told him everything. He was so different from my other doctors, who always seemed rushed and barely listened to what I had to say. Dr. Yonker actually listened and interacted with me, asking me important questions so he could get to know my case. He made me feel comfortable and at ease as I detailed my symptoms and concerns. By the end of my appointment, I was pretty sure I was in love with Dr. Yonker—as far as doctor-patient relationships went.

"Let's schedule an appointment for the end of the year, after your Evoking Ceremony," Dr. Yonker suggested. "I want to see how you're doing once your magic awakens."

"Sounds good," I agreed.

I could hardly wait until my Evoking Ceremony so I could start on the road toward remission.

☽

"How'd your doctor's appointment go?" Grammy asked the following night when I came to visit for dinner.

"Really well, actually," I told her as I took a bite of casserole. "I really like Dr. Yonker."

"Good. He's a very talented Alchemist."

"You know him?" I asked.

Grammy gave me this side-eyed look. "Honey, I know everyone in my Cast."

"But there must be thousands," I argued.

Grammy tapped the side of her head. "I've got a great memory. Plus, he dated your mom for a while in high school."

My stomach sank at the mention of her. It was easy to forget Mom had a life before me and that she used to live in Octavia Falls. She never talked about her past, so I didn't know much. What hurt most was knowing she and my dad had no future.

The room went silent at the mention of my mom. Grammy dared to speak first. "You know what? I think I still have some photo albums of hers upstairs. What do you say we take a look after dinner?"

I wanted to tell her no. Acknowledging my mom's past was acknowledging the accident. It was easier to pretend it didn't happen.

But I didn't dare tell Grammy I felt that way. So instead, I just nodded.

Grammy finished her dinner quickly, but I poked at my food. Eventually, I finished, and I helped her with the dishes. Then she led me upstairs to a closet in the second guest room. She pulled out a big box and opened it. It was filled with at least a dozen scrapbooks.

"Wow, Grammy," I said, staring down into it. "That's a lot. I didn't know you were so into scrapbooking."

She grabbed one of them and flipped open to the first page. "It's nothing fancy. Come sit."

Grammy walked over to the bed and sat on the pink comforter with her back to the door. She patted the spot beside her, and I sat.

"Here's your mom at one month old." Grammy pointed to the first picture. It was a photograph of a baby in a studio setting. It didn't look anything like my baby pictures, though. The photo was faded, and my mom wore a frilly dress I'd never be caught dead in.

"She was really cute," I said, but inside, my guts were twisting.

"Of course she was," Grammy laughed. "She gets it from me."

I turned the page, wanting to get this over with as soon as possible. The next photos showed my mom in the grass, playing with an older woman I didn't recognize. "Who's that?"

Grammy leaned over to get a better look. "Oh, that's your great grandma."

I ran my fingers over the photo. "You look like her."

Grammy nodded.

"So, Mom *actually* got her good looks from Great Grandma?" I teased, trying to lighten my mood.

Grammy frowned. "Tread carefully, Nadine."

I laughed. "Right. Great Grandma got it from you. My bad."

"Now you're getting it," Grammy joked.

The doorbell rang, and we both looked up from the scrapbook.

"I'll get it," Grammy said as she stood.

I turned back to the scrapbook and flipped through the pages, but it felt like each flip of the page was another dagger to the heart.

She's gone, I thought. *This is all that's left of her... Pictures.*

Tears pricked at my eyes. I stopped on one picture where my mom must've been only a year old. She was standing on a step-stool at the counter, helping Grammy mix something in a bowl. She had a huge smile on her face, like she was enjoying herself.

I sighed. Mom had been preparing to become an Alchemist for years, and she'd left it all behind. It seemed really sad. It was hard to believe she gave it all up for my dad. Of course they loved each other, but she'd left behind her entire culture to marry him—

My thoughts halted in their tracks as a dark piece of fabric was thrown over my eyes from behind. I let out an earth-shattering scream as hands grabbed my shoulders and dragged me backward. My heart hammered against my rib cage.

"Grammy!" I shrieked.

No answer came. Oh, fuck! Whoever had been by at the door must've hurt Grammy.

I waved my arms and kicked my feet out, trying to get out of my attacker's grasp. My wrist broke free, and I hurled my elbow backward. It sank into my attacker's gut, and I heard them let out a pained *oof!*

Hold on. I knew that voice.

I stilled. "Grant!?"

"Let her go," Grant said in a strained voice.

The blindfold lifted from my eyes, and I turned to see Talia and Lucas standing beside Grant. They both had looks of amusement on their faces. Grammy was in the doorway, trying to hold back a laugh, while Grant was clutching his stomach.

"You've got a good swing," he groaned.

"Jesus Christ," I cried as I sat up straight on the bed. "What the hell are you guys doing?"

"We're abducting you," Talia said proudly.

I pushed my hair out of my eyes. "A little warning would've been nice."

"A warning wouldn't be any fun," Lucas replied with a smirk.

"What are you abducting me for?" I demanded.

"Your initiation." Grant's voice was back to normal.

"Initiation?" I looked to Grammy.

She waved her hand. "Go have fun. We'll look at the scrapbooks later."

Thank God! I needed a distraction.

I turned back to my friends. "Does everyone get an initiation?"

Grant chuckled. "Lucas did one for me, so I thought we should keep the tradition going."

"Why doesn't Talia get one?" I argued.

"I was born in Octavia Falls," she reminded me. "You weren't."

"Technically, I was, too," Grant said. "But I left and came back."

"Why would you leave?" I asked.

"My mom married into the coven," he explained. "When my parents split, my younger brothers and I left with my mom. I came back after high school to learn my powers."

"Dude, I miss your mom," Lucas said. "She was the best cook ever."

Grant chuckled. "Why do you think she opened her own restaurant?"

"Grant's a good cook, too, by the way," Lucas said, obviously for Talia's benefit. "His mom's family emigrated from Costa Rica, and she runs a Latin American restaurant. Grant spent high school working there, so he knows all the secret recipes."

"Well, you'll have to cook for us sometime," Talia suggested.

Grant's eyes lit up.

Talia turned to me and held out the blindfold. "Now put this on."

I groaned. "Do I have to?"

"Yes," Lucas insisted. "It's part of the ceremony."

"A *fake* ceremony," I shot back. I knew my friends were only trying to have fun, but they could've gone about it another way. My heart was still racing.

"Please," Talia begged. "It'll be fun."

I glanced to Grammy. She had this knowing look on her face. Had she been involved in planning this? Well, she should've told them abducting me wasn't a good idea. I'd have drawn blood if I had to.

I caved. "Okay."

"You have to wear the blindfold, though," Lucas insisted.

"How will I know where I'm going?" I asked.

Talia let out a fake evil laugh. "You won't. That's what's fun about it."

I rolled my eyes. "Let me at least walk down the stairs by myself."

Lucas nodded. "Agreed."

I took the blindfold and started for the door. Grammy stepped aside to let me through, but I leaned over and hissed at her. "No cool, Grammy. Not cool."

Talia heard me and patted Grammy's shoulder on the way out of the room. "She's a liar, Helena. You're the best."

"I appreciate your vote of confidence," she replied playfully. "Can't say the same about my granddaughter."

I didn't look back as I flipped Grammy off while I descended the stairs. Her laughter rang out through the house.

"Love you, Nadine," she called.

"Love you too, you traitor!" I said with a chuckle.

"Have fun." Grammy waved from the top of the stairs.

That was all I saw before Lucas took the blindfold from my hands and pulled it up to my eyes. My heart fluttered as his fingers brushed across my hair.

"You ready?" he asked, placing one hand on my shoulder. His touch sent tingles all throughout my body. I wondered what it'd be like if he touched me other places…

I cleared my throat, pushing the dirty thoughts from my mind. "Yeah, let's go."

Lucas kept hold of me as he guided me outside and down the porch steps. It was dark outside, so I couldn't see anything behind the blindfold. Lucas took my hand to keep me from falling. At the bottom of the stairs, neither of us let go of each other, so he led me across the lawn holding my hand. It was kind of weird, but felt natural at the same time. I felt a little lightheaded and disoriented as we walked, and it wasn't just from the blindfold. Lucas's scent surrounded me, and all I wanted to do was sit under the stars while he held me.

I was getting ahead of myself. He probably didn't even like me that way. I wonder if he thought I was at least bangable. Apparently my ex didn't.

My thoughts were interrupted when Lucas spoke. "We're headed into the forest. Watch your step."

"Watch my step?" I asked. "I can't see a damn thing."

Talia snickered from up ahead. "That's the point."

I rolled my eyes, even though none of them could see it. "This better be worth it."

We walked for another ten minutes or so. The whole time, Lucas held me close so I wouldn't trip over anything. Grant was trying to flirt with Talia, but I missed most of what he'd said because I was so focused on Lucas next to me. My mind was fighting a fierce battle on whether or not I should ask him out.

Don't do it, the dominant voice argued. *It could ruin your friendship. What if he doesn't like you back?*

Screw you. I can do whatever I want, I shot back at the voice.

"We're here," Talia announced.

Lucas leaned over to whisper in my ear. "Sit down."

"What? Right here?" I asked. I could still hear the sound of the wind in the trees above us and feel the cool air on my skin.

Lucas guided my hand over, and I felt the back of a chair. It was soft fabric, like a camping chair. He helped me sit, then said, "Don't take your blindfold off yet."

Lucas's hand disappeared from mine, and cool air rushed in to take his place. I could hear the shuffling of feet and the soft rustle of fabric.

"What's going on?" I asked.

Nobody answered for a few seconds, until Talia spoke in an ominous voice. "You may now remove your blindfold."

I reached up and tugged the blindfold off my eyes. In front of me stood three cloaked figures. Their hoods shaded their faces, and it was so dark out that I couldn't see their eyes. I could still tell who was who by their height. Behind them, a fire burned in the forest, and a cauldron bubbled above the flames.

I couldn't take my eyes off Lucas, who stood on the right. He looked so mysterious. It was fucking hot. I just wanted to rip that cloak off and see what was underneath...

"Nadine Evers," Grant said in a deep voice, like he was trying to sound like someone else.

"Um… yes?" I said.

Grant cleared his throat. "You have been called by the Goddess to join the Miriamic Coven. How do you respond to this request?"

"Um, I accept?" I said it like a question. My friends were acting really weird.

Grant dropped his shoulders and spoke in his normal voice. "Nadine, come on."

I sighed and made my voice serious. "Fine. I accept."

"You will be gifted magical abilities unlike any other," Grant said in his deep voice. "But you must undergo grueling obstacles to prove yourself worthy. Are you willing to undertake the task?"

I sat a little straighter and played along. "I am."

Grant's voice grew in intensity. He was starting to sound like a drill sergeant. "Are you willing to do anything to serve the Goddess, no matter what she asks of you?"

"I am."

"Will you protect and serve the coven, no matter the cost?" Grant practically yelled.

"Yes," I replied.

The three of them took a step back and bowed their heads in unison.

"Then you may step forward and drink from the Cup of Life," Grant said. "Pledge yourself to Mother Miriam, and drink the blood that flows through her veins."

I stood and followed my friends to the fire. Inside the cauldron was a bubbly liquid that looked a lot more like soda than blood.

"Is this for real?" I asked.

Lucas pushed his hood back. "Consider it a perk of being friends with Grant. He has a wild imagination. There is no Cup of Life."

"Shut up and put your hood back up," Grant scolded. "We're not done."

"Can we be? Please?" Talia asked, dropping her hood. "I can't see under this thing."

Grant sighed and stripped off his robe, then tossed it aside. "Fine. You're all losers. You're no fun."

"You say that now," Talia teased, raising an eyebrow at him. She was totally joking about getting into bed with him. Once she stopped lying to herself about liking him, it was only a matter of time before that condom box was empty.

Talia and Lucas took their robes off and put them on top of Grant's. We all sat on the ground in a circle around the fire. Talia sat across from me, and Grant and Lucas were on either side.

Grant reached for the ladle in the cauldron and conjured a plastic cup in the other hand. He ladled one scoop of the potion into the cup and handled it to me. "The blood of Mother Miriam, in the Cup of Life."

"Wow," I said flatly. "I thought the Cup of Life would be... prettier."

Grant laughed as he ladled another cup. I started passing mine around the circle toward Lucas.

"Whoa!" Talia exclaimed, while everyone else froze. Lucas held his hands up, like he was refusing the cup.

I pulled it back toward myself. "What? What's wrong?"

Lucas relaxed. "It's customary to only accept a potion from an Alchemist. It's how you know it's safe."

"Oh," I said. "I didn't realize sharing was sacrilegious."

Talia snickered from across the circle. "I wouldn't go that far. It's just considered bad luck to take a potion from a non-Alchemist."

The way everyone looked at me, you'd think I'd just sacrificed a cat or something. I ducked my head. "Sorry."

Grant shrugged as he handed Lucas a cup. "You didn't know. Now you do."

I relaxed. "So, what is this anyway?"

I looked down at my cup and sniffed it. It smelled sweet.

Grant handed Talia the next cup, then sat back on his heels and smiled. "I call it Fizzy Bubbly."

I raised an eyebrow. "Sounds good, but that doesn't really answer my question."

"It's a little concoction I made myself," Grant said. "It tastes great without affecting your blood sugar."

"Is it alcoholic?" I asked.

"Nope," Grant said. "That's the beauty of it."

I didn't drink alcohol because of my lupus. Maybe this would be different.

"But it does have a little kick that'll make you tipsy after a few," Grant warned.

At that, Talia threw her head back and chugged her drink. She smacked her lips and held out her cup. "In that case, pour me another one."

Grant smiled. "Gladly."

I leaned over to Lucas. "Is it safe?"

He took a sip. "Would I drink it if it wasn't?"

"Depends," I said. "Are you trying to get me drunk?"

He smirked. Good God. I loved that smirk. "What would happen if I was?"

Hopefully a make-out session, I thought.

I brought the cup to my lips. "I don't know. Let's find out."

I figured it didn't hurt to try. I kept it to one drink for now just to be safe.

The drink was sweet, with hints of citrus to it. It bubbled on my tongue but was smooth at the same time.

"What do you think?" Grant asked after I'd tried it.

"Really good," I said.

Grant took a swig. "You're lucky. When Lucas *initiated* me, he made me strip down and skinny dip in Lake Santos."

"Lucas!" I scolded.

His jaw dropped. "I did *not*. You're the one who decided to go skinny dipping. You're all like, *'I'm such a fast swimmer. Look how fast I can go naked.'*"

Grant snickered. "Whoops. I forgot."

"Hey, that's a great idea!" Talia cried, lifting her empty cup. "Let's go skinny dipping."

"Talia—" I started, but Grant cut in before I could finish.

"That sounds fantastic. I can show you how fast I can swim!"

Lucas groaned. "Guys, I'm not stripping down."

"Good," Grant jabbed at him. "No one wants to see that."

"I do," I blurted. My face went beet red as all eyes turned to me. Lucas's eyes widened in shock. I tore my gaze off his and glanced to my drink, which was almost gone. "Holy shit. What's in this thing?"

Grant nearly died laughing. "That was all you, Nadine. I don't make my drinks that strong."

Talia stole Grant's attention by holding her cup out. "Can I have another?"

"You might want to slow down," he warned her.

"I thought you didn't make it *that* strong," I teased.

"Can't slow down," Talia said. "I need the courage if we're going skinny dipping."

"You don't have to," Grant assured her in a genuine voice.

She shrugged. "I want to. It'll be fun. I've never been. This is college, isn't it?"

Grant shrugged, like he couldn't argue. "It is."

As Grant filled Talia's cup a third time, Lucas leaned over to me to whisper softly. "So, you want to see me naked, huh?"

My gaze traveled down his torso. *Hell yeah*!

"It's the Fizzy Bubbly talking," I claimed.

"Doesn't make it untrue," he pointed out.

I took another gulp. It was really tasty and actually might've been making me feel better. "Perhaps."

"So what's the answer?" he challenged.

"Mm… I think I'm gonna keep you guessing," I teased.

He frowned. "Not fair."

"Totally fair," I shot back. "You didn't answer my question."

"What question?" he asked.

It was only a moment later that I realized I hadn't asked him anything. Tipsy my ass. Grant's Fizzy Bubbly was some strong shit.

I went for it anyway. "Do *you* want to see *me* naked?"

Lucas stilled, and his eyes flickered toward my boobs. I leaned over a little, making my cleavage more obvious.

"I'm, uh, not answering that," he said breathlessly.

"Why not?" I pouted.

"Because if I answered like a gentleman, I'd be lying."

Holy shit. He *did* want to see me naked! Every nerve in my body came to life as heat spread over my skin. This Fizzy Bubbly was seriously messing with my courage. I'd kiss him right then and there if he let me.

"Nadine…" Talia dragged out my name. I'd been so focused on Lucas that I didn't realize she'd come up behind me. She tugged on my arm. "Let's go."

I didn't take my eyes off Lucas as I shot him a smirk. The challenge was on!

"How far is the lake?" I asked.

"It's right down there." Talia bounced on her toes and pointed down the path. "Let's go!"

Talia and I ran off giggling. I glanced back to see if the guys were following us, and they were. They whispered to each other, though I didn't know what they were saying.

Talia's version of "right down there" was at least ten times longer than mine. It felt like we were walking for a mile before the trees parted and a clearing gave way to a rocky beach. Beyond that was a huge lake that reached nearly halfway to the horizon. It must've been a couple miles across. I was exhausted by the time we arrived.

"I'm going in!" Talia sang as she stripped off her top.

"Oh my God. Talia!" I shouted at her as she sprinted toward the water. "You're drunk."

"Am not!" she shot back. "I'm just having fun."

The quarter moon illuminated her silhouette. I caught a glimpse of her breasts before I quickly looked away. The guys were still in the trees, thank God, so they didn't see anything.

Talia squealed as she entered the chilly water, but it didn't seem to bother her, because she dove in a second later. Her head broke the surface, and she inhaled a big gulp of air. "Come on, Nadine. The water's great."

I glanced back to the trees. I could hear the guys' distant voices, but I didn't see them yet.

"Don't be nervous," Talia said. "I have a sister, and we shared a bedroom. It's no big deal."

I looked back to her, trying to work up the courage to slip my clothes off. It *did* look like fun. But we were talking about being naked in front of Lucas. It was one thing to dream about and another to actually do it.

"Quick!" Talia said with a laugh. "They're coming."

I decided to go for it. I kicked off my shoes and unbuttoned my jeans. They fell to my ankles, and I stepped out of them. I pulled my shirt over my head and reached for the waistband of my panties, before I heard a loud whistle from behind me.

I whirled around to see Grant and Lucas frozen at the edge of the trees. Lucas's eyes were glued to my ass, but it'd been Grant who'd whistled.

An involuntary squeak left my throat, and I suddenly lost all my courage. Instead of throwing my clothes back on like a normal person, instinct took over. I ran to jump into the water to hide myself, but I tripped on a rock and face-planted into the water. I inhaled a deep breath, and water filled my nostrils, burning my nasal passages.

I pushed off the shallow bottom with my arms, and my head broke the surface. I inhaled a greedy gulp of air. Suddenly, a pair of hands were on me, helping me out of the water.

I looked up to see Lucas's green eyes staring down at me. "Nad, are you okay?"

"Fine," I said, though I was still sputtering.

His hands left mine, and I sank deeper into the water so it would conceal me. My eyes traveled downward, and I started laughing. Lucas was standing in the water fully clothed, and his shoes were completely soaked.

"What?" he asked in alarm.

"You're funny," I giggled. Okay, the Fizzy Bubbly was officially hitting me. "It's not like I was drowning."

Lucas stood up straighter and shrugged. "Better safe than sorry."

I leaned into the cool water and floated on my back, then ran my hands through it to pull me out deeper into the lake. "You should come in. The water feels nice."

"Cannonball!" Grant shouted.

I glanced over, only to see a naked ass right next to me. Grant landed a few feet away from me, spraying water up into my face. I shrieked at the cold shock and stood up straight. The water came to my belly button.

Grant came up for air and wiped his eyes, then rubbed his tailbone. Thank God the water reached his hips. "Ow. A little shallow for a cannon ball."

"Dude, personal space," I snapped.

"What? You don't want my naked ass anywhere near you?" he teased.

"No, I don't," I said.

"I want it over here!" Talia called. She was low in the water so that it covered her shoulders.

Grant smirked and started wading through the water over to her. He stopped a good ten feet way to respect her space.

I turned back to Lucas, who was sitting on the beach and stripping off his wet shoes. "Are you coming in?"

"I don't want to get naked," he said.

"Come in with clothes on," I encouraged. "Like me."

Lucas sighed and rose to his feet. "If I *have* to."

He reached for his jeans and started unbuttoning them. Heat pooled between my thighs. Pretty sure I was making the lake even wetter than it already was. I couldn't take my eyes off him as he pulled his shirt over his head. Holy hell. He was toned as fuck. All I wanted to do was run my hands across those muscles. To kiss him. To... do other things to him.

Lucas stripped down to his boxers and stepped into the water until it was up to his knees. "There. I did it."

I rolled my eyes and swam closer to him. Grant and Talia were in their own little world splashing each other. They didn't notice Lucas and me.

"That doesn't count," I claimed. "You have to get wet."

He glanced down to the water beneath him. "I am wet. This counts."

"Does not." I splashed him, and the water landed on his stomach. Droplets dripped down his toned abs to his waistband. I couldn't help but think what *I* wanted to do to that waistband.

Lucas dropped his jaw dramatically, then bent down to splash me back.

"Hey!" I cried, wiping my eyes of the water. "I'm already wet."

In more ways than one. I was fucking swimming, and I didn't mean in the lake. Lucas was hot as hell.

"Turnabout's fair play," he teased.

"In that case..." I swam straight up to him and reached out for his wrist, then tugged him into the water.

Lucas stumbled and landed right on top of me. My heart lifted in my chest as his body pressed against mine. I didn't even care that my head had dipped below water. I'd hold my breath forever just to stay in this position.

Lucas's arms wrapped around me, and he pulled me out of the water. I pushed wet strands of hair out of my face and giggled. I couldn't help it. He did things to me that no one else ever had. I felt like I was floating, even though the water was so shallow that we were both on our knees.

Lucas didn't let go of me, even though I was no longer in danger of drowning. I figured it was some sort of signal, so I decided to play along. I wrapped my arms around his neck.

"See?" I said innocently, like we weren't sitting here in an intimate embrace. "The water's nice, isn't it?"

He stared down at me, never taking his eyes off mine. His chest rose and fell rapidly in shallow breaths. "Yeah, it is nice."

His gaze flickered down to my lips, then further down to my breasts. I inhaled, purposely lifting my chest out of the water a little so he could get a better look. In the cool water, my nipples were rock hard, though he couldn't see through my push-up bra. My mouth went dry as my eyes roamed over him. They locked on his lips, and my whole body felt magnetized toward him.

The Fizzy Bubbly had made me bolder than normal—a helluva lot bolder. I dragged myself closer to Lucas and wrapped my legs around his middle, until our bodies were pressed tightly against each other. Lucas seemed like he was in another world, totally oblivious to Grant and Talia's laughter across the beach as I drew closer. My hips pressed into his, and I could feel his erection through my panties. My heart was hammering so hard that I was sure he could feel it. I could hardly believe this was actually happening.

"You're so warm," I whispered.

Lucas's arms tightened around me. He licked his lips, staring at my mouth like he was in a trance. "You, too."

"Well, what are you going to do about it?" I asked.

His hands trembled on my back, like he wanted to move them across my body but was too scared. He swallowed. "I, uh, I…"

I leaned in closer. My breasts pressed up against him, and my heart hammered so hard it rocked my entire body. I didn't know how I could feel this way when we hadn't even kissed yet. All I knew was that I wanted Lucas more than I ever wanted anyone. It wasn't just because he was hot, either. I really, *really* liked him.

"You could kiss me," I whispered in his ear.

He shook his head. "Nadine…"

"What's wrong?" I asked. "Are you nervous?"

Then, because I had absolutely no inhibitions at the moment, I pressed my lips to the corner of his jaw. Lucas froze against me, his breath cooling the side of my neck. Testing his limits, I ran my lips along his jawline and pressed a kiss to his cheek. My pulse quickened. I was so close to kissing him for the first time.

Lucas closed his eyes and turned his head, until his warm lips brushed across the side of my face. He was so close to my lips that he almost touched them. My heart skipped a beat. I burned for more, to have his lips all over me, his tongue inside my mouth. I tilted my head toward him, anticipating the kiss.

But it never came. Lucas's eyes snapped open. In an instant, his hands left my back and pressed against my shoulders. My stomach dropped as he pushed me away from him.

Lucas gazed at me with sad eyes. His face had paled, and he looked like he was going to be sick. Because of me? "I'm sorry, Nad. We can't."

That floating feeling in my chest disappeared as a heavy weight came crashing down. What just happened?

I dropped my legs from around his waist and pushed away from him in the water. "What's wrong?"

Lucas turned away from me. He wouldn't look me in the eye. "I can't do this, Nad. It isn't fair to you."

"Wait, Lucas."

He stood and started for shore. My limbs felt so heavy that I couldn't bring myself to follow him. I thought we were having a good time. Wasn't he flirting back? Or had I misread his signals?

"Lucas, what's wrong?" I asked in a small voice. I barely noticed that Talia and Grant had stopped goofing off to stare at us. "What did I do?"

Lucas stopped on the shore to look back at me as he reached for his jeans. "Nothing, Nad."

My eyebrows knitted together as I searched his expression for explanation. But I couldn't find any. A thousand thoughts ran through my head. Was he not attracted to me? Did he already have a girlfriend? Had he promised Grammy he wouldn't get involved with me?

No, that was all stupid. So what was the problem?

I blinked a few times, feeling the weight of the rejection getting heavier. God, I was so immature. It's not like we were breaking up. We weren't even dating!

Lucas sighed. He dropped his jeans and stepped back into the water. He reached out for me. "Nad…"

I pushed off the bottom of the lake and swam around him. "Whatever. It's cool."

I tried to keep an even tone, but it didn't come out that way. "I didn't realize… I thought…"

I couldn't finish my sentence. Instead, I started toward shore, barely caring that my panties were on display for him. *Maybe it'll get him to change his mind.*

"Nadine, please," Lucas begged. "Let me explain."

"Lucas, it's fine," I practically snapped, though I didn't mean to. "We're just friends, and I'm not myself right now. Neither of us are. So let's just forget this happened and go back to normal tomorrow?"

It wasn't true. I was being myself, just with a little extra courage. I *wanted* the kiss to happen—and so much more. I was stupid and crazy. There was still so much I didn't know about him—which incidentally only drew me closer. I wanted to know it all.

Lucas stared at me like a deer in the headlights. "Nad, I just don't think—"

"You don't owe me an explanation," I said as I started pulling on my clothes. I didn't know why I told him that, considering an explanation was all I wanted. I just wasn't sure I could hear it right now. What if it was worse than I was thinking?

"If that's what you want," Lucas said softly.

It wasn't, but I nodded anyway.

Talia and Grant had come to the shallow end, though they kept their distance from each other.

"Hey, guys," Talia said softly. "What happened?"

"Nothing," I told her as I put my shoes on. "I think it's time to go."

"Yeah, sure." Talia sounded more like herself now. "Can you toss me my clothes?"

I gathered her clothes and held them out to her where she was crouched down in the shallow end. The guys turned their eyes away as she got out of the water and started to dress. I averted my eyes out of respect.

The whole time, I couldn't stop replaying what had just happened in my mind. It was obvious Lucas and I had chemistry. He clearly wanted to kiss me back, and yet he insisted on pushing me away. The only explanation I could think of was that Lucas was playing some sort of game with me.

A game that I was going to win.

NINE

I hated my fucking gift. I had Nadine in my arms. I was going to kiss her. If we'd been alone, we probably would've gone a lot further, too. The second my lips touched her cheek, the nausea hit, and a thought from the recently departed came to me, shattering the moment.

"We were never right for each other," the female voice said. She sounded younger than most, but I didn't want to think about how she died. I hoped it was an accident, but there was a hint of fear in her voice that suggested something more was going on.

And that chilled me to the bone. What if it was some sort of sign? I had to admit, it couldn't have come at a worse time. It was like a reminder that I wasn't any good for Nadine. And so I pushed her away, because if I let this happen once, I didn't think I could ever stop. She deserved better than me—better than someone whose mere existence could hurt her in ways I couldn't imagine.

So as much as it killed me to do, I kept my distance from her.

It was literal torture. I didn't know why, but when I was around Nadine, the weight of my gift seemed to ease. Now that I was avoiding her, it seemed to weigh heavier and heavier.

The voice I'd heard at the lake ended up being a woman named Emily Robinson, who'd died after being pushed down the stairs. The jackass who'd pushed her had already been arrested, but that didn't bring me much peace from the thought, if any. That one stuck with me for days, because every time I pictured the girl, I saw my mom. I'd even called Mom to check up on her, and she assured me she was fine. I wasn't sure I believed her.

Over the next few days, the nausea grew worse. On Thursday after lunch, I was taking a piss at the urinal when another thought struck.

"Is it playtime?" a child's voice whispered in my mind.

Though it was quiet, the weight of the thought crashed down on me like a tidal wave. I swayed on my feet, spraying urine all over the floor. I quickly shoved my dick back inside my pants, then made a beeline for the stall behind me. I fell to my knees so quickly that a sharp pain shot up through my legs. But I barely noticed as my attention was stolen by the ache in my gut. It felt as if someone had stuck a fork into my stomach and twisted my intestines around like spaghetti. I hunched over the toilet, waiting for my lunch to come back up, but all that came out were dry heaves.

"Shit," I groaned as I curled up into a ball on the floor. I was hot all over, but freezing cold at the same time. A sheen of sweat covered my body, and I shivered. The child's voice just kept echoing over and over again in my mind.

"Is it playtime? Is it playtime?"

Fuck, the kid didn't even know he was going to die. I wish I could've taken his place.

No! You're not allowed to think like that, I reminded myself. In times like this, it was difficult not to.

It took another half hour for the nausea to pass, which was unusual. Usually it was gone in only a few minutes. I pushed myself up off the cold tile, my arms shaking. Taking a deep breath, I leaned my head back against the stall door, waiting for the last of it to fade. Eventually, I felt like I could move again, so I conjured my journal and added the thought to it. I wished I could've added something to the positivity journal Professor Warren was forcing me to make, but all I wanted to do was rip the pages out of it and tell him to go screw himself. Listening to little kids die was the furthest thing from what I'd call a *gift*.

I did a quick scroll through my social media accounts to see if anyone had reported on the death yet, but it was too soon. My stomach sank when I noticed the time on my phone. I only had a few minutes to get to my Introduction to Incantations class.

Ugh. I forced myself to my feet—I was a little shaky, but stable—then started for my Incantations classroom. I took a seat in the back row of the lecture hall, so I could slip out easily if the nausea hit again. I spotted Ryan and the other Tarantulas sitting toward the middle of the room. They were laughing loudly and shooting spitballs through a straw.

Our professor walked in just as one of the balls was flying toward the front. She waved her hand, and the spit wad changed course and snapped back in the direction of the Tarantulas. It landed square on Ryan's forehead. He swatted it away and mumbled a few crude words about Professor Loren under his breath.

Professor Loren strolled to the front of the room without even glancing back at Ryan. She was an older woman with long silver hair who frequently wore flowing black dresses. She was wise and pretty much knew everything about everything—and she didn't take anyone's shit. Everyone really loved her classes, unless they were the one causing trouble.

"Last week, we covered basic incantations all witches and warlocks should know," Professor Loren began her lecture. For a woman as old as dirt, she had a surprisingly strong voice that projected all throughout the lecture hall. "You've learned basic defensive magic, like stunning spells."

Nolan, one of the Tarantulas, raised his voice. "When do we learn battle orbs and shields?"

Professor Loren frowned. "Not until you're much more mature with your magic, Mister Kowalski. Those spells are far too advanced for this class."

She turned toward the other side of the room, ignoring him. "Today, we will be talking about the theory behind incantations. Why do you think incantations work for all Casts and not just a select few?"

Felicia Green's hand shot up at the front of the room. She was in all my classes last semester and always had an answer for everything. She was the real Hermione Granger of Miriam College. She was pretty, with long blonde curls and nice skin, but her lack of humility left a lot to be desired.

"Yes, Miss Green?" Professor Loren called on her.

Felicia spoke like she was reading out of a textbook. "Incantations are universal to all Casts, because the *tasks* generated by them are universal. Incantation magic comes not from the incantation itself, but from within you."

"Exactly," Professor Loren said proudly.

Ryan leaned forward in his seat and shot another spit wad at the back of Felicia's head. Her hand slapped over it, and she whirled around to shoot daggers Ryan's way. "Do that again, and I'll incant your ass all the way to the Abyss, dickhole."

A chorus of *oohs* traveled around the room. I couldn't see Ryan's face from here, but he sounded amused. "Savage, Felicia. I like it. You wanna take the trip with me?"

"Screw you," she spat.

"Yeah, I bet you'd like to," Ryan teased.

Felicia shot him a look of disdain before turning back around in her seat.

"Let's behave ourselves," Professor Loren scolded. "You're not children anymore, for Alora's sake!"

Ryan leaned back in his chair, and his buddies laughed around him. What a fucking loser.

Professor Loren turned away from them and continued her lecture. "Incantations serve to alter your mindset. Later in the semester, we'll be writing our own incantations for simple tasks. By the end of your senior year, you should be able to perform the same tasks without incantations at all."

Felicia's hand shot into the air again, and the Tarantulas shared a collective groan. "What about group spells? Isn't it dangerous to try them without an incantation?"

"Yes," Professor Loren responded. "We'll be getting to that unit later in the semester, but since you asked, I will warn you all that group spells should always use incantations. It's the only way to ensure you're all on the same page. If not, your magic could clash. Any other questions?"

Another hand raised at the far corner of the front row.

"Yes, Mister Walker?" Professor Loren said.

Gregory Walker was a straight-A student like Felicia. If the school had some sort of geek squad, they'd both be on it. Gregory was a tall, skinny guy with a long neck and glasses. His hair stood up in all directions. I wasn't sure if it was some sort of fashion statement or what, but it looked like a mess.

"What about curses?" Gregory asked. "Can those be cast through incantations?"

Professor Loren's face fell. "Curses are very dangerous, Mister Walker."

"It's all theoretical, of course," Gregory quickly clarified.

Professor Loren's lips pressed into a thin line. Finally, she spoke softly. "A curse—or a spell cast with malicious intent, to hurt someone else—can be cast through incantations. However, curses are difficult to cast. They stem from hatred and very deep, terrible emotions. Curses are against Miriamic law. Since the Curse Breakers died out, there isn't a witch or warlock in the world who can break them. It's best if you never utter a curse at all."

Everything in the room seemed to come to a chilling halt. It was so quiet I couldn't even hear the people beside me breathing.

After a moment, Professor Loren cleared her throat and returned to her lecture. She covered things I already knew, so I took to ignoring her. Instead, I conjured my positivity journal and opened up to the first page. That child's voice was still nagging at me. Maybe if I could find the positive in it, it wouldn't hurt so bad.

I sat there the rest of class, staring down at a blank line on the page and waiting for something to come to me. But nothing did. I was so engrossed in my own little world that I didn't even realize when class ended. Ryan and his gang were headed out of the lecture hall when he stopped beside me.

"What's this, Taylor?" he asked in a harsh tone.

My gaze snapped upward to see him peering down at me. His massive arms were crossed over his chest, and he looked like he was about to start something. I bet he needed to let out some of his anger after Felicia called him out in class. And I was an easy target.

I brushed the hair out of my eyes. "Nothing. Get lost."

"Nothing, huh?" Ryan pressed. "Then why don't you let me see it?"

Before I could jab back, his hand shot out and snatched the journal out from under my hands. I was on my feet in a second, reaching for it. "Give it back!"

Ryan shoved an arm in my direction, holding me back. Using his magic, he made the journal hover just out of my reach, while he commanded the empty pages to flip. He hadn't noticed the writing on the first page, so the notebook just looked empty.

I grabbed for the journal again, but Ryan tossed it to Nolan, one of his gang members, who then passed it to Finn. The five of them laughed as they passed it around out of my reach. I bet they were so fucking proud of themselves.

I backed off and crossed my arms. By now, we were the last ones left in the classroom. "Aren't we a little old for Monkey in the Middle?" I snapped.

Ryan let out a deep belly laugh. "We're never too old to piss you off. What's so special about this stupid little notebook?"

My hands turned into fists, and my jaw tightened. "None of your damn business, that's what it is, jackass."

Ryan fucking lost it. He grabbed me by my shirt and shoved me up against the wall in the back of the room. He landed a heavy forearm to my chest to hold me there.

"Talk to me like that one more time, Lucas," he dared. "It'll be fun showing you what I can do about it."

Ryan raised his other hand, and magical swirls the color of night rose out of his palm. His magic twisted like smoky, burnt fingers. One of the fingers elongated until it reached my jaw, then skimmed along it threateningly. A magical chill spread where it touched me. I wanted to open my mouth to give him a piece of my mind, but my jaw was clamped shut tight by his Mentalist powers. My nostrils flared.

Fuck you, asshole!

I didn't take my eyes off his. Time and time again, I'd watched warlocks drop their gaze in submission to this sorry excuse of a human being. I wouldn't let him win like that.

Ryan stared me down, until his buddy Declan said, "Hey, look at this."

Ryan turned and snatched the journal out of Declan's hands. He started reading off my list. "*My gift led me to Nadine. Muffins in the Lounge. We met Talia. Grant seems happy.* What the fuck is this, Taylor? Some sappy poem? Sounds like garbage to me."

He released his magic on me, and my jaw finally freed.

"Yep," I said through gritted teeth. "That's me. A bad poet."

Ryan scoffed and shoved the journal at me. "At least you're right on that one, loser. Have fun with your sucky poetry."

Ryan walked off without looking back. The rest of the Tarantulas followed him. They all laughed like it was the best insult they'd heard all week. Probably was, considering Ryan's complete lack of creativity.

Whatever. I didn't have time for idiots like them. I had real problems to deal with.

Like my gift. This was one of the reasons I hated it. When I wasn't on the verge of vomiting, it was getting me into trouble in one way or another.

I subconjured my journal. It disappeared out of my hand and went into my stash, where I kept all my junk so I wouldn't have to carry it around.

I decided to head to the disc golf park to take my mind off everything. I was so stuck in my own head that I nearly walked straight into Professor Loren on my way out of the classroom. She was standing in the hall talking to Professor Richards, who was an Alchemist.

"Do you think you could brew me something?" she asked him a moment before I nearly trampled her.

"Sorry," I mumbled.

She grabbed my shoulder to steady me. Her face immediately fell. "Lucas, are you okay? You look a little pale."

I shook my head. "I'm fine. Are *you*?"

She furrowed her brow. "Yes, of course. Why do you ask?"

"You said you needed something brewed," I pointed out.

Professor Loren waved her hands. "It's nothing but old age, I'm sure. Just a little blip of magic waning here and there. Nothing to be worried about."

I narrowed my eyes. "Is that usual? Professor Warren wasn't feeling well a few weeks ago. He said his magic was weak, too."

Professor Loren and Professor Richards shared a glance, but it was Richards who spoke. "I'll be sure to check on him, Lucas. Thank you for letting us know."

"Yeah, no problem," I said before heading on my way.

The way they looked at each other worried me a little, but there wasn't anything I could do about it.

I headed toward the Main Foyer and stopped dead when I spotted

Nadine. My heart fluttered before I could tell it to calm down. I'd nearly forgotten I wasn't supposed to be drawn to her.

She was walking toward me with a pile of books in her hands, as if returning from outside after a study session. She wore long sleeves and a wide-brimmed hat. Her hair spilled around her shoulders, and she looked really nice, but I'd promised myself I'd keep my distance.

I took a second to admire her. She radiated beauty as she smiled and waved to Mandy and Amy across the foyer. I tried to slip back down the hall before she saw me, but I didn't make it fast enough.

Nadine's eyes met mine, and the bright look on her face darkened. She hurried over to me before I could slip down the hall.

"Lucas," she greeted coolly. Her lips pressed into a thin line. She was obviously upset with me. I couldn't exactly blame her, after the way I blew her off.

"Uh, hi." I shoved my hands into my pockets. *Awkward.*

"Can we talk?" she asked.

I shrugged. "Yeah, sure."

What else was I supposed to do? Tell her no?

Nadine led me to a secluded sitting area in the corner where no one would hear us, and I took a seat on one of the plush red chairs. Nadine set her books down on the coffee table next to us and removed her hat. It caught on her hair, which made it stick up in a couple places. I found the messy look kind of hot. She tamed it with her fingers, then sat across from me with the hat in her lap.

"What's up?" I asked casually, even though I already knew what she wanted. It was obvious we were going to have to talk about the night at the lake eventually.

Nadine sat up straight in her chair. "Look, we're friends, right?"

I nodded, though I wasn't sure. Were we?

"And friends tell each other the truth?" she asked.

Fuck. I already knew where this was going. "Yeah, they do, Nad."

Nadine looked me straight in the eye. "Then tell me what happened at the lake, Lucas. Why have you been avoiding me?"

I dropped my gaze. There were a million reasons I couldn't get involved. Even if I weren't the Reaper's Apprentice, she wouldn't want me once she figured out who I really was. Who would be happy with me if I wasn't happy with myself? Worse, I couldn't put the burden of my gift on her, and it was inevitable if we got together.

Shit, look at me getting ahead of myself. Who said we were going to get together?

"Nad, it's not you," I assured her.

She frowned and gave me a disappointed look.

Hell, was I seriously going to go and make things worse? *It's not you, it's me.* How lame could I get?

I was quick to clarify. "I can't get into a romantic relationship. There's stuff you don't know."

"Then tell me," she begged, her tone softening.

I sighed. "Nad…"

"At least give me something, Lucas." She looked at me with these big puppy dog eyes I couldn't refuse.

"What do you want to know?" I asked.

There was so much I wasn't ready to talk about. My parents. My brother. My gift. And worst of all, the dying thought I'd heard about her. That secret was something I'd have to take to the grave.

"Your Cast, for starters," she said sheepishly.

I smirked. "Isn't the mystery a little fun?"

She shook her head. "Not for me. You're a mystery I can't figure out, and I want to know everything, Lucas."

"Really?" My voice was a few pitches higher than normal.

"Yes." She blushed a little.

My smirk turned into a light smile, and tension eased out of my shoulders. It was hard to leave her alone when it felt this good to be near her.

"Maybe we can start with what everyone else already knows about me," I offered.

Nadine's eyes lit up, and she sat straighter. "Okay."

I took a deep breath. "My Cast is Mortana. I'm the Reaper's Apprentice."

Nadine blinked a few times, but otherwise, her face remained blank.

"You know what that is, right?" I asked.

She cleared her throat. "I, um… think I heard about it?"

Good. I didn't have to explain it to her. Talking about my gift was almost as bad as experiencing it.

"That's why we can't get involved," I told her bluntly. "Even if I liked you, I couldn't be with you."

Nadine swallowed. "O-okay," she stammered.

It was obvious she *wasn't* okay with it, but I couldn't find the words to explain myself. Instead, I found myself saying, "Thanks, Nad. Why can't everyone be like you?"

She chuckled nervously. "Because I'm perfect."

She placed her hat back on her head, then rested her chin on her fist and fluttered her eyelashes like she was posing for a camera.

Damn it all if that didn't make her look even sexier.

I laughed. "The hat suits you."

She touched the brim. "You think? I thought it was ugly."

I furrowed my brow. "Then why do you wear it?"

Nadine's face fell, and she set the hat aside on top of her books. "I wasn't going to tell you this yet, but since you asked…"

My heart slammed against my rib cage. The sad look on her face had me worried, like she was about to break some terrible news. I had no idea what it could possibly be.

Nadine knotted her hands together in her lap and took a deep breath. "I have something called lupus."

Her words knocked the wind out of me. I didn't wish a chronic disease like that upon anyone. "Nad…"

"If you tell me you're sorry, I might lose it," she threatened playfully.

My mouth slammed shut.

She laughed lightly as she watched my eyes go wide. "I just mean, it's what I hear every time I tell someone. You don't have to be sorry. It's not your fault."

"Well, I don't feel good about it," I admitted. "Nadine, I had no idea."

She shrugged. "Why would you? Most people don't even know what lupus is."

"If there's anything I can do to help, you have to tell me," I said.

Nadine forced a smile. "Thanks for being nice about it. Most people just tell me I don't look sick, then throw their pity at me when I explain it to them."

"My cousin has lupus," I said. "So I know a little about it."

It didn't mean I understood what she was going through, though, because I didn't.

She seemed relieved, like she didn't want to have to explain it all. "So you must know I'm sensitive to the sun."

I nodded. Inside, my guts sank. I wished there was something I could do to help her—some way to take all the pain and symptoms away.

"That's why I cover up when I'm outside," she explained. "When I get too much sun exposure, my symptoms flare up. Like, right now my joints are really sore."

She held one hand with the other and flexed her fingers. The way they moved in a stilted way suggested she was in more pain than I knew. My instinct hit, and I reached out for her. She didn't protest as I took her hand in mine and gently massaged her joints. The warmth from her hand seemed to consume me, radiating up my arms and all throughout my body. Once I started, I couldn't stop. I just wanted to be near her, to touch her.

She shot me a nervous smile. "That actually doesn't hurt."

I shrugged. "My mom broke her hand when I was a kid, and it never quite healed right. She used to ask for massages all the time, so I kind of got good at it."

I didn't tell her how Mom had broken it during one of Dad's fits.

Nadine relaxed into her seat as I continued massaging her hand. She closed her eyes and rolled her head back. "Oh my God. Can I pay you to be my personal masseuse?"

I chuckled. "What are friends for?"

"Most of my friends wouldn't do this for me," she joked.

I couldn't take my eyes off her perfect skin as I stared down at my fingers moving over her. Her eyes were closed, so she couldn't see me admiring her beauty. There was so much I wanted to do with these fingers—for these hands to do to me.

I dropped her hand before my imagination could run too wild on me. But even that didn't slow my heart. Just being this close to her and smelling the rosy scent on her skin, it made my body go wild. I longed to be back in that position at the lake. I'd freeze the moment in time as her legs boldly wrapped around my waist, her half-naked body pressed tightly against mine. Maybe instead of pushing her away, I'd actually kiss her...

In a perfect world, where the Reaper's Shadow didn't exist.

Nadine cleared her throat, calling me back to reality. "Thanks, Lucas. That really helped."

I sat up straighter. "Are there other things that help with your symptoms?"

"I already told you about the yoga," she said, "but someone needs to kick my ass, because I haven't been doing it lately."

"Why not?" I asked. "If it helps?"

Nadine's shoulders dropped. "It's hard to convince myself to do it with all the stress."

"What do you mean?" I asked.

Nadine eyed me curiously. "You don't know, do you? I thought everyone knew."

"Know what?"

She swallowed, and her voice came out small. "Lucas, my parents died."

If her telling me she had lupus knocked the wind out of me, this one was a double whammy. Why hadn't Helena mentioned it to me?

I knew someone in her life had died recently, because I'd heard the woman's last thought, which was about Nadine. But I didn't know it'd been her mom. I should've put the pieces together. And now I'd learned that her *dad* died, too. Holy shit!

Her mom's last thought echoed through my mind. There was more to her last thought than I could ever tell Nadine... a dark, ominous warning that could get Nadine hurt. Which was why I hadn't spoken of it—and wouldn't.

What could I possibly say to Nad if she didn't want to hear *I'm sorry*?

Like an idiot, I spat out, "My brother died, too."

What the hell? Why was I making this about me?

"I just mean, I get what it's like to lose a family member," I quickly added.

Her expression softened. "It's nice to have someone my age around who understands. Most people don't get it."

"Tell me about it," I said, feeling a little more of that weight on my shoulders lift.

She played with a thread on the chair and didn't meet my eyes. "How long ago?"

"Almost a year," I answered.

"Mine was this summer. It was a car crash." She didn't say anything more than that. She just stared down at the loose thread, poking it with her finger while we sat in silence. It killed me to watch. I wished that I could shoulder all that pain, just to see her happy.

I decided to change up the subject. "Well, if you're looking for help with your yoga, you should check out the fitness center."

She finally looked to me. "They have yoga?"

"Yeah. We could head over there and pick up a schedule if you want," I offered.

Damn it. I was supposed to be staying away from her, not inviting her on walks with me.

Screw it. This one time wouldn't hurt anything.

"Okay," she agreed.

She reached for her hat, but I grabbed her books for her before she could get them.

"I can carry those," she protested.

I shrugged. "So can I."

Nadine huffed a little, but she didn't put up a fight.

"This way." I cocked my head, and we started down the hallway toward the pool and fitness center.

She walked a step ahead of me, so she didn't see how I was eyeing her from the side. She had a beautiful profile, and that hair... I couldn't stop staring at that long brown hair that looked so soft. I just wanted to run my hands through it and—

Nausea hit me.

Aw, fuck.

I didn't want Nadine to notice, so I kept up pace beside her.

"Five more minutes..." the thought said.

The thought was there and gone in a matter of seconds. I'd collected a lot of thoughts like that over the months. Most people would sell their souls just for a few more minutes with their loved ones. This guy was no exception.

It was only when the wave of nausea passed that it hit me how smoothly that one had gone. It was nothing like earlier. I didn't even have to double over and catch myself against the wall. How could that be when just a few hours ago I was writhing on the bathroom floor?

And then it hit me.

The difference was Nadine. I didn't know what it was about her, but being around her made everything better. I didn't feel as hopeless when she was nearby.

I quickly conjured my journal and a pen, then scribbled something down on the next line before Nadine saw.

She makes it all bearable.

She looked in my direction, but I'd already sent the notebook away to my stash.

"What?" I asked innocently.

She shrugged and offered a kind smile. "Nothing."

Well, fuck. How was I supposed to stay away from her now?

nadine

TEN

I was a filthy liar. I don't even know why I lied to Lucas. It just slipped out.

Oh, yeah, Lucas. I totally know what the Reaper's Apprentice is.

Ugh.

I guess I didn't want to sound totally clueless around him. And then I had to tell him I understood? WTF? I didn't. Not really. I just couldn't bear to see him looking all sad like that and everything.

I was still thinking about it days later on my way to my Introduction to Tarot class. It was a small class with only thirty students. The subject was interesting, but Chloe was in this class, and I couldn't stand her. She always had to call people out for their interpretation of the cards, even though Professor Wykoff said in our first lesson there were no right or wrong interpretations.

We'd already covered the basics of Tarot, how there were twenty-two Major Arcana cards in a deck that spoke to your life-long spiritual journey, and fifty-six Minor Arcana cards that represented everyday challenges. We learned about the four suits—that cups represented emotions and relationships, swords referred to behaviors and the mind, pentacles were about finances and career, and wands were about spirituality. From there, Professor Wykoff said, all we had to do was interpret the images.

Professor Wykoff was younger than most of my other professors. She must've been in her thirties. She had long caramel-colored hair and always wore multi-colored dresses and sandals. She spoke in a soft tone so that the class had to be dead silent to hear her.

Today, she stood at the front of the room, shuffling the cards in mid-air with her telekinetic abilities. "I'd like to start our lesson today with a fun exercise. Each of you will come up and pick a single card that represents *you* and your life's journey. As a class, we will work to interpret the card together. Who'd like to go first?"

Chloe's hand shot up at the front of the room. I sank down in my seat. I wasn't looking forward to getting up in front of everyone else. They all knew tarot way better than I did.

Professor Wykoff smiled brightly. "Miss Olson, come on up."

Chloe breezed to the front of the room. As much as I hated to admit it, she looked graceful in her high heels.

Professor Wykoff held out her hand, and the cards fluttered out of the air into a neat pile. She held it out to Chloe. Chloe tilted her chin up confidently and split the deck, then pulled a card from the middle. She smiled proudly as she turned it over.

"Hold it up so everyone can see," Professor Wykoff encouraged.

Chloe held the card high over her head and announced, "I got the Hierophant."

I remembered him from our readings last week. He was like a priest, a spiritual leader. He sat on a throne in front of two subjects, with a set of keys placed at his feet.

"An excellent card," Professor Wykoff said. "What do you think it means?"

Chloe lowered the card to study it closely. "Well, I know he's a teacher. The keys represent his ability to unlock the mysteries of the world, and these two guys here represent a group identity."

Damn, I was hoping she'd be wrong, but she sounded like she knew what she was talking about.

"How do you think that fits into your life?" Professor Wykoff asked.

Chloe held her head up confidently. "It must mean that I'll become a spiritual teacher someday. Perhaps I'll serve on the Imperium Council like my grandmother."

Professor Wykoff nodded. "Very good. Would anyone like to challenge this interpretation?"

I sat a little straighter. Last week, Professor Wykoff had told us each card had multiple different meanings. Chloe didn't really come off to me as the *teacher* type. Maybe the card had a different meaning for her.

"Nobody?" Professor Wykoff prodded. Her eyes turned to me. "Miss Evers?"

I didn't know why she called on me. Maybe she sensed something in my expression. My pulse quickened, but I answered anyway. "Well, I was just thinking… the card could mean that you *need* a teacher, instead of becoming one, right?"

Professor Wykoff nodded, but Chloe's features darkened.

I tried my best to ignore her. "Or perhaps it's not about the teaching aspect at all. Priests are all about tradition, aren't they? So couldn't this card be encouraging you to honor your traditions, to not break the rules?"

"I'm not breaking any rules," Chloe snapped.

"Turning someone into a toad sure sounds like breaking the rules to me," I snarled back.

Gasps traveled around the room, and it took me a second to realize what I'd said. I didn't mean to. It just slipped out.

Chloe narrowed her eyes at me, as if trying to figure out how I knew about that. "I don't know what you're talking about."

Liar.

"Ladies," Professor Wykoff quickly stepped in, pretending like she didn't notice the hostility between us. "These are both very valid interpretations. Miss Olson, I suggest you take into consideration Miss Evers's suggestions as you weigh the possibilities of this card on your life."

Chloe looked Professor Wykoff up and down, then scoffed as she tossed the card back at her. "I know my tarot. I'm not wrong."

She stomped back to her desk and flipped her hair over her shoulder while she sat.

Professor Wykoff turned her gaze back to me. "Miss Evers, perhaps you'd like to go next?"

It didn't sound like a suggestion. Taking a deep breath, I stood on shaky knees and walked to the front of the room. Professor Wykoff shuffled the deck again, then held it out to me. I cut it as Chloe had and picked a card out of the middle. I was a little taken aback by what I got.

After a few moments, Professor Wykoff said, "Hold it up for everyone, please."

My pulse raced as I flipped the card over and showed the class. "The Eight of Swords."

This card depicted a woman bound in cloth, with a blindfold over her face. Eight swords were sticking out of the ground around her.

"What do you think it means?" Professor Wykoff asked.

I studied the card before answering. "Well, we know that swords represent behaviors. She's bound and can't see where she's going. So it might mean that my behaviors and mindset are holding me back."

"Very good," Professor Wykoff praised. "This is the card of negative thoughts."

I furrowed my brow. "That doesn't sound good."

Chloe's hand shot into the air.

"Yes, Miss Olson?" Professor Wykoff called on her.

Chloe straightened her spine. "On the contrary, this card is quite positive if you look at it correctly." She shot me daggers as she emphasized the word *correctly*. "Notice how her feet are unbound. She has the ability to go in any direction she chooses. The woman in this card is bound by her own doing. All she has to do is stop playing the victim."

Chloe glared at me. Was she seriously accusing me of victim mentality when she didn't even know me? Yeah, my life sucked, but I wasn't a victim. I dealt with my shit.

"Excellent," Professor Wykoff said. With her, I didn't think anyone could interpret the cards wrong. "It seems the power to escape your issues is in your hands, Miss Evers. Remove the blindfold, and everything shall be made clear."

I gave her back the card and returned to my seat. The whole time, Chloe's eyes followed me. I sat, wondering if maybe I'd chosen the wrong card. Was I really holding myself back? I didn't play the victim, did I?

I was contemplating it all class, so I didn't really pay attention to the rest of the readings. All I knew was Chloe had to challenge them all, and Professor Wykoff praised her each time.

As I was walking out of the classroom, Chloe grabbed my wrist and dragged me down the hall. I ripped my arm out of her hold and glared at her. "What the hell?"

She lowered her voice, but her tone was as harsh as ever. "You think it's funny challenging me like that?"

"Professor Wykoff called on me," I growled. "I followed the assignment."

Chloe pointed a manicured finger in my face and leaned close. "Don't *ever* insult me like that again. Understand?"

"I'm so scared," I said flatly. "Try not to act so offended next time… unless it's true?"

Her lips tightened. "Screw you, Nadine. No one wants you here anyway. Why don't you just leave?"

"I don't know. Why don't you come up with a better insult? I've heard that one before," I said coolly.

Chloe didn't like that. She stepped closer, until she was looming over me. "I'm going to have so much fun driving you out of town."

I raised an eyebrow. "Yeah? I'd like to see you try."

Chloe scoffed. "You're on."

She breezed away. I stared after her, narrowing my eyes at the back of her head. It wasn't until she turned the corner that I breathed a sigh of relief. Whatever. She didn't deserve my attention anyway. What I really needed right now was a nap.

I turned and started back toward my dorm room. When I got there, the door handle didn't move. I twisted harder, but it wouldn't budge.

"What the…?" I glanced down to my wrist, and my gut sank. My bracelet! It was gone! That was the key to my room.

I pounded on the door, feeling a red-hot energy rise inside of me. How could I have lost my enchanted bracelet?

Talia answered a few moments later. She furrowed her brow and tilted her head. "You didn't have to knock."

"I did." I held up my wrist to show her it was empty.

She gazed at my wrist in shock. "What happened to your bracelet?"

I entered the room and plopped down onto my bed. It felt really good to lie down. "I don't know."

Talia sat on the couch. "When was the last time you saw it?"

I racked my brain, trying to recall. "I definitely had it at lunch. I fell asleep in the study area outside the fitness center between classes, but I'm pretty sure I still had it on me when I woke up. Which means I must've gone to my tarot class with it on."

"Should we retrace your steps?" Talia asked.

I was too tired to move. I shook my head. "Maybe in a bit."

Talia's face fell. "You know what? I'll go look for it."

"No, Tal," I said quickly. "You don't have to do that."

She grabbed her bag. "Well, I'm going to go for a walk. If I happen to stumble upon it, I'll let you know."

I'd already closed my eyes. I was drifting off so quickly that I barely heard her. "Yeah, okay. Have fun on your walk."

I was out before I heard the sound of the door shut.

I woke at least an hour later to the sound of three voices entering the room. It felt like I'd barely slept at all. I pushed past the pain in my joints and sat up in bed to see Talia, Mandy, and Amy entering the room. Mandy wore a plum dress with a plaid skirt that fell to her knees, with dark tights and high heels. Amy dressed more casually, in jeans and a *Miriam College* hoodie.

"Bad news," Talia said. "I didn't find your bracelet, but I *did* find these two wonderful ladies who want to go shopping with us and take us out to dinner."

"Anywhere but the Chinese buffet," Amy said. "I'm sick of rice and egg rolls. My mom hasn't stopped making them all summer. She's trying to replicate my grandmother's famous recipe."

"In that case, no Indian food, either," Mandy added. "Curry's the only thing my mom knows how to make."

"Your family has a secret recipe?" Amy asked her.

"Just the one," Mandy replied. "That recipe was the one thing my grandma brought with her from India."

"Same," Amy said. "Except my grandma came from China."

Mandy turned to me. "So, what do you say, Nadine?"

I forced a smile. As much as I loved shopping, it was beyond tiring. I hated to miss out, though. "Sounds like fun. You'll have to give me a few minutes to get ready."

"Sure," Talia said, before walking over to her bed to pick up her cat. "Hey, you guys want to meet Gus?"

"Oh my gosh! He's sooo cute," Mandy raved. "Nadine, do you have a cat?"

I grabbed my hairbrush and started brushing my hair into a high ponytail. "No, not yet."

The girls either didn't notice how slowly I moved, or they didn't care, because they didn't rush me. It was kind of nice.

Talia leaned against the bathroom door while I was fixing my makeup. "I can't wait until we get our magic. Hair and makeup will be so easy."

"We can do magic makeup?" I asked as I smeared mascara across my eyelashes.

She nodded proudly. "Makeup and hair. It'll make my morning routine super fast."

I tightened my ponytail and turned from the mirror. "It will definitely be a perk of magic."

We took Mandy's car into town and parked along a street with a bunch of cute shops. I noticed various signs advertising free samples of things like honey, maple syrup, and apple cider. There were plenty of cute clothing shops and metaphysical stores. I didn't know where to start.

Amy noticed me eyeing the street curiously as we stepped out of the car. "Haven't you been here before, Nadine?"

I shook my head. "I haven't had the time yet."

Mandy inhaled a sharp breath. "Girl, you're missing out! You *have* to try Grandma Dee's Apple Cider. It's the best."

"We could start here and work our way to the end of the street," I suggested, pointing to the closest store, which sold crystals.

"Good idea." Talia looped her arm through mine, and we entered the shop.

It was quiet inside, though a soft melody played over the speakers. Various incense smells hit my nose all at once. Beneath the counter in the middle of the shop, crystals big and small glittered under the light. There was an entire section dedicated to different tarot decks, and another for candles. The entire ambiance soothed me...

Until I caught sight of Gwen and Camille. They were filling small draw-string bags with different colored stones. I was pretty sure I saw Gwen slip one of the smaller ones into her pocket. The two of them shot daggers my way when they noticed my eyes on them. I quickly glanced away and followed my friends to the other side of the store.

I pulled a box of tarot cards from the shelf. "I should probably get myself my own tarot deck. It's not required for my class, but it might help me study."

The artwork on this deck was beautiful, but I didn't recognize the cards shown on the back.

"Those are oracle cards," Talia said.

"What's the difference?" I asked.

"Tarot is more standard," Talia explained. "Tarot decks should have seventy-eight cards, with Major and Minor Arcana, and four suits. Oracle cards can basically be anything the creator wants them to be. There's more flexibility in the oracle cards."

"Interesting…" I mused as I studied the artwork on the front. It depicted a beautiful woman with the full moon behind her. She looked as if she was praying. I didn't know why, but I felt drawn to her. "I think I'm going to get these ones."

"Oh my gosh! Check these out," Mandy cried. She was hunched over the front counter looking down at one of the crystals inside. The three of us came over to join her. Below her was a beautiful orange and red crystal set into a silver ring. It shimmered in the light. "It's beautiful, isn't it?"

"I like this one," Amy said, pointing to a midnight blue crystal. "Don't let me buy it, though. I have at least a dozen of these already."

"Seriously guys?" Talia teased. "It's pink all the way."

"Check this out!" Amy cried, flapping a hand. She pointed to a green stone beneath the glass. "This is supposed to ward off curses. I hear it's the best thing since Curse Breakers."

"Curse Breakers?" I asked.

Mandy's face fell. "Oh, honey. You have so much to learn. Curse Breakers are the fifth Cast."

My eyebrows knitted together. "They died out, didn't they?"

Mandy nodded. "Yeah, I think… well…"

She hesitated.

"What?" I pressed.

Mandy played with the strap on her purse. "I'm just surprised no one mentioned it to you. I'm pretty sure your grandpa was the last one."

Shock hit me. Why hadn't Grammy told me?

"What exactly is a Curse Breaker?" I asked carefully.

"Exactly what they sound like," Mandy said. "Witches who break curses."

"There's more to it than that," Amy added. "They could transfer magic from one place to another. That's how they broke the curses. Plus, they can absorb magic."

"That sounds really cool. I wonder why there aren't any left," I mused.

"It's always been kind of rare," Talia explained. "I mean, being able to absorb magic takes a lot of responsibility. Mother Miriam wouldn't want that kind of power to be put in the wrong hands."

"I guess that makes sense," I said.

Talia gestured to the stones below us. "Which one is your favorite?"

I peered into the glass. They were all so gorgeous. Some shimmered like diamonds, while others were smooth. I was drawn to a light blue one, but it was hard to pick a favorite.

"Will that be all for today?"

My thoughts were interrupted by the sound of the cashier checking out a customer. I looked up to see Headmistress Verla setting a huge crystal on the counter next to us. It was orange and reminded me of a Himalayan salt lamp, but it was solid and looked hella heavy. She had a large bag draped over her shoulder, and Odin's black head poked out the opening.

She brushed her brown hair out of her eyes. "Yes, that's it."

The cashier started ringing her up. Headmistress Verla lifted her head and caught my eye. "Girls, how are you?"

"We're good," I said.

"Nadine, I'm actually really glad I ran into you," Headmistress Verla said. "I wanted to talk to you about your Evoking Ceremony training."

"Oh?" I pushed my hair behind my ear. "How exactly does that work?"

She gave a polite smile. "Each freshman is assigned a mentor who will help prepare them for the ceremony."

"Have I been assigned?" I asked eagerly. I was excited to hear who I'd been assigned to.

"Yes," she said brightly. "Me."

I blinked a few times. "You're my mentor?"

"You sound surprised, Nadine."

"I just thought it'd be one of my professors," I said.

"Well, it was, but there were some... reassignments." I didn't know what she meant by that, but I sensed something in her tone.

"What do you mean?" I asked curiously.

She waved her hand nonchalantly. "It's nothing. I just thought... maybe we could get to know each other. You know, since I was so close to your mom."

"Yeah, I'd like that," I told her.

"Excellent," she said brightly. "I suggest we meet at least three times before your Evoking Ceremony. How does the first week of October sound?"

"Sounds great."

"I'll see you then." She paid for her crystal, then left the shop with it cradled in her hands.

Talia, Mandy, and Amy all turned to me with wide eyes.

"What?" I asked innocently.

"You're so lucky," Talia said. "She never mentors anyone."

I furrowed my brow. "She doesn't?"

"No," Mandy confirmed. "She's super good, too. You'll pass your Evoking Ceremony for sure."

Relief washed over me. "That's encouraging."

"You should get a crystal to celebrate," Amy suggested.

I eyed Talia and Mandy. "Is that what witches do?"

Amy laughed. "No. I just *really* like crystals."

Mandy frowned. "I feel so bad for the headmistress."

My heart sank. "Me, too. Talia told me what happened. She lost her sister *and* her baby."

Mandy leaned in to whisper. "It wasn't just any sister, either. It was her twin."

"Wow, that must've been hard," I said in a soft tone.

Talia shook her head. "Worse than that. Identical twins share a soul. She literally lost half her soul."

My jaw dropped. There were no words for this kind of thing. "Is there anything we can do?"

Talia shook her head. "There was a memorial for her baby after it happened. The whole town came. I would hate to reopen old wounds."

"You're right," I told her. I felt the same way with my parents. The grief was personal. I didn't want to talk about it, and I bet Headmistress Verla didn't want to, either.

Mandy seemed to sense the tension in the air and made a point to break it. "Well, I'm going to get this ring and another palm reading book for my collection. Anyone else getting anything?"

I bought the oracle cards, then we went next door to a cute shop that sold fudge and salt water taffy.

I chuckled as I read through the names of the taffy flavors. "These are great. Eye of Newt. Witch's Brew. Midnight Reaper."

I stopped in my tracks when I saw the one labeled *Midnight Reaper*. It was a deep black and probably licorice flavored, but the name reminded me that I'd been meaning to ask Talia about what Lucas had said.

"Midnight Reaper tastes amazing," Talia said. She reached for a bag to start filling it with candy.

I cleared my throat. "Speaking of reapers, I heard of something called a Reaper's Apprentice, but I'm not sure what it means."

Mandy paused as she reached for a taffy labeled *Pumpkin Spice*. "You hang out with Lucas Taylor, don't you?"

I nodded. "He told me he was the Reaper's Apprentice, and I said I knew what he meant, but I didn't."

Amy came up close to me to explain in a low voice. "There's one Reaper's Apprentice every generation. They collect the last thoughts of the dead, so that the spirits can move on to the afterlife. When he dies, he'll become a reaper."

My eyebrows shot up. "Like the Grim Reaper? A scythe and everything?"

"There is no Grim Reaper," Talia said. "Just reapers. Lots of them."

A heavy weight settled on my chest, and I suddenly felt for Lucas. He dealt with death day in and day out. It sounded like a huge burden to bear.

I quickly became intrigued. "Do all magical races have reapers?"

Talia shrugged. "Depends on what you call it. In some societies, their ancestors come to lead their spirits to the other side. In ours, specially trained reapers help you cross over."

"Mm..." I mused thoughtfully. "So, why can't a Reaper's Apprentice have a girlfriend?"

Amy tilted her head to the side. "What do you mean?"

"Lucas said we couldn't get involved because he was the Reaper's Apprentice," I explained. "Any idea why?"

The three of them stared back at me blankly.

"It sounds like an excuse to me," Talia said bluntly.

"Totally," Amy agreed. "I bet he's scared or something."

My teeth gritted. "If he doesn't like me, why doesn't he just say that?"

No one had an answer for me.

We bought our candy and left the store. As we were leaving, two women in beautiful velvet robes passed by us. In unison, Mandy, Amy, and Talia all bowed their heads and politely said, "Priestesses."

The women bowed their heads back, then continued on their way. My eyes followed them. They were both decades older than us. One had salt and pepper hair, while the other had a mane of red hair tied into a long braid. They held their heads high, like they were important. I noticed a cauldron tattoo on the back of one lady's neck, and a skull on the other's wrist.

I turned to my friends. "What was that about?"

Mandy and Amy exchanged a glance, but it was Amy who spoke. "They're Imperium members."

"Imperium?" I asked. Chloe had mentioned the Imperium Council, but I hadn't asked what it meant.

"Our government," Amy explained as we entered the next shop down, which was a cute boutique that sold dresses. "The Imperium is made up of one High Priestess from each of the coven's Casts."

I smiled. "The coven's run by women?"

Talia ran her hands down a pink dress. "Absolutely."

"Awesome," I said. "How are the priestesses chosen?"

"Oh! We just talked about this in my sociology class," Amy piped up excitedly. "When a priestess dies, the remaining Imperium members nominate and vote on the next priestess to take their place. Usually, they choose the strongest members of the Cast."

"What if there's a disagreement or a tie vote?" I asked.

Talia's gave me this dead serious look. "Then it's a fight to the death."

My face fell. Talia and Amy burst into a fit of laughter.

"I'm kidding!" Talia giggled. "I don't think there's ever been a tie vote. They definitely pray to Mother Miriam before they vote, so it's usually unanimous."

I pulled a black floral dress off the rack and held it up to my body. "It sounds so easy."

"You should try that on," Talia encouraged.

"You think?"

"Yeah, and I'll try this one." She grabbed the pink dress she'd been eyeing. "This would look hot for the Midnight Formal."

"Midnight Formal?" I asked.

Mandy beamed. "A winter tradition! It's the best dance of the year."

"I didn't know colleges held dances," I said.

"You think we're all done dancing after senior prom?" Mandy asked. "No way. We love our dances around here."

"Okay, so which one of you can I take?" I joked. "I doubt I'll find a date."

"Don't talk that way, Nadine," Amy scolded. "I'm sure there are tons of guys who would love to take you."

Problem was, there was only one I wanted to go with.

I shrugged. "I guess we'll see."

We made our way back to the fitting rooms. The black dress was light and flowy on me. It was a little too girly for me, but my friends liked it, so I decided to buy it. Mandy bought three, all in different colors. We stopped at a dozen more shops before we ordered dinner at a cute café that was famous for its assortment of pies. I got to try some of the cider I'd heard so much about, and it was amazing. Finally, we decided to call it a night. By the time we got back to campus, my arms were full of shopping bags.

"You think those shoes I wore yesterday will go with my new dress?" Mandy asked Amy as we crossed the foyer.

Amy thought about it for a second. "The black sandals with the strap?"

"Yeah. I don't know if those will work or if I should buy new ones," Mandy said.

Amy scrunched up her nose. "Buy new ones anyway."

Mandy's jaw dropped dramatically. "Girl, you are no good for my credit card."

Amy flipped her dark hair over her shoulder. "What do you think I'm here for?"

I gripped hard to the banister as we climbed the stairs. All the walking we'd done had really tired me out. Talia noticed, but she didn't say anything. She made a point to walk behind me, in case I passed out or something.

"Bad Mandy," Talia snickered. "You already spent too much today."

Mandy groaned. "I know. My parents are gonna kill me."

We reached the top of the steps, and my stomach sank when I saw Chloe, Gwen, and Camille standing there. They were huddled in a small group and giggling about something I couldn't hear. Their laughter instantly died when Chloe lifted her head and caught me staring. I was pretty sure she was trying to flip us off with her eyes.

Mandy shot her a disgusted look, then flipped her hair over her shoulder and continued on her way. "Sorry, guys," she said when we were out of earshot of the Lucky Three. "I kind of attract hostility from that chick."

I scoffed. "Believe me, it's not just you."

I reached for the door handle on room 112, but when I twisted, nothing happened. "Whoops. I forgot I lost my bracelet."

"That's okay. I've got it," Talia said.

When the door swung open, my jaw dropped.

Talia's hand shot over her mouth. "Good Goddess."

The room had been totally trashed. I was too shocked to say anything. All the dresses in our closet had been ripped out and were strewn across the entryway. In the bathroom, my Epsom salts littered the floor, and Talia's shampoo had been poured over every surface. All the books from my dresser were on the floor. Some of them lay open, with the pages crinkled at the corner. Our bedding was all messed up, and the cushions were thrown off the couch. Dresser drawers were open, and our clothes were scattered all around the room. All the condoms from Talia's jewelry box had been ripped open and were hung from the knobs on our dressers. A small cry came from under the bed.

"Gus!" Talia screeched. She rushed over and dropped her shopping bags at her feet, then reached under the bed to pull out her suitcase. She flipped the top up, and Gus jumped out. He purred as she set him free.

My hands shook as I leaned down to pick up my books.

"Oh my gosh," Mandy said breathlessly. "Who would do this?"

Talia held Gus close and gently stroked his white fur. "I don't know."

I placed one of the books back on my dresser, and that's when I noticed it. My enchanted beaded bracelet sat neatly on the middle of my dresser. I picked it up and turned to Talia. "This definitely wasn't here when we left."

Talia's jaw dropped. "Someone must've found it and done this…"

Red hot rage tore through me. Something from earlier flickered through my mind, how Chloe had grabbed my wrist after our tarot class. My nostrils flared. "I don't think they found it. They *stole* it."

"Oh, no," Amy whispered as she reached down to pick up one of my books. She flipped it over, only for me to see that the cover had been ripped off of my Agatha Christie paperback. Amy held it up in two pieces.

That's when I fucking lost it. I tore the book out of her hand and stomped out of the room. Screw my fatigue and aching joints. I didn't care how much it hurt to punch this bitch in the face. She deserved it. She was going to pay for this!

I ignored Talia's voice calling my name as I marched down the hall. Chloe looked to me with false shock in her eyes, but I could tell she was holding back a laugh.

"Oh, no, Nadine," she feigned. "What happened?"

I thrust my arm out and shoved Chloe so hard that pain shot through my wrist. She stumbled back a step, but quickly straightened.

I shoved the book into her face. "Look what you did, you fucking bitch!"

"I have no idea what you're talking about," Chloe said coolly.

Gwen and Camille snickered from behind her. Chloe just looked amused. In the foyer below, all eyes turned to us.

"This was the last thing my mom gave me before she died!" I shouted, my hand curling into a tight fist. "And you've ruined it!"

Chloe's eyebrows knitted together. She spoke loud enough for the onlookers in the hall to hear. "But Nadine, how could I have gotten into your dorm?"

"You know damn well how you did it!" I snarled, getting up in her face. "You stole my bracelet and went in while Talia and I were in town. I bet you sent your back-up bitches to keep an eye on us."

Gwen and Camille only laughed harder—like they took the insult as a badge of honor.

Chloe crossed her arms and leveled me with a challenging gaze. "Prove it."

"Nadine." I felt Talia's hand on my elbow, but I shrugged her off.

"Are you seriously going to stand here and tell me it wasn't you?" I growled at Chloe. "No one's going to believe you!"

She leaned forward and spoke in a low voice. "Leave town, and it won't happen again."

"Leave town...?" My fist tightened. "How about you tell me what the fuck it is you have against me?"

Chloe eyed me up and down, then scoffed. "You don't know, do you?"

"Know what?" I snapped.

She smirked. "Maybe you should ask your grandma. Anyway, good luck cleaning up."

Chloe turned on her heel and started walking away from me, but I dropped my book and lunged forward. My fingers tangled in her hair, and I jerked so hard that she stumbled backward and landed on the ground. I was about to jump on top of her when three pairs of hands held me back.

Chloe cradled her head where it'd hit the ground and quickly got to her feet. "You're crazy!"

"And you're a fucking liar!" I seethed. Tears began to stream down my face as I struggled out of my friends' hold. But I couldn't get away from all three of them. "That was my mom's book, you bitch!"

I screamed more obscenities at her, but they flew out of my mouth without me really realizing what I was saying. I was pretty sure I called her a bitch at least three more times. It was loud enough for practically the whole school to hear. I probably looked insane as spittle flew from my mouth and I struggled away from my friends. But I didn't care. I just wanted her to pay.

Professor Wykoff rushed up the stairs. "Nadine, Nadine," she said softly. "You need to calm down."

"Calm down!?" I shrieked. "Did you see what she did?"

Professor Wykoff didn't raise her voice at all. I had to quiet down to hear her. "Why don't you show me?"

I was still seething, but it was enough to get me to stop struggling. My friends let me go, and I led Professor Wykoff back to our room.

"Oh, dear," she said once she saw the mess. "Let's... let's get some help."

She turned from the room, presumably to find some other professors. Talia led me over to my bed, and I sank into it.

"Nadine, what *was* that?" she asked.

I took a deep breath and wiped the tears from my eyes. "Don't you want to punch her, too?"

"Yeah, of course I do, but that..." Talia hesitated. "That didn't seem like you at all."

I sniffled as Mandy handed me my book that I'd dropped in the hall. I hugged it close to my chest. "I just... get that way sometimes. I can't explain it. It's like..." I choked up as a sob rose in my throat. "It's like I have this darkness inside of me. Most of the time it's fine, but other times it's like… like I want to rip somebody's head off."

Amy's shoulders fell. "We all get that way sometimes, Nadine."

I shook my head. She didn't understand. When I got this way, I could get downright murderous. It was way overly dramatic, and I knew I was totally out of line, but I couldn't control myself. I was beyond furious.

"Deep breaths, Nadine," Mandy encouraged.

"No." I got to my feet, but I stood too fast. The room spun around me, and I flopped back onto the bed.

"Nadine, you need to slow down," Talia insisted.

I pressed the heel of my palm to my forehead, waiting for the dizziness to pass. "I don't want to calm down, Tal."

"Okay, but you can't keep acting like this," she stated sternly.

I dropped my hand and looked her in the eyes. "Fine. Then I want to go see my grandmother."

Talia exchanged a nervous glance with the other girls.

"We'll stay and clean up," Amy offered.

Talia turned back to me. "Okay, Nadine. We'll go visit your grandma."

I was still fuming on the car ride over, but Talia had insisted she drive, so I managed to cool down a little by the time we pulled into Grammy's driveway. Grammy rushed out of the house when she saw my car pull up.

"Nadine, what happened?" she demanded. There was a look in her eye that told me she already knew.

"Who told you?" I asked as I stepped out of the car.

Grammy frowned, but she wrapped an arm around my shoulders and led me up the walkway. Talia followed close behind.

"Clarice called," Grammy admitted.

I groaned. Headmistress Verla knew? Was I going to get suspended or something?

"I heard you made quite a scene," Grammy stated. I expected her to sound disappointed, but her tone was impossible to read.

"It was justified," I said bitterly.

Grammy led me into the living room, and I took a seat on the couch. Talia sat beside me with a worried look on her face.

Grammy sat in the chair across from us. She adjusted her long skirt and folded her hands in her lap. "Why don't you tell me what happened?"

My blood heated as I pictured that satisfied look on Chloe's face. What a fucking bitch. I took a deep breath before jumping into my explanation. "There's this girl at school who hates me—I don't know why—and she broke into our dorm room and tore the whole thing apart."

My hands shook the longer I spoke. "She ripped the book Mom and Dad gave me for my birthday, and I just… I lost it. She's lucky I'm going through a flare-up, or I would've pummeled her fucking—"

"Nadine." Grammy held up a hand to stop me. She spoke so calmly, like my anger didn't faze her at all. "I understand that you're upset, but getting into fist fights is not the answer."

I groaned. "What was I supposed to do, Grammy? Sit there and take it?"

Grammy sat silently, unmoving, though Talia shifted uncomfortably beside me.

Finally, Grammy's stoic features turned into a frown. "I'm sorry about your book, Nadine. Perhaps we can get you a new one—"

"I don't *want* a new one," I snapped.

Grammy's eyebrows tightened.

I quickly adjusted my tone. "It's not just any book, Grammy. Mom and Dad signed it to me. It's… it's—"

I choked up again.

Talia inched closer to me and pulled me into a hug. "It's going to be okay, Nadine. No one got hurt, and that's what's important."

I melted into the hug, letting it cool some of the heat raging through my body. Slowly, the tension in my shoulders began to ease. Finally, I drew away from Talia, feeling like my head was a little clearer. "I'm sorry. I know I could've reacted differently. And you're right, Tal. No one got hurt. I just don't get why she did it in the first place."

I turned my gaze back to Grammy. "She told me to ask you."

Grammy's face fell, and she completely froze up. "Me?"

"Yeah, she acted like there's something I should know, and she thought you might be able to tell me," I said.

Grammy furrowed her brow. "What's this girl's name?"

"Chloe." I cleared my throat. "Chloe Olson."

Grammy huffed, but it was barely audible. Her lips pressed together tightly, and her eyebrow twitched, but I couldn't read the look in her eyes. It was like she was trying hard not to give anything away. "I have no idea what she meant."

I crossed my arms and glared at Grammy. It was obvious she was lying to me. "Are you sure? Because she seemed pretty certain you knew something."

Grammy sucked on her teeth and hesitated. "I know that years ago, before Grampy died, he didn't get along well with the Olson family. But that's over now."

My eyebrows knitted together tightly. That couldn't be what this was about. Grampy had died over forty years ago, when Grammy was still pregnant with Mom. Whatever she was talking about had nothing to do with Chloe and me.

"What did they fight about?" I asked.

Grammy shot to her feet. There was anger etched in her eyes, like she was furious I had the nerve to ask. "That's in the past, Nadine. There's no reason to go opening old wounds. Stay away from this Olson girl, and you'll be fine. Now come eat some cookies. They're fresh."

I gaped up at Grammy. "Actually, I'm not hungry—"

"I'm not going to ask you again, Nadine," she snapped. "I made too many, and I need your help eating them."

Holy crap. Grammy could get sassy when she wanted to. Talia and I shot each other wide-eyed gazes, then quickly got to our feet to follow Grammy to the kitchen. It was obvious Grammy wasn't willing to talk about this thing with Grampy. But she couldn't keep it from me forever.

One way or another, I'd figure out what she was hiding.

☾

Grammy's secret hovered at the forefront of my mind during classes the next day. I could hardly concentrate knowing she was keeping something from me, but I knew how stubborn she could be. She wouldn't spill unless she wanted to, and it drove me nuts.

Talia and I had returned to school the night before to a clean dorm and a note from Amy and Mandy that said we could thank them with an order of Barry's Enchanted Muffins. We'd left a dozen outside each of their dorm rooms that morning, along with a personalized thank-you note to each of them. Talia had made some inappropriate drawings inside that she assured me they'd both appreciate.

At lunch, I was filling my plate in the buffet line when I caught sight of

Lucas and Grant entering the cafeteria. The school's cafeteria wasn't like the lunch room back at my old high school. Instead of long tables with benches and bright, fluorescent lighting, the college's cafeteria was set up more like a restaurant, with red carpet, dark walls, and dim lighting. The room was so big that it had three full buffet lines, and the high ceiling featured beautiful black chandeliers.

Seeing Lucas brought a whole other issue to mind—one that I *was* going to get answers to.

I abandoned Talia and intercepted Lucas on his way to grab a plate. "Hey."

My tone was less than friendly, but his eyes lit up when he saw me. "Hey, Nad. What's up?"

"I need to talk to you." I wasn't giving him a choice this time.

Lucas shot a glance to Grant. "Um, sure…"

He filled up his plate, then followed me to a secluded corner of the room at a table set for two. Grant looked more than eager to share Talia's company for lunch, so he didn't seem bothered that I dragged his friend away from him.

"What do you want to talk about?" Lucas asked. His voice was steady, but I sensed a hint of uncertainty in his eyes. He wouldn't look at me directly.

"I want to know the truth," I stated.

He finally looked at me. "The truth about what?"

I sighed. "If you don't like me, just tell me."

"Whoa." Lucas's spine straightened. "Where's this coming from, Nad?"

I gaped at him. Was he serious? "You said we couldn't be together. I want to know what that means."

He furrowed his brow. "I thought you said you knew."

I swallowed. "I lied to you."

His face paled. "What do you mean you lied?"

Now I was the one who couldn't meet his gaze. I poked at my food. "When you told me the other day that we couldn't be together because you're the Reaper's Apprentice, I said I understood, but I didn't. Not really. And my friends… they don't seem to understand either."

When I finally lifted my gaze to his, he had this sad look on his face. It was barely there, but I could sense it.

"Nad, I'm sorry," he said softly. "It's something we cover in Mortana Studies. I assumed others knew."

"What does it mean?" I begged. If I couldn't be with him, I wanted a good reason.

Lucas glanced around, and although no one was seated near us, he leaned in and lowered his voice anyway. "Nad, you have to understand that being the Reaper's Apprentice is a very difficult calling. There's a reason the dead leave their last thought behind with me. It's because…"

"Because?" I pressed.

Lucas swallowed. "The nature of what I do can be a bit… morbid. Dark. And sometimes, that darkness is passed on."

"Passed on?" I asked.

"Like, to children," he clarified.

"Whoa!" I held my hands up and leaned back in my chair. I mean, I liked Lucas, but I wasn't seriously thinking about having his babies just yet.

"Goddess, no," Lucas said quickly. "I didn't mean us. Around two hundred years ago, a Reaper's Apprentice fathered a child, and that child was born with a darkness inside of him that no child should be burdened with. As he grew, so did that darkness. He was literally pure evil."

I could feel the crease between my eyebrows deepening. "So you're afraid of having kids? Lucas—"

He held up a hand to stop me. "Let me finish."

I snapped my jaw shut and listened.

"Anyway, this kid, he grew up to resent his parents," Lucas continued. "I don't know the full story, but I guess all those bad emotions built up, and one night, he lost it. He…"

I leaned in closer, intrigued.

Lucas swallowed. "He snapped and murdered his own mother."

I audibly gasped.

Lucas shuddered. "Apparently, it was so brutal that he accidentally cast a curse upon all future Reaper's Apprentices."

My stomach sank. Lucas was cursed?

"There must be a way to break the curse," I said hopefully.

Lucas shook his head. "There isn't. Without a Curse Breaker, it's impossible. Even with one, it'd be tricky."

A beat passed as I considered the weight of his words. "So, what does the curse do?"

"If I was with you, Nadine, you'd…" He hesitated and glanced down at his food.

"What, Lucas? I'd what?"

He cleared his throat. "You'd become the Reaper's Shadow. I couldn't do that to you."

A shiver ran down my spine. "What—what's the Reaper's Shadow?"

He took a long breath. "The Reaper's Shadow is the mate of a Reaper's Apprentice. The sacrifices involved are too much."

"What sacrifices?" I shifted in my seat. I was burning for all the answers.

Lucas hesitated, like it was too painful to even think about. "There are three stages. If the Reaper's Apprentice has sex with the Reaper's Shadow, she will experience a great illness."

I snorted, and Lucas gave me a strange look. I was already sick enough to fit that description. So I was keeping sex on the table. Yeah, like, on this table. I'd like to do him on it.

What the hell? That came out of nowhere.

"Go on," I encouraged, pushing the dirty thoughts aside.

"If the two get married, the Reaper's Shadow will experience severe trauma," he explained.

Nothing I hadn't gone through before. So far, he wasn't exactly scaring me off.

"And the third stage?" I asked.

Lucas closed his eyes. He didn't answer for a moment. "If the Reaper's Apprentice fathers a child… the child will have no choice but to kill the mother."

My breath stalled in my chest. So Lucas was saying that if this turned into something serious, I'd either have to give up kids or die.

That was a big decision to make, but we *weren't* serious. There wasn't any reason to worry about that right now.

"Okay," I said slowly, mulling it all over. "I can see your hesitation. But I mean, the first stage only starts at sex. That doesn't mean you can't have a girlfriend—and I'm not just talking about me," I added quickly when he looked at me.

He scoffed. "What do you think boyfriends and girlfriends do, Nad?"

"What? You're never going to kiss someone?"

"I've kissed people," Lucas grumbled. "And I've done enough to know that kissing leads to other things. *We* almost kissed. I'm not going to risk it, Nad. I don't care how much I want you."

He pressed his fingers to his lips, like he hadn't meant for the confession to spill out.

I blushed a deep pink. "You… you want me?"

Lucas's lips twitched, but the rest of his body had gone still. "I just meant… in general."

Fucking liar! Lucas liked me. I'd bet my ass he wanted to take me right here on this table, too. Damn it. His confession only made me want him more.

"Nadine," he said softly. It caught my attention, because he'd used my full name.

"Yeah?" I responded past the lump in my throat.

"You have to understand why I've chosen to remain celibate." He ran his fingers through his hair, looking flustered. "It's not because I don't want… it's not because…" He took a deep breath. "Look, the truth is, I—"

He cut off, like he couldn't bear to tell me the truth.

"You what?" I asked. I was dying to hear the last half of that sentence.

He dropped his hands to the table and looked me straight in the eye. "The truth is, I'll never have a real relationship like that. I can't do that to someone."

There was such sorrow in his eyes. The way he looked at me, it burrowed deep down into my soul. I felt my own sadness streaming out from my chest. I just wanted to hold him in my arms and tell him that it was all going to be okay. That even if he couldn't have someone *like that*, there were still people who would love him.

But I choked up, and I couldn't say any of that. Instead, I simply smiled and said, "If that's what you really want, Lucas."

Even as I said it, I heard the lie in my voice. I wanted more. Lucas wanted more.

Lucas shifted in his chair, looking like he had more to say. Finally, he lifted his gaze and whispered, "All I want is for you to be safe, Nad."

My heartbeat quickened, and my body heated. The room spun, but not in the scary kind of way. It was exhilarating, like the thrill of reaching the crest on a roller coaster. The problem was, once you stepped onto a roller coaster, you had no choice but to ride it to the end.

Something told me Lucas and I had a long ride ahead of us.

ELEVEN

Talking to Nadine about the Reaper's Shadow wasn't easy.

I'll never fall in love or have sex.

Total pick-up line. I bet she wanted me so badly right now.

At least I'd managed to finish the assignment Professor Warren had given me, to fill the page in my journal. It was all bullshit, but he didn't look at it long enough to make sense of what I'd written.

"Good job, Lucas," he said proudly before class one day. He handed the book back to me. "I'm glad to see you're making progress."

Ha! Progress.

If anything, I'd gone backward this past week. I'd considered skipping classes just to sleep all day. If it weren't for Grant literally dragging me out of bed, I would've.

Professor Warren clapped me on the shoulder. "Take a seat."

I sat in the back of the classroom as the rest of my classmates filed in for Necromancy Safety. Professor Warren started the lecture right away, while I pulled up the *Miriamic Messenger* on my phone.

This week had been hard on me. I never did find out how that kid died. The family probably wanted their privacy at this time.

I was scrolling through the obituaries, not really paying attention to the lesson. Professor Warren was going on and on about how necromancers had to be careful to only reanimate a soulless being. If you started playing around with the body before a reaper came to take their soul, bad things could happen. It was like that with all Mortana. Our magic was touchy, and if you didn't do things the right way, it could backfire.

Honestly, I wasn't even sure why I was in this class. I wasn't a necromancer. I couldn't create an army of zombie rats or whatever. But they didn't have a class for reapers, and Professor Warren was my mentor, so I guess they just threw me in here with him.

I was hardly listening when a hand shot up at the front of the room.

"Theoretically, could a necromancer bring someone back to life?" a girl asked. It was Lena, my ex-girlfriend from high school. We were on good terms, but I didn't care about her like that anymore. We'd only dated for a few months and never got past second base. "I mean, if they tried reanimating them before the reaper got there."

"No," Professor Warren said firmly. "It's been tried many times, and each time, it fails. You are forbidden from even attempting it. That kind of magic can do great damage to the soul—and bind it here on the earthly plane."

Another hand went into the air. This time, it was a girl named Samantha. "I heard there was a guy in the coven who was brought back to life like, two hundred years ago or something. So there must be some Mortana who can do it, right?"

Professor Warren hesitated. "I'm sure that's just a story."

"But if someone could do it, who's the most capable?" she pressed.

Professor Warren paused, but I barely processed it since I was still reading my phone. "*If* someone could do it, it'd be very difficult—almost impossible. And they'd have to do it before the soul crossed over."

"Who?" Lena demanded.

The room went dead quiet until Professor Warren cleared his throat and said, "The Reaper's Apprentice."

That finally got my attention. All eyes turned to me, and a chill ran down my spine.

"Of course, it's just a theory," Professor Warren was quick to clarify. "A theory one would hope they never have to test."

His stare felt as if it bore a hole in my forehead. The look he gave me was so intense—like he was warning me not to even think about it. *Of course* I wasn't thinking about it! Like hell I wanted someone to die in front of me just to see if I could bring them back. No, thank you.

Samantha raised her hand again. "So let's say the Reaper's Apprentice *could* do it. How would that work? Could they do it to anyone, or does it have to be at a special time, like during the Reaper Moon?"

My spine straightened. I'd never heard of the Reaper Moon before, but it sure sounded important. "What's the Reaper Moon?"

Professor Warren's lips tightened. "We don't cover reaper lore in this class."

I leaned forward in my seat, my hands tightening into fists. This was so unlike Professor Warren. He was the kind of guy who'd give you a lecture about anything just to hear himself talk. It was almost like he was hiding something from me.

"Tell us what the Reaper Moon is," I demanded.

Samantha tossed her long black hair over her shoulder as she turned to me. "It's an astronomical phenomenon that happens every hundred years or so—"

"It's nonsense," Professor Warren insisted, cutting her off.

Samantha acted like she didn't hear him and continued. "When the moon aligns just right, the Reaper Veil lifts and—"

"Miss Stone!" Professor Warren snapped.

Samantha's face paled, and she turned around to face the front of the room again.

Professor Warren crossed his arms. "The Reaper Moon is nothing more than myth, Miss Stone. You're wasting our class time by discussing it. Now let's get back to business."

I didn't hear the rest of the lecture, because I was too hung up on what Samantha said about the Reaper Moon. I wanted to know more, especially since Professor Warren thought I shouldn't. I tried searching for it on my phone, but nothing came up.

The second class let out, I shot out of my chair and ran into the hall to catch up with Samantha.

"Hey, Samantha!" I called.

She turned. Her face fell, and she held her textbooks tight to her chest. "Hey, Lucas. Sorry about bringing up the Reaper's Apprentice in class. I didn't mean to embarrass you."

I shook my head. "You didn't embarrass me. Can you tell me more about the Reaper Moon?"

Samantha glanced back to the open classroom door, then nodded. "Yeah, but not here. Come on."

I followed her to a small study area off the main hall. It was nothing more than an alcove with three plush chairs. I sat across from her and leaned forward, resting my elbows on my knees.

Samantha set her books on her lap and pushed her hair behind her ears. "Let me preface this by saying I don't know all the details about the Reaper Moon. I only know what my grandpa told me. He used to be a history professor here before he retired."

"I want to know everything," I said.

"The Reaper Moon is pretty rare—a once in a lifetime kind of thing," she explained. "Usually, reapers can only step through the Reaper Veil on assignment—when someone dies and they have to step onto our plane to help them to the next."

"Right. I know that," I told her.

Samantha sat up straighter. "Okay, so the Reaper Moon does away with the Veil for just that night. All the reapers are free to roam our plane. Think of it like Halloween, but for reapers."

I furrowed my brow. "Why haven't I ever heard of it? Why isn't there a big celebration for it?"

She frowned. "Well, because it's rare, and most people, like Professor Warren, don't think there's any truth to it."

"Why not?" I asked. It didn't seem that implausible.

"Because people don't believe things they can't see with their own eyes," Samantha asserted. "On Halloween, Seers can see the spirits, speak to them, sometimes even touch them. The Reaper Moon's not quite the same. The only one who can see the reapers is—"

"Is me," I finished for her. "The Reaper's Apprentice. But why would I be able to see them during the Reaper Moon when I can't see them all the time?"

She pressed her lips together. "I'm not entirely certain. I would guess it has something to do with the Veil."

Her eyes brightened. "You'll get to see for yourself, though. It's been a hundred years since the last one. The next Reaper Moon is coming soon —on December twelfth."

My eyebrows shot up. "So soon?"

She frowned. "Yeah, which is why I don't get why Professor Warren wouldn't talk about it."

"Yeah," I agreed. "It doesn't sound dangerous. Unless there's a reason he doesn't want me to see the reapers or get in contact with them."

Samantha glanced down to the books in her lap, but she didn't say anything.

"Wait, do you know something else?" I asked.

She bit her lower lip. "I have a theory."

"What is it?" I didn't like that Professor Warren was keeping something from me.

Samantha hesitated before answering. "Well... my grandpa told me this story about the last Reaper Moon."

I practically squirmed in my chair. The anticipation was killing me. "And...?"

"The Reaper's Apprentice who was alive at the time... he went to one of the reapers, and he asked them to take away his power and assign it to someone else."

I gasped. "Is that even possible?"

No wonder Professor Warren didn't want me to know about the Reaper Moon. He wanted me to suffer with this gift forever. He knew if there was a chance to get rid of it, I'd take it.

"It must be, because it worked," Samantha said. "The reapers all came together and used their magic to take the gift away from him. He lived another forty years or something without ever hearing another person die."

My mouth had gone dry, and I stared blankly ahead. I couldn't believe I had a chance to get rid of this thing—to silence the voices!

"Lucas, are you all right?" Samantha waved her hand in front of my face.

I snapped out of it and shot to my feet. "Yeah, I'm fine. Thanks for the information. You're a lifesaver."

I abandoned Samantha and rushed back to Professor Warren's classroom. The room was empty and silent, but I found him sitting behind the desk in his office. The curtains were closed, and it was a little eerie.

"I know what the Reaper Moon is," I stated as I burst into the room.

I fell down into the chair across from him without so much as a hello.

The dick didn't deserve it. He'd been lying to me for months. *Find the good in your gift, Lucas. You're stuck with it for the rest of your life.*

What a load of crap!

Professor Warren looked shell-shocked as his gaze followed me to the chair.

"Why didn't you tell me there was a way to get rid of this… this curse?" I demanded.

Professor Warren leaned back in his chair. "For one, the Reaper Moon is nothing but fiction."

"You don't know that," I snapped. "Most would say that about our magic."

Professor Warren tilted his head as if to say *touché*. "The truth is, Lucas, I didn't want to put ideas in your head. Even if it worked, it would have great consequences."

"Like?" I challenged with a raised eyebrow.

Professor Warren sighed and sat up straight. "For one, your powers would be passed on to someone else."

"Yeah, to someone who wants it," I shot back.

He raised an eyebrow. "How can you be sure of that? Are you truly willing to take that risk and let someone else carry this burden?"

My jaw tightened. Honestly, I didn't really care. Let them have it.

"Mother Miriam chose you for a purpose," Professor Warren reminded me.

"Yeah, yeah," I grumbled. "I've heard that one before."

His lips tightened. "Don't you think it's a little… *dishonorable* of you to refuse the gift she's given you?"

"That's what I'm saying!" I cried. "This isn't a gift. I can't do cool shit like the rest of you. I can't brew potions or see the future. I hear people *die*, Professor Warren! Every single day, I take their secrets and their regrets, and I shove them as far down as possible so they can't hurt anybody anymore!"

I shook, but Professor Warren barely seemed fazed.

"Perhaps that's the problem, Lucas."

I gaped at him. "Excuse me?"

"You're pushing them down, instead of facing them—*accepting* them."

I slammed my hands down on his desk, my nostrils flaring. "Don't tell me what I'm facing. You don't know shit."

Professor Warren backed off a few inches. "Please understand, Lucas, I'm only trying to help. If you refuse Mother Miriam's gift, she won't let you into Alora."

"Who says?" I growled. "Giving my gift back isn't a sin."

Professor Warren sighed. "That depends on how Mother Miriam sees it. If you displease the Goddess—"

"This isn't about her!" I roared.

Professor Warren's eyes went as wide as golf balls. It was like he couldn't believe I had the gall to take a jab at my own goddess. For a second there, I couldn't believe it, either.

But she's the one who wanted me to spend the rest of my life under the weight of this mental trauma. She hadn't sent me a real mentor—someone who actually knew shit about reapers. She hadn't told me what to do, or given me any real way to deal with it. Professor Warren's attempts be damned. Maybe I'd take my chances in the Abyss.

I whirled around and stomped out of his office, but his voice followed behind. "The coven needs a reaper, Lucas!"

I grumbled on my way out of the classroom. "The coven's got enough."

☽

"HOLD UP. You're telling me there's a way to *stop* being the Reaper's Apprentice?" Grant asked.

"Yep." I stepped up to the concrete disc golf platform.

Grant let out a puff of air. "And I thought *my* day was bad."

"What happened to you?" I asked.

Grant frowned. "The whole Alchemy department's in an uproar because someone broke into the supply closet and stole a shit ton of potion ingredients."

"I hope they caught the idiot." I threw my disc as hard as I could. I held my breath as it flew through the air, praying it wouldn't land in the trees on either side of us. It soared in a perfect arc and landed five feet from the basket.

"They haven't caught him yet. Good throw, man," Grant said as he stepped up to the platform. He took a running start and threw his disc, flicking his wrist at the last second. His disc landed in line with the basket but too far away to make it in the next shot. "Anyway, I can't believe Warren didn't tell you about the Reaper Moon. Like, the dude just *forgot?*"

"No." My teeth ground together as we walked down the fairway. "He purposely didn't tell me. *The coven needs a reaper, Lucas.*"

Grant laughed. "That's a pretty good impression of him. Why are you so desperate to get rid of it, though? I mean, if Mother Miriam wanted you to be the Reaper's Apprentice…"

I shook my head. "I'm not cut out for it. I'm too weak."

"You're *not* weak," Grant insisted, punching me lightly in the shoulder.

I dropped my gaze to my feet. "I don't know. Maybe I am."

Grant stopped beside his disc and picked it up. "You know what I think? I think this has less to do about your gift and everything to do with a certain someone whose name starts with an N and ends in an Adine."

I let out a puff of air and rolled my eyes. "This isn't about Nadine. But I'm not going to lie to you, it's definitely crossed my mind. Fuck man, I'm cursed to be a virgin my whole life."

Grant chuckled and tossed his disc. It bounced off the corner of the metal basket and ricocheted back at him.

"That's what you get for laughing at me, douche," I teased.

Grant stepped forward and swapped out his driving disc for a putting disc. This time, the chains *clanged* as he landed it inside the basket. "Technically, you're not cursed. You could fuck whoever you wanted and be fine."

"Yeah, but at their expense!" I conjured my putter and tossed it into the basket. "I'm not going around fucking girls I don't care about just to get laid, only to curse them with a terrible illness."

We both grabbed our discs and headed to the next platform.

"You're too soft," Grant accused.

"Dude, you're awful," I shot back.

Grant rolled his eyes. "It was a joke, Lucas. So, what are you going to do about Nadine? Are you going to get rid of this thing so you can date her?"

I frowned. "I don't even know if she wants to date me."

"What are you talking about?" Grant asked. "She totally likes you."

"I don't get why," I grumbled.

Grant stepped up to the platform, flipping his disc in his hands. "Well, you could ask her."

"I'm not going to ask her!"

Grant rolled his eyes. "Say she wanted to date you. Would you contact the reapers at the Reaper Moon?"

I hesitated. My instinct was to say yes, but Professor Warren had made some good points. Now that I had time to consider what he said, I feared he might be right. Mother Miriam trusted me with this gift. If I gave it back, I'd be banished and sent to the Abyss. So my choices basically came down to Nadine or Alora.

Fuck.

"I don't know," I admitted. "It's kind of a big decision. I've got to weigh the pros and cons. To be honest, it's looking pretty appealing right now. I wouldn't have to carry these thoughts around anymore. And I know there's no way to break the Reaper's Shadow curse, but this is the next best thing if I'm ever going to date. But… the Abyss, man."

Grant shuddered. "Yeah, that's tough."

I gaped at him. "That's all you have for me? *That's tough?*"

He shrugged, then threw his disc and watched it soar through the air. It hit a tree and bounced into the forest. He sucked a sharp breath between his teeth, then turned to me. "If it were up to me, I wouldn't risk the Abyss. An eternity of damnation? No thanks. But I can't make that decision for you."

"Why not?" I joked. "It'd be easier."

Grant frowned. "Nothing about this is easy. If you're not going to go through with the Reaper Moon, you need to stay away from Nadine."

My eyebrows slammed together. "What? No way. She makes me happy. I actually smile around her, and the voices are quieter when she's around."

Grant frowned. "You know that never works. One of these days, you're going to cave."

I narrowed my eyes at him. "And what do I do if she wants to stay friends with me? I can't just avoid her."

Grant shrugged. "Be an asshole, and *she'll* be the one avoiding you."

I scoffed and stepped up to the platform. "Uh, no thanks."

I swung my arm around and flicked my wrist, and my driver went flying toward the basket. It narrowly missed a tree and landed just a few yards from where I was aiming.

"How about I tell her you've been keeping secrets?" Grant suggested.

"You promised!" I growled.

It'd been weeks ago that I'd told Grant where I'd heard Nadine's name before—in her mom's last thought. Nadine didn't know, and I couldn't tell her. It could put her in danger.

Grant held his hands up in defense. "I'm not going to tell her! Not unless you decide you want to drive her away. What'd this last thought say, anyway?"

I shook my head firmly as we started toward our discs. "Nope. Not telling. Reaper's Apprentice privileges only."

"It's killing me why you won't tell her," Grant said. "What's the big secret?"

"I've already told you too much."

"Fine," Grant sighed. "Your secret is safe with me. So, can we invite the girls out for a round of golf?"

"What's with you, man?" I complained. "One second you're telling me to stay away from her. The next you're inviting her to our bro day."

Grant cocked an eyebrow. "Bro day? You *just* said you're not going to avoid her. So pick one."

"Whatever. Invite them if you want."

Grant conjured his phone and started poking at the screen.

Grant and I worked our way through the rest of the course. The last hole ended close to the parking lot. Grant chucked his disc above a wall of tall bushes, and we heard it skid along the gravel.

When we stepped out of the forest and into the parking lot, my blood ran cold. Next to our vehicle sat a sleek black sports car. It was the only car here besides ours. Just thinking about all my rides in that thing made me want to hurl. I couldn't believe I was ever friends with those assholes.

Grant turned up his nose. "What are the *Tarantulas* doing here?"

I frowned. "Dunno. But I guarantee it's not disc golf."

I'd only ever seen Ryan play once, and I kicked his ass so badly he made a big deal out of how disc golf wasn't a real sport and I was a sissy for playing instead of working out in the gym like a "real man." I can't believe I took that jerkwad's verbal abuse. I guess growing up with my dad, you just learned those kinds of things were normal.

Grant chuckled. "I bet their drug drop-off is somewhere around here."

The sad thing is, he wasn't kidding.

"Let's find my disc and get out of here before they come back," Grant said. He still hadn't forgotten the prank they'd pulled on him last year. Neither of us wanted to face those losers.

Grant and I glanced around the parking lot, but his disc was nowhere in sight.

"That's weird," Grant remarked. "I didn't think I threw it *that* far."

He walked to the other side of the parking lot to see if his disc had landed in the grass. Meanwhile, I bent over and tilted my head to look beneath the cars. Sure enough, Grant's green disc was lying in the gravel beneath Ryan's shiny black car. I groaned and lowered myself onto my stomach to reach under the car for the disc.

"Hey!" a deep voice boomed across the parking lot.

My whole body gave a jolt. Several pairs of footsteps began racing across the gravel all at once. I quickly pushed myself out from under the car and tried to get to my feet. But I didn't get there before Ryan dropped a backpack beside his car and grabbed me by the collar.

"Stop!" Grant cried as he sprinted over to me. Nolan and Finn stepped in front of him and held him back.

"What the fuck were you doing to my car?" Ryan roared. Spittle flew onto my face, and his nostrils flared.

My whole body shook in rage. What I wouldn't give to punch this jerk in the face. I shoved him away with my forearm so hard that he stumbled backward and let me go. "Get off of me, man. I didn't touch your damn car. We lost a disc."

I held up the disc as evidence, but Ryan didn't seem to buy it. He was back on me in less than a second, his forearm pinning me to the side of the car.

"I don't believe you," he growled, his dirty breath skimming along the side of my face.

Grant tried to side-step the other Tarantulas, but the third and fourth gang members stepped forward to block his path.

"Now tell me what you did to my car!" Ryan shouted in my face.

My lips tightened, and I held his gaze. "I told you. We lost a disc. That's all. I wouldn't touch that filthy thing anyway."

Ryan's lips curled into a sneer. He grabbed a fistful of my shirt with each hand, then slammed my back against the car again so hard it nearly knocked the wind out of me.

"I'm not in the mood today, Taylor," Ryan threatened. "If you cut my brake lines or some shit like that, there's going to be hell to pay."

I scoffed. Did this loser really think he could scare me? The only time we'd ever gotten into a fist fight, I'd won. "I've already served my time. Being friends with you was hell enough."

Before I saw it coming, Ryan's fist slammed into my mouth. A shock wave went through my teeth and down my jaw. Warm liquid and the taste of copper filled my mouth. For a second, I couldn't believe he'd actually done it.

I was done. I was *so* done with this asshole. I dropped the disc and retaliated quickly.

"I've had enough of your mouth—" Ryan started.

He was cut off by my fist cracking into the side of his jaw. Pain shot through my knuckles, but I didn't care. It was totally worth it to watch him stumble to the side clutching his face. A wave of pride washed over me, but it was short lived.

Ryan righted himself and shot daggers my way. "You're gonna pay for that, Taylor."

Ryan gathered midnight blue magic in his hands and muttered an incantation under his breath. He thrust the defensive magic forward. I ducked and lunged, slamming my shoulder into his middle. We both fell to the ground the same time the sound of shattering glass came from behind us. The idiot had smashed his own window.

Everything moved so fast that I barely knew what was going on around me. All I heard was the sound of feet slamming into flesh and Grant's pained grunts not far from me. I had to get to him pronto, but I couldn't while Ryan was trying to rip the flesh off my face. Fingernails dug into my skin as he muttered an incantation and ran his nails down my cheek. A burning sensation—like acid—ignited across my face. Whatever magic he was using wasn't anything we'd learned in class. It was probably illegal.

I gathered magic in my hand to retaliate with a defensive spell, but Ryan was quicker than me. He shot his hands out and used his telekinetic powers to throw me backward.

My elbows skidded along the gravel. Ryan was quick to get to me. He jumped on top of me to hold me down and punched me straight in the nose. Red flashed across my vision, and blood spurted everywhere.

I grabbed him around the neck and threw him off of me. I used the momentum to slam his body into the dirt. I jumped on top of him and wrapped my hands around his throat. I squeezed tightly, enjoying the satisfaction of shock cross his features. He grabbed my wrists and tried to twist them off him, but I wouldn't budge. His lips curled into a rage-filled sneer.

A second later, an invisible force slammed into my wrists, throwing my arms outward and catching me off guard. Damn Mentalist powers.

I could feel Ryan trying to lift me off him with his magic, but he wasn't strong enough yet to do it. I regained control of my hands and grabbed his shirt.

"What the fuck's your problem?" I shouted.

"You are," he spat. "I'm not letting you ruin this."

"Ruin what?" I demanded.

Ryan never got a chance to answer. A foot slammed into my guts, launching me off of Ryan. I rolled a couple of times in the gravel. When I looked up, Declan was standing over me, fury etched in his features.

"Traitor!" he snarled, cracking his knuckles.

Why were these idiots still hung up on that? So I left their group. Why couldn't they just leave me alone?

I swung my leg out and knocked Declan off his feet, but I didn't have time to stand up before all five of the Treacherous Tarantulas were surrounding me. One quick glance toward their car, and I saw they'd finished with Grant. He was lying there clutching his stomach and groaning in pain.

I held my hands up in surrender. "Guys, please. We were really just—"

A heavy boot smashed into my face. All I saw was a shadow coming closer and closer, then felt the ungodly pain shooting through my face. A *crunch* sounded, and my ears rang. When the darkness cleared from my vision and refocused, Ryan's bruised face was right in front of me.

"This beating's long overdue, Taylor," he seethed. "And for once, your brother's not here to stop it."

Heavy footfalls began to rain down on me from all directions as each of the Treacherous Tarantulas took their turn beating me to a pulp. It was hard to tell where the pain was coming from. Everything hurt.

"How's it feel, Lucas!?"

I squeezed my eyes shut tightly and brought my hands up to protect my face, but Ryan's voice sounded like it was coming from all around me.

"How's it feel to finally be the one on the ground?" Ryan taunted. "I bet Eric's looking down on you from Alora thinking what a pussy you are. He was a pussy, too—"

The sound of tires crunching across the gravel was like music to my ears. All five of the Tarantulas halted at once. They whirled around, but I just lay there trying not to spew my guts.

Ryan started laughing, and the other four quickly joined in. I finally peeled my eyelids back to see what was going on. My heart lifted at the sight of Nadine's silver sedan stopped in the middle of the parking lot. Nadine and Talia shared a similar wide-eyed expression, like they couldn't believe what they were seeing. Nadine's gaze met mine from behind the wheel, and her features quickly shifted. Her eyebrows dropped over her eyes, and her lips pressed into a thin line.

Ryan chuckled and stepped in front of the vehicle with his arms held wide. "What are you going to do, bitches? Come at me?"

Nadine shot one look at Talia, and Talia gave her a subtle nod. Without hesitation, Nadine narrowed her gaze on Ryan and stepped on the gas. The car hurled through the parking lot, speeding straight toward the Tarantulas.

Ryan must've thought Nadine was playing chicken with him—or he was trying to stop the car with his powers and failing miserably—because he didn't back down until the very last second. Ryan and his cronies leapt out of the way.

"What the fuck, you crazy bitch!?" Ryan screamed as he jumped back to his feet and dusted the dirt off his leather jacket.

Nadine yanked on the wheel, and the tires spun as she turned the car around back in Ryan's direction. She shot him the finger, then placed her hands firmly back on the wheel.

"Crazy hoe!" Finn yelled.

"Let's get out of here!" Ryan shouted at the same time.

Ryan grabbed the bag he'd dropped, and the five of them scurried into his vehicle. Nadine's car hadn't moved an inch, but she kept her narrowed gaze on them and her hands tight on the wheel. The Tarantulas tore out of the parking lot without so much as a glance back.

Grant groaned and pushed himself to his knees, shaking a fist in the air. "Not so tough now, are you?"

Of course, they didn't hear him.

Nadine shifted into park, and she and Talia jumped out of the car before she'd even cut the engine.

"Lucas!" Nadine cried as she ran over to me.

I clutched my stomach and pushed myself to a sitting position, but it was difficult. It felt like I was bleeding out everywhere.

Talia sprinted toward Grant. "Goddess, let me help you. We should get you to the hospital."

Talia pulled Grant to his feet and supported him as he limped over to Nadine's car.

"Lucas," Nadine said breathlessly. She dropped to her knees beside me and gazed into my eyes with deep concern. She placed her hands on either side of my face.

When Nadine laid her hands on me, it was like magic. My heart lifted, and all the pain seemed to melt away. I couldn't even feel the gravel beneath me, as if I was floating.

"Nad…"

"Shh, Lucas." Nadine stripped off her zip-up sweatshirt and balled it up to place beneath my head like a pillow.

I must've been really out of it, because when I lay back and looked up at her, it looked like there was a halo surrounding her. She truly glowed.

Without thinking about it, I reached out and ran my fingers across the side of her face. "Nad, you're here."

"Yes, I am," she said in a rush. "And you have a broken nose. We're going to the hospital."

"We will," I assured her. "Just let me rest a moment."

"Lucas, what hurts?" she asked frantically. "Tell me what hurts."

I shook my head. "Nothing, Nad. It's all good now."

Nadine threw herself over me and buried her face into my shoulder. Her knee brushed up against a bruise forming on my hip, but I didn't care. She was hugging me, and that made everything better.

"Lucas, I was terrified for you." Her voice was muffled in my hoodie. "When we drove in and saw them, I…" Nadine drew away to look me in the eyes.

I grabbed the sides of her face. "You got here just in time."

Her eyes began to sparkle with tears. "If we'd gotten here just a little sooner—"

I swallowed. I was pretty sure I was swallowing blood, but it didn't really register. "No use in worrying about what could have been. Thank you."

Before I knew what I was doing, I dragged Nadine's face close to mine, and I pressed my lips to hers.

nadine

TWELVE

Kissing Lucas was beyond anything I ever imagined it would be. You know in the movies when the guy gets the girl and he sweeps her off her feet, then everyone starts clapping and this beautiful, teary-eyed music starts playing? Then they cut forward a few months and he's carrying her out of the church on their wedding day, everyone's throwing rice and is all happy, then they drive off into the sunset and nothing can ever hurt them again?

That's what Lucas's kiss felt like, but better. It was like nothing bad could ever touch me.

Lucas's hand came up to cradle the back of my neck. A fire ignited deep within my belly, and I relaxed into the kiss. My lips parted, and his tongue slid inside my mouth.

It felt as if the ground had dropped away, like we were spinning in midair and the whole world had ceased to exist around us. My heart lifted in my chest before the adrenaline settled in and sent my heart pummeling against my rib cage.

My hands tangled in Lucas's hair, and I dragged him closer to me. He kissed me harder, like I was the very breath he breathed. My nipples hardened beneath my shirt, begging for more.

Lucas drew away, and his soft eyes roamed over my face. I was frozen in place, unable to move, blink, or breathe. Several quiet moments passed as we stared deep into each other's eyes, until I thought my lungs might burst.

It was the only indication I had that time was still moving forward.

"I'm sorry," Lucas whispered. "I shouldn't have done that."

I shook my head and finally took a breath. "It's okay, Lucas. I'm glad you did."

I hesitated as my gaze roamed over his bruised features. I longed to kiss him again, but right now wasn't the time. "Let's get you to a hospital."

The next few hours passed at an ungodly slow pace as Talia and I waited in the emergency room for Grant and Lucas. When they were finally released, Grant had four stitches above his eyebrow, and Lucas's broken nose had been set. We took the guys back to their dorm room, then brought them ice cream before turning in for the night.

We didn't see them the rest of the weekend. I tried visiting Lucas on Saturday, but no one answered the door, even though I was pretty sure I heard footsteps behind it. I could hardly sleep over the weekend as the kiss replayed over and over again in my mind. Every time I thought about it, my heart lifted in my chest.

And then I remembered that I hadn't seen Lucas in days, and my pulse quickened for entirely different reasons. He was obviously avoiding me again, and I was ticked off about it. One minute he's kissing me like his life depends on it, and the next he falls completely off the map. I was getting really sick of his mixed signals.

Tuesday morning, I awoke with a terrible shooting pain in my left hand. My whole body was stiffer than normal, and it took at least fifteen minutes of lying in bed trying not to scream before I could shift and get into a more comfortable position.

Lupus was like that sometimes. I had good and bad days, and it was all totally unpredictable.

Talia noticed I was lying in bed longer than usual. "Hey, girl. Are you going to take your bath this morning?"

My neck was so stiff I couldn't even work up the strength to shake my head. Screw my body. Why did it hate itself so much?

"Eventually," I told her.

"Well, you better hurry up," she said as she brushed her hair. "Miriamic History is in half an hour."

I groaned and reached for my phone on my bedside table. She wasn't lying.

"I think I'm going to skip today," I said. I didn't want to, since it was the one class I struggled the most with, but I hadn't skipped all semester, and I figured I deserved a pass at least once. Today just wasn't happening.

Talia turned from the mirror and shot me a concerned expression. "Are you going to make it to Conjuring Basics later today?"

"Yeah, I'll make it."

Talia frowned and grabbed her bag. "Okay. Feel better."

I scoffed. "I'll try."

It was another hour before I got out of bed, and another hour after that before I finished my bath and got dressed. I was feeling a lot better, but all I wanted to do was go back to sleep. I had a few hours before Conjuring Basics, and I needed to get some homework done before I went, but I couldn't bring myself to work up the energy. I couldn't recall a day this bad since before my diagnosis.

Eventually, I got so hungry that I knew if I didn't head down to the cafeteria soon, I'd end up passing out before I got there. I ate, then headed off to Conjuring Basics.

"Before we jump into our next lesson," Professor Carlisle said, "let's review what we already know about conjuring."

Professor Carlisle was a short, elderly Seer with salt and pepper hair and an equally gray cat who looked like he was on his last life. You'd think at first glance Professor Carlisle was too, but he had this energy about him that suggested he had many years left.

He continued. "Earlier in the semester, we learned that conjuring is bound by many rules. You can't conjure something out of nothing, and you can't make one thing disappear from somewhere and end up in another. Imagine a pocket universe that follows you around everywhere you go. To *subconjure*, you take an object from your hand and place it into this pocket universe. To *conjure*, you take something from that universe and place it into your hand."

Professor Carlisle held out his hand, and a cane materialized out of nowhere. "Conjured."

He smiled brightly and did a little tap dance at the front of the room. At the end, he kicked the cane and made it spin around in his hand. It disappeared right in front of our eyes. "Subconjured. See? Simple."

A few people clapped at the demonstration, but it was half-hearted.

I couldn't wait until I had magic so I didn't have to lug around my textbooks wherever I went. It'd be so convenient to have my wallet at my fingertips without having to actually carry it around. I mean, I'd be fine with it if the fashion industry just gave women pockets, but I guess that was more of a stretch than actual magic.

"What we haven't talked about yet this semester is conjuring's limitations," Professor Carlisle said. "Let's say I wanted to fill my pocket universe to the brim. How many items do you think I could take with me?"

A hand raised at the front of the room. "Five?" the girl guessed timidly.

Professor Carlisle pressed his index finger to his lips. "Mm… not exactly."

"Ten!" someone else shouted, but Professor Carlisle shook his head.

"A hundred!" another voice came.

Professor Carlisle didn't stop shaking his head as more and more students piped up with their guesses, the numbers growing each time. I couldn't help but think that my classmates were idiots. This obviously wasn't the kind of answer Professor Carlisle was looking for.

I raised my hand, and his eyebrows shot up. "Miss Evers?"

The room went quiet, and I cleared my throat. "Wouldn't it depend on the size of the objects and not the amount?"

His eyes brightened, and he smiled. Professor Carlisle had one of the most expressive faces I'd ever seen. "Precisely. But how big do you think our invisible bag is? Could I, say, fit a car in it? Or an entire library of books?"

He looked directly at me, but I didn't know how to answer his question.

Professor Carlisle clicked his tongue. "No guesses?"

Some jock in the front row leaned back in his seat. "I bet you could fit a car."

Our professor cocked an eyebrow. "You think so, Mister James?"

"Sure," he claimed. "I'll betcha ten bucks after my Evoking Ceremony I'll subconjure a car."

Professor Carlisle smirked and stepped up to him with his hand out. "You're on."

The two of them shook on it, then Professor Carlisle turned to the door at the front of the lecture hall. He stepped behind it and put a door stopper in front of it to keep it open. Practically the whole class craned their necks to see what he was up to. I couldn't see anything, until he shot back into the room sitting on a chest of drawers that was on wheels. He sat with his knees crossed and his arms held in the air, like he was making a grand entrance to a Vegas show or something. The chest of drawers spun once. He jumped off and nearly stumbled over his cat, but he made a clean landing. The class clapped and cheered for him.

"Ladies and gentlemen, a chest of drawers!" Professor Carlisle gestured to it. It was dark mahogany and looked a lot like the dressers we had in our dorms, except it was longer and shorter. "This is approximately the size of your unique pocket universe. So by all means, Mister James, if you manage to subconjure a car, I'd be very interested to see that."

Professor Carlisle turned back to the chest of drawers and conjured his cane, then started tapping it against the drawers. "This is all the space you get, ladies and gentlemen. In my opinion, it totally beats a duffel bag, and it definitely saves you money when you fly."

The class chuckled.

A girl at the front of the room raised her hand. "What happens if you try to subconjure too much, if your space gets full?"

"Let me ask you this," Professor Carlisle replied. "What would happen if I tried to fill this chest of drawers too full?"

"Well... the drawers wouldn't close, obviously," she said.

"Exactly," Professor Carlisle said. "It'll push back. Things will start spilling out. Simple as that."

The jock eyed the chest of drawers. "So, what happens if you subconjure a person?"

Professor Carlisle raised an eyebrow. "Why, Mister James? Do you have plans to kidnap somebody?"

James sent a nervous glance around the room at the people who were laughing. "No. I just wondered, you know, could you survive it? The pocket universe?"

"I don't know," Professor Carlisle answered. "That's another limitation to conjuring. You can't subconjure a living thing."

One of James's friends leaned over to him. "There goes your kidnapping plans."

"Shut up." He shoved his friend.

I raised my hand, and Professor Carlisle called on me. "I'm curious, can things get lost? Like, if I wanted to subconjure something to hide it from someone, would they ever be able to find it? Or say I subconjured a valuable family heirloom, but I died before I had a chance to pass it on. Would it be lost forever?"

Professor Carlisle pressed his lips together firmly. "That's a very good question, Miss Evers. And this is why I advise you never subconjure anything of value. That said, there *are* ways to retrieve items from someone else's personal stash. However, it is a very complicated spell that requires more than one individual to perform and is only done on rare occasions. Why, Miss Evers? Is there something you'd like to retrieve?"

I shook my head. "No. I was just curious how it works is all."

"Snooping into someone else's pocket universe is dangerous," Professor Carlisle warned. "You may not like what you find. Don't let your curiosity get you into too much trouble, Miss Evers."

I chuckled under my breath. Professor Carlisle didn't know me at all.

☽

AFTER CLASS, I made my way to Headmistress Verla's office for my first Evoking Ceremony training session. I turned down a short hall, but it was deserted. I glanced down to my campus map to confirm I was in the right hall, then walked to the end. There sat a pair of double doors with a plaque that read *Headmistress Clarice Verla*. I raised my fist to knock when I heard a deafening *bang* sound from the other side of the doors. My heart leapt up to my throat, and I swayed on my feet as the ground shook beneath me.

I heard the sound of doors swinging open from the adjacent hall, then came the many footsteps. A second later, white smoke began to billow out through the cracks around the doors. It was unusually thick and didn't smell of fire. I eyed the smoke curiously and reached my fingers out to touch it. A stinging pain shot though my fingers, and I jerked away like I'd been burned.

Professor Wykoff—my Introduction to Tarot professor—rounded the corner. Her usual calm demeanor was replaced by a terrified look in her eyes.

"Dear Goddess!" she cried. "What's happened?"

"I-I don't know," I stammered, stepping away from the smoke creeping out into the hall. My fingers stung like I'd been attacked by a bee.

Professor Wykoff whirled around as two other professors came running. "Get Professor Richards."

The other professors went running to get help, while Professor Wykoff turned back to me. She grabbed me by the elbow and spoke gently. "Come, child. You must stay away."

"Wait, what's going on?" I asked, terrified that I'd just encountered some sort of chemical weapon. "Is Headmistress Verla going to be okay? What is that?"

Professor Wykoff pulled me into the next hall and guided me to stand next to the wall to let a group of professors pass. I noticed Professor Richards among them, clutching a flask full of a blue liquid.

"Tell me what you saw," Professor Wykoff instructed.

My jaw dropped, and I rubbed my aching fingers with my thumb. I think I was still in shock. "I-I didn't see anything. I'd just walked into the hall when I heard a bang. Then I saw the smoke, and you were there a second later."

Professor Wykoff grabbed my wrist and inspected the ends of my fingers. They were bright red, but otherwise looked fine. She breathed a sigh of relief. "Child, what are you doing in this part of the school?"

Voices yelled down the hall, and it took me a second to process her question. "I came to meet Headmistress Verla. We have an appointment."

"Okay," she said with a frown. "You stay right here, Miss Evers."

I didn't really know what was happening, so I did as I was told. After Professor Wykoff turned the corner to join the other professors, I heard them start to argue.

"We need to figure out who did this," a male professor said.

"Agreed," Professor Wykoff replied. "This is a threat."

"How do we know it's not just a prank?" a second female professor asked.

"We don't," the first guy responded in a clipped tone. "But until we know, we must treat it as an attempt on the headmistress's life."

Professor Wykoff gasped. "Who would do that?"

I was breathing heavily, unable to process what they were saying. Was someone out to *kill* Headmistress Verla?

"Relax, I've got the perimeter secure," Professor Richards said. "The antidote is working, but it will take a few hours."

The sound of clicking heels caught my attention. I looked up to see Headmistress Verla breezing down the hall. Her black cat ran behind her, but he was so fat that he more or less waddled. I breathed a sigh of relief, grateful that she hadn't been in her office when that thing went off. Her eyebrows hung low over her eyes, giving her this dark look that seemed strange on such a beautiful woman. She walked past me, like she didn't even see me, and stomped straight up to the other professors. I inched my way along the wall to peek around the corner and get a good look at them.

"What in the name of Mother Miriam is going on here?" she cried.

"A sting bomb," Professor Richards said. "But not to worry, Headmistress. This potion should take care of it in a few hours."

He held up the blue potion I'd seen him run past with. Most of it was gone.

Professor Wykoff's jaw dropped. "A stink bomb?"

"No," Professor Richards replied. "A *sting* bomb. It's a defense potion brewed using stinging nettle. It's fairly harmless but hurts like a son of a bitch. Thank Alora Headmistress Verla wasn't in her office when it was set off."

"Did anyone see who did it?" Verla demanded. Odin stepped toward the cloud of smoke and hissed.

The professors all glanced to each other and shook their heads. Professor Wykoff's eyes brightened, and she looked to me. My face paled as I was caught eavesdropping.

"There was a witness." Professor Wykoff gestured to me.

Headmistress Verla's face fell as she turned to me. "Nadine, tell us what happened."

Timidly, I stepped out from around the corner and joined the professors. The double doors were open. All I could see behind them was a wall of white smoke, but it just hung there in the air instead of creeping into the hall.

"I actually didn't see anything," I admitted. "I only just arrived when it went off."

An older male professor who looked cocky as hell gazed down his nose at me. He wore an ironed suit, and his gray hair was combed into a neat style. "Who's to say *you* weren't the one who set it off?"

He reached out and snatched my wrist.

"Ow!" I cried.

"Oh, please," he sneered. "I barely touched you. Proof!"

He held my hand up to all the other professors to show them my red fingers. He pointed an ugly finger at me. "You've been caught red-handed! Did you think this was some innocent little prank, half-blood?"

I gaped at him. Did he seriously just have the nerve to call me a half-blood in front of all these other professors?

"Professor Daymond!" Headmistress Verla shouted.

He dropped my hand, and I held it to my chest protectively. If I had any strength in it at the moment, I might've curled it into a fist and sucker-punched that smug sneer off his face. I prayed to Miriam I'd never have this professor. He seemed awful.

Headmistress Verla stepped forward to get up in Professor Daymond's face. "How dare you accuse a *student* of this. She is my mentee."

"Well, I-I," he stammered.

Headmistress Verla scoffed at him. "Go do something useful with your time, Archibald."

Professor Daymond narrowed his gaze at her before huffing and stomping off.

Headmistress Verla turned to me. "I'm very sorry, Nadine, but I'm afraid we're going to have to reschedule while I deal with this. I'll get back to you on our next session."

"Okay," I said. "I'm sorry this happened."

Headmistress Verla shook her head. "Don't worry about it. Unless you saw something happen…"

She eyed me, like she too was a little suspicious. If she was, I wasn't sure why she'd stood up for me.

"I didn't," I said. "I swear."

Headmistress Verla looked at me a moment longer, then dropped her shoulders. "You may go."

I walked away feeling really confused. Did Headmistress Verla seriously suspect me of trying to sabotage her? Why would I do something like that? The only person in this school I knew who had the balls to sabotage someone like that was Chloe.

Speak of the devil...

I exited a long hallway to see Chloe, Gwen, and Camille huddled in a group and snickering at each other. Can you say *déjà vu*? They'd done the exact same thing after they broke into my dorm room.

I stomped straight up to them. Chloe noticed my approach and shot me a death glare. She placed her hand on her hip. "What's *your* problem?"

I crossed my arms and stood just inches from her. She was a lot taller than me in her heels, but I liked to think I intimidated her nonetheless. "A sting bomb just went off in Headmistress Verla's office. You don't happen to know anything about that, would you?"

Chloe scoffed and rolled her eyes. "Please. I've been standing here for the last ten minutes. My girls will back me up."

Camille pursed her lips in my direction. At the same time, Gwen tossed her blonde hair over her shoulder. It was the first time I noticed a cauldron tattoo on her chest. It definitely wasn't there before, which meant she must've gone through her Evoking Ceremony recently—and that Chloe now had a right-hand Alchemist to do her bidding.

"So, what? You put it on a timer or something," I accused.

Chloe shot an innocent look to the other girls. "I don't know. Can you do that with potions?"

The other two shrugged in unison.

Chloe leaned forward so I could feel her breath on my face. "You don't know *anything* about this coven, Nadine. You don't want to leave on your own? Then I'll *make* you."

My hands tightened into fists, but my fingers were still burning from the sting bomb. "Is that a threat?"

Chloe stepped away without acknowledging my question. "Good luck passing your Evoking Ceremony without any training."

She flipped her hair over her shoulder and started walking in the other direction. I gaped at her. That was a confession if I'd ever heard one. No one had tried to hurt Headmistress Verla. Chloe had set off that sting bomb to sabotage my lesson! She knew I had it this week because Camille and Gwen had been in the metaphysical shop when Headmistress Verla and I talked about it. That bitch would do anything to drive me out of town, including ensuring I failed my Evoking Ceremony. And all for... what? A dead feud between our grandparents?

"Get a life and stop trying to ruin mine!" I shouted down the hall.

Chloe continued on her way, swaying her hips as if she never heard me. I'd bet anything she was the one who'd raided the Alchemy lab last week, too.

"Gah!" I screamed, turning on my heel and storming in the opposite direction.

I was passing by the cafeteria when I caught sight of Grant sitting alone at a table near the door. I walked in and plopped down across from him. He glanced up to me, but he didn't have any food in front of him. I shot him a curious expression.

"What's got your panties in a bunch?" he asked.

I huffed. "Chloe's at it again."

Grant frowned while he poked at something beneath the table. "What'd she do this time?"

"Well, I don't have any proof, but I'm pretty sure she's responsible for setting off a sting bomb in Headmistress Verla's office to sabotage my Evoking Ceremony training," I said.

"It *does* sound like her." He winced, then stuck his finger in his mouth and sucked on it like it hurt.

I eyed him curiously. "What are you doing?"

"Oh, this?" Grant held up a small device with digital numbers on it. "I'm checking my blood sugar before I eat."

I tilted my head, and the knot in my chest loosened. "You have diabetes?"

He nodded as he took his bag from his lap and placed it on the table. It opened flat like a wallet and was filled with his medication. "Not a big deal. I can hardly remember a time I didn't have it."

I suddenly felt an instant connection with Grant that wasn't there before. Obviously diabetes and lupus weren't the same thing, but I always got a jolt of excitement when I met someone with a chronic illness. It was like they were the only people who even remotely understood what I went through.

"How long have you known?" I asked.

"Since I was fourteen," he replied as he grabbed a needle and started filling it with insulin.

"I was fifteen when I was diagnosed," I blurted. I usually didn't talk about my disease to just anyone, but I felt like Grant would understand.

He raised a curious eyebrow. "Diabetes?"

I shook my head. "Lupus."

"That's autoimmune, isn't it?" he asked casually.

I smiled. Usually I was met with, *"Oh, Nadine, I'm so sorry,"* or, *"Have you seen a doctor about that?"* But Grant just wanted to know more, like I was telling him about one of my classes.

"Yeah, my doctor says it's common in the coven," I said.

He injected his shot, then nodded. "Yeah. It comes with being half human."

A silent beat passed between us, but I broke it. "Do you want to get dinner together?"

"Sure. I just have to wait a few minutes for the insulin to kick in," he said.

I folded my hands in my lap. "I can wait. Are Lucas or Talia joining us?"

He shook his head. "Lucas is meeting his mentor, and Talia has a study group."

I frowned. I wasn't sure if Grant was covering for Lucas or if it was the truth.

"What's wrong?" Grant asked, sensing my discomfort.

I hesitated a moment, but I couldn't stand not knowing. "Does Lucas *really* have a meeting with his mentor?"

"Yes," Grant answered honestly. "Why wouldn't he?"

I pressed my lips together. "Well, I haven't seen him since..." *Since our kiss,* I wanted to say. Instead, I said, "Since the hospital. He has a habit of avoiding me, and I'm worried—"

"Don't worry, Nadine," Grant assured me, but I sensed uncertainty in his tone. "Lucas just needs... time."

My stomach sank. *Time to decide how he truly feels,* I thought.

I tried not to let my disappointment get to me, but it was hard when all I could think about lately was that kiss. Lucas said he didn't want to be with me, then he kisses me like that—the best kiss of my entire life. What the hell was his deal?

"Well, I guess it's just us two then," I said.

"Yep, just us." After a moment of silence, Grant said, "Hey, do you think if we put our immune systems together, we'd have a working one?"

I laughed. "I don't know about that. Mine's trying to kill me."

"Mine, too. But in a different way." He started putting his supplies away in a bag that held it all. "I've got Type 1 diabetes. My immune system attacks the cells in my pancreas that produce insulin. I have to eat regularly and inject myself to regulate my blood sugar. There's no cure, but at least life's pretty normal, as long as I plan ahead."

"Same here," I said. "Do you have to use an insulin pump?"

I was too curious not to ask questions.

Grant subconjured his supplies, and they disappeared from the table. "I could if I wanted to, but then I'd have to wear it all the time, and I'd have to take it off when I'm active, which is a pain, especially with how much I swim. With the shots, it's in, out, and done, and there's a lower risk of infection."

"That makes sense. So, I'm curious about something. If mixed kids in the coven like us end up with autoimmune diseases, how'd the first generations survive?" I asked. "I mean, there was no treatment for this type of thing back then, and I'm pretty sure they weren't all purebred."

Grant leaned forward, looking interested by the question. "Back then, they didn't have their magic suppressed in childhood like we do now."

"They didn't?" I asked.

"No," Grant said. "Mother Miriam started suppressing our magic when she saw what a danger it could be to children. That's when the Evoking Ceremonies began. Anyway, back before the kids had their magic suppressed, their bodies became accustomed to the magic faster, before their immune system could be triggered. But..."

Grant sighed. "Mother Miriam had to make a trade-off to control children's magic. In the long run, I guess a few sick witches and warlocks are better for the coven than hundreds of kids running around with unpredictable magic."

I chuckled. "Yeah, I guess it is. Turns out we just drew the short straw."

Grant rolled his eyes. "I always seem to draw the short straw. It's like I'm cursed or something."

"I guess you could be," I joked, "considering curses are real."

Grant pressed his hand to his heart and dropped his jaw. "Now who would want to curse me? I'm a darling."

I cocked an eyebrow. "Are you? I've heard horror stories from Talia."

He dropped his jaw further. "What did she tell you?"

I threw my head back and laughed. "Nothing. I was joking."

Grant blew out a breath of relief. "Oh, good. Hey, maybe you can work in a good word for me."

"With Talia?" I asked.

He nodded.

I scoffed. "Uh, you're going to have to do the work yourself."

"Come on," he begged. "At least give me a hint. How do I get the girl?"

"I don't know. Serenade her?" I joked.

Grant tapped his chin. "That just might work. You're a genius."

I pressed my palm to my forehead. "I wasn't serious."

"Well, it's worth a try, isn't it?" he asked.

"Yeah, I guess," I admitted.

The truth was, I was pretty sure Talia enjoyed the chase. Eventually, she'd cave, but not before Grant jumped through hoops to get to her.

Grant finally said he was ready to eat, so we made our way through the buffet line. He went straight for various dishes instead of contemplating them, like he'd planned out his meal beforehand. We returned to our table and chatted. Halfway through dinner, Grant's eyes focused on something behind me.

I turned to see the gang of idiots who'd beat up him and Lucas sitting at a table in the corner of the room. They were wearing their stupid Treacherous Tarantula leather jackets, and one of them was trying to see how many peas he could shove up his nose. Totally badass.

Not.

Heat flared in my bones, and my eyes narrowed their way.

"Idiots," I mumbled under my breath.

Grant scoffed. "No kidding. Did you know the Imperium did nothing to punish them?"

My jaw dropped. "You're kidding! There were witnesses. You have *stitches* above your eye."

Grant shrugged. "Yeah, well, apparently they have better things to worry about than *some petty fight*."

My nostrils flared. "That wasn't a petty fight! That was battery!"

"Shh…" Grant glanced around the cafeteria. "I know. I'd like to get back at them too, but I can't justify going after them when they could just beat me to a pulp again."

"It was five against two," I said. "It was hardly a fair fight."

My hands clenched into fists as I thought about all the terrible things I could do to get back at them. The gears started turning in my head, and a wide smile spread across my face.

Curiosity filled Grant's eyes. "What's going on in that pretty little head of yours, Nadine?"

I leaned forward. "Tell me, Grant. How badly do you want to get back at them?"

He eyed me. "Depends on what you have in mind."

I crinkled my nose. "I've got a plan."

☾

"This is dangerous," Grant hissed at me. "Lucas would kill us if he knew we were doing this."

I smirked. "Why do you think I didn't invite him?"

He grabbed me by the arm and pulled me behind a black sedan. I kept my gaze on the five Tarantulas across the school parking lot. They were piling into Ryan's black sports car. It was past nightfall now, and the only light we could see by was the moon.

I cocked an eyebrow at Grant. "So what? I thought you wanted to get back at them."

"Not by *following* them," he said. "Nadine, you don't know these guys."

I rolled my eyes and zipped my leather jacket all the way up. "I've known enough guys like them. Now let's go before we lose them."

I hurried out of my hiding spot and raced a few cars down to my own vehicle. I unlocked the doors and tossed my backpack on the floor below the passenger seat. Grant hesitated, then ran after me and climbed in beside me.

I threw the car into reverse. "Did you see where they went?"

Grant pointed to the right. "That way."

I tore out of the parking lot and followed the Tarantulas down the road. I caught up quickly, but was careful to keep my distance so they wouldn't notice my headlights following them.

"Lighten up, Grant." I nudged him in the side. "I thought you of all people would be thrilled to get back at them."

"Hell yeah, but I don't want *you* getting in the middle of it," he said.

I smirked. "You have a lot to learn about me."

Grant looked at me for a few seconds, then caved. "Okay, Nadine. I'm all in, as long as you understand what you're getting yourself into."

I scoffed. "I'm not scared of these assholes."

Grant clicked his tongue. "I think we need to hang out more often. I already like you ten times more."

I chuckled. "That's because I'm awesome. Where are these guys going, anyway?"

"I don't know," Grant said, "but it looks sketchy to me."

I glanced to either side of the road, but there was nothing but trees. I didn't recognize where we were. Wherever the Tarantulas were going, it wasn't into town.

The Tarantulas turned into a long driveway. I slowed and tried to take in as much as I could about the property, but we could hardly see anything from the road. All I saw were more trees.

"What the...?" I whispered. Hairs rose on the back of my neck, and I was getting a little creeped out. Whatever this was couldn't be good. Which meant I definitely had to check it out.

I pulled off to the side of the road and cut the engine.

"What are you doing?" Grant glanced back to the dark driveway.

I smirked at him as I opened my door. "We're going to check it out, of course."

Grant frowned. "You sure, Nancy Drew?"

I smiled at the nick name. "Positive."

I shoved my car keys in my pocket, then grabbed my bag and swung it over my shoulder. Grant stayed by my side as we entered the woods and crept through the trees.

"What do you think they're doing back here?" he asked, looking amused.

I shrugged. "Sacrificing babies?"

Grant chuckled. "Probably."

I half expected to walk in on them around a bonfire conducting some dark ritual. Instead, we came upon a run-down house with their car parked out in front. It looked like nothing more than a small weekend cabin, no bigger than two bedrooms. I'd kill to know what they were doing inside.

I swung my bag off my shoulder and opened it. Contents clinked together and fell to the ground. My heart lurched at the noise. I froze and glanced to the house to make sure no one had heard.

"Shh…" Grant hissed. He looked down to all the boxes and aluminum spray cans I'd run back to my room to get after dinner. "What *is* all this, Nadine?"

I gathered the contents and shoved it all back in my bag, then handed him a can of spray paint. "I bought it at the joke shop in town after Chloe trashed my room—just in case."

Grant read the spray paint label in the moonlight. He smirked and started shaking the can like he had a good idea for it. "What else have you got in there?"

I started digging through my bag to show him. "Unpoppable bubbles, multiplying silly string, and these beads that smell awful when you touch them."

An evil grin spread across Grant's face. "I like how you think, Nadine. Like an Alchemist."

I shrugged. "I have my moments."

"I might have something we can use, too." Grant conjured a collection of firecrackers.

"Put those back," I whispered. "We don't want to let them know we're here. Now let's go before they come back out. I want to get those jerks back for what they did to Lucas's face."

Grant's jaw dropped. "What about mine?"

I smiled. "Yours too. For you and Lucas."

"For me and Lucas," he repeated.

Grant and I crept through the shadows toward Ryan's car. Grant started spraying the back window with hot pink paint, while I threw the stink beads through the open driver's side window. They scattered across the front seats. I threw the rest of the container in the back. When that was empty, I pulled out a can of unpoppable bubbles. They rushed out of the container like spray paint, covering the seats with big, soapy-looking bubbles.

I smiled proudly as I emptied the can. Adrenaline pulsed through my body, and my heart slammed against my rib cage. It was exhilarating.

Next, I pulled out the can of multiplying silly string. I sprayed that all over on top of the bubbles, then touched it just for fun and to test it out. Beneath my fingers, the silly string started growing, twisting into new strings everywhere I poked it. Grant snickered as he sprayed the tires with paint.

"I think that's good," he hissed through the darkness.

"Hang on," I said. I pulled my keys from my pocket and dragged one along the side of Ryan's car. It made a satisfying *screech* as it dug into the shiny black paint.

I smiled proudly. "Okay, let's go."

We shoved our supplies back in the bag and started toward the forest. But we didn't make it there before the front door of the house banged open.

"Hey!" one of the Tarantulas shouted, making my heart leap up into my throat.

Grant grabbed me by the hand, and we sprinted into the trees. My knees groaned in protest, and I couldn't keep up with Grant. I slowed and caught myself on a nearby tree. Not far from us, we could hear the Tarantulas screaming about what we'd done to their car.

Grant tugged at my hand. "Come on, Nadine. We've gotta go."

I knew he was right, despite my body telling me otherwise. I suddenly regretted following the Tarantulas on a day I was so wiped I could hardly walk.

"Give me a second," I gasped.

Grant seemed to realize I wasn't completely myself, because a look of concern came over his face. "Get on my back, Nadine."

I didn't have a moment to question it, because Ryan was shouting at his Tarantulas to split up and find whoever vandalized his car. If I didn't get moving fast, they were going to catch up with us.

I climbed onto Grant's back, and he started moving through the woods. He stopped in his tracks when he turned toward the road and we saw orbs hovering in the forest ahead of us.

"They're going to see us if we go that way," I said.

"I have an idea," Grant whispered.

He turned around in the opposite direction and doubled back toward the house.

"What are you doing?" I hissed.

"They're not going to look for us over *there*," he pointed out.

"Good point."

Grant moved quietly through the trees toward the back of the house. From what we could see, Ryan was angrily trying to clean out his car, but the multiplying silly string was getting tangled in his hands. He swore and flailed his arms around angrily, making it clear he was going to strangle whoever had done this. I thought it was hilarious. The other four Tarantulas were in the trees looking for us, without a clue that we'd slipped past them.

Grant set me down. I steadied myself against a tree and sat on the ground. He crouched beside me, keeping close watch on all the Tarantulas.

"Are you okay?" Grant asked.

I was a little lightheaded and could feel that the blood had drained from my face. I felt like curling into a ball and falling asleep right there. But I couldn't say that to Grant. My disability never gave me any rational reason to feel the way I did. These waves of fatigue hit randomly, and there wasn't much I could do about it.

"I'll be fine," I told him. "Thanks for asking."

We sat there for another ten minutes, and I started to feel the blood return to my face, which was a relief. Ryan had managed to pull most of the bubbles and silly string out of the car, and it just lay there on the gravel in a heap around the vehicle. He was still pissed about the spray paint.

The four Tarantulas returned. "Whoever it was got away," one of them said.

"Shit!" Ryan growled in rage and kicked one of his tires. "Incompetent fucks. Get in the car. We're leaving."

Grant and I breathed a sigh of relief at the same time. He turned to me with a smile. "Good work, Nadine. You've successfully pissed them off."

I shrugged. "It's a gift."

Ryan tore out of the driveway like he was ready to raise some hell of his own. I snickered as we watched their lights disappear through the trees, but I held my breath when they reached the end of the driveway. I prayed they wouldn't turn to the left, where my car was parked. Luckily, they took a right back the way we came. We were safe.

"Come on." I gestured to Grant and got to my feet, then crossed the small clearing to the side of the house.

"Nadine!" he hissed through the darkness. "What are you doing?"

I reached for the side door and turned back to him. "Aren't you the least bit curious?"

"Someone could be in there," he pointed out.

I shrugged. It was unlikely, since there weren't any other cars here and the lights were off. "Don't you at least want to find out?"

I turned back toward the door and twisted the handle. It didn't budge.

"Guess we're not getting in," Grant said.

I eyed him. "Don't you know a spell to unlock it or something?"

Grant glared at me, like he wasn't using it even if he did.

"Not a problem," I said. "I brought my lock pick set."

I pulled my lock pick out of my bag, and Grant's eyes went wide. "What do you have *that* for?"

I shrugged. "It's a hobby."

Despite Grant's obvious unease, he looked impressed when I picked the lock in under a minute. "I didn't know breaking and entering was a hobby."

"I really am a bit of a Nancy Drew," I teased. "Come on."

Grant groaned and followed behind me.

"A little light?" I suggested.

An orb formed in Grant's palm, lighting up the stairwell in front of us like a flashlight. We were standing on a landing, where a few stairs went up to a kitchen on our left and the rest went downward to the basement.

"Come on." I waved my hand, and Grant and I started upstairs to the main level.

Like I guessed, there was no one here. It was eerily quiet, and apart from a few empty soda cans and a bag of chips lying on the ground, it looked like no one had been here in years. There was hardly any furniture —just a couch in the living room and an old mattress in one of the bedrooms. Everything was covered in a thick layer of dust.

"Why do you think they came here?" I whispered to Grant. We were alone, but the place gave me the creeps, so I kept quiet.

"I don't know," he replied. "To hide a body? To talk to the ghost who haunts this place?"

"You think it's haunted?" I asked.

He shrugged. "I'm not a Seer."

I glanced into the second bedroom, but it was empty. "Let's check out the basement."

Grant stopped me at the top of the stairs. "Let me go first, Nadine."

I stepped out of his way, and Grant took the stairs first. I followed close behind. When we got far enough down the stairs to see in the light of his orb, I inhaled a sharp breath. The basement was nothing but endless counters, all covered in various alchemy supplies. There was even a huge shelving unit in the corner with tons of ingredients packed haphazardly into it.

Grant's eyes grew wide. He tossed his orb into the air, and it split into a million tiny stars, lighting up the room like it was daytime.

It took me a second to find my voice as I took in all the cauldrons and vials. "What is all this? Those guys aren't even Alchemists."

Grant was too shocked by what we'd found to say anything. He walked over to the supply shelf and started reading the labels. "Dragon scale. Breath of a kirin. Hunpedskin venom. I don't even know what that is or what it's used for, but it's definitely not something these guys should be able to get their hands on."

Grant continued talking while I walked around the room inspecting all the supplies. "Mermaid scale. Blood of a vampire. *Wolven tooth*? Nadine, none of this stuff comes from the coven. These are all from other magical societies—like the Elementai and Arcanea. To get your hands on this stuff… Goddess, you'd have to be the Imperium. Or at minimum, the alchemy supplies director at school."

I came up behind Grant to look at all the vials. I could hardly believe what I was seeing—a real phoenix feather, and a hair from a unicorn. And to think. Just a few months ago I thought *witches* were nothing but fiction.

"You mean you can find this kind of stuff at school?" I asked.

Grant nodded.

I raised an eyebrow. "Isn't it obvious, then?"

Grant's jaw dropped. "Nooo. You think *they're* the ones who raided the Alchemy lab?"

I gave him a bored frown. "No. It's too unlike them," I said sarcastically.

Grant picked up a vial that had a thick blue liquid in it. "What do you think they're going to do with all this?"

I pressed my lips together. "Well, they're not Alchemists, so my guess is they're going to try reselling it."

An evil grin spread across Grant's face. "They can't sell it if there's nothing to sell."

I was instantly intrigued. "What are you suggesting? We steal it back?"

Grant rubbed his hands together mischievously. "I've always wanted to play Robin Hood."

"Steal from the rich and give to the poor?"

Grant crinkled his nose. "More like steal from the assholes and put it back where it belongs."

I smiled. "Count me in."

Lucas
THIRTEEN

"You. Did. *What?*" I growled.

Grant sat on his bed and sucked air through his teeth. He knew he was in deep shit with me. "Nadine and I followed the Tarantulas to an abandoned house and robbed them…?"

I paced around the room, my hands fisting at my sides. "Is that a question, Grant?"

He shook his head. "No. We definitely robbed them. But we only did it to give the stuff back to the Alchemy department. We dropped it off in Professor Richards's room. No one saw us."

I raked my fingers through my hair. "So you put Nadine in danger?"

Grant gaped at me. "It was her idea."

"When did this happen?" I demanded.

Grant shrugged. "Over a week ago. I wanted to tell you, but…"

"But?" I cocked an eyebrow.

Grant frowned. "I thought you'd be mad."

"Of course I'm mad!" I yelled. "I don't want Nadine anywhere near Ryan—or any of the Tarantulas. What were you doing hanging out with her, anyway?"

"I don't know," he said vaguely. "She wasn't feeling well, and I guess she just—"

My jaw dropped. "She wasn't *feeling* well? Like how?"

Grant furrowed his brow. "I don't know. She didn't give me a detailed list of her symptoms."

I covered my mouth with my hand as realization struck. "It's my fault," I muttered, thinking back to the kiss.

"What's your fault?" Grant asked.

My teeth ground together. "The kiss. I never should've kissed her."

"About that…" Grant hesitated.

I stopped pacing and faced him. "About that, *what?*"

Grant sighed. "Well, Nadine's kind of upset you haven't talked to her since then. She thinks you've been avoiding her."

"Oh, so now you've been talking to her behind my back?" I fumed. Today was *not* a good day. My temper was all over the place.

"Come on," Grant said. "You know it's not like that."

I *had* been avoiding Nadine, but I only did it to protect her. I still hadn't decided if I was summoning the reapers at the Reaper Moon and risking the Abyss. And if I didn't, I couldn't take things any further with Nadine and make her the Reaper's Shadow.

"I have good reason," I said.

"*I* know that," Grant told me. "But Nadine doesn't. You should talk to her."

I groaned. "You know what happens when I talk to her."

"You turn into a love-sick puppy?" Grant teased.

"Shut up." I grabbed my pillow and threw it across the room at him.

Grant checked the clock on his nightstand. "It's almost noon. You should go ask her out to lunch."

"*You* should go ask Talia out to lunch," I shot back like a child.

Grant crossed his arms. "Tell you what. I'll one-up you. I'll *serenade* Talia if you have just one lunch with Nadine."

I scoffed. "*That,* I'd like to see."

Grant shrugged. "The sooner you go ask Nadine to lunch, the sooner I can get to serenading."

I groaned, but I snatched my hoodie up off the bed anyway. "Fine. I'll do it."

I could hear the sound of Grant laughing in delight as I left the room. I shoved my arms through the sleeves of my hoodie and sauntered down the hall with the hood up. This was going to go absolutely fantastic.

Not.

I raised my hand to knock on Nadine's door, but I hesitated. After waiting two weeks since the kiss to talk to her, she probably never wanted to see my face again. Goddess, what was I thinking? Girls were so emotional. She probably took it super personally, which I guess I couldn't blame her for.

Before I could talk myself into knocking on her door, it swung open. The sound of piano music spilled out into the hall, and Nadine's bright eyes stared back at me.

When I saw her, it was like a dark storm cloud lifted from above my head. My hood fell to my shoulders. She was so pretty, with her hair down in waves and tight skinny jeans hugging her curves. How had I managed to steer clear of her for two weeks? This girl drew me in like a magnet.

She stumbled back a step, surprised to see me standing there. "Lucas?"

"Nadine, I, um…"

Fuck, why couldn't I talk? I spit it out before I could make a total fool out of myself. "I came to see if you wanted to come to lunch with me."

Nadine's features hardened. She didn't say anything for several long seconds. I half expected her to yell at me considering the death glare she shot my way. It was preferable to the silence. I had no idea what she was thinking.

"So you're not avoiding me?" she finally asked sharply.

Ouch.

"Well, I'm here," I replied.

Nadine hesitated, but her tone softened. "I was just headed down there anyway. Hang on."

She left the door open and hurried back inside the room. Talia sat at her piano bench playing the keyboard, and she hummed under her breath. Nadine returned moments later.

"Is Talia coming to lunch?" I asked, holding my breath. I liked Talia, but I kind of wanted to be alone with Nadine.

"No," she said as she shut the door behind her. "She's stuck in the zone."

We started down the hall side by side. I noticed she was clutching her fist tightly, like she was holding something. "What's that you've got there?"

She bit her lip and looked up at me. "It's for you."

Nadine held her fist out, and I placed my hand beneath it.

"For me?" I asked in surprise.

Nadine opened her hand and a small, cool object fell into my palm. It was a blue stone.

"Um… thanks," I said lamely.

Nadine raised an eyebrow, like my indifference amused her. She stopped at the top of the stairs and turned to me. "It's celestite, Lucas."

I blinked at her a few times. I knew that was supposed to mean something, but I hadn't taken Crystal Studies yet.

"It's a calming stone," Nadine explained without me having to ask. "You know how you can't sit still and you're always fidgeting?"

"I am?" I asked. I'd never noticed, but I guess she was right.

She nodded. "I bought it for you at the hospital gift shop, but I haven't had a chance to give it to you. I thought it might help you feel better."

My heart instantly melted at the sentiment. I didn't care what the stone was meant for. The fact that it came from Nadine made all the difference.

"Thank you," I said genuinely as I curled my hand tightly around the celestite. "That's very thoughtful."

That's very thoughtful? Who was I? The pope?

I wanted to say something more, but Nadine turned away and started down the stairs. She gripped tight to the railing—like she was afraid she might fall.

"Are you okay?" I asked.

"Fine," she told me. "Why?"

We reached the bottom of the stairs, and I breathed a sigh of relief. "It's just… Grant told me you weren't feeling well."

Nadine scoffed and continued toward the cafeteria. "I never feel well. I have my good days and my bad."

"What's today?" I questioned. "A good day or a bad day?"

A weight like a rock settled in my stomach. I dreaded the answer.

Nadine frowned. "How about we don't ask questions we don't want to know the answers to?"

Now *that* pissed me off. I grabbed Nadine's hand and stopped her just outside the cafeteria. She scowled at me and jerked away. I gaped down at her for a second, shocked that she was so offended by my touch. I guess after avoiding her so long, I deserved that.

"I *do* want to know the answer," I assured her. "I always want to know how you're feeling, Nad."

She crossed her arms, and her eyes darkened. "Really? Is that why you haven't spoken to me in two weeks? You want to know how I feel, Lucas? I feel confused. I feel abandoned."

Holy shit.

"Nad, I—"

"I feel like I did something wrong, and I don't know what it was." Angry tears rose to her eyes, and it was like a knife through my heart. "I feel like we had something going, but when we kissed, it was like... like you just decided I wasn't worth your time anymore."

Fuck, I'd really screwed up. That stone in my stomach grew heavier and heavier by the second.

"That's not it at all," I insisted.

A few people slipped by us on their way out of the cafeteria, and I realized we were blocking the doors. I took Nadine by the shoulder and led her down the hall where we could talk in private. She didn't shy away from me this time.

"Look, Nad." I pressed my fingers to my eyes. "The reason I've been staying away is because I'm concerned about you."

She scoffed. "For real, Lucas? Because you say stuff like that, but it doesn't *feel* like it."

"It's true," I promised. "You already know we can't be together because of the Reaper's Shadow."

"Screw the curse!" Nadine shouted, earning us a few stares from people in the hall. She quickly lowered her tone. "The curse has nothing to do with you not talking to me."

My face began to heat, and my lips pressed tightly together. She didn't get it.

"Yes, it does," I snapped.

I hated myself for the harsh tone I was taking. I never wanted Nadine to be on the receiving end of one of my freak-outs. But if this was what made her understand—and kept her away from me—then maybe I had to hurt her a little. Maybe I had to be the asshole to save her.

"The curse has everything to do with this," I said. "Because every time I'm near you, I just... I just..."

"You just, what?" Nadine snapped.

Before I knew what was happening, I grabbed her face and pressed my body up against hers, pushing her back against the wall. My lips swooped down, but I stopped a millimeter away from her mouth. I was dying to claim it as my own, to kiss her one more time, but I became a statue stalled in fear.

Nadine's chest rose and fell rapidly. Her eyes were practically begging for it. My dick wasn't cooperating either, as it hardened in my jeans. What I wouldn't give to get rid of the clothes between us.

I swallowed, and my voice lowered to a soft whisper. "Every time I'm near you, Nadine, I just want to kiss you."

Nadine inhaled a sharp breath. She wrapped her hands around my back, pulling me closer until her breasts were pressed against my chest. Images of the night at the lake flashed through my mind. I wanted to be back there—to feel her skin on mine again.

Nadine's breath wavered. "So kiss me, Lucas."

By the Goddess, I almost did. Then all these warning bells went off in my mind, and I couldn't bring myself to do it. I couldn't keep hurting her.

I stepped back and dropped my hands from Nadine's face. "I'm sorry, Nadine, but I can't. Look what happened last time I kissed you."

Nadine laughed—but it wasn't the kind of laugh where she was having fun. It was like she couldn't believe what I was suggesting. "You mean I got sick?"

"Exactly," I said. "The curse causes illness the closer we get physically."

Nadine blew out an exasperated breath and spoke firmly. "Let me make something very clear. I have lupus. I am sick *all* the time. Nothing you do—now or ever—will change that. This is not your fault."

"But what if—?"

"Exactly, Lucas," she cut me off. "You're basing this all on *what if*. Well, I have a question for you. What if Lucas Taylor just wanted to be my *friend*? What if we just hung out and—gasp!—he *didn't* expect sex from me?"

I gaped at her. Is that what she thought? That I believed hanging out with her meant she *owed* me sex? I didn't expect a damn thing from her.

"I'd love it if we could just be friends, Nadine," I said harshly. "But how can we do that when you keep leading me on? You're the one who tried to kiss me at the lake. You just asked me to kiss you now. Do you get some sort of thrill out of this?"

"Thrill?" she bit.

Aw, fuck. I was making this worse. Right now, it was hard to keep my mouth shut after what she just accused me of.

"It's like you're addicted to danger or something," I accused. "Like you're trying to see just how far you can push it. Just like you did when you followed the Tarantulas!"

Her eyes went wide, like she couldn't believe I'd throw that in her face. "I went after them because of what they did to you. Because I care."

I rolled my eyes. "Don't say stuff like that, Nad."

She scoffed. "Why not? It's true."

I raked my fingers through my hair. For the first time since I met her, I was seriously frustrated with Nadine. "It's *not* true," I insisted. "People don't care about me."

She gaped at me, like I'd just insulted her. "Are you serious right now? Grant cares! Professor Warren cares! I'm standing right here telling you I care, and you still can't believe it?"

"No, I can't," I growled. "I can't believe you would put yourself at risk just to be with me."

She pursed her lips. "Maybe I would."

"Why?" I cried. "You know the risks of getting involved with me. And you still want to take things further."

"Maybe you're worth it," she argued, fuming.

"But I'm not! The further we go, the sicker you get. You must love the pain!"

The hall went dead silent. For a second, it was as if time stood still. Then I realized what I said, and my stomach dropped.

Nadine's lips pressed into a thin line. "You think I like being in pain? You think I *like* being disabled?"

I sighed. "Come on, Nad. I didn't mean—"

"Screw you, Lucas," Nadine spat. "You don't know me at all."

Nadine slammed her shoulder into mine as she stomped off into the cafeteria to eat lunch alone. My heart felt like it was breaking into a million pieces, and that heavy stone in my stomach had all but consumed me.

I guess I didn't have to worry about avoiding Nadine anymore. I'd done exactly like Grant suggested and been a complete ass. Nadine would be the one to avoid me from now on.

☾

I TOSSED and turned all night. How could I have acted like such an idiot?

Jerk. Total and complete asshole.

That's what I was, and I hated myself for it. I wanted to do better. I wanted to be a better person. But I didn't know how.

My eyes shot open in the darkness to the most excruciating nausea I'd felt since I'd heard the kid. I curled into a ball on my bed, waiting for the thought to come and the nausea to pass.

"I bet no one will notice. They never cared anyhow."

Aw, fuck. Not another suicide.

I tossed the covers off myself and made a beeline for the bathroom, but I didn't make it that far. I doubled over at the trash can and heaved. The stench of puke filled the room, and Grant stirred in his bed as I made gagging sounds.

I'd never handled suicides well, but this one was particularly taxing. It echoed the exact thoughts I'd had when I considered offing myself.

No! I screamed at myself internally. I didn't let myself think about that. I'd decided long ago I wouldn't go back down that road.

I had to take my mind off it somehow, so I crawled back into bed and put my headphones in to listen to music. But tonight, even the heavy beats that usually drowned out my thoughts didn't work.

I hated myself, and it wasn't just because of my gift. Even if I got rid of it, it wouldn't fix the way I felt about myself. Nothing could.

In that moment, I truly meant it. I had no hope. I didn't want hope. Without it, I could never be disappointed.

I wished I could've said I slept that night, but I didn't. I just lay there, shivering in a ball as the darkness of my own mind closed in around me. I hated feeling this way, but I deserved it.

I didn't know how much time passed, but eventually, I heard the sound of the door slamming and Grant squealing as he came into the room. I hadn't even noticed he left.

I groaned as I pulled the blanket down from my head. The daylight coming through the window was blinding. "What the...?"

Grant ran across the room and jumped on his bed a few times. He didn't even notice me. He ran back to the door and double checked the peephole for Goddess knows what.

218

"Grant, jeez," I sighed, still trying to find my bearings as I stirred awake. "What's going on? You're acting like a girl."

Grant's eyes went wide. "What are you still doing in bed?"

I pressed my hand to my pulsing forehead. "Don't feel well. What happened?"

Grant bit his lower lip. "I was going to serenade Talia. I had everything set up in the Lounge and was going to play the grand piano and everything—"

"You can't play piano," I reminded him flatly.

"But I chickened out!" Grant groaned, like he hadn't even heard me.

I rolled my eyes and threw the covers back over my head. "So try again and don't chicken out this time."

"You don't get it," Grant said. "Ugh, I'm a total fool."

I shrugged. At least he and Talia were still on good terms. He wasn't a total loser like me. He didn't know how good he had it.

Grant sighed and stomped out of the room. Thank the Goddess for some peace and quiet.

Except I quickly realized the peace and quiet was just as excruciating, if not more. My thoughts were racing far too quickly, burying myself into a deeper, darker hole than I was already in. I knew the only way to drag myself out of it was to get out of bed. I told myself that all I had to do today was take a shower, but I couldn't even manage to do that much.

It wasn't until late afternoon when I finally decided I couldn't hold my piss any longer and dragged myself out of bed.

After showering, I eyed the bed. It called to me, but I knew if I crawled back under the sheets, I might not get out for a week. I decided to leave my room and grab some takeout from the cafeteria. I wasn't really hungry, but I could practically hear my mother's voice in my head.

"Do they feed you at that college, Lucas? You're getting too skinny."

Speaking of my mother, today was as good a day as any to visit her. I hadn't seen her all semester, and I knew Dad would be down at the bar drinking away his troubles before he had to go back to work for the week.

I left the school and let my feet carry me home. I wasn't really watching where I was going or paying attention to how long it took me. Even the chill of the October air didn't register.

Eventually, the small black house came into view. My family's little three-bedroom was nothing compared to the elaborate gothic houses along the main stretch of road through town. Ours shared the same architecture, but was practically a dollhouse compared to the other houses in town.

I breathed a sigh of relief when I didn't see Dad's car in the driveway. Mom didn't have her own car, but I bet she was home anyway. Dad never let her go anywhere on her own.

I didn't knock. Even after all this time, it didn't seem right. I opened the front door and—

My mother gasped. "Lucas, don't come in!"

But it was too late. I'd already witnessed the damage. Across the living room and through the kitchen doorway, I saw my mother on her knees. Huge chunks of glass lay at her feet, surrounded by a giant splatter of Shepherd's pie and little drops of blood.

My stomach bottomed out. I rushed over to her, kneeling at her side to help clean up. By the looks of things, I'd just missed my father.

"Mom," I sighed, looking down to the broken dish and her wrapped-up hand. "A casserole dish? What was his problem this time? The casserole was too salty? Not salted enough?"

"No," she said, wiping her gauzed hand across her nose. "It was my fault. I dropped it and cut my hand cleaning up."

She could tell me that all she wanted, but I'd never believe it. What terrified me was that she actually believed it herself.

"You don't have to lie to me, Mom," I said as I placed broken bits of glass in the garbage beside us. "I remember how he is."

My mother pressed her lips together, but she continued to clean up as an excuse not to meet my gaze. "You don't remember him as well as you think, Lucas. We had good times, too, but you choose to focus only on the bad. Why do you demonize him so much?"

I gaped at her as I tore a wad of paper towel from the roll. "Because he's a jackass, Mom."

Before I could blink, my mother huffed and snatched the paper towel from my hand. She looked as if she might slap me, though I knew she'd never lay a hand on me.

"How dare you!?" she snapped, catching me off guard. "How dare you talk about your father like that. You know he can't control it."

My breath grew hot. How could she keep telling herself that after all this time?

"Of course he can, Mom," I shot back at her. "He tells you that so you'll excuse his behavior."

"I do not excuse it," she argued.

I sighed. Mom hadn't changed at all these past few months. She was still in denial, and no matter how much I tried to tell her otherwise or how much space I gave her, there was nothing I could do. I guess I thought that I could change her mind somehow. It was just another person's burden I carried. She was so deep in denial she didn't even know the burden was there.

I took a deep breath and placed my hand on Mom's shoulder to get her to look at me. She sniffled and glanced up. "Mom... you know I'll always be here for you, right?"

The crease between her eyebrows deepened. "No, Lucas, I don't. I haven't seen you in months, and then you show up here out of the blue just to insult your father? I don't want to hear it."

I froze in place. My own mother didn't want me around? She preferred my sorry excuse of a dad to me? Tears brimmed Mom's eyes, and she placed a hand over her mouth so I wouldn't hear her sobs.

"Hey, Mom," I said softly, reaching out for her.

She shrugged me off. "It's just so hard to see you here, Lucas," she admitted. "I've already come to terms with the fact that my son is dead."

My guts twisted. "I know, Mom. We've all dealt with Eric's death in different ways."

Mom shook her head and placed her hand on the side of my face. "Not Eric, Lucas. You. The night we lost Eric, it was like... like we lost you, too."

Every muscle in my body tensed. Her words were like a knife through my heart. Maybe I hadn't been lying to myself all this time.

Maybe it was true that no one wanted me around anymore.

FOURTEEN

Lucas Taylor was a jerk.

I couldn't believe I fell for him. And yet, at the same time... I couldn't stop thinking about him. I flipped between the two moods so quickly it could give me whiplash.

No, no. He's *definitely* a jerk.

I tried to put him out of my mind in Demonology the following week.

"Today, we move into our unit on demon deals," Professor Daniels announced. She was a middle-aged woman, with flowing brown hair and a beautiful Bengal cat that lounged on her desk during every lesson. "Before we begin, let me lead off with a warning. The one and *only* reason we cover this unit is to warn you of the dangers of making deals with demons. I will not be teaching you how to summon a demon, and I *strongly* advise you never do so. The consequences can be... dire."

A shiver ran down my spine. Though I'd never seen a demon before, my mind brought up horrible images of creepy, black-eyed men—the spirits of those who followed evil gods. In my head, they were followed by demonic monsters. Professor Daniels had shown us drawings of some of the monsters, and I hoped to never encounter one in my life. They were terrible creatures created by the gods or mutated from magical creatures. There were canines that were nothing more than skin and bones, creatures with the skull of a deer for a head, and three-headed lions with black manes and golden eyes. She didn't have to tell me twice. I wouldn't be caught dead summoning one of those things.

"As we all know, our history is rooted in the summoning of demons," Professor Daniels continued. "With demon blood in our ancestry, it is easier for Miriamic people to summon demons than it is to summon other spirits, as the demons are more willing to show up. That said, demons only appear when they can strike a deal that will benefit them."

Someone spoke up from behind me, though I didn't see who. "But what about Santos? He helped Mother Miriam, even though there was nothing in it for him."

Professor Daniels cocked an eyebrow. "Is that something you'd wish to risk? Demon deals always come with a price."

I raised my hand. I was too curious not to get in the middle of the discussion. "What kind of price? Can you give an example?"

Chloe shot me a scowl from across the room. What? I wasn't allowed to talk now? I ignored her.

Professor Daniels hesitated, then cleared her throat. "An extreme example might be making a deal for more magic. This kind of deal would require..."

She hesitated and got a faraway look in her eye. "Well, it'd require a soul."

My muscles tensed. There was something deep and dark in her tone that suggested such a thing was worse than giving up your own soul. Almost like... like you'd have to *kill* to make the deal.

Who could do such a vile thing like that?

☾

HEADMISTRESS VERLA CALLED me into her office that afternoon. She stood from her desk and straightened her blazer when I walked in. Odin purred from his spot on her desk. "Nadine, I'm so glad we finally get to prepare for your Evoking Ceremony. Have a seat."

She gestured to a chair across from her. My hands shook as I sat. I shouldn't have been so nervous, but I was. My Evoking Ceremony would determine my magic and where I fit in within the coven. I couldn't mess this up.

Headmistress Verla rounded her desk and leaned against the corner, placing her hands in her lap. "I'm sorry we had to cancel our previous lesson. How are things going here at school?"

I relaxed a little as she spoke in a casual tone. "They're fine. My history class is a lot to take in, but I'm really enjoying all the others."

The corners of her lips turned into a frown. "Is that something I can help with? I could set you up with a tutor."

"No," I said quickly, though I appreciated the kind gesture.

"Let's get started then." She returned to her seat behind her desk and stroked Odin's fur. He closed his eyes and swished his tail, enjoying the gentle massage. "Let's begin with any questions you have. It'll help me get a feel for what we need to cover."

Headmistress Verla spoke to me like I was her equal. I should've felt better about it, but it put me on edge. Did I perhaps remind her too much of my mother?

I didn't want to think about my mom, so I pushed the thought out of my mind.

"What exactly happens during an Evoking Ceremony?" I asked.

Headmistress Verla gave a bright smile, like she was happy to answer the question. "It's quite simple, really. You'll lie on the ground in a circle of five candles—one to represent each of the Casts. Another witch will perform the ceremony by repeating an incantation."

"Who will that be?" I asked. "You?"

She gave a slight nod. "If you want it to be, but you can ask anyone you choose, as long as they've already been through their ceremony. Your grandmother, for instance, would be a perfect example."

I let out a deep breath. I'd really like for Grammy to be there with me. "Can other people be there, or just the one witch?"

"You can invite anyone," she answered. "Some witches throw huge parties for their ceremonies, while others prefer to keep it strictly to family and friends."

I was already forming a list in my mind of who I wanted to be there, but the list pretty much stopped at Grammy, Talia, and Grant. Lucas's face flashed through my mind for a second, then I remembered that I was mad at him.

I shifted in my chair. "What happens after the incantation is spoken?"

"You will fall into a trance," Verla explained. "This trance is so deep you won't even realize you're in it."

"Then how can I prepare?" I balked. Nerves ignited deep within my belly. How could I pass the test if I didn't know I was being tested?

Verla held up a hand to calm me down. "Not to fear, Nadine. If your heart is in the right place, you will pass."

I swallowed. What if my heart *wasn't* in the right place? I didn't even know what that meant.

"What if...?" I trailed off. I had so many questions I didn't even know which one to start with. Verla raised a curious eyebrow, and I knotted my hands in my lap. "What if I decide not to do it?"

Verla frowned. "Why wouldn't you go through with your Evoking Ceremony, Nadine?"

Because I'm scared. I don't want to fail. I can't let Grammy down.

Instead, I just shrugged.

"If you don't go through with this, you won't receive your powers," Verla stated.

"Is my birthday my only chance?" I asked.

Verla pressed her lips together and nodded regrettably. "It's the one and only night the veil lifts for you and allows you to contact Mother Miriam. Contacting her on any other night would be nigh on impossible."

A knot formed in my chest. Usually I wasn't so afraid to take chances, but this was different. This was terrifying.

Verla eyed me, and her features softened. "Nadine, what's wrong? Perhaps I can ease some of your worry."

My eyes locked on her cat so I wouldn't have to meet her gaze. I took a moment to breathe, then forced the confession out. "What if... what if I don't have the power to be part of the coven?"

Verla furrowed her brow. "What do you mean?"

I forced down the lump in my throat as my anxiety reached the surface. "Well, I'm only half witch. My mom was a witch, and my dad was a human, right? So what if I don't have enough power to pass Mother Miriam's test?"

Amusement crossed Verla's features for a moment before settling into a sympathetic expression. "I assure you, Nadine, Mother Miriam doesn't work that way. As long as you have her blood running through your veins, she will accept you as any other. When a witch has a child with a human, their children have the same potential as the parent. You can be just as strong of an Alchemist as your mother, Nadine."

"You think I'll get Alchemy?" I asked.

"It runs in your family," she stated. "Mother Miriam almost always assigns families to the same Cast, as the coven is very family-oriented. In some instances, she may assign you a different Cast if she sees fit, but it's quite rare."

"What about if the parents are from different Casts?" I questioned. "Can you end up in two?"

Verla shook her head. "No. There's never been a witch or warlock assigned to more than one Cast. Mother Miriam will pick the one that's the best fit for you regardless."

"So, what do I have to do to become an Alchemist?" I asked.

"I'd like to run you through a few scenarios," Verla said. "Of course, we can't predict what scenarios Mother Miriam will put you in, but we can—"

Screeeech!

My heart leapt into my throat as Odin jumped to his feet and let out a terrifying meow that sounded more like a scream. His back arched, and his hair stood on end. Verla gasped as Odin jumped off the desk and tore across the room like he was being chased. He ran around in circles, crying out like he was in pain. My stomach bottomed out as I watched the creature sprint from one end of the room to the other. A chill ran down my spine as he yowled.

Before I could really process what was happening, Odin's head slammed into the wall, and he slumped to the ground.

"Good Goddess!" Verla cried. She leapt out of her chair and rushed over to Odin's limp form. She cradled him in her arms.

Meanwhile, I was still trying to process what had happened. It was like he'd been possessed or something.

I cautiously stood and draped my bag over my shoulder. "Is he okay?"

Headmistress Verla kept her head down, and she stroked Odin's black fur. She shook him, but he didn't move. "I—I have no idea what happened."

She lifted her gaze to mine, and her features were so heartbreaking it made me want to cry. "I'm sorry, Nadine, but I've got to get Odin to the infirmary. We'll have to reschedule again."

"Don't apologize," I said, my heart still hammering. "Go take care of your cat!"

Headmistress Verla hurried out of the room with Odin cradled in her arms. I slumped out of the office behind her, thinking how strange and out of the blue that all was.

And then it hit me. Maybe it wasn't so random after all.

Curling my hands into fists, I headed down the hall in the opposite direction that Headmistress Verla had gone. When I passed by the Lounge, I spotted the Lucky Three inside. They were sitting in the coveted chairs around the biggest TV. Chloe had her feet up on the coffee table and was inspecting her nails.

"It's been two weeks since my last manicure," she complained. "I totally need a new one."

"Let me see," Camille offered, holding out her hand.

My nostrils flared as I stomped into the Lounge toward them. "It was you, wasn't it?" I growled.

Chloe turned from Camille and looked up at me with utter disgust. "What are you going on about?"

A few people in a nearby seating area looked our way, but I didn't care.

I crossed my arms. "What was it this time? Some poison slipped into Odin's food bowl this morning? A curse one of your friends cast on him?"

Chloe rolled her eyes and stood so that she was a mere step away from me. "I seriously don't know what you mean."

I narrowed my gaze at her. "I know you had help. You don't have magic of your own yet."

Chloe faked a frown and spoke in a mocking tone. "Oh, dear. Didn't you know I don't *need* magic to get my way?"

"Screw you," I growled. I wanted to rip her hair out, but with two other girls behind her, I didn't think it'd get me anywhere. "You can mess with me all you want, but you don't get to touch other people—or their cats."

Chloe chuckled, but her laughter instantly died as she stepped forward. She was so close that our noses almost touched. "You don't make the rules."

"Oh yeah?" I growled. "We'll see about that."

I turned on my heel and stomped away from her, fuming.

Chloe's laughter echoed through the room. "You can't touch me, Nadine. But have fun trying."

Oh, bitch. I will.

I didn't really know where I was going, until I passed through the Main Foyer and saw Talia. She clutched her books tightly to her chest with one hand. She held the other out in the direction of a very tall, very handsome warlock. He must've been a senior, but she looked up at him with dreamy eyes like he was a god. He had dark hair that fell into his eyes and a strong jawline. He traced his finger over her hand as she giggled.

"And this line here means you've got a hot date coming up," he teased. "On Friday night. With me."

Talia snickered. "Well, the palm doesn't lie. I guess I can't say no."

I furrowed my brow as I approached. "What's going on?"

Talia finally tore her gaze from the guy. "Oh, Nadine. This is Cody. He was just…"

"I was just enjoying Talia's company," he said slowly, deliberately. He didn't take his eyes off her when he spoke. She practically drooled.

"That's great, but I kind of need you right now, Tal," I said.

Talia's face fell when she noticed my tight expression. "Yeah, sure. I'll see you later, Cody."

"See you." He winked at her and walked away.

Talia turned to me. "What's wrong?"

"Wrong with me?" I balked. "Who is that guy? What about Grant?"

Talia shrugged. "I can't wait around for him forever. Cody asked me out, and I said yes."

I frowned. That was too bad. I was rooting for her and Grant.

"Never mind that," she said. "What's up with you?"

"Chloe," I scoffed, like that explained everything. I looped my arm through hers. "We need to gather the girls. It's time to raise some hell."

☾

"ARE you sure this is safe, Amy?" Mandy asked as the four of us gathered around a cauldron in one of the Alchemy labs.

"Totally," Amy assured us. She pulled her dark hair into a ponytail. "Though that depends on your definition of *safe*."

Mandy was sitting on one of the tables, swinging her feet beneath her and tapping the table top with her long, manicured fingernails. She blew a bubble with her gum, and the *pop* sounded throughout the empty room. "What's your definition?"

Amy chewed her lower lip. "Well, it's not going to *hurt* Chloe, but it will give her some serious nightmares."

I picking up various ingredients Amy had signed out from the supply closet and began reading their labels. My guts twisted as I thought about what we were going to do to her. I mean, Chloe deserved it, but was it worth it to stoop to her level? She'd done the same thing when she asked Amy to help her brew a revenge potion.

My hesitation passed quickly, as I reminded myself that getting back at Chloe was the only way to stop her from sabotaging my lessons. If I didn't ruin this bitch, I wasn't going to make it through my Evoking Ceremony.

"How does it work?" I asked.

"Once it's brewed, we'll sprinkle the potion in front of her dorm room door," Amy explained. "When she crosses the line, it will trigger night terrors."

Talia rubbed her hands together and smiled mischievously. "How long does this stuff last?"

Amy pressed her lips together in thought. "A few weeks, maybe?"

"Perfect," I said. "Let's make it real potent. I want to scare her panties off."

"Ew. No," Mandy joked. "Let's keep those on. I've heard horror stories from Ryan."

Talia chuckled. "Do you think this is good enough payback? Or should we like, make her hair fall out?"

"In patches," I added.

"Or boils," Mandy teased. "She could cover up the bald spots with a wig. Let's give her something she can't hide."

"Ooh, or hair like, all over her body," Talia laughed. "Like Bigfoot."

I snickered. "How about a beard?"

"Come on now," Amy joked. "You're getting a little out of my paygrade here."

I calmed my laughter. "Okay. Nightmares it is."

"Perfect," Amy said. "Nadine, I need an extra hand. Talia, can you get me a spoon from the wall over there?"

"What about me?" Mandy asked.

Amy smirked. "You can just sit there and look pretty."

Mandy lay on the table top with her head propped up on her elbow and the other hand on her hip. She batted her eyelashes. "Like this?"

Amy's eyes roamed over her. "That's perfect. Here, Nadine. I need you to pour these two vials into the cauldron the same time I do these two. We have to pour at the same rate. Got it?"

"Got it." I took the vials of liquid from her hands. One vial read *Basilisk Venom* while the other read *Cockatrice Blood*. A shiver ran down my spine. Neither of those sounded like friendly creatures.

"Here you go." Talia returned holding out a big wooden spoon.

"Perfect," Amy said. "Can you stir while we pour?"

"Sure." Talia stood beside me and placed the spoon inside the cauldron. As Amy and I poured our vials together, Talia began stirring. A strong, putrid stench filled the lab, and dark gray steam started to rise from the cauldron.

Mandy sat up straight and pinched her nose. "Is it supposed to do that?"

"Sure is," Amy said brightly, looking proud. "The smell will go away once we've finished brewing."

She picked up another container full of dried herbs. She took a pinch and sprinkled it into the brew. It turned a thick, murky black, and big bubbles started snapping in the bottom of the cauldron like tar. A thrill went through me when I realized I was brewing my first potion.

Amy added another spoonful of dried herbs, and the potion instantly cleared. It became thin and looked a lot like tomato juice. Amy took the spoon from Talia's hands and stirred while she waved her hand over top of the steaming cauldron and muttered an incantation under her breath.

Mandy watched in deep interest. She noticed my eyes on her and said, "She's really good, isn't she?"

I nodded.

Amy finished the incantation. She leaned over the cauldron and inhaled deeply. "That's more like it."

"That was it?" Talia asked, looking impressed.

Amy scooped a spoonful of potion into an empty vial and held it up. "That's all there is to it. Who wants to do the honors?"

☾

To say I was excited to see Chloe get what was coming to her was an understatement. She'd used Amy to try to turn Mandy into a frog, torn apart mine and Talia's room, sabotaged my lesson with Headmistress Verla, then went after Verla's cat. She deserved every ounce of terror she got in her sleep tonight.

I'd been given the honors of pouring the potion over the carpet in front of Chloe's dorm while my friends kept watch. No one spotted us, and we hurried away before we could get caught. Talia and I invited Amy and Mandy to stay in our dorm in case anything interesting happened. It turned into a full-on slumber party, with pizza, manicures, and guy talk. Amy's cat, Stormy, and Talia's cat, Gus, snuggled up together on Talia's bed.

Mandy had twisted my hair into a pair of French braids, and she was working on painting Amy's nails. Talia stood in front of the mirror, pushing her boobs up to see how much cleavage she could get out of them.

"Do you guys think I should wear a push-up bra on my date with Cody on Friday?" Talia asked. "Or is that just setting him up for disappointment?"

Mandy laughed. "That depends. He can only get disappointed if he sees what's underneath the bra."

"Or feels it," Amy added.

"See, that's the thing," Talia said. "I don't know if things are going to go that far or not. Should I play it safe?"

I looked up from filing my nails. "If you want to play it safe, you're going to want to bring the condom box with you."

Talia's jaw dropped. "The whole box?"

"Hold up," Mandy said. "Condom box?"

Talia smirked and went to her dresser. She opened her jewelry box, and a bunch of condoms spilled out. "Yep. We had to restock after the Lucky Three trashed our room."

"Oh, *that* explains all the condoms," Amy said.

"Either of you need one?" Talia offered.

Mandy scoffed. "That would be a miracle right now. I'm going through a serious dry spell."

"You?" Talia held out a condom toward Amy.

Amy crinkled her nose from where she sat on the floor. "That's kind of useless for a girl like me."

"What do you mean?" Talia asked.

Amy raised her eyebrows. "I thought you knew."

Talia tilted her head to the side. "Knew what?"

"That I like girls." Amy glanced from Talia's shocked face to mine. She burst out in laughter. "Oh Goddess, you guys. You should see your faces."

I quickly righted my expression. "I didn't mean to assume anything."

"No, it's fine," Amy assured me. "I really thought you guys knew. Just as long as you're still my friends."

"Of course we are," Talia said, placing the condoms back in the jewelry box. "It just means more condoms for us."

Amy chuckled. "You can have all the condoms you need, girl. I'm not going to use them."

Before anyone else could say anything, a high-pitched scream echoed down the hall. It shocked me at first, but my pulse quickly slowed as a proud smile spread over my face. "Looks like it's show time."

Talia smiled mischievously and headed for the door. Mandy screwed on the cap to the nail polish, and Amy blew on her fingers. We all followed behind Talia as she opened the door. Down the hall, we could hear the sound of doors swinging open.

Gwen rushed out of one of the dorm rooms as the scream came again. She pounded on the door next to hers and shook the handle. "Chloe!? Chloe, what's going on?"

Camille stepped out of the room behind Gwen in nothing but tiny shorts and a skimpy tank top. "What was that?"

"Chloe!" Gwen screamed again, pounding on the door.

Chloe's door swung open. She looked like a total mess, with no makeup on and her hair in disarray. Her silk nightgown hung off her at an odd angle. "What the hell are you doing, Gwen? It's like, one in the morning."

Gwen blinked a few times in shock. "You were screaming. I thought—"

"You thought wrong," Chloe snapped. Her eyes scanned the hallway, and she noticed a bunch of girls watching curiously. She raised her voice. "What are you looking at? Go back to sleep, losers."

A few people murmured to their roommates as they shut the doors. I, on the other hand, stepped out into the hall and crossed my arms. I leaned against my door frame, proudly admiring our handiwork.

"Are you okay?" Camille asked Chloe.

"Yeah, just a bad dream," Chloe admitted. "I haven't had a dream like that in—"

She cut off as she noticed me standing there. She pushed past Gwen and Camille, her nostrils flaring. "What did you do, Nadine?"

"Me?" I asked innocently. "What ever do you mean, Chloe?"

Mandy and Amy snickered from behind me.

"You cursed my sleep!" she accused, pointing a finger in my direction.

A few girls were still peeking through the cracks in the doors. Good. Let them enjoy the show. I hoped Chloe looked as crazy to them as she did to me in that moment. It was *so* satisfying to watch her stand there shaking.

I tilted my head to the side. "How could I do that, Chloe? I don't have magic yet."

She turned her angry gaze on Amy. "It was her!"

"Me?" Amy feigned. "You really think I'd do anything to you, after you kidnapped my cat and threatened to kill her?"

Chloe's eyes darted from door to door. She noticed a few onlookers. "I would never threaten a cat, Amy. Everyone knows that."

Heat flared deep in my belly. No way was she getting away with such a bold-faced lie. I straightened and stepped forward. "Really? Is that why Headmistress Verla's cat is in the infirmary? Oh, wait. Let me guess. That wasn't you, either?"

Chloe cocked an eyebrow, but she couldn't hide the fury etched in her features. "I told you I don't know anything about that."

"Too bad you're not a very good liar," I said.

Chloe's features hardened. She seemed to forget about all the other onlookers. "Fine, Nadine. You want to curse me with nightmares. I'll show you just how much of a nightmare I can be."

She whirled around and stomped back toward her room. Camille and Gwen stepped forward to join her, but Chloe slammed the door in their faces.

When I turned back to my friends, Talia's eyebrows were raised. "Wow. She's really intense, isn't she?"

I shrugged. "Doesn't matter to me. I'm not scared of her."

☽

"I HEARD you and Chloe went at it the other night," Grant said to me after class on Friday. I hadn't meant to meet up with Grant again, but he happened to be sitting in the same study area in the Main Foyer I usually sat in after Introduction to Tarot.

I scoffed as I settled into one of the plush red chairs. "Believe me, if we *went at it*, she'd have a chunk of hair missing."

Honestly, I couldn't believe she'd gone all week without retaliating. At least Verla's cat was back to normal, but I still didn't know what Chloe might do next. I'd been watching my back for days, and she had yet to strike. I figured it was all part of some elaborate plan to put me on edge. It was working. Between my feud with Chloe and everything going on with Lucas, I barely had a chance to breathe all week.

I didn't want to ask Grant about Lucas, so I asked about Talia instead. "So when are you planning to ask Talia out?"

Grant frowned. "About three weeks ago. Every time I get close, I chicken out."

"Why?"

"Because she already rejected me once," he admitted.

I sat straighter in my chair. "What? When?"

"On move-in day," he reminded me. "I asked her out, and she said we should all go out for muffins instead. I'm afraid she'll reject me again."

"I wouldn't call that a rejection," I told him. "She's been waiting for you to ask you out again and has gotten sick of waiting. She's got a date with some guy named Cody tonight."

Grant groaned. "Cody White. Are you kidding me? How am I supposed to compete with *him*?"

Grant sank down in his chair. "She never would've gone for me anyway if she's got guys like *Cody* asking her out."

"Hey, don't say that," I scolded.

Grant ran his fingers through his dark hair. "Damn it. I missed my chance, didn't I?"

"No," I reassured him. "She can't date him forever."

"You don't know that," he grumbled.

Grant's eyes went wide as they connected with something behind me. He sank even further in his chair until he was practically hiding.

"What?" I turned around to see what he was looking at.

"Speak of the devil," he murmured.

My eyes landed on Talia. She looked really cute in a casual red dress that fell to her knees and black boots. She wore her hair up in a high ponytail. Cody walked alongside her and tugged playfully at the ponytail.

"You look like a freshman with your hair up," he told her. "You should wear it down."

Talia reached up and touched her ponytail. "You think so?"

"Yeah, you'd look so much hotter," he said. "Here, let me show you."

He reached into her hair and pulled the elastic out of it. Talia's hair fell around her shoulders. She ran her fingers through the strands to straighten them. "How's this?"

"Perfect," Cody said, shooting her a smile. "Let's get out of here."

"Can I have my elastic back?" Talia asked.

Cody looped it over his wrist. "And risk you putting your hair back up? No way. It's mine for the night."

Talia walked alongside Cody toward the doors. She noticed us as she was passing and waved. *Good luck,* I mouthed.

As soon as Talia was out the door, Grant straightened. "What a jackass."

I raised an eyebrow at him. "Is someone a little jealous?"

Grant's face fell. "That's not what I meant. The way he took her ponytail down like that… It's an asshole thing to do."

"It was harmless," I argued.

Grant crossed his arms. "If I were dating Talia, I'd let her wear her hair any way she chooses."

Before I could respond, Grant's face fell as his eyes connected with something else across the foyer. "Uh oh."

I turned to see Lucas across the room. My heart lifted in my chest, then started pounding furiously. I hadn't seen him since that day I snapped at him by the cafeteria. I hoped he didn't come over here to talk to Grant. I didn't know what to say to him.

And then I saw *her.* I didn't know who she was, but she was walking alongside Lucas and laughing. She was a tall blonde, with legs that went for miles and a tiny little waist. Her hair flowed around her in perfect curls. She looked like she belonged on the runway.

"Who's that?" I asked Grant before I could stop myself.

"Lena?" he asked. "She's nobody. A necromancer in one of his classes. They're writing a paper together."

Grant said it like it should've eased my nerves, but it did the exact opposite.

"If she's nobody, why did you say *uh oh* when you saw them?" I demanded.

Grant bit his lower lip. "Because Lucas told me you two got into a fight. If you want my opinion—"

"I don't, thanks," I snapped.

I felt bad as soon as I said it. I didn't mean to take my frustrations out on Grant, but seeing Lucas with Lena made this red-hot jealousy ignite inside of me that I didn't know was there. I'd never met Lena, and already I wanted to slip a potion into her lunch that would turn her into a frog. I mean, the girl was too pretty for her own good. There was no way she and Lucas were just *writing a paper* together.

"They look awfully comfortable together." I tried to keep the bitterness from my voice, but it didn't work.

Grant shrugged. "Well, yeah. They went out in high school."

My body went rigid, and Grant noticed. He was quick to add, "But they weren't serious. Not like *that*."

I wasn't sure I believed him. The way Lena looked at Lucas, it was like she still had feelings for him… Fresh feelings.

Lena threw her head back in laughter at something Lucas said, though I didn't hear what it was. She reached out and casually touched his arm. My teeth ground together. Lucas's gaze darted in my direction, and my heart jumped as our eyes locked. He looked away quickly and pretended like he hadn't seen me, but it'd been as clear as day.

Lucas reached out for Lena's hand, and my jaw dropped. He entwined his fingers in hers and whispered something I couldn't hear. It felt as if time stood still, but I must've been the only one frozen in time, because Lucas and Lena continued up the grand staircase hand-in-hand. Grant gasped from beside me.

Lucas shot one last glance over his shoulder, and he looked straight into my shocked eyes. It was in that moment that I realized he'd done it on *purpose*. I could feel a fault form in my heart at the blatant rejection.

I took back what I said about Lucas being a jerk. Rubbing this rejection in my face to intentionally hurt me entered entirely new territory.

Congratulations, Lucas Taylor. You've just graduated to full-level asshole.

Lucas

FIFTEEN

I saw the way Nadine looked at me when I passed through the Main Foyer with Lena. Her expression was full of longing, but it quickly shifted to unadulterated loathing when she spotted Lena at my side. I couldn't explain it, but that look in her eyes tore my fucking heart in two. I hated how much I'd hurt her, but I had to protect her.

And so I did what I had to do to keep her away. I grabbed Lena's hand.

Nadine's features darkened, and a heavy weight dropped on my stomach. But I couldn't back down now. Nadine had to know we could never be anything more than friends. If acting like the asshole was what got her to get over me, then I'd do it.

"Just go with it," I leaned over and whispered to Lena.

Lena smiled back at me as we started up the stairs. "Just go with it? Lucas, are you *flirting?*"

"Believe me," I said. "You'd know it if I was flirting."

Lena batted her eyelashes at me, and my stomach sank. I didn't want anything to do with Lena. But here I was, holding her hand.

I really was a jerk, wasn't I?

I watched for Nadine over the following week, but I didn't see her. I was pretty sure *she* was the one avoiding *me* now. It was probably for the best.

On Thursday, I stayed in bed, my head buried under the pillow. It was

Halloween, a sacred holiday for the coven, which meant we had off school for the festivities, but all I wanted to do was sleep.

"That's it," Grant said from across the room.

I was awake, just not moving.

"It's time for you to get out of bed." Grant grabbed my ankle and tugged.

I jerked it away. "Get off me, man," I snapped. "You're not my mother."

Not like I'd let my mom drag me out of bed, either.

"It's *Halloween*," Grant emphasized. "You have to get out of bed."

I pulled the pillow off my head and rubbed my eyes. Grant stood beside my bed in a suit and cape. His hair was slicked back, and he wore fake vampire fangs.

"You're ready already?" I groaned. "The festival isn't until dark."

Grant shrugged. "No, but there's plenty to do before then. We could hit up Main Street and shop the sales."

"That crowd is worse than Black Friday," I complained.

"But we can get free cider!" Grant exclaimed.

He was way too fucking cheerful. Didn't he realize this day was all about the dead? It was too depressing to handle.

"I don't want free cider," I grumbled, putting the pillow back over my head.

Grant yanked it off me. "You have to at least *eat* something today."

"Not hungry," I told him. My stomach felt hollow, but I didn't want to eat.

Grant eyed me curiously, and his tone softened. "Dude, what's up with you? Last year you couldn't wait for Halloween."

I pulled the blanket up over my head. "Last year was different."

"Why?" Grant asked.

I didn't answer.

Grant huffed. He grabbed my blanket and tore it off from me, throwing it on the floor. It was really cold without it, so I curled up into a ball to stay warm.

"Lucas, talk to me," Grant demanded in a harsh tone.

"I don't want to talk about it," I told him.

"I'm your best friend, man," he said. "Let me help you."

I swallowed the lump in my throat and turned my gaze up to him.

Thinking about what this day meant only made my guts twist. But Grant wasn't going to give up until I gave him something.

I pushed myself upright in bed. "I'm not sure I want to attend the festival tonight."

"Is this about your gift?" Grant asked.

It was obvious by his tone. He worried I'd faced too much death this past year and didn't want to celebrate. But that wasn't it at all.

I shook my head.

"Then what?" Grant asked, spreading his arms out in question. "You love Halloween. The hay rides, the apple bobbing, the costume contests. You could even go to one of those Seer booths and—"

Grant stopped in his tracks, and realization crossed his eyes. "Oh," he said flatly, eyeing the fallen expression on my face. "You don't want anything to do with spirits today."

I curled my arms around myself, because it felt like my guts would spill out otherwise. "There's a reason I haven't gone to a psychic since he died."

The words felt heavier than I thought they would. *He died.* Eric was gone. I knew it, and still it was hard to wrap my head around. Because he wasn't totally gone. His spirit was out there somewhere. I was just too afraid to figure out where.

"You don't want to talk to him," Grant whispered, sinking into a spot on the couch.

"It's not that," I told him. "It's just…"

I hesitated. I wasn't good at sharing my feelings. With Grant, we could talk about girls and crap like that, but I couldn't talk about the heavy stuff. I couldn't talk about my brother.

The truth was, Eric hadn't reached out to me in the past year. If he wanted to talk to me, he could've contacted a medium and relayed a message. But he hadn't. Which either meant he was at peace with everything that happened… or he'd ended up in the Abyss.

It was easier to believe he was at peace. I'd rather not seek out confirmation.

"You don't have to visit a Seer," Grant said. "Just dress up and go to the festival with me. That's all I ask."

I shrugged. "I don't know, Grant. I'm not feeling very festive."

"Here's an idea," Grant said brightly. "The veil's thin tonight, which makes séances super easy. You'll get an A for sure."

I cocked an eyebrow at him. "You want to help me do a séance for my Afterlife Studies class?"

"For sure," Grant said. "It'll be fun, and you have to do it sometime this semester."

I sighed. "I guess you're right. But I don't have a costume."

Grant smiled. "I have the perfect thing."

☽

GRANT'S IDEA of *perfect* was far from my definition. I lifted the hem of the robe I wore, ready to tear the freaking thing off because I couldn't stop tripping over it. It was one of the black robes we wore the night of Nadine's initiation. Grant said I should dress as a reaper.

"Not cool," I'd told him, rather harshly.

"I didn't mean it as a joke," Grant promised. "It's an easy costume."

I grumbled about it all day, before finally giving in. At least I could hide beneath the hood.

It was dark by the time we finally left the dorm. I held the celestite stone Nadine had given me in my hand. It was supposed to calm me, and our goddess knew I needed some serious help in that area. So far, it didn't seem to be working. I slipped the stone in my pocket and instead focused on not tripping over my robe. Who the fuck were these things made for? The Harlem GlobeTrotters? I wasn't exactly a short dude.

"Dear Goddess," Grant groaned. He stopped in the middle of the sidewalk and knelt down. He grabbed the hem of my robe and tied the corner into a knot, so that it hung just above my feet.

"There." He stood and cocked an eyebrow at me. "Can we get to the festival now?"

"Geez," I said. "Someone's in a hurry."

"Trick-or-treating is already over," Grant pointed out, gesturing around the dark street. There were cars parked in every slot, which was why we decided to walk. "I don't want to miss the bonfire, too."

"So, you're gonna dance?" I asked.

"Hell yeah," he said as we started walking again. "What do you think Halloween's about?"

We turned the street corner, and it was like stepping into an alternate dimension. The last street was so quiet and deserted, but Main Street was bursting with life. All the shops were open, and there were strings of orange and white lights above us.

People walked up and down the road, since it was blocked off to cars. They were dressed in creepy costumes like ghouls, demons, and scary clowns. I saw at least a dozen people in costume as slasher film villains, and there was an entire family dressed up as characters from the *Addams Family*. One girl had done her makeup to look as if her skin was falling off. Her boyfriend made it look like his head had been severed. Everywhere I looked there was some sort of dead something or other—a dead bride, dead prom queen, and a dead nurse. One kid walked around looking like a talking ventriloquist doll, which was creepy as hell. I even saw a girl dressed up as a Ouija board, with the planchette painted on her eye and the letters on her chest. A trio of girls from school had dressed up as the Sanderson Sisters from *Hocus Pocus*. I noticed Lena was the one dressed as the pretty blonde.

Up and down Main Street, the shop owners had gone all out with decorations. Skeletons hung from signs, and cobwebs had been stretched across windows. Jack-o-lanterns of all shapes and sizes were set up along shop stoops or on bales of hay in front of windows.

We passed by the four Imperium priestesses. They wore long, flowing robes and were handing out suckers shaped like their Cast's symbol to all the kids.

As Grant and I made our way through town and to the park, the Halloween decorations only became more prevalent. Plastic bats had been hung from the trees, and fake blood was smeared all over tree trunks. The vendor booths in the park were even more elaborate than the shops on Main Street. One looked like a gingerbread house, and a lady dressed as an ugly old witch invited kids inside for candy. A haunting melody came from the bandstand, and I could see the bonfire burning down by the river.

"Candy!" Grant cried. He ran over to the first booth and grabbed a handful of chocolate from the bowl sitting there. He subconjured it, then grabbed another handful and shoved it in his pocket.

I eyed him with a frown, and he stopped dead in his tracks. He pulled the candy from his pocket and held a piece out to me. "Sorry, bro. Did you want some?"

"No, thanks," I said.

Grant shrugged. "More for me. So, you want to start with apple bobbing, or the hay bale maze?"

"They're both for kids," I pointed out.

Grant clapped me on the shoulder. "There's a kid inside all of us. It's your fault if you refuse to embrace it."

Grant really wanted to do the apple bobbing, so we wove through the maze of booths to find it. Each booth had a different activity, like pumpkin painting or pumpkin carving. There were photo booths, pumpkin tosses, and all sorts of carnival games with Halloween themes. One booth had aisles made out of hay bales, and people were rolling pumpkins down them at plastic bowling pins. Beside that, miniature pumpkins had been set up on a giant checkerboard. Not far from us, a Halloween movie was playing on a projector, and kids were snuggled in blankets on the grass watching.

If the booths weren't hosting some activity, they were selling food. My favorites were the hotdogs wrapped in dough and made to look like miniature mummies, and the brain-shaped Jell-O.

Grant stopped at the apple bobbing booth and rolled up his sleeves. "Watch the champion at work."

"Yes, Grant, because they give out trophies for apple bobbing," I teased.

He frowned. "They should—oh my Goddess."

Grant's eyes locked on something across the way, and he ducked behind me. I looked to where his gaze had gone, but I didn't see anything. I turned toward him, but he just moved with me to stay hidden.

"Hey, dude, what's up?" I asked.

Grant hid his face. "Talia's coming. Hide me."

I scanned the crowd again, and sure enough I spotted Talia and Nadine coming our way. Talia was dressed in a short green dress and faerie wings. Her cat wore a sack with something written across the side, though I couldn't read it.

Nadine looked absolutely stunning in a plaid shirt, overalls, and a straw hat. Her hair had been twisted into braids, and her makeup was done up to look like a scarecrow. I didn't know what it was about her outfit—maybe the way the overalls hugged her curves—but she looked amazing.

It took me a few moments to tear my gaze off of her.

"Relax," I told Grant. "They're not coming over *here*."

Except they were. They hadn't seen us yet, but they stopped beside the booth next to us, where a dozen other college girls were giggling. At first I didn't know why, until Grant inhaled a sharp breath.

"That's the matchmaker booth," he pointed out. "Do you think Talia will get me?"

I shot him a side-eye look. "You'd have to be dating her first."

"It could happen," Grant shot back.

"Come, come, ladies." Professor Wykoff gestured Nadine and Talia forward. She was dressed in a medieval Celtic dress and was running the matchmaker booth. The booth drew in high school and college girls, and they performed various rituals that would tell them about their future relationships.

"Come," she said again. "Open your minds, and your future husband shall be revealed."

Nadine shot Talia a skeptical look, but she giggled like she was having fun. She stepped up to the booth. "How does this work?"

"Well, my dear, there are many rituals performed on the night the veil is thin," Professor Wykoff said in a mystical voice. "The spirits of our ancestors will guide you and tell your future."

Talia nudged Nadine forward. "It's worth a shot."

"Okay," Nadine agreed, though she didn't sound sure of herself.

"Start with the mashed potatoes," Professor Wykoff said, holding out a small bowl to each of them.

"Oh, this one's fun," Talia said chipperly.

"You've done this ritual before?" Professor Wykoff asked.

Talia's cheeks blushed pink. "Once, but I didn't get the ring."

"What do you mean?" Nadine asked. "What's supposed to happen?"

"We've made a large batch of mashed potatoes," Professor Wykoff explained. "And I've hidden a ring inside. Whichever young lady finds the ring is said to be married by next Halloween."

Nadine chuckled. "If I find the ring, I think it'll come as a shock to all of us. I don't even have a boyfriend."

Professor Wykoff smiled. "Well, you never know, my dear. Things can move quickly when they're meant to be."

She handed each of the girls a spoon, and they both took a scoop of mashed potatoes. I didn't know why, but I found myself holding my breath. I breathed a sigh of relief when Nadine swallowed—no ring to be found.

Nadine handed back the bowl. "No ring, but that was delicious."

"Thank you," Professor Wykoff said. "Not to worry, my dears. We have plenty of other rituals for you."

Professor Wykoff offered them a bowl of hazelnuts. "In this ritual, you'll name each hazelnut for each of your suitors. You'll place them into your fire at home. The nut that burns to ashes will represent your future husband."

Nadine hesitated. "Oh, um… I don't really have any suitors right now."

Grant stiffened beside me, like he hoped Talia might take a hazelnut and name it after him. But she refused the bowl as well. "We don't have a fire in our dorm."

"Not to worry, not to worry," Professor Wykoff said. "Let's try the apple peels."

Professor Wykoff held out another bowl, which was filled to the brim with apple peels.

"What do we do with these?" Nadine asked.

Talia bounced on her toes. "Oh, I like this one. I never got a good reading on it, though."

"It's simple," Professor Wykoff told them. "Take a handful of apple peels and toss them over your shoulder. The shape they land in will reveal to you your future husband's initials."

Nadine laughed. "I guess I'll try it."

She and Talia both took a handful of apple peels and tossed them over their shoulders on the count of three. Grant grabbed my robe and tugged on it, but when I glanced over to him, his eyes were locked on Talia. He didn't seem to notice he had a hand on me at all.

"Mine doesn't look like anything," Nadine said.

She was right. It just looked like a mess.

"I think mine worked!" Talia exclaimed.

Grant tugged on me harder, until my robe was practically choking me. I coughed, and he let go, but he couldn't tear his eyes from Talia.

"That could be a G…" Talia said thoughtfully, pointing down to her apple peels.

Grant gasped.

"Or a C," Nadine added.

Grant sighed.

Talia tilted her head to the side, inspecting the peels. "True. I can't make out the last initial, though."

"Did you hear that?" Grant said to me. "*It might be a G!* That's me!"

"Or a C," I reminded him. "Could be Cody."

Grant frowned. "Screw that asshat. He doesn't deserve her."

I shrugged. "Then ask her out."

Grant ignored my suggestion and tugged on my sleeve again. "Good Goddess, Nadine's doing the mirror!"

I looked back to Nadine, and sure enough, Professor Wykoff had guided Nadine in front of a full-length mirror. It was pointed in our direction, so I could see her reflection perfectly. She looked nervous as she stepped up to it, but there was curiosity in her eyes, too.

"Take this and concentrate on the spirits around you," Professor Wykoff instructed. "Ask them to guide you to see your future husband's face."

Professor Wykoff placed a lit candle into Nadine's hand. Nadine took a deep breath and closed her eyes. Talia stood off to the side, peering curiously at Nadine.

"What if Talia sees me?" Grant whispered from beside me.

"Shh…" I hissed at him.

I shouldn't have cared what Nadine saw in that mirror when she opened her eyes. Whichever guy she saw, it wasn't going to be me. That shouldn't have bothered me, since I knew we'd never end up together, but for some reason, it did.

Nadine's eyes shot open, and she gasped. "Lucas!"

My heart jolted in my chest. No, she didn't see me. She couldn't have.

She whirled around, and her eyes locked on mine. Shock was etched into her features for a moment, until a darkness akin to anger took over.

"Lucas," she snapped. "You ruined my spell!"

I was so stunned by the accusation that I just stood there for a moment. "I—I what?" I stammered.

"What are you doing standing there?" she demanded.

It was only then that realization hit. She *had* seen me in the mirror, but it wasn't because of the spell. It was because I was standing right there, the mirror pointed straight at my face.

"I didn't *try* to mess up your spell," I defended. "Grant wanted to apple bob." I gestured to the booth we stood next to.

"No, I didn't," Grant said quickly, shooting a glance over at Talia. "Apple bobbing is for kids."

Talia chuckled. "No, it's not. It sounds fun."

Grant's features brightened. "Oh, well… I'm pretty good if you want to challenge me."

Dear Goddess. I resisted the urge to roll my eyes.

Talia stepped toward him and raised a challenging eyebrow. "Maybe I will."

"Don't forget these!" Professor Wykoff shoved a small bag of treats into the girls' hands. "It's walnuts, hazelnuts, and nutmeg. Eat it before you go to bed tonight, and you'll dream of your future husband."

"Um… thanks," Nadine said, glancing down to the bag. She eyed it like she wasn't quite sure of this *future husband* ritual, since I'd screwed the last one up.

"Maybe after apple bobbing, we could dance around the bonfire?" Grant suggested to Talia.

"Sure, that sounds great!" She sounded really excited.

Grant suddenly didn't sound so shy. "Cool. So, what are you supposed to be? An Arcanea?"

Grant was careful with his words. It was offensive to dress up as other races for Halloween, and we all knew it.

Talia frowned. "I'm Tinkerbell. Gus is my bag of fairy dust."

Gus was licking his paw. He stopped when he heard his name.

"You're not a Midnighter, are you?" Talia asked, eyeing Grant's costume.

He looked disappointed she didn't recognize him. "I'm *Dracula*."

"Ah, I see it now," she teased. "You're missing the receding hairline."

"I know, my hair's just too perfect for Dracula," Grant joked, running his hands through his gelled hair. "Anyway, shall we?"

Grant and Talia ditched us to take their turn apple bobbing, leaving Nadine and me alone. Neither of us said anything. I couldn't stand it. I think I would've rather stabbed myself in the stomach with a chef's knife than stand there in awkward silence.

"So, um… a scarecrow?" I said to kill the silence. If anything, I only made it worse.

"Yep," she said, popping the P at the end of her word. She shoved her hands into her pockets. "And you're… a reaper?"

I nodded. I couldn't look at her, so I kept my eyes on Grant and Talia as they dipped their heads into the water.

"Creative," Nadine said flatly. I couldn't read her tone, but it sure felt like an insult.

Several minutes passed, and we just stood there. I swear I'd never waited longer in my life. Grant was taking forever. I thought about saying more to break the silence, but Nadine hadn't said anything, either. I got the feeling she didn't want to talk to me. I wanted to apologize, but I could hardly find my tongue. Something told me that'd just end in a fight, and I didn't want to ruin her night.

Finally, after what felt like seven hours of excruciating silence, Grant and Talia returned. They were both laughing, and Talia was running her fingers through her wet hair.

"You were right, Grant," she said. "You *are* good at apple bobbing."

Grant puffed his chest out proudly. "Got one on my first try."

"So, Talia, you wanted to dance?" Nadine said quickly, like she was dying to escape as much as I was.

"Yeah," Talia said brightly. "It's the best part of Halloween."

Nadine looped her arm through Talia's and said, "Show the way."

Grant practically skipped behind them, and I followed along at a distance.

"Come on," Grant hissed at me.

Ugh. Why'd he have to invite Talia and Nadine of all people? This was too weird.

We reached the bonfire, where people in costume were already dancing and having a good time. There were large logs set up around the perimeter. I took a seat on one, because I wasn't much of a dancer.

"Party pooper," Grant joked, before running off to dance with the girls.

Grant took three stocks of dried yarrow off one of the picnic tables. St. John's Wort flowers were woven around the stems. He handed one to each of the girls.

"What's this for?" Nadine asked.

"We dance with it, to keep the faeries away," Grant explained.

Nadine raised an eyebrow. "Faeries? Like the Arcanea?"

"Yes, but also their ancestors," Grant clarified. "The veil between all realms is thin tonight. We don't want any tricksters in our midst."

The three of them hurried off to join the dancing. From the bandstand, a female voice sang a slow, melancholy tune played in a minor key. She was backed by a piano and bells. Everyone danced to their own muse. There was no choreography, except they all moved around the fire in a counterclockwise rotation. Talia and Nadine swayed their hips slowly to the music, while waving their arms seductively. Grant looked like he was doing a poor rendition of *Swan Lake*, though at least he looked like he was having fun.

I couldn't take my eyes off Nadine. It was like that every time we were together, but tonight especially. She smiled and laughed, like she was having the time of her life. It made my heart lift, even though I wasn't participating. All I wanted was for her to be happy.

After a while, Nadine stepped away from Talia and Grant. She breathed a heavy sigh as she came to sit beside me. She looked totally wiped.

"You okay?" I asked.

I could pretend to be an asshole, but I still *cared*. So sue me.

"Just need to catch my breath," she said.

"Are you having fun?" I asked.

"I am," she replied. "So, what's the deal with Halloween around here?"

"What do you mean?" I asked.

She waved her hand and gestured to the people dancing around the bonfire. "You guys seem to take it really seriously. I thought Halloween was all superstition."

I chuckled lightly. "You're a witch, and you think superstitions aren't real?"

She shrugged. "I don't know. *Is* it all real?"

"Most of it," I told her.

She raised an eyebrow. "So, do the gates to hell open on Halloween or something?"

I rolled my eyes at her. It was cute how little she knew. "No, but the veil between the living and dead is thin."

She turned to face me, looking intrigued. "Why tonight, though, on All Hallows Eve?"

"We don't call it that," I stated.

She furrowed her brow. "Really? I thought that was the traditional name of Halloween."

"Our traditions date back *way* further than that," I said. "All Hallows Eve ties into All Saints Day, which is a Christian tradition that coincided with Halloween. Our traditions date back to Celtic culture and the Samhain festival."

Nadine tilted her head. "The coven isn't Celtic, though, is it?"

"No," I told her. "But we adopted the traditions of Samhain because they were so effective."

"Effective at what?" she asked curiously.

It was weird that she was talking to me so casually again after I'd been such a jerk to her. But she always got this way when she was curious about something. Her curiosity was one of the things that drew me to her.

"At keeping away the evil spirits," I told her simply. "The end of October marks the end of the harvest. It's the midpoint between the fall equinox and the winter solstice. Cultures around the world believe that this is the day of the year when the veil between the living and the dead is the thinnest. That's why Professor Wykoff was making you do all those rituals at the matchmaking booth—because they work best when the veil is thin."

"So, evil spirits can really get through to the land of the living on Halloween?" she asked.

I shrugged. "Sure. They all can, if they want to. The point of all these Halloween traditions is to scare away the evil spirits and welcome the good ones."

"Scare them away? That's why everyone dresses up so scary and people hang creepy decorations?" she asked.

I nodded. "Right. It's why we dance and sing around the fire and burn our crops, too. Ages ago, we used to burn cattle, but we don't do that anymore."

Nadine's eyebrows shot up. "If you do this all to ward off spirits, how do you welcome the good ones?"

"A lot of people will set an extra plate at dinner so their ancestors can dine with them," I explained. "After the festival, people will bring flames from the bonfire back to their houses to light their own fireplaces. Then we'll all light candles so the spirits can find their way back to the afterlife when the night is over."

It was actually cool to explain this all to her, because her eyes lit up with intrigue with every little piece of information I gave her. She was obviously a really big fan of Halloween.

"What's the deal with all the candy and crafts, then?" she asked, gesturing to the booths in the park behind us.

I shrugged. "That's just for fun. The Seer booths are real, though. If you want to talk to anyone who's crossed over, now's the best time."

Nadine's features fell, and she stared into the bonfire. I couldn't read her expression, but she looked deep in thought.

She cleared her throat. "I, um… think I might prefer the haunted house tonight."

Nadine got really quiet after that.

"There's no one you want to talk to?" I asked.

I could've sworn I saw tears in Nadine's eyes, but I couldn't tell for sure because she wouldn't look at me. Great. I was the asshole *again*.

"Thanks for telling me about Halloween," Nadine said without looking at me. "But I'm going to get back to dancing."

Nadine stood and walked over to Talia and Grant. She barely danced, though. She picked up Gus and made it look like he was the reason she wasn't dancing, but I could tell she was really tired.

"Lucas," a voice hissed through the darkness. It was so chilling that it made me freeze on the spot. I glanced around, wondering if anyone else had heard it, but everyone kept on dancing and laughing.

"Lucas," the female voice sounded again, louder this time.

I whirled around, and I nearly fell out of my seat when I saw a woman dressed in black crouched at my level. Her face was only inches away from mine. She was dressed as a night hag—a creature of lore who could invade your dreams and caused sleep paralysis. She wore a black veil over her face, but red eyes glowed from beneath it.

"W-what do you want?" I asked.

"Fear not, child, for I am only a Seer," she said.

I knew it was a costume, but I'd be damned if it didn't scare the living daylights out of me.

"A spirit has visited me tonight," she whispered. "He has seen the future, and he has a message for you."

The woman reached out and pressed a piece of paper into my palm. When I glanced down at it, I saw it was a tarot card. Not just any card, either.

Death.

My stomach dropped to my toes. I glanced back up at her. "Is this some sort of joke?"

She shook her head. "Death follows you wherever you go, Lucas."

A shiver ran down my spine.

"Of course it does," I snapped at her. "I'm the Reaper's Apprentice. What does this mean?"

The card could literally mean anything. I dealt with death on the daily, but I knew the Death card had many other meanings. Usually, it wasn't literal.

"You must stop this," the Seer warned.

"Stop what?" I demanded.

"Lucas!" Grant called.

Instinctively, I looked toward him. He waved his hand in my direction as he passed by me. "Come dance! It's fun."

Grant turned back to Talia and grabbed her around the waist. She giggled as he bared his fake fangs and pretended to bite her neck.

I ignored him and turned back toward the Seer… but she was gone. The card still sat in my hand, but it was as if the woman had never existed.

Whatever. I was sure it was nothing more than a joke.

I tossed the card into the grass behind me, and it tumbled in the wind.

Even after the card disappeared from view, I still had this feeling of dread settled deep in my stomach. What if the Seer had really meant something by it? The whole encounter had me shook.

Grant and the girls made it around the bonfire again, then plopped down on the log beside me. "Man, is it fun warding off evil spirits!" Grant exclaimed.

"Gus had fun," Talia said, stroking her cat's head.

Nadine shot a glance my way, but she didn't say anything. Silence settled over our group, and I could feel the awkwardness creeping in again. I just wanted to get out of there—away from the creepy Seer, and away from this awkwardness with Nadine.

I cleared my throat. "Well, Grant. We should probably get going."

"Get going?" he balked. "But I'm having so much fun."

"And I have that paper to write," I reminded him.

"Right. The séance." Grant's shoulders fell. He didn't sound as enthused about it as he had been earlier.

Nadine's spine straightened, and her eyes lit up. "You guys are doing a séance?"

"Um, yeah," I said nervously. She sounded like she wanted to come, but I'd been using it as an excuse to leave.

"Yeah, Lucas needs to do one for his Afterlife Studies class," Grant said. "Do you two want to join us?"

I pinched his arm the same time Talia and Nadine answered in unison, "Yes!"

"That's not necessary," I said. "You guys enjoy the festival. Grant and I are fine on our own."

Grant shot me a look the girls didn't see. *Come on, bro!*

"Ooh, I'd love to see it!" Nadine's eyes were so bright and hopeful.

I still felt bad about the first séance we did. I supposed I owed her a descent séance that didn't end in her getting hurt.

I spoke before I could talk myself down. "If you want… you can come," I offered timidly.

My guts twisted as soon as I said the words. Something told me I was about to regret this decision.

☾

THE CEMETERY WAS creepy at night, but it was particularly chilling on Halloween. The front gates had been left unlocked, and they creaked on their hinges. The moon was nothing more than a sliver, which cast the cemetery in almost complete darkness. Cold air brushed across my skin, raising the hairs on the back of my neck. There wasn't a soul in sight, but I could feel death in the air.

Nadine and Talia clutched each other, and Gus took cautious steps forward.

"Is there a reason we're doing this in the cemetery?" Nadine asked. If it were any other girl, I'd expect her to sound terrified, but Nadine wasn't. Her voice was steady, and she sounded intrigued.

"It's easier to contact someone who's recently deceased," Grant explained. "And since we don't have anything personal, we figured a grave would do."

"Who are we contacting?" Nadine asked.

I shrugged and gestured to the newest plots. "Take your pick."

Nadine walked up to a fresh gravestone. The ground sank a little beneath her feet. The grass hadn't even started growing over the plot.

"Nadine!" Talia exclaimed. She grabbed Nadine by the arm and dragged her back onto the grass.

"What?" Nadine asked innocently, glancing between the three of us.

"It's rude to step over someone's grave," Talia told her.

Nadine pressed her fingers to her lips, and her eyes went wide. "I'm sorry. Did I already ruin the séance?"

I shook my head. "No. We can still contact… Emily Robinson."

My heart stopped when I read off the name on the gravestone. It was the girl who'd died in that domestic attack a few weeks ago. I thought for a moment it'd be better to contact someone else—someone who hadn't left with such a sad last thought. But then I realized pretty much everyone died with some sort of baggage. Emily was as good of spirit as any to contact.

I eyed the date on the stone, then glanced down to the freshly turned earth. Something about it made me uneasy, though I couldn't put my finger on it.

Talia's face fell. "What is it, Lucas? Do you know her?"

I cleared my throat. "No. Let's get this over with."

The four of us sat around the gravestone, being careful not to sit directly on Emily's grave. Gus snuggled up in Talia's lap, looking positively content.

"Anyone happen to have a candle or two on them?" I asked. I'd totally forgotten about it before we left.

"Yeah," Nadine said, grabbing at her pockets. "I've got a whole stash right here in my overalls."

I looked at her hopefully, then realized she was joking. She chuckled, and I rolled my eyes at her.

Not amused.

"I've got you." Grant conjured a candle and set it at the base of the grave marker, then lit it with a lighter. He looked to me for further instruction, since this was my class assignment.

"Everyone join hands," I said. I hesitated when I realized Nadine had sat on my left, which meant I had to hold her hand.

She noticed my hesitation and frowned at me. "I'm not contagious."

"Didn't say you were," I replied, a little harsher than I meant.

Nadine's eyes narrowed. She looked like she was about to say something, but thought better of it. She didn't want to get kicked out of the séance.

I took her hand, but I must've squeezed a little too tight, because she winced. I let up a little, until I was just barely touching her, but it didn't matter. Her touch sent an electric shock straight through me. It took me a few moments to find my voice.

"Try to relax," I told everyone.

Pft. I was one to speak. I really didn't care for this assignment. I mean, who was I to disturb the dead? But I was barely scraping by in Afterlife Studies. If I missed this assignment, too, I'd have to repeat the semester.

"Focus on Emily," I instructed.

Nadine peeked an eye open. "Focus how? We know nothing about her."

I shrugged. "Think about how she loved her Grandma Bea. Or how she used to weave blankets and loved singing karaoke."

Nadine furrowed her brow. "I thought you didn't know her. Did you just make that stuff up? I don't think that's how séances work."

Grant shot me a knowing look. I'd never met Emily in my life, but I'd read her obituary at least fifty times. I knew enough about her to summon her.

"Just go with it," I said flatly.

Nadine closed her eyes again, and the four of us inhaled a collective breath.

"Emily," I called out to the darkness. "We seek to contact you. If you can hear us, please make your presence known."

A light breeze rustled through the trees, but nothing about it felt particularly spiritual.

"Emily," I repeated her name. "All we want is to know how you are. Show us a sign—any sign—that you've made it to the other side all right."

Nothing but silence met us in the night. After several minutes of calling Emily's name, I was starting to wonder if I was doing it wrong. But I couldn't be. Séances were easy. It should've been simple tonight of all nights.

"Emily?" I called again. I tried not to let the irritation in my tone show, but something told me this wasn't going to happen tonight. Emily's spirit wanted nothing to do with us. She was probably hanging out at her Grandma Bea's house. Why would she bother visiting us when she could go anywhere tonight? This was a dumb idea.

I tried one last ditch effort to get her to appear. "Emily, please show yourself—"

An earth-shattering scream cut through the night, sending my heart up into my throat. My eyes shot open, and I jumped away from Grant and Nadine.

Talia sat across from me, screaming like a banshee. Her face had gone paper white, and she pointed to something behind me. Grant scrambled away from where he'd been sitting, looking like he might've shit his pants. Nadine's eyes went wide.

I whirled around and nearly dropped dead at what I saw. A woman in a black dress limped toward us through the shadows. Her face was pale as death, and there was a sickening gray tone to her skin. Her eyes stared forward without focusing on anything. At first, I thought it was some chick from the festival dressed as a zombie, until the moonlight crossed her face. I realized I recognized her from her obituary picture.

Holy shit! It was Emily, but this was no fucking ghost. She was here in the flesh.

How the hell was that possible?

I shot to my feet, my heart racing. "Stand back, everyone!"

I threw my arms out to push everyone behind me.

Emily limped forward. She moved her lips, but nothing came out. I'd seen Professor Warren reanimate animals in Necromancy Safety, but I'd never encountered a human corpse. To say it chilled me to the bone was an understatement.

Nadine grabbed my robes and peeked over my shoulder at Emily. Unlike my hands that were shaking fiercely, Nadine's held steady.

"Emily?" I asked the walking corpse.

She reacted by twitching her head at me. It moved unnaturally, like a creepy demon child from a horror movie. She was almost close enough to touch now, but I didn't want to freak her out—especially if I wanted answers. How was this happening? Was there a necromancer hiding in the trees laughing at us right now or something?

"Emily, what happened to you?" I asked. I didn't know why I was asking. If this was a necromancer's prank, she wouldn't be able to speak. But it was too much of a coincidence that we'd been trying to summon her spirit and her body showed up. Something deeper was happening here. The thing was... did I really want to stick around and figure it out?

Emily reached out for me. Two things happened at once. Emily's cold, dead fingers brushed against my robe, and it was like death itself had touched me. I felt the emptiness of death within my gut.

At the same time, Emily parted her lips. Black smoke began billowing out of her mouth. I'd never seen anything like it. All I knew was that it could only mean something bad. Like, *black magic* bad.

Nope!

We were out of here. To hell with answers.

"Debilito!" Grant cried. Green magic shot out of his hands and slammed into Emily's chest. It was a simple defense spell meant to cripple your opponent.

Emily's body crumbled to the ground, but that black smoke continued to billow out of her mouth.

"Run!" I shouted to my friends.

The four of us whirled around and started sprinting toward the cemetery gates. My heart pummeled against my rib cage. I didn't think I'd ever run so fast in my life.

We only made it a few gravestones down when I heard Gus screech. I took a few more paces before I realized Nadine had disappeared from my side. I spun back around and gasped.

Nadine had tripped over Gus and lay in the grass, groaning. Emily's corpse had risen from the ground and had gone straight for her. Nadine rolled over, and Emily reached out toward the silver star necklace Nadine always wore. She tried to say something again, but it was nothing more than a chilling moan.

"Nad, get up!" I shouted as I raced back toward her.

But Nadine hardly needed my warning. She lifted her foot and slammed it into Emily's gut. Talia and Grant gasped in unison as Emily went stumbling back. I reached Nadine and grabbed her under the shoulders to drag her to her feet.

Nadine held on to me, but she didn't move. She inhaled several breaths and stared at the live corpse like it was the most fascinating thing she'd ever seen.

"Iactus!" I screamed. My purple magic sent Emily flying back a few feet, but it barely fazed her.

"Nad, come on." I tugged at her.

I was about to toss her pretty little ass over my shoulder to get her out of there, but I didn't act in time. Emily recovered and lunged toward Nadine again.

Nadine screamed and curled into me. I wrapped my arms tightly around her. I expected Emily's body to slam into both of us, but she didn't reach us before a sleek black cat as dark as midnight sprinted into view. It hurdled over the nearest gravestone and hissed as it jumped through the air. The cat's claws sank into the flesh on Emily's face.

Nadine's eyes went wide, but we didn't have time to sit around questioning it. I grabbed her around the waist and tossed her over my shoulder.

"Let's go!" I demanded.

Talia and Grant were holding each other, and Gus had scurried on ahead. They both wore a deer-in-the-headlights expression, but they quickly snapped to attention when I hurried past them.

"Lucas!" Nadine protested, slapping me on the back. "Lucas, we have to go back!"

"Screw that!" I cried. We were almost to the front gates now, and there was no way I was going back to face that dark zombie. Sure, she moved slowly, but there was something terrifying about her. Whatever this was was way out of our paygrade.

"Lucas, you don't understand," she cried, kicking her feet.

We passed through the front gates, and I set Nadine on solid ground. I noticed she'd lost her costume hat at some point.

She brushed the hair out of her eyes. "We have to go back for—"

"We don't have to go back for anything," I stated firmly. "Whatever that was wasn't just some everyday reanimant. There was something dark."

"Necromancy gone wrong?" Talia asked curiously. Gus approached her, and she bent down to pick him up.

Grant pulled the gates to the cemetery shut and whispered an incantation to lock them.

"I'm not sure." My heart continued racing as I stepped up to the gate and wrapped my hands around the bars. My pulse slowed as I looked over the cemetery. I didn't see the zombie anywhere.

"Lucas," Nadine pressed.

I whirled around and pressed my fingers to my eyes. Usually, her curiosity turned me on, but right now, it was downright irritating. "I don't care what you want to go back for. Want to see if she's really dead? Want to know what that black smoke was coming out of her mouth? Too bad."

Nadine placed her hand on her hip and looked at me with a pissed expression. She raised an eyebrow. "You done? I was *going* to say, we have to go back for the cat. She saved us."

"Are you kidding me?" I balked. "That cat can clearly take care of itself—"

The rattling of the cemetery gates startled all four of us. Emily had returned from seemingly out of nowhere, and she was violently shaking the cemetery gates. Her features twisted into rage, and she moaned at us like she was some sort of rabid animal trying to escape.

The four of us took a collective step back.

"She can't get to us," Talia stated, though her voice shook.

Grant reached for Talia and stepped in front of her protectively. "Who knows? Our stunning spells didn't work."

"Well, we have to do *something*!" Talia insisted.

"We trapped it," Grant pointed out. "What more can we do?"

Nadine huffed, then stomped over to the side of the road. She grabbed a thick stick and started toward the zombie.

"Hold up." I grabbed for the stick before she could get too far. I didn't want her anywhere near that thing. "I'll do it."

Nadine stepped back. "Be my guest."

I hesitated as I walked up to the corpse. She continued to rattle the gates like a madwoman. My stomach felt hollow as I considered what I was about to do. But it wasn't like she was *alive*. I wasn't going to *hurt* her.

I flexed my fingers around the stick, testing how it felt in my hand.

"Grant?" I cocked my head at him, though I kept my eyes on the raging zombie.

He stepped forward. He kept his voice steady, and I guessed it was for Talia's benefit. "What do you need, man?"

"A little help with the *validus* incantation," I told him. "I can't do it myself."

"I've got you." Grant wrapped his hands around the stick with me.

"*Validus,*" we spoke together.

The stick glowed purple and green as we pooled our magic to make it stronger. It felt like a steel rod in my hands, and I could feel the power emanating from it.

"On three?" I asked.

Grant and I stepped closer to the corpse.

"One…" he said.

"Two…" I added.

"Three!" we cried together.

We lifted the stick and aimed it between her eyes.

"Sorry," I whispered to her.

Grant and I slammed the end of our enchanted stick straight forward through the bars. It connected with Emily's face so hard that it snapped her head back, and her moaning ceased instantly. Her eyes rolled back into her skull, and she collapsed onto the ground.

I thought that was the end of it, until her back arched instantly. The sound of bones snapping met my ears, and black smoke erupted out of her eyes, mouth, and ears. It swirled into a ball above her head, and a high-pitched shriek that wasn't quite human echoed across the cemetery.

"Get back!" I screamed, my heart racing. The four of us stumbled down the road, but we couldn't take our eyes off the strange phenomenon happening in front of us.

Then all at once, the smoke dissipated, and the shrieking stopped. I gasped for breath as my heart rate slowed.

"Let's get out of here," Grant said.

"Wait." Nadine grabbed Grant's arm to stop him. "We can't just *leave* her here."

"Well, we can't touch her, either!" I pointed out. "We don't know what that was."

"Then we need to tell someone," she insisted.

"Yeah, let's freak *everyone* out," Grant said sarcastically.

She frowned. "Someone has to take care of this."

She had a point.

"Headmistress Verla's house is just ahead," Talia said. "We can tell her."

I glanced to each of them, and they all looked in agreement. "Okay."

Headmistress Verla's house was tucked back in the trees. It was pretty elaborate for just one person, with two stories, a three-car garage, and a balcony at the top of the gothic turret. Verla owned like, twenty acres out here at the edge of town, but she was headmistress. She was loaded.

The house was dark when we stepped up to the front door. There was a chill in the air that was even more apparent here in the trees. Two huge door knockers hung from the black double doors. They were shaped as skulls and kind of creepy.

"She's probably not home," I said, like the pessimistic guy I was. "I bet she's at the festival."

Nadine rolled her eyes. "It doesn't hurt to check."

She stepped forward and grabbed the door knocker shaped like a bone. She slammed it hard against the door.

Silence.

I glanced around the forest, as if searching for any signs that the corpse would reappear.

Nadine knocked again, but no one came to the door.

"Maybe we should go," Talia suggested, eyeing the trees. "There are lots of people in town we can tell."

"Yeah," Grant agreed. He seemed eager to get out of here.

Nadine turned from the door. "Okay, let's go."

The four of us stepped off the porch, but the sound of a door swinging open caught our attention. We turned around in unison.

Headmistress Verla stood in the doorway, looking positively surprised to see us there. She wasn't wearing a costume, just a black cardigan she pulled around herself. Her eyes fell on Nadine. "What are you doing here?"

Nadine cleared her throat and spoke like this was an everyday thing. "There's a zombie in the cemetery. We thought you should know."

Headmistress Verla's eyes went wide.

"I think we killed it," Nadine added. "But the corpse is lying by the entrance, and we didn't want to touch it."

Verla's face paled. "Necromancy?"

I stepped forward. "It was something different. Something... *dark.* Black smoke came out of the corpse's mouth."

"I'm sure it's nothing more than a harmless Halloween prank. I'll handle this." But there was something akin to recognition in her eyes, like she knew there was more to what we'd just encountered than that. It was like she recognized the magic we spoke of, but couldn't tell us because we were students.

I realized then what had made me uneasy about Emily's grave. The plot was too fresh. Someone had intentionally grave robbed her and raised her tonight.

The question was who, why, and how the hell were we getting those answers?

nadine

SIXTEEN

The events of Halloween had me shook. I didn't know what to make of what we'd seen.

"Verla's probably right," Talia said as we headed back to our dorm after midnight. Grant and Lucas had walked us back to school, and we split up at the top of the stairs. "It was just a harmless prank... right?"

"Yeah, but who would do that—?"

Talia raised an eyebrow.

"Chloe!" I realized.

Talia shrugged. "I wouldn't put it past her."

My lips pressed into a thin line. "She *would* find a necromancer to freak us out."

"Well, there you go," Talia said. "Mystery solved—"

Talia cut off when Gus jumped out of her arms. He ran down the hallway toward a black cat that sat just outside our door. He crept toward it and sniffed it curiously. The black cat sniffed him back and started purring.

"Um, Talia?" I said as we got closer. I couldn't take my eyes off the cat —or rather, kitten. It looked only a couple months old. It had a short black coat, and there were no unique markings on it. But there was something about those piercing green eyes. "Is that the cat from the cemetery?"

She took a cautious step forward. "I think it is."

"What's it doing here?" I asked. It had to be more than coincidence.

There was something about this cat that left me enamored. I had the strangest feeling the cat felt the same connection with me.

It looked up at me, then walked over and started rubbing itself against my leg. My heart melted, and I bent down to pet it. A warm sense of peace settled over me. "She's *so* sweet."

Talia eyed me curiously. "Nadine, can you describe to me what you feel?"

I stroked the kitten's fur. "I don't know."

I couldn't put it into words. There was a sense of familiarity there that didn't make any logical sense. I wanted to dress her up in little aprons and decorate sugar cookies with her. I could practically taste the dough melting in my mouth when I touched her. And there was this scent to her that made my mouth water—like the delicious scent of baking bread. I wanted to snuggle her tight and never let her go.

And then it hit me. I gasped and threw my hand over my mouth. Talia smiled from above me, like she already knew.

I let out a shaky breath and dropped my hand. "Talia, could this cat be reincarnated?"

"I think you already know," she replied softly.

Tears pricked at my eyes. "Is this cat my mom?"

Talia shrugged, but she looked happy for me. "Only you can tell."

"But… how do I know?" I asked.

"You just… *feel* it," she said. "Like when I first met Gus, he came to me with a chickadee in his mouth."

"What does that mean?" I asked.

"My grandpa Jimmy was a birdwatcher," she told me. "He taught me bird calls, and he called me Little Chickadee. I just *knew*."

I couldn't explain it, but something deep within my soul knew this cat was my mother. I picked her up and cradled her in my arms. She nuzzled against me, and my entire body felt warm with love. "I'm keeping her."

Talia and I entered the room, and I sat on my bed and stroked the kitten. "Does she remember me?"

"Not quite in the same way," Talia explained as she began to strip off her costume. "It's the same soul, but she's still a cat. She'll have a strong connection with you that spans lifetimes, but you'll create new memories with her."

"A strong connection?" I questioned.

"Why do you think she protected you in the cemetery?" Talia pointed out. "And that you wanted to go back for her? It's probably how she found our dorm room, too. Reincarnated cats are different from regular cats. They have a high sense of intuition that will draw them to their loved ones, and they'll act to protect them."

I pressed my nose into the kitten's fur, inhaling the sweet scent that reminded me of my mom. A tear fell from my eyes and soaked into her fur. For a moment, all my fatigue washed away, and I knew without a doubt that my mom had returned. She was here to take care of me again.

I sniffled. "I guess that's why the séance didn't take. My parents souls must've been reincarnating or something."

Talia looked thoughtful as she placed her costume on the hanger. "That might explain it."

The kitten began kneading my stomach. I swooned. "Aww... so, what do I name her? Do I name her after my mom?"

Talia pulled an oversized t-shirt over her head. "It's customary to give them a new name. It differentiates this life from their last."

"Mm..." I mused. "Then I think I'll call her... Isa."

Talia sat on her bed and stroked Gus. "Isa? That's pretty."

"It's my mom's middle name," I told her. I squeezed Isa tight to my chest. "I'm so happy to have her back."

☾

Isa turned out to be a godsend over the next week. My symptoms had flared so bad I couldn't get out of bed and ended up missing a few days of class. She kept me company while I waited for the pain to settle.

By Friday, I was feeling better. I went to Demonology in the morning, then headed to Introduction to Tarot after an early lunch. I noticed Chloe walking my way. I slowed my steps so I wouldn't run into her, but she did the same thing. We ended up at the classroom door at the same time. Chloe stepped in front of it so I couldn't pass and placed a hand on her hip. At my feet, Isa hissed.

That a girl.

"I heard you were sick," Chloe sneered.

I shrugged. "I'm always sick. What's your point?"

She narrowed her eyes. "You don't look sick to me."

Good Goddess, didn't this girl have anything better to do than to torment me?

"If you could tell I was sick, it wouldn't be called an *invisible illness*," I snapped.

"If you want to be invisible, you might as well just leave Octavia Falls," she said. "It's too bad. I'd kind of been hoping that's what happened to you."

I scoffed. "You really think your stupid Halloween prank could scare me away?"

Her lips tightened. "I don't know what you're talking about."

"You said the same thing about Verla's cat," I reminded her.

She rolled her eyes. "Okay, *maybe* I slipped something into his food. But I didn't do anything on Halloween. I take Halloween *very* seriously."

"Right," I said sarcastically, dragging the word out. I didn't believe her. "You would *never* break the rules. Black magic's *way* outside of your comfort zone."

Chloe's gaze darted up and down the hall, as if making sure no one else heard, then she narrowed her eyes at me. "Go die in a ditch, Evers."

She whirled around and entered the classroom. I just laughed from behind her, while Isa let out another hiss.

"That a threat, Chloe?" I called. "Or are you working on casting a curse?"

She ignored me and pulled her tarot cards out of her bag. She started shuffling through them as I took my seat. She pulled a card from the top and started laughing so loud that the other students stopped talking to look at her. Chloe turned the card toward me and beamed.

It was the Death card, but I didn't really care. I knew she'd picked it deliberately to try to freak me out, but I was totally at ease. I pretended I didn't see it and faced the front of the room. Isa purred in my lap.

Class continued like normal. We were studying the symbolism in various cards within the suit of Wands, which was all pretty easy to pick up at this point in the semester.

At the end of class, I waited until everyone else had left, then approached Professor Wykoff.

"Nadine," she said brightly. "What can I help you with?"

"I missed a couple days of class, and I was wondering if there was any makeup work to do," I said.

"I noticed you were out of class," she said solemnly. "Is everything okay?"

"Fine," I told her. "Just been feeling a little under the weather."

She frowned. "Must've been a nasty little bug."

I chuckled under my breath, though she didn't notice. "Yeah, it's pretty awful."

"At least you're better," she said. "I mean, it could be worse. Could be chronic."

My stomach sank at her words. She had no idea.

"Yeah," I said flatly. I didn't have the energy to explain to her it *was* chronic. I quickly changed the subject. "So, is there any makeup work?"

"We studied the Ace of Wands through the Ten of Wands," she told me, "but there's no homework."

"Okay, thanks." I turned and left the room with Isa in my arms. I knew Professor Wykoff had been trying to make me feel better, but I couldn't get her comment out of my mind. Who was *she* to assume what I went through?

I was walking back to my dorm, barely paying attention, when I passed through the foyer. Tons of students were hanging around, but it wasn't until Isa growled lowly that I actually paid attention.

I lifted my gaze and saw Lucas chatting with that blonde chick, Lena, next to the fireplace. She laughed at something he said, which was dumb, because he wasn't even that funny. When she laughed, she reached out and touched his arm. He glanced down at her fingers, but he barely acknowledged that she touched him, like it was totally natural for those two.

Lena pushed a strand of hair behind her ear and fluttered her eyelashes at him. I just stood there frozen, watching, my stomach turning into knots. If he held her hand again, so help me...

Lena's eyes darted around the foyer, and for a second, they landed on me. She didn't look at me long, but something sparked in her eyes when she saw me. I couldn't even explain what it was. Jealousy, maybe?

Which made no sense, because if anyone was allowed to feel jealous, it was me. Lucas clearly didn't have a problem hanging out with *her*.

Lena said something I couldn't hear. The next second, she reached up and placed her hand on the side of Lucas's face. She leaned in and planted a kiss right on his lips. *In the middle of the fucking foyer!*

I went completely still, and the room spun around me. Rejection settled like a knife in my gut. This was a hundred times worse than when he held her hand. This was confirmation of everything I'd worried about the first time I saw them together.

Lucas didn't want me.

But apparently, he didn't care about the Reaper's Shadow curse when Lena was involved. Those two could have it *all.*

How could I have been so stupid? Why had I fallen for Lucas in the first place? And why the hell was I so mad that he was kissing Lena? It wasn't like I *owned* him.

Rationally, I knew that. But deep down, I felt a connection there that screamed of possession. He was mine, and I was his. We were two broken puzzle pieces that fit perfectly together—if only he wanted to.

Except Lucas didn't want that with me. He wanted it with *Lena.*

Screw him! He didn't know what he was missing out on. I was going to have to get him to see that for himself.

I couldn't make sense of what dark energy overcame me in that moment, but I felt nothing like myself. Jealousy, rage, and revenge bubbled up inside of me. All I knew was I had to do *something* to let off some steam.

I whirled toward the stairs. One second, I was stomping toward the banister, and the next, I was in my room. I hardly knew how I'd gotten there.

Talia was playing music at her piano but stopped abruptly when I entered the room. "Is something wrong?"

A maniacal laugh bubbled out of my throat. "Try everything. I just saw Lucas kissing that *bitch* Lena."

Talia's jaw dropped. "He didn't."

"He did," I stated. "And I'm getting back at him."

I dropped Isa off on my bed, then flung open my dresser and went for the skimpiest outfit I could find. I pulled on a black crop top and matching shorts that showed off my ass cheeks. I didn't even know where the outfit had come from, but I felt empowered in it. I let my hair down and slipped on a pair of high heels.

Talia's jaw dropped. "Nadine, are you sure about this? You're really emotional right now."

"Hell yeah, I am!" I cried. "Lucas can reject me all he wants, but he can at least tell me the truth, jackass. See you later, Tal."

I waved over my shoulder and left the room.

"Nadine, wait!" she called, but the door was already closing behind me.

I didn't know where I was going—just that I was looking for trouble. I passed through the foyer, expecting to show off my new look to Lucas, but he was gone.

Shame.

I swayed my hips as I walked down the hall as if I was on the runway. I could practically hear the bad-chick music in my mind. I pursed my lips and floated down the hall like a hella confident goddess. All eyes turned my way, and power exuded out of me. I felt like I could lift a mountain.

I stepped into the lounge, where my gaze narrowed in on what I was looking for—the one thing that would piss Lucas off the most.

Ryan.

He sat alone in the corner by the TVs, his arms stretched across the back of one of the couches. There was something in the way Ryan sat that made it look like he was on a throne. Confidence rolled off him in waves. He seemed like a king turning his nose up at all his peasant servants.

He was the total opposite of Lucas, and right now, it totally turned me on.

I walked straight up to Ryan, and let me tell you, when he noticed me, he *noticed* me. His eyes roamed up and down my body in such a seductive way that it already felt like his hands were on me. I should've felt dirty— and I did, in a way. But something about it exhilarated me, too.

Well, hellooo, danger.

"Mind if I sit?" I asked in a tone that wasn't my own.

Ryan straightened his spine, and his eyes traveled straight down to lock on my breasts. "Go ahead, sweetheart."

He gestured to the cushion beside him, but I didn't take it. I caved to the bad girl inside of me and sat straight on his lap, wrapping my arms around his neck.

"Where have you been hanging around, handsome?" I asked.

Ryan wrapped an arm around my waist. "I could ask you the same thing. Have we met?"

I found it hilarious he didn't recognize me, considering I nearly ran him over with my car. But that was the kind of guy he was. He only noticed a girl if she was spewing sex pheromones his way.

I ran a finger across his chest. "I think I'd remember *you*."

Ryan smirked. "I'll give you something to remember."

"How about a broken jaw?"

My heart fluttered at the sound of the voice, and I couldn't help it when a smile spread across my face. I turned to see Lucas standing there, his hands curled tightly into fists. A dark shadow crossed his eyes, and he looked like he was about to strangle Ryan.

My, my, my… looks like Lucas couldn't handle a little jealousy after all. And it *thrilled* me.

SEVENTEEN

Lena was kissing me. What the hell?

One second we were talking about our class assignment, and the next her lips were on mine. I'd kissed Lena before, back when we were dating in high school, but this was different. This was empty.

I felt nothing—absolutely *nothing*. Her lips were cold, and her hand felt like ice on my face. For all I knew, she could've been a ghost.

It took me a few seconds to realize what was happening, because no *way* was Lena fucking kissing me. But it was happening, and I totally wasn't okay with it.

I pressed against Lena's shoulder and pushed her away from me. "Lena, what the hell?" I hissed, glancing around the foyer. No one seemed to notice—or simply didn't care.

Lena tossed her blonde hair over her shoulder. "What's wrong, Lucas? We've kissed like, a million times before."

"When we were *together*," I snapped.

She pursed her ruby red lips and shrugged. "I thought you'd like a taste of what you were missing."

I scoffed. "I gotta say, Lena, it wasn't that sweet."

"So, what?" she challenged. "You've had sweeter?"

I raked my hands through my hair. "Come on, Lena. You know I don't date."

She lifted a manicured eyebrow. "Really? Because word around these halls is you have something going on with that Nadine girl."

"There's nothing going on…" I trailed off. Lena wore a pleased expression, but I didn't understand it at first.

Then it hit me. She'd kissed me because of Nadine.

"She saw, didn't she?" I growled. "You made sure of it."

Lena shrugged. "I don't know. Why don't you go ask her?"

"Lena," I groaned. I started to walk away—because I just couldn't take her right now—but I realized a second later I had more I wanted to say. I whirled back toward her. "You know what? I'm not some piece of property you can go around *marking*."

"You know I don't think that," she said, but there was no emotion behind her voice. She was as cold as ice—always had been.

"What do you want with me anyway?" I demanded. "You know nothing will ever happen between us."

She just stood there staring at me with complete confidence written across her face. Then it hit me—if she couldn't have me, no one could.

To hell with her. I could hang out with whomever I pleased.

I stomped away from Lena and headed down the hall in search of Nadine. I'd never seen her in the foyer, so I didn't know which way she'd gone. Heck, I didn't even know for sure if she'd seen. It could all be a stupid manipulation tactic from Lena to get me to tell Nadine I kissed another girl.

Yeah, I got that I was supposed to be playing the asshole, but I wasn't *that* kind of asshole. I had to explain to her what happened.

I wandered down the hall and checked the cafeteria, then tried a couple study areas, but I didn't spot Nadine. I turned around and headed in the other direction toward the Lounge.

My stomach flipped when I caught sight of her, but it immediately dropped when I noticed everything else about the scene. It was all *wrong*.

Nadine was dressed in sexy little number that left little to the imagination. It seemed like something Chloe or Lena would wear—not my sweet Nad. I barely recognized her.

It wasn't just the outfit she was wearing, either. It was this look in her eyes I'd never seen before. Something dark and sinister lurked beneath the surface—like she was under some sort of spell.

The worst part, though, was Ryan. Nadine sat in his lap, her arm draped around his shoulder. His hand rested so low on her hip he was practically touching her ass.

"I think I'd remember *you*," Nadine said in a voice that wasn't quite her own.

Ryan practically undressed Nadine with his eyes. "I'll give you something to remember."

Red-hot rage ignited inside of me. "How about a broken jaw?" I snapped.

Nadine turned toward me, and she smirked proudly.

Ryan chuckled. "You really think you can take me, Taylor? Don't forget what happened last time."

"Your backup's not around this time," I pointed out. "Let Nadine go."

Ryan smirked, like my attempt to rescue her was nothing short of amusing. "You act like I'm the one who initiated this. I think the girl can speak for herself."

I crossed my arms and looked to Nadine, a single eyebrow raised. "Nad?"

She practically beamed. "Ryan and I were just hanging out."

Ryan and Nadine would never just *hang out*. Someone must've slipped her a potion or something.

"You're not thinking straight," I insisted. "Let's go."

I reached for Nadine's wrist, though I was careful to be gentle with her. Nadine got to her feet, but so did Ryan. He took her other wrist, like he was laying his claim on her. She glanced between the two of us, looking mildly pleased.

Ryan puffed out his chest. "You're gonna have to fight for her—"

Thwack.

My fist connected with Ryan's jaw before he could finish his sentence. Hell yeah, I was going to fight for Nadine! And I was going to get a good swing in before he went all telekinetic crazy on me.

Pain shot through my knuckles, but it was worth every ounce. Ryan's head snapped backward, and his eyes rolled into his skull. His body slumped onto the couch. A girl sitting nearby gasped, while the guy next to her beamed at the sight of a fight.

Nadine's eyes went wide as she looked down to Ryan's unconscious body. "Lucas!"

At first, I thought she was scolding me, but she turned to me with an expression of exhilaration written on her face.

I shook my hand out. "Lucky shot, I guess. Let's get out of here."

I took Nadine's hand, and we hurried out of the Lounge. She followed without resisting. I dragged her into a dark, empty room down the hall and took her face in my hands. I searched her eyes for dilation, but they looked normal.

And yet, I couldn't help but get lost in them. Once my eyes began to roam her features, I couldn't look away.

Nadine shot a glance toward the door. "Um, Lucas. What are you doing?"

"I'm checking to see if you've been drugged."

"What!?" Nadine slapped my hands away. "I haven't been *drugged*."

"Then what the hell is wrong with you, Nad?" I snapped. Heat flared deep in my belly just thinking about her with Ryan.

She crossed her arms. "Nothing's *wrong* with me. That was all me back there."

"This isn't you," I argued. I eyed her up and down. The new look was... stunning... but it wasn't her. I much preferred her usual look—tight jeans and long sleeves. "You don't dress like this, and you don't act like *that*."

"I could say the same about you!" she yelled. "I thought you didn't date."

My breath caught. I didn't need any more confirmation than that. She'd seen Lena kiss me.

I raked my fingers through my hair. "Nad, it's not what you think."

She raised an eyebrow. "Oh? What is it that I think?"

I frowned. "I know you saw me and Lena in the foyer."

She pursed her lips. "Yeah. How *is* the new girlfriend?"

"She's not my—" I blew out a breath of exasperation. "Lena kissed *me*, okay? I didn't kiss her back, and I'd never want to."

Nadine's features fell, and she blinked a few times. "Oh. Well, that's..."

She trailed off, looking deeply contemplative.

A few moments passed before I broke the silence. "So, do I get an explanation, or—?"

"Where is that motherfucker!?" a voice sounded down the hall, cutting me off.

Instinctively, I grabbed Nadine's shoulders and pressed her up against the wall, pushing both of us deep into the shadows.

The two of us held our breaths as we listened to the sound of Ryan's footsteps pound down the hall toward us. I finally let out a breath when he passed. It was only then that I became acutely aware of how close Nadine and I were. I'd sandwiched her between myself and the wall, and I could feel her heartbeat against me. Her breasts were pressed firmly against my chest, and my jeans started to tighten.

I jumped away from her quickly, and I cleared my throat. My eyes darted around the room—anything not to look her in the eyes while my dick calmed the eff down.

It was the first time I noticed what room I'd dragged her into. It was one of the fitness rooms, complete with those big yoga balls, towels, and a shelf packed full of rolled up yoga mats. My eyes fell on a box marked *Lost and Found*, and I noticed a black fleece and yoga pants inside.

I grabbed them and shoved them at Nadine. "Put these on."

She gaped at me. "I'm a big girl. I can wear whatever I want."

I looked to her arms, which were covered in goosebumps, then shrugged. "Suit yourself."

She wrapped her arms around herself, like she'd just noticed how cold she was. She glanced to the clothes, then narrowed her eyes at me. "I'm only doing this because I'm cold."

She snatched the clothes up and started putting them on. I peeked out into the hall. Ryan stood at the end of it, his hands curled into fists. He twitched his fingers, and the door next to him swung open. A loud *bang* sounded through the hall.

I whirled back to Nadine. "Ryan's coming."

She zipped up the fleece and shrugged. "Then we're going to have to make a run for it."

My gaze roamed over the room. "Want to take the window?"

Nadine smirked. "I *do* love sneaking around."

"Then let's hurry." I started across the room with her, but I stopped mid-stride. Something about the yoga mats called to me. I remembered how much Nadine said she liked it. I turned back to the shelf and grabbed two mats, then sub-conjured them.

"Lucas," she hissed. She already had the window open and was straddling the sill. "That's stealing."

Bang!

Another door crashed open, closer this time.

"We'll bring them back. Let's *go!*"

I nudged Nadine out the window, and she jumped to the ground. I stuck my head out the window to see her catching her balance.

"You okay?" I asked.

Nadine didn't get a chance to respond.

"Taylor!" Ryan growled from behind me.

We hadn't been quick enough.

I whirled around just in time to see Ryan lifting his hand toward me. A dark ball of defensive magic formed inside of it. I wasn't sticking around to see which spell he wanted to use on me. I jumped out the window and landed in the grass beside Nadine.

"Hurry!" She chuckled under her breath, like running from a madman thrilled her.

Nadine and I locked hands and ran toward the forest. A ball of magical energy whizzed past us, missing my head by a hair. Ryan was pretty set on revenge, but the trees were thick and made good cover.

"This way," I said.

I tugged on her hand and pulled her behind a thick tree. The two of us crouched down beside each other. I braced myself against the tree, and Nadine pressed her back to it. I couldn't help but notice how close we were again. Her chest rose and fell rapidly, and her breath touched the side of my face. It sent my heart beating double time. While Nadine's eyes darted around the forest, I kept my eyes on her.

What I wouldn't give to lean in and kiss those sweet, soft lips of hers…

"I think he's gone," she whispered.

I breathed a sigh of relief, though all I wanted was to stay in this position—to be as close to her as I could without touching her. If only I could, I wondered where we'd be now. The images that crossed my mind were dangerous.

I cleared my throat and stood. Now that I had a moment to calm down, I realized how cold it was. There'd been snowfall after Halloween, but it was nothing more than a light dusting. Still, tonight was pretty chilly.

I reached out to help Nadine to her feet. "You okay?"

She brushed her hair out of her eyes. "Yeah, I'm fine. You?"

"Good… for now," I told her. "Ryan's not going to rest until I pay for that."

She winced playfully. "Yeah, it must've really hurt his pride."

"What were you *doing* with him?" I asked.

She dropped her gaze. "Honestly?"

I nodded. "Honestly."

She bit her lower lip, which only made me want to kiss her more. "Honestly, I don't know."

My eyebrows shot up. "You don't know?"

"Yeah," she snapped. "I'd really like not to talk about it right now."

My heart dropped. I didn't know what she meant by that, but she sounded pretty serious. Her face fell, and I realized in that moment that a lecture from me was the *last* thing she needed. I didn't know what was going on with her, but I could see it in her eyes. Right now, all she needed was a friend.

"Okay, we won't talk about it," I agreed.

The sound of leaves crunching in the distance caught my attention.

"We should hide," Nadine suggested.

I placed my index finger over my mouth. "Shh… you like haunted houses, don't you?"

Her eyes lit up, but her features quickly turned into a mock scowl. "Not if it's anything like last time."

"It won't be," I promised with a smirk. "This one's not actually haunted."

She narrowed her eyes, like she couldn't figure out what I had in mind. But like the curious soul she was, she agreed to come with me. "I want to see it."

Good Goddess, this girl would do anything to satisfy her curiosity. It was going to come back and bite her in the ass some day.

"This way." I cocked my head, and Nadine followed beside me.

I navigated through the woods by sheer intuition and a vague memory. We walked for at least fifteen minutes, until I finally spotted the clearing in the trees.

"Is this another kidnapping attempt?" Nadine teased as she ducked under a tree branch.

"Indeed," I told her.

She rolled her eyes. "You've gotta stop doing that, Lucas."

"But you're just so easy to kidnap."

She shrugged. "You know how to intrigue a girl."

I turned serious again. "You're free to go whenever you want, but we're here."

I pulled back a tree branch, and Nadine's eyes sparkled in wonder. In the clearing stood an abandoned gothic mansion. It looked a lot like the school, with the sharp, peaked roofs, tall turrets, and thick wooden doors, but it was smaller. The walls were made of stone, which was probably why it'd stood so long. Ivy grew up the side of the house. This place was absolutely stunning when the clearing was in full bloom and the ivy blanketed the house in green, but right now everything was just kind of dead and sad.

And yet Nadine couldn't take her eyes off it. It was like she saw beauty in the house I couldn't quite see myself.

"Wow," she breathed. "This place is amazing. Can you imagine if someone fixed this place up, how beautiful it would be?"

"Yeah. I bet it was really nice when it was built," I said. "Want to see the inside?"

Nadine nodded eagerly.

We stepped up to the house and entered through the front doors. Hardwood floors spanned in front of us, and the banister that led upstairs was intricately carved, interweaving all the five Cast symbols in a beautiful work of art. There wasn't any furniture, and all the cupboards were empty. Like on the outside of the house, ivy grew on the inside, too, weaving its way through broken windows and overtaking practically everything.

Nadine's jaw dropped. "This architecture is amazing. Look at the archways and crown molding. What is this place?"

I explained as we walked through the rooms. "It used to belong to one of the headmasters of the school. It was abandoned when he died. Legend has it, the house will only reveal itself to those who wish not to harm it."

Her eyebrows shot up. "I guess that's why it makes a good hideout from Ryan."

"Exactly," I stated. "That idiot would fuck this place up. Anyway, Grant and I found it last year."

Nadine reached out a hand and ran her fingers across the wall. "How often do you come back?"

"I haven't been back," I admitted. "We explored, saw what there was to see, and left."

"But this place is just so beautiful," she whispered.

It was, but it was just a *house*. And it was on the cusp of collapse.

Nadine's eyes continued to wander as we entered the sitting room. It was my favorite room in the house because of the massive fireplace. The black mantle was intricately carved, making it the clear centerpiece of the home.

The rest of the room was empty, save for a pile of firewood someone must've brought in a few years ago. There was a thick layer of dust over all the firewood, though it hadn't started to rot.

Nadine drew a breath when she saw the fireplace, then turned to me. "Are you sure the house isn't haunted?" She sounded a little disappointed.

"I'm sure. Let me show you." I took Nadine's shoulders and guided her to stand in the middle of the room. "Close your eyes."

Nadine did as I instructed and inhaled a deep breath. I found myself walking in a circle around her, inspecting her features from every angle. She looked so at peace, so alive and eager for answers. There was this spark inside of her that glowed bright—and like a moth to a flame, I couldn't resist being drawn in.

She took another calming breath. "Now what, Lucas?"

I stopped behind her. We were so close we nearly touched. My pulse quickened, though I resisted the urge to pull her into my arms.

"What do you feel?" I whispered in her ear.

I could've sworn I saw her shiver, but it must've been from the cold.

"I feel... at peace," she finally said. "I feel like I could be happy here forever. There's this warmth inside the house, like it was built on happiness. But... there's something missing. It's like it's fading, like it's losing its memory. All it needs is someone to nurture it."

I stepped around her to look at her from the front again.

Her eyes opened, and her cheeks blushed pink. "Was that the wrong answer?"

I shook my head. "There are no wrong answers."

"What does it mean?" she asked.

"For one, you're intuitive," I said.

She tilted her head to the side. "Aren't most witches?"

I nodded. "True. It also means there are no malevolent spirits hanging around."

"I'm not a Seer, though," she pointed out. "I can't tell when there are spirits around."

"Not the way a Seer can, but even humans can feel the negative energy of a malevolent ghost," I explained.

"Good to know we're in the clear." Nadine spun around again, taking in all the little details she didn't see the first time. "It's a shame that no one is taking care of this place. I just want to… sweep it or something."

"I've got it." I stood in the middle of the room and raised my hands. *"Peppermint patty and grass so green, make this room sparkling clean."*

Purple magic swirled out of my hands, causing dust to rise off of the floor. It gathered into a cloud at the base of the fireplace, then swept up through the chimney and out of the house. I looked to my feet and ran the tip of my shoe across the floor. It was totally clean.

Nadine's eyebrows shot up. "I can't wait until I learn cleansing spells."

I shrugged. "Cleansing incantations are easy. You just make shit up."

She looked amused. "Oh, so you're a poet now?"

"You get a feel for it," I said.

Nadine wrapped her arms around herself.

"You cold?" I asked.

She nodded. "November's not exactly known for its warm temperatures."

"Hold on." I knelt at the fireplace and started building a fire with the bits of tinder next to it. I conjured a lighter and lit it, then added bigger pieces of wood.

Nadine knelt beside me and warmed her hands. She breathed a sigh of relief. I watched her for several moments, until she lifted her gaze and caught me staring.

I cleared my throat and stood, then did the only thing I could think of to keep my hands busy. I conjured the two yoga mats I'd borrowed from school and laid them out on the floor in front of the fireplace. Nadine talked so much about how she liked yoga and needed to get back into it. Maybe this would help her—or at least give me a chance to apologize.

She eyed the yoga mats. "What are you doing?"

I kicked my shoes off and stood on one of the mats. I placed my hands together at my heart and closed my eyes. I lifted one foot and tried to balance on the other, but my balance was shit. I stood back on two feet and peeked an eye open. "I'm doing yoga. What does it look like?"

Nadine laughed and stepped onto the yoga mat beside me. "Need some help?"

I resisted the urge to smile. I really liked that we were getting along for once. "You're the expert."

Nadine lowered herself onto the mat and crossed her legs. I mirrored her posture.

"Let's just breathe for a minute," she suggested.

Nadine went silent. For the first minute or so, it was really hard not to let my mind wander and my body wiggle. But the longer Nadine just sat there breathing, taking in the moment, the more I came to appreciate it, too. I felt grounded, rooted right here with Nadine. My mind wasn't on my gift, my brother, my mom, my classes—any of that. I was just right here, drinking in every second I could with Nadine.

How could I have been such a jerk to her? She didn't deserve any of that. She deserved to be loved.

Nadine shifted and got onto all fours on the mat. She arched her back, pointing her belly toward the floor. I couldn't help but steal a glance at her ass, which made my pulse quicken.

"Do you know any yoga?" Nadine asked, snapping me out of it.

My eyes shot back up toward her face. "No."

"This is cow pose," she told me. "Then you arch your back the other way…" She brought her chin inward and curled her spine. "And you have cat pose."

I tried it along with her, and I was surprised at how much it stretched my back. It actually felt really good, like I could breathe easier.

Nadine walked me through several other simple poses—downward facing dog, cobra, and my favorite, mountain, since we just stood up and it was really easy. She explained each one, until she seemed to disappear into her own little world. Soon, she was moving slowly to her own muse without speaking to me at all.

She stopped in a pose that had one foot forward and the other pressed firmly to the floor. She held both arms out parallel to the floor.

"What's this one?" I asked.

She inhaled a deep breath, like she was enjoying herself. "Warrior two. Feels good, doesn't it?"

"Yeah," I whispered. It felt *really* good to be around her.

Nadine opened her eyes, then stepped out of the pose. She straightened her fleece and sat on the ground again. "Thanks for doing this, Lucas. I forgot how much it helped."

I didn't even realize what I was doing when I sat beside her and took her hand. I began massaging it like she said she liked. I knew her joints always hurt, and I just wanted to help.

I shrugged. "I didn't do anything."

She got really silent after that, but she didn't pull away from me. She just let me run my fingers over her hands. They were so soft and small. She seemed so fragile.

"Do you have any other poems?" Nadine asked to break the silence.

"Poems?" I asked. Then I realized she was talking about spells. "You mean incantations?"

"No," she replied. "Like, actual poems. You seem like you'd be good at them."

I kept my gaze on her hands and shrugged. Deep down, my heart warmed. No one had ever said I'd be good at poetry, and I really wanted to impress Nadine. I knew whatever came out was going to sound like shit, but I just started spewing words without thinking about it.

"Your eyes are like the stars, twinkling so bright. Your smile is like the sunrise, bringing light to night. Your laugh is like the soundtrack to Alora's great divine. But if one thing lights the world at all, it's your soul that really shines."

My cheeks flames when I realized what I just said. Did I seriously just improv poetry in front of Nadine? She must've thought I was such a nerd.

She didn't say anything at first, which made me really nervous. I lifted my gaze to hers, and that's when I noticed her eyes sparkling with tears.

My stomach twisted into knots. "What's wrong?"

She shook her head and pulled her hand away from mine to wipe her eyes. "Nothing. It was really good."

I was stunned. Was she just staying that?

Nadine looked like she was going to add something, but she hesitated.

"What is it?" I asked. I was dying to know her every thought.

She took a few moments to respond. "Why do you act like such a jerk?"

My heart fell. That wasn't exactly the kind of thing a guy hoped to hear.

"I don't know," I lied. The truth was, we both knew exactly why. But it was hard to be a jerk all the time, because that wasn't who I was. Apparently, I was somewhat of a poet-writing romantic. Who knew?

"You're not a jerk, though," she said softly. "Not for real."

My heart felt like it was turning to stone in my chest. I felt really guilty for the way I'd treated her. "Well, I act like one. Doesn't that make me one?"

Nadine swallowed. "It depends on the intentions."

Fuck, even Nadine could see straight through me. Was it this connection we had, or was I really that transparent?

The truth was, I was sick of pretending to be a jerk all the time when all I wanted to do was be near her. But could we really just stay friends?

We had to, because there was no other alternative. By the grace of Mother Miriam, I couldn't stay away from Nadine. It was like we were pushed together by some divine force that wouldn't freaking give up. I wasn't sure I really had a choice anymore. I was just making it harder on both of us.

"I'm sorry." My voice came out so small I wasn't sure Nadine heard me.

She perked up. "What?"

I shoved my pride deep down inside of myself and cleared my throat. "I'm sorry," I said more clearly this time. "I'm sorry I was such a jerk to you. It wasn't fair to you, and I said things I never should've said."

She took a deep breath. "So did I."

"What you said was fair, though," I pointed out.

Her lips tightened. "Why do you do that?"

"Do what?" I asked.

"You just… I don't know… *accept* the worst-case scenario," she said. "You put yourself down and focus on the negative."

"That's not true," I argued.

"Really?" She raised an eyebrow. "When was the last time you focused on the positive?"

I opened my mouth to answer, but the words halted on my tongue. It seemed the only time I was ever positive was around her.

That was the moment it hit me, why I craved Nadine's company so much. When I was around her, I felt a positive spark in my heart. She literally brought to life parts of me I long thought were dead and buried. I wasn't just bull-shitting with that poem earlier. She literally brought light into my life.

I didn't know how to tell her that, so instead, I answered her first question. "I guess I act like a jerk as a defense mechanism."

Nadine's shoulders dropped, and sympathy crossed her face. "I wish you didn't feel like you had to defend yourself."

The knots in my abdomen eased. Her words were a relief, an invitation to let life flow through me instead of bottling it up all the time. It was strange—like she was going against everyone else's unwritten rules. Another reason why I couldn't keep myself from falling for her.

"It's okay, Lucas," she whispered. "You don't have to defend yourself around me. You don't have to hide."

"Neither do you," I assured her softly.

She knotted her hands together in her lap. "So, you've noticed?"

"Noticed what?" I asked curiously.

Her voice cracked, and it broke my heart. "That I hide. That there's this piece of me that I push deep down inside until my walls crack and she comes flooding out."

"She?" I wasn't sure where she was going with this. Sure, sometimes Nadine acted out of character—like earlier with Ryan—but she spoke as if she was hiding a secret identity or something.

Nadine didn't look at me when she spoke. "She doesn't have a name. I just know she's not... me."

Oh, shit. I had no idea that Nadine was hurting this much. I didn't know what kind of secrets she was hiding. But that was the thing about this coven... it was full of secrets.

If there was one thing I learned as the Reaper's Apprentice, it was that everyone had secrets. I wanted to know Nadine's, but I feared if I pressed her, it'd only push her away.

"In what way?" I asked, trying my best to be gentle with her.

Nadine kept her gaze on her hands. "I've learned to control it... mostly. But sometimes, this dark side of me just comes out, and I can't stop it until she's satisfied."

All I wanted to do was rip the demons out of her and make them my own. I reached out and gently brought her chin up so she'd look at me. Our eyes searched each other's for several long moments before I finally spoke.

"Don't hide from me, Nad," I said. "I'll never judge you."

A smile touched the corners of her mouth, then suddenly, the confessions started spilling out. "It's hard to explain, but I've always felt like I had this darkness inside of me. When I was a kid, my teachers called me a *problem child*. If I got upset, even over the littlest thing, I'd freak out. Someone sat too close to me? I'd hit them. Someone took the jump rope I wanted at recess? I'd pick a fight. I can't tell you how many times I was sent to the principal's office. I got kicked off the bus for pulling a girl's hair out. My parents eventually started homeschooling me when I stopped doing my work."

She continued like she couldn't stop herself. "I went through a couple years of therapy, but it was really my lupus that changed me. I guess on some level, it was sort of a blessing. My diagnosis was a huge wake-up call. I had to learn to control myself to keep my symptoms from flaring. It was like the angrier I got, the more pain I felt."

She took a breath. "Eventually, I returned to public school for high school. I learned how to control my temper, but it still comes out sometimes. I just wish I could get rid of it, you know? It's not me. Like when I almost ran Ryan over with my car. Or how I acted with him today. I don't even know why I did it. It already feels surreal—like a dream."

I pressed my lips together, contemplating her story. That darkness she spoke of was far from the Nadine I knew.

"I'm sorry, Nad," I said. "No one should have to deal with that."

She shrugged, like it wasn't that big of a deal, but I knew she was underplaying it. Constantly watching her own behavior had to be taxing on her.

"It is what it is," she said. "Can I ask you something?"

"Anything," I replied.

She spoke slowly, like she was choosing her words with care. "What's the deal with you and Ryan? Do you two have a history or something?"

Oh, boy. Here we go.

I didn't really want to talk about it, but Nadine didn't want me to hide around her. Just the opportunity to lay it all out there on the table was freeing. I wanted her to know everything. I just hoped it didn't change her opinion of me.

I sighed. "Ryan and I were buddies in high school. We formed the Treacherous Tarantulas together."

Nadine's eyebrows shot up. "You were a Tarantula?"

I chuckled. "I wasn't just one of them. I was their *leader*."

Nadine's jaw dropped further. "Lucas Taylor, the lone wolf, in a gang. Who would've guessed?"

I was shocked by her reaction. She didn't look like she thought less of me. In fact, she eyed me up and down like the thought intrigued her, maybe even—dare I say it?—*turned her on.*

"I wasn't always a lone wolf," I said. "But the Tarantulas weren't always the low-life gang they are now. When we formed, it was about brotherhood. We stood to protect other people. When we saw something we didn't think was right, we'd stand up to it—you know, guys pushing other people around in the locker room, pressuring girls in the hallways, that sort of thing."

"That sounds incredible," Nadine praised. She looked at me with dreamy eyes, like she was picturing me walking down the halls in my leather jacket and whipping other kids into shape. "What happened to the group?"

"After graduation, Ryan got into the drug scene," I explained.

"Shocker," she said flatly.

"Right?" I chuckled. "Anyway, he got the other guys to agree to dealing. They were all enticed by the money—and the drugs—but I couldn't do it. I tried to stick it out, but then they pulled this sick prank on Grant and stole his insulin. That was the last straw. I left the group, and they've had it out for me ever since. They call it a betrayal, but I call it a mutiny."

Nadine frowned. "I'm sorry, Lucas. I had no idea."

I shrugged. "It's good, I guess. I've got Grant now, and he's a better friend that all five of the Tarantulas put together."

"He *is* cool," she agreed.

A silent beat passed. Neither of us knew what to say next.

Nadine hesitated, then broke the silence. "So, what were you like... before the Tarantulas ditched you? Were you happier?"

The question hit me hard in the gut. *Was* I happier? Yes and no.

"In a different way," I admitted. "But a lot has happened since then. There are other reasons that I'm so... I don't know... *me.*"

"You can tell me," Nadine offered. "You didn't judge me, and I'm not going to judge you."

I knew Nadine was being honest, but I had a hard time talking about this at all. I pretty much tried not to think about it myself. But pushing it down made the memories stew, made them that much more painful. I knew it, and yet I couldn't face them.

Nadine reached out and touched my hand. My breath caught.

"It was my brother." The words spilled out. "I loved him so much, and when he left, it was like… like a part of me left with him."

"I get it," Nadine whispered, her eyes twinkling with tears. "I feel the same way about my parents."

A lump rose to my throat. I started talking to get it to budge, and I just couldn't stop after that. "My brother and I were really close growing up. My dad was a total asshole, always yelling and starting fights with my mom. She excuses his behavior because he never touches her, but he gets his work in. He's a Mentalist—has telekinesis. When he gets mad, glasses break, things start flying around the room, and… he takes it out on Mom."

Nadine's hand went to her mouth.

"The worst one was when Dad got in one of his fits. Mom *says* she tripped, but Eric and I both knew Dad used his magic to push her down the stairs. She broke her hand."

"Lucas, I'm so sorry you had to grow up with that," she said.

"Don't be," I told her. "It's not your fault. Anyway, Eric and I bonded over our fear of our father. We didn't spend a lot of time at home, since he didn't want us around anyway, so we spent all our time together."

My entire body tensed at the memories. "Things changed after his Evoking Ceremony. He became a Seer. He couldn't see ghosts, but he could hear their thoughts. He described it to me as this constant, annoying chatter he couldn't turn off. I mean, maybe I should be grateful. At least I only hear a couple thoughts a day. With Eric, it was constant. I guess he just couldn't take it anymore. The night I did my Evoking Ceremony…"

My breath halted. I didn't know if I could say it out loud. But maybe it would help.

"That night, Eric hung himself in the garage," I spat out.

Nope. Not better. Not better *at all.*

The confession was like knives through my heart. I didn't think I'd ever said it out loud. I knew that Eric was gone, but I didn't think I'd come to terms with the fact that he killed himself. It wasn't like it was an accident. He left me by choice.

That single thought made me want to hurl. It was selfish to think that way. Eric had been struggling, but I couldn't help him. Yet here I was blaming *him*. I wasn't being fair.

I didn't even know I felt that way until now. I pressed my face into my hands to hide myself from Nadine. I was supposed to be strong, not some emotional wreck for her to piece back together. This was why I didn't open up—because when I did, it all came flooding out all at once.

"Lucas…" Nadine's voice was like a song—a soft, comforting song that kept me grounded to reality.

She reached out and took my wrists, then pulled them down from my face. I was embarrassed for her to see tears dotting my eyes. But she stared straight at me like she saw past them—like she saw *me*.

"You don't have to hide from me, remember?" she asked.

I choked back a sob. "You don't know the worst part, Nad."

"I want to," she whispered. "I want to hear it."

I turned my head away from her. She waited. The silence was almost more agonizing than the confessions.

"You know how I hear the last thought of the dead?" I asked her.

She nodded.

I forced down the lump in my throat. "Well, the night my powers awakened, Eric's last thoughts were the first I heard."

Tears spilled over Nadine's lids, which only caused mine to flow. I dashed them away.

Sure, open up to Nadine. See what she thinks of you now.

I bet she thought I was a freaking *joy* to be around. If I wanted to chase her away, I should've started crying sooner. Who wanted to be around the guy who was so weak he couldn't even hold his tears in?

Nadine reached for my hand again. She pulled it away from my face so I couldn't wipe the tears.

"Don't do that," she said.

"Do what?" My voice cracked. "Cry?"

She shook her head. "No. Don't push it back in."

"I have to," I argued. "Otherwise, I'm weak."

She ran her thumbs across my face and wiped the tears for me. They only continued to fall harder.

"Crying doesn't make you weak," she said. "It's an opportunity to grow."

I laughed nervously. "And you call *me* the poet."

"Shh..." Nadine whispered. "Let's not talk."

And then the strangest thing happened. Nadine crawled into my lap. I didn't know where it came from, but here she was snuggling close to me, not because she wanted something from me—but because she wanted to comfort me. I wondered for so long what that might feel like—for someone to love me unconditionally and expect nothing in return. It was the most amazing feeling in the world, but it felt wrong, too. It felt like I was stealing from her. Stealing what, I didn't know. This moment, perhaps. She could be anywhere doing anything right now, and she chose to be in my arms.

I wrapped her close to me, holding her to my chest. And yet somehow, it felt like *she* was holding me.

Nadine's rosy scent surrounded me, and her warm body sent the chill away. Though my eyes were closed and my nose pressed into her hair, I could swear I could *see* the light radiating off of her. Peace washed over me, and for the first time in my life, the tears stopped on their own. I didn't have to force them.

I drew away from her and whispered, "Why are you doing this, Nad?"

She looked into my eyes, which made my heart melt. I never knew how freeing it would be to hold her in my arms like this.

"Doing what?" she asked.

"Why are you here with me?" I questioned. "Why do you like me?"

Nadine shrugged, but it was obvious she was stalling. There was an answer behind her eyes. I just couldn't read it.

"I like being with you, Lucas," she finally said.

"But why?" I pressed.

She sniffled. "When I'm with you, I forget that my parents aren't alive."

It was such a simple answer, but I felt it deep within my soul. Maybe Nadine and I were more alike than I thought. Maybe we weren't total opposites—light and dark.

Maybe I brought a spark of light to her darkness, too.

No, that was ridiculous. I had no light to share.

"But I'm broken," I told her.

"Not broken," she said softly. "Just growing."

No one had ever put it that way before. If I wasn't broken, maybe I didn't need to be fixed. If I was growing, then maybe the wounds would heal. Maybe it wasn't about putting the shattered bits back together and hoping the glue would stick. Maybe it was about growing new branches.

I pressed my face back into her hair. I was quickly realizing it was the one place in the world where I felt my problems couldn't touch me. "You have no idea what it means to hear you say that."

Nadine wrapped her arms tight around me. "There's more, you know."

"More what?" I mumbled into her hair.

"More reasons why I like you," she said.

"There are?" I asked curiously.

Nadine reached up a hand and started running it through my hair. "I like to think I see the real Lucas beneath the layers."

I didn't even know what that meant. "I *am* the layers."

"No," she said. "You're not your past. You're not your darkness. That's what my therapist always told me. You, Lucas… you're kind and protective and fun. You have a heart so big it should have its own satellite."

I chuckled lightly. Part of me actually believed what she was saying.

"You are selfless," she continued. "You have this desire to take on everyone else's pain just so they won't suffer. If you could, you'd take on the sins of the world."

I stared down at her. I searched for the lie, but it wasn't there. She really believed everything she was saying.

"You… you *see* all that in me?"

She nodded. "I just wish you did, too."

I told myself I'd resist, but I couldn't anymore. Everything Nadine had said was what I needed to hear and more. She was beyond anything I could ever imagine, and I'd be damned if I hadn't fallen head over heels in love with her.

I brought my lips to hers. She melted into my kiss like ice on a warm summer's day. The thought to pull away, to resist, never crossed my mind. All I wanted was this moment. If I was to steal anything from her, it was this kiss, right now.

Kissing Nadine was like standing on top of a cliff. My toes lined up with the edge, and my arms opened wide. She was that moment as I raised my heels from the ground and tilted forward—the split second you thought you had before you could stop the freefall. Her kiss was that wild adrenaline rush, suspended in time. I was safe here—and I was free.

Nadine parted her lips, and my tongue slid into her mouth. My heart beat frantically, and my jeans tightened. She was so warm in my arms that I never wanted to let her go.

I thought I'd have to, but the kiss didn't end. Nadine wrapped her arms around my neck and continued making out with me. Her breasts pressed tight against my chest, and that was the moment I lost it. I went free falling down that cliff, and I couldn't catch my balance.

The room spun around me, and I couldn't hold Nadine up any longer. I gently lowered her to the mat beneath us. She moaned as my kisses continued across her lips. Her noises were like a symphony to my ears. I loved every sound she made.

Nadine's hands continued to roam through my hair, and it felt amazing. I couldn't stop my hands from running up and down her sides. I wasn't on top of her—more or less propped up at her side—but I wanted to be. I wanted to be with her in every sense of the word. I wanted to fight for her tooth and nail.

But I couldn't. And I knew that.

In this moment, though, it didn't seem to matter. I didn't push her away like all the other times. Because if this moment was all I ever had with Nadine, I was going to bask in the warmth of every second I could get from it. I wasn't going to ruin it this time.

Eventually, Nadine pulled away. I pushed myself onto my elbow and hovered above her. The light from the fire flickered off her face, and I'd be damned if it wasn't the most beautiful thing I'd seen in all my life.

"Is something wrong?" I asked.

"No," she said softly. "Would you just… hold me?"

She didn't have to ask twice. Nadine rolled onto her side. I lay next to her, my front pressed against her back. I draped one arm over her. She fit so perfectly into my arms, like it was where she was meant to be.

Nadine went quiet for a long time. After a while, I noticed she was shivering.

"Are you cold?" I asked. I didn't know how. I was radiating so much heat I was practically sweating. Being near her made me hot all over.

"No," she said. "I just… want to ask you something. I don't know how."

"You can ask me anything," I told her.

She shifted and rolled over to face me. She rested her face on her hand, and her hair spilled across the floor. We just lay there staring at each other. It was a beautiful moment I wished would never end.

"I've wanted to ask you for a while, but I know you don't like to talk about your gift," she said.

"Ask me anything," I offered. I wasn't so scared to share with her anymore.

She took a deep breath. "I know it's a long shot, but... did you hear my parents when they died?"

My body tensed. This wasn't the first time someone had asked what their loved ones' last thoughts were. I didn't like to answer, because it usually wasn't what they wanted to hear. That, and last thoughts were Reaper's Apprentice privileges only. It violated the integrity of the job if I went around telling everyone what I heard.

But this was Nadine. I didn't want to lie to her.

I answered carefully. "Your father was never part of the coven, so I didn't hear him."

"And my mother?" she asked.

I nodded slowly. "I heard her."

Her eyes filled with hope. "Can you tell me what she said?"

This was where things got hard. Her mom's last thought was complicated—a mix of good and bad all wrapped into one.

The coven's in danger. Stay safe, Nadine. I love you.

This thought had been weighing on me for months. I didn't know what it meant. I couldn't investigate, either, because I didn't know where to start. For all I knew, her mom was as confused as Old Man Keller.

I couldn't tell Nadine. I didn't want her to know her mom died worrying about her. If I told her the truth, she'd want to fix whatever danger her mother spoke of. She'd get herself hurt looking for answers.

I wanted to tell her, but I couldn't until I knew what it meant.

"She said she loved you," I told her honestly. It was only half of it, but it was true nonetheless.

Nadine's eyes glistened. "Is that true, or is that just what you tell everybody?"

"It is what I tell everybody," I admitted. "But in this case, it's true."

She sniffled. "Thank you, Lucas. I love her, too."

I couldn't bear to see her upset. I leaned forward and kissed her again. She reached up and placed her hand on the side of my face, and that warmth ignited in my heart all over again.

The kiss didn't last long, though. A few moments later, she drew away.

Her eyes searched mine. "Why are you kissing me, Lucas?"

I was struck by the question. "Don't you want me to?"

"I do, but… you're kind of sending me mixed signals," she said. "Do you want this or not?"

I hesitated. Of course I did. I wanted every moment with Nadine and more. But I didn't want her to get hurt.

"I do," I told her honestly. "I wish there was a way we could be together, but…"

"But if we were, this is as far as we could go," she finished for me. "We can't have what every other couple has."

Her voice was so sad, so melancholy. When we first met, I thought she was just chasing me for the thrill of it. I thought she'd get over me once I turned her down. But it wasn't like that between us. Nadine and I were drawn like magnets. And now that we'd come together, nothing could come between us, not even this stupid curse.

"Are you okay with that?" I asked.

I held my breath, awaiting the answer. Part of me feared both options.

"I don't know," she finally said. "I think I need time to figure that out."

"Then we won't make any decisions right now," I promised.

"Okay," she agreed. "At least now we can be friends."

I smiled—a real, genuine smile. I didn't know how she did that to me. "Agreed. We're done arguing. I'm done pushing you away."

She closed her eyes and sighed blissfully. "That sounds good."

I reached out and took Nadine's hand. She lay there, looking perfectly content, while I ran my thumb across the back of her hand.

It was in that moment that I realized it didn't matter which decision Nadine made. There would never be anyone else. Nadine would always be it for me.

I just hoped I could handle her decision.

EIGHTEEN

I needed Lucas in my life. It didn't matter that we couldn't be together in the way that I wanted. I needed him near me the way I needed the very air I breathed. Without him, I was caged. But when he was around, I was a free bird soaring the skies. I could almost believe the two of us were capable of anything together.

Something changed when Lucas brought me to that abandoned house. I didn't know if it was a change in him, or me, or both of us. It was like we could finally breathe again.

The house was gorgeous, and there was a beautiful energy surrounding it that made it feel like home. It was crazy, considering the state of the place, but I just felt like I didn't have to hide anything there.

I'd never felt so close to Lucas. When he stood next to me, I couldn't help but shiver. When he kissed me, the world seemed to tilt on its axis. It was magic.

I walked through the school hallways the following week on this amazing, magical high. I felt energized, and my joints moved with ease. It was like Lucas's touch had a way of healing me.

He was still waiting for an answer from me. Truth be told, I didn't want to think about that right now. We could figure out where we wanted to go with this later. Right now, I just wanted his company.

Lucas met up with me in the hall after class on Wednesday. He carried my books, and I took his hand. It was instinctive now. It was like we couldn't be together without attaching ourselves. It turned a few heads, but I didn't care. Screw the haters.

Let it be known that Lucas Taylor and Nadine Evers were a thing.

A non-official thing, but a thing nonetheless.

"How was class?" Lucas asked.

I shrugged. "Chloe drew the Seven of Swords. I think that means she's planning to act on her threat soon."

Lucas's face paled. "That's not good."

"It's okay," I said honestly. "Now I have some warning. I can't say I'm surprised, though. I have a meeting with Verla today. I expect Chloe to do something."

"Yeah, she's kind of predictable," Lucas said. "But I'm not going to let her hurt you."

My heart fluttered. "Oh? How are you going to do that?"

He smiled. "By not letting you out of my sight."

"I don't think Verla's going to let you in on my lesson," I pointed out.

He shrugged. "Then I'll stand outside the door."

"For how long?" I asked, though I was really enjoying his offer.

He slowed his step and turned to me. He pushed a strand of hair behind my ear, which made butterflies dance in my stomach. "However long it takes. Consider me your personal guard for the day."

My heart totally melted. "Thank you."

"No need to thank me," he replied gently.

Lucas and I returned to my room to put my books away. Talia, Amy, and Mandy were there. Amy and Mandy poked at their phones, while Talia flung around a string for Gus, Isa, and Stormy to chase.

"Hey," I greeted as I entered the room. "What are you guys up to?"

Mandy looked up from where she lay on the couch. "Looking at dress ideas for the Midnight Formal. I'm thinking full-on gothic."

"I was thinking of going with something white and sparkly," Amy said.

Mandy's eyes lit up. "Ooh, it could be a theme. You could be like, the good witch, and I'll be the bad witch."

Amy laughed. "I love it."

"Consider me the Good Witch of the South," Talia said. "I've got my pink dress picked out already. Do you have any ideas yet, Nadine?"

I shook my head. Lucas looked oddly uncomfortable with all the dress talk.

"I'll figure something out," I said. "In the meantime, I have a meeting with Verla today."

Talia's spine straightened. Isa grabbed ahold of the string with her paw and ripped it out of Talia's hands. She barely noticed. "Uh oh. Does that mean another sabotage?"

I crossed my arms and smirked. "I was thinking so. Except this time, maybe we could be the ones doing the sabotage."

Mandy beamed as she stood and gave me a salute. "We're on it, girl."

Talia and Amy jumped to their feet. "You don't have to worry about Chloe," Talia promised. "Go have fun at your lesson."

"Wait," I said. "You mean I don't get to watch?"

Talia frowned. "That would beat the point of distracting her for your lesson."

I made a face. "True. Any ideas?"

Amy stepped forward and patted me on the shoulder. "You let us take care of that."

"You guys are the best." I reached out to hug each of them in turn, then turned back to Lucas.

"Are you ready?" he asked.

I took a deep breath. "Yep. Let's get this over with."

Lucas took my hand and walked me to Headmistress Verla's office. Isa followed at my feet. She seemed to sense my discomfort. The whole time, I kept watch for Chloe, but I didn't see her anywhere. Maybe she'd finally given up.

I knocked on Verla's office.

"Come in," she called.

Lucas stood guard outside while I stepped inside.

Verla shot me a kind smile, but she wasn't the only one there. Professor Daymond, the jerk who'd called me a half-blood, sat in one of the chairs next to her desk. He barely looked my way.

"I hope I'm not interrupting," I said as Isa and I approached the desk. "I'm here for my lesson."

Verla gestured to the chair next to Professor Daymond. "You're not interrupting anything at all. In fact, we were waiting for you."

I couldn't keep the disgust from my voice. "What's *he* doing here?"

"I'm here to help," he replied in a less than friendly tone. Something told me he wasn't very interested in helping me.

I sat but remained at the edge of my seat. "How?"

Isa looked to Odin, who was perched on a cat tower beside Verla's desk. She gave a low growl, then jumped into my lap. I stroked her to calm her down, but she kept throwing glances at Odin.

"I'd like to start where we left off last time," Verla said. "I've invited Professor Daymond here to help run us through some scenarios. Hopefully we won't be interrupted."

"I think we'll be okay," I told her. I trusted my friends to deal with Chloe.

Verla straightened in her chair. "Excellent. As you know, an Evoking Ceremony tests your emotional state. Everyone is tested differently, based on their strengths and weaknesses. I thought we could talk about that before we try out some scenarios."

I looked to Professor Daymond, who held his nose high. I wasn't really interested in talking about my strengths and weaknesses in front of him.

I scratched Isa behind the ears to keep my hands busy. "Isn't that, um... kind of private?"

"Well, yes, but—" Verla started, but Professor Daymond spoke at the same time.

"You want to pass your Evoking Ceremony, don't you?" he sneered.

What a prick.

"Yes," I said.

"Then let's get on with it," Professor Daymond said.

Verla looked a little shocked by his tone, but she brushed it off. She picked up a tablet on her desk and began scrolling through it. "Nadine, I want you to rate the following statements from one to five, one being strongly disagree, and five being strongly agree."

"Okay." That didn't seem too hard.

Verla cleared her throat and began reading off the list of questions. *"When I see someone being bullied, I feel the need to step in."*

"Five," I answered automatically.

Verla pressed her tablet, then moved on to the next question.

"I find it easy to forgive other people."

I thought about that for a moment. "Um... four."

"I often feel like other people don't like me."

"One," I said. I was a joy to be around.

"I get envious of other people easily."

I paused for a moment. Usually, I'd answer one to this question—strongly disagree. But I couldn't help but recall how I felt when I saw Lena kissing Lucas.

"Three," I decided on.

Verla went on like this for at least another fifteen minutes. Most of the questions I felt pretty comfortable with. Professor Daymond's lips pressed into a thinner and thinner line as the minutes ticked by. It was almost like he was unhappy I wasn't a total train wreck.

It wasn't until Verla neared the end that I started to feel the questions weighing on me. "*I find it easy to bounce back from hardship,*" she said.

My stomach twisted into knots. I *wanted* it to be true, but I'd be lying if I said it was.

"Two," I told her.

Professor Daymond seemed pleased by that, though I didn't know why. Wasn't he supposed to *support* his students?

"*My moods are greatly affected by my situation,*" Verla continued.

"Five," I answered. I mean, who *wasn't* affected by their situation?

"*I feel lonely when my loved ones aren't around.*"

My gut sank at the mention of *loved ones*. All I could think about was my parents, and Verla's statement felt shockingly true in that moment. I sank deeper into my seat.

"Five," I said in a small voice.

Verla eyed me, like she sensed my discomfort. "Just one more, Nadine. *Memories of the people I've lost upset me.*"

Okay, now it felt like she was doing it on purpose.

"Of course memories upset me," I said, suddenly feeling very defensive. "I mean, who wouldn't be upset by losing someone?"

Verla kept her eyes on the tablet. Her expression didn't give anything away. "So, where would you rate that?"

I hesitated, though I knew the answer. Finally, I spoke so soft I wasn't sure she heard me. "Five."

Verla took a deep breath and set the tablet aside. "I think it's clear what we need to work on."

"What's that?" I asked, a little scared to hear the answer.

Verla gave me a sympathetic look. "Your grief."

My breath halted. I knew I had work to do, but the way she said it… it was like I shouldn't be allowed to feel this way. But I should! I lost my parents, for Alora's sake.

Unless… unless Mother Miriam didn't want people like me in the coven.

"Am I not allowed to grieve?" I asked in a small voice.

"Of course you are," Verla said kindly. "But you can't shove it aside. You must work through it."

I didn't want to. I wasn't ready.

"And I have to do that before my ceremony?" I asked.

Verla nodded. "Mother Miriam will test your weaknesses."

My bottom lip quivered. It felt as if the air was being sucked from the room. "So, if I can't get over it by then, that's it? I'm banished?"

I couldn't be! This was the only place where I had family and friends. I wasn't leaving the coven.

"Relax, Nadine," Verla said softly. "I'm not asking you to get over it. All I'm asking for is progress."

"But I'm not ready." My voice cracked.

Beside me, Professor Daymond smirked, like he was getting great joy out of this. What the fuck was his problem?

"You must try," Verla said. "You must trust that Mother Miriam has a plan. If you don't show her that you're willing to change, your magic won't come."

Headmistress Verla was really starting to scare me. How could I be asked to get over my parent's death so quickly? Surely, Mother Miriam would understand.

Yet part of me feared she wouldn't.

I swallowed. "I'll do anything to pass my ceremony."

"Then let's try our first scenario." Headmistress Verla gestured to Professor Daymond. "Professor Daymond is a unique type of Mentalist. He can imprint pictures into your mind. It's a lot like the visions you'll see during your Evoking Ceremony."

I turned to him, clutching the armrests of the chair so hard my knuckles turned white. I had to believe he was here to help me, because there was no alternative. Either he helped me get past this block, or I failed Mother Miriam's test.

That wasn't an option. I'd do anything to stay here with Grammy, Lucas, Grant and Talia.

"Okay," I said, my voice strong. "How does this work?"

Professor Daymond reached out a hand. "My powers work through touch."

I hesitated. "Is it just visions, then? Or can you see other things in my mind?"

I wasn't about to let this stranger poke around in my head.

"I can project visions using memories of your past," Professor Daymond explained. "But I can't see anything you don't want me to see."

"It's perfectly safe, Nadine," Headmistress Verla assured me.

I trusted her, and I really wanted to pass my ceremony, so I placed my hand in his.

Immediately, the room around me disappeared. Instead, I stood at the edge of the road. It was nighttime, with nothing but the moon and stars above to light the landscape. Forest surrounded me at several angles, save for a clearing that gave way to a cliff. Below that spanned a large lake. The road curved along the outer edge of the lake, and a guardrail bordered the edge of the cliff.

I glanced around. There was no motion, no sound.

"I don't get it," I called out to the darkness. I didn't know if I said the words aloud, but I sensed that Professor Daymond could hear me.

I waited another beat, and then I heard the sound of a vehicle approaching at high speed. The headlights flickered past trees in the forest, and the vehicle twisted and turned with the road. I expected the driver to slow, but they didn't. They just kept picking up speed. I knew that if they didn't hit the brakes soon, they wouldn't make it past the turn I stood at.

I have to stop this, I thought.

That was the answer to the test, right? Professor Daymond wanted to see if I'd save them.

Except there wasn't anything I could do. There wasn't enough time. I began running up the road. My heart slammed against my rib cage. I began to wave my hands in the air.

"Slow down!" I cried, even though the driver couldn't hear me. "There's a turn up ahead. You won't make it!"

The car sped by me so fast that it was there and gone in the blink of an eye.

"No!" I cried hopelessly, running out into the middle of the road as I watched the car speed away.

Horror struck when I spotted the license plate. It was so familiar, and it left this gaping hole in my heart. Professor Daymond had dug into memories he shouldn't have!

"Mom! Dad!" I screamed.

I could hardly hear the sound of my own voice over the screech of the tires. Red brake lights lit up the night—a color that I sensed would haunt me for many nights to come.

It was already too late. The car lost control and slammed into the guard rail. My stomach ached so badly, it was like the car had hit *me*.

The guard rail crumpled like a piece of paper, and the car launched over top of it.

"STOP!" I screeched. I threw my hands over my ears, but the sound of my parents' screams filled the vision. I heard the car hit the water, and then… silence.

My ears rang, and my vision blurred. I didn't want to witness the aftermath, but my feet moved beneath me involuntarily. I stumbled toward the edge of the cliff. Somehow, I made it to the guard rail, and my hands splayed across the cool metal to steady myself. I leaned over to look, but I couldn't bring myself to do it. Bile rose to my throat as I squeezed my eyes tightly shut.

"Stop it!" I cried. "I want out. Get me out of here!"

"Nadine? Nadine!" Verla's voice sounded just feet away from me.

I felt the weight of Isa in my lap again, and I opened my eyes to see I was back in Verla's office. Sobs bubbled out of my throat, and my head pounded.

Verla shot Professor Daymond a hard look, but he wore an expression of indifference.

"That was horrible," I spat.

"What did you do, Professor Daymond?" Verla demanded.

"My job," he told her simply, before turning to me. "Believe me, Miss Evers. If you can't handle a simple vision such as this one, you won't pass your Evoking Ceremony."

My hands trembled. "I doubt Mother Miriam would be so heartless. That's not something *anyone* should ever witness."

Professor Daymond smirked. "This just goes to show you're not ready, Miss Evers."

I shot out of my chair so fast that Isa fell to the ground. "Who are *you* to judge that?" I snapped. "You're cruel!"

"Nadine, calm down," Headmistress Verla said softly. "Let's discuss what happened."

I opened my mouth, but nothing except a sob came out. I covered my mouth with my hand. I thought closing my eyes would help get rid of the image I'd just seen, but it only made it worse. The vision of the car falling off the road assaulted me. Then came flashes of other memories—real memories. I saw the caskets, then the gravestones, then the empty house.

Even if I wanted to talk about it, I couldn't. My chest wound so tightly that I couldn't get a word out.

"Nadine?" Headmistress Verla pressed.

All I could do was shake my head. This was so embarrassing. I just wanted to hide in a hole. It felt like I was being buried in one already.

"I'm sorry," I managed to get out. "I-I can't."

I whirled around and ran for the door. Isa followed at my feet as I flung the door open and stormed out of the room.

"Nadine!" Headmistress Verla called, but I ignored her.

Lucas was leaning against the wall outside her office. I'd almost forgotten he was waiting for me.

He straightened when he saw me and reached out for my arms. "Nad, what's wrong?"

I heard the sound of Headmistress Verla's heels against the carpet, and I knew she was on her way across the room to follow me.

I grabbed Lucas's hand. "Let's go."

Lucas didn't inquire any further. He followed me as we rushed away from Verla's office. It wasn't until we turned two other halls and I was certain we'd lost her that I finally slowed. Isa purred and rubbed herself against my leg.

Lucas turned to me and took my face in his hands. "Nad, what happened?"

I wiped my nose and sniffled. I tried to keep my voice steady, but it cracked. "Professor Daymond showed me a vision. It was supposed to be like one of Mother Miriam's tests, but it was awful."

Lucas frowned. "I'm so sorry, Nad."

I took a breath, but I could hardly breathe. "Lucas, he made me watch my parents die."

His eyes went wide, then he wrapped me into a tight hug. His spicy scent surrounded me, and his chest felt warm against my cheek. After a few moments, I felt like I could breathe again.

"I wish I could make it better, Nad," Lucas whispered.

"You *are* making it better," I replied. "Just being here with me is enough."

My heart rate slowed, and I finally drew away to look up at him. "I'm sorry I freaked out. I didn't mean to."

"Don't apologize," Lucas said. "You're allowed to feel upset over this."

I sniffled and wiped my nose again. "Yeah, but if I can't handle this, how am I going to handle the ceremony?"

Lucas squeezed my hands. "One step at a time, Nadine."

The sound of heavy sobs came from down the hall. Lucas and I looked up to see Amy and Mandy walking our way. Mandy was hunched over and sobbing uncontrollably, while Amy supported her.

"How did this happen?" Mandy wailed.

"I don't know." Amy's voice cracked. "We're going to get answers. We just need—"

Amy lifted her gaze, and she stopped dead in her tracks when she spotted Lucas and me. Her eyes widened, and her jaw dropped. She looked like she'd seen a ghost.

I glanced around the hall briefly, wondering if she really *had* seen a ghost. The hall was empty.

"Hey, guys," I said. "What's wrong—?"

I barely got the question out before Mandy squealed and raced over to me.

"Nadine!" She flung her arms around my neck and drew me close.

Amy came up beside her and pulled me into a group hug. "Goddess, Nadine! You're okay!"

I drew away from them. Lucas looked just as confused as I was.

"I'm fine," I assured them. "What's going on?"

Amy and Mandy exchanged a grave look.

My face fell. "What did Chloe do this time?"

Mandy wiped her tears. "We're not sure if it was her, but considering you're standing right here..."

Lucas crossed his arms impatiently. "Will you guys tell us what's going on?"

Amy hesitated. "It's probably better if we show you. Just… don't freak out."

Yeah, because that was *totally* the way to stop me from freaking out.

"We can't make any promises," I told them.

Amy and Mandy led us toward the foyer. When we got there, we saw that the front doors were open. Cold air rushed into the room, and the flames in the fireplace flickered. A huge crowd had gathered outside, and we couldn't see anything beyond them.

I craned my neck. "What's going on?"

Mandy took my arm. "Come on. They'll make way for us."

Mandy led me out the front doors and through the crowd. People murmured quietly, but they went dead silent when their eyes turned toward me. The sound of a woman's wail traveled across the yard. Above us, the clouds were dark, and the air was so cold it made me shiver.

"Mandy, what's going—?"

I stopped dead in my tracks. The crowd parted enough that I finally caught a glimpse of what was happening. Two figures knelt at the base of a large oak tree. They were both sobbing. That's when I realized the wailing was coming from Talia.

For a split second, I didn't realize why she was crying, or why Grant was next to her, trying to comfort her. Then my gaze lifted, and I saw what everyone was staring at.

I saw the boots first—black boots, just like mine. Then came the ripped skinny jeans, then the leather jacket, and then finally… my own face.

I didn't know how it was happening, but my body hung from a noose in the tree. I was standing right here, and yet my lifeless body was spinning in the tree. Isa hissed and ducked behind me.

I got so suddenly nauseous that I could hardly stand. I braced myself against Lucas, but he seemed equally weak on his feet. He turned his gaze away from the hanging body and kept his eyes on me. I was almost certain I'd just witnessed my own death, but it didn't make any sense.

"It isn't real, Nad," he said, but it sounded more like he was trying to convince himself.

"Is this another test?" I asked. "Did I ever leave the vision?"

"This is real," he assured me, gesturing between the two of us. "We're standing here for sure. But whatever *that* is…" He pointed to the hanging corpse, but wouldn't look at it. "That's not you."

"Then how is this happening?" I asked, my heart racing. I wasn't sure which was worse—watching my parents die, or seeing myself hanging from a noose. Both were equally horrifying.

"I don't know," Lucas whispered.

I swallowed hard and looked back to Talia and Grant. Their backs were to us, so they hadn't spotted us. It broke my heart to hear Talia cry like that.

"Give me a minute." I stepped away from Lucas and walked over to Talia. I didn't know how to break the news to her that I was still alive. I feared I'd only scare her, but she had to know this wasn't real.

I stopped behind her and cleared my throat. Grant turned first, but he more or less looked *through* me. He turned back to Talia to comfort her, before doing a quick double take.

"Nadine!?" he cried.

Talia turned, and her sobs instantly ceased. She went totally still, like she couldn't believe what she was seeing. After a moment to let it sink in, her gaze darted between me—the real Nadine—and the other me—the fake, dead Nadine.

Her eyes grew wide, and she scrambled to her feet. "Nadine! What's going on?"

"I could ask you the same thing," I told her.

She threw her arms around my neck and hugged me so tight it practically choked me.

Grant got to his feet beside her and wiped the tears from his face. "We thought—"

"I know," I said, cutting him off. I didn't want to hear him finish that sentence. "But I'm here."

Talia's eyes darkened, and she looked out toward the crowd, who still hadn't taken their eyes off us. There must've been a hundred people gathered around, like my life was some sort of freak show.

"Who did this?" Talia demanded. I'd never heard her talk in such a loud, stern voice.

Nobody responded. They all looked as shell-shocked as we did. Isa growled at the onlookers.

Mandy's nostrils flared. "You fuckers better start talking!"

She stomped up to the nearest guy, whose face was hidden in his jacket. She grabbed the back of his hood and yanked it down, then got up in his face. "Are you enjoying this, Gregory?"

He was a lanky guy with glasses and messy hair. His hands instantly shot up in surrender, and he cowered away from her. "I don't know anything, I swear."

Lucas crossed his arms and loomed over Gregory. "What do you know about this kind of magic?"

"Nothing!" he repeated. "I said I don't know anything."

A muscle popped in Lucas's jaw. "Come on, Gregory. You know everything."

Gregory's eyes twinkled for a second, like he appreciated the compliment, but it was gone a moment later. He shot a dark look at Mandy, who still had a tight hold on his hood. "Let me go and I'll talk."

Mandy narrowed her eyes at him, then finally dropped him. As Gregory straightened out his jacket, Mandy looked out to the rest of the crowd.

"Well?" she growled. "What are you all still doing here? Show's over!"

The crowd started to disperse. We turned back toward Gregory, awaiting his explanation.

"M-my guess is it's an illusion," Gregory stammered. "It's the only explanation."

"Witches can't cast illusions," Lucas stated bluntly.

"No, but the Arcanea can," Gregory reminded him. "The school's got enchanted objects from all over the world. I wouldn't be surprised if they had a fae object from Malovia that could do this sort of thing."

"But why would anyone want to make it look like Nadine…?" Grant started to ask, but he trailed off. The six of us looked at each other, and it was as if we all already knew the answer.

Talia's hands curled into fists, and her nostrils flared. "*Chloe*," she snarled, like the name was poison.

"I thought you guys were keeping an eye on her," I said.

"We *were*," Talia replied. "Then this happened, and…"

Her eyes locked on something toward the front doors, and her features darkened. I turned to see the Lucky Three standing in the open doorway. Chloe's hands were on her hips, and she stared toward the oak tree with unadulterated pride on her face. I bet she fucking *loved* watching my friends and I squirm like this.

Chloe's proud stance lasted only a moment, just long enough for us to spot her and pin her as the evil mastermind behind the illusion. Once her eyes connected with mine, she turned back into the school, her two side bitches following behind her.

Amy gasped from behind me, and I turned to see the illusion was gone. A stuffed dummy hung from the tree, but my face was no longer on it. It wore clothes like mine, but that was it. There was no hair or face—just stuffed canvas.

"She's not going to get away with this!" Talia yelled. She started across the lawn faster than any of the rest of us could react.

We hurried behind her, but Talia sprinted so quickly she was inside the school before I made it halfway back. When the rest of us reached the doors, Talia was running up the grand staircase behind Chloe. She flung herself forward and grabbed Chloe around the neck, then yanked her back.

My hands flew over my mouth as the two went tumbling down the stairs. Gasps traveled around the crowd that continued to linger. The two girls landed at the bottom of the stairs, but Talia barely seemed fazed. She scrambled to her knees and pulled her arm back, like she was about to pummel Chloe's face.

But her fist never made it. She just froze.

Her face contorted in anger, like freezing up wasn't of her own free will.

"You think you can threaten my best friend like that!?" Talia shrieked. "You think you can go around doing whatever you—*who the fuck is doing this to me!?*"

Several things happened at once. Grant, Lucas, and I rushed over to Talia the same time Ryan stepped forward with a proud smirk on his face. He held his hands up toward Talia, and I knew he was the one controlling her. Poor Talia was so petite that she wasn't strong enough to push past his telekinetic hold. Before I reached her, Ryan twitched his wrist, and Talia's fist shifted course, slamming straight into her nose.

At that, the room broke into utter chaos. Chloe scrambled backward, laughing like a maniac. I grabbed Talia and dragged her behind the stairs, and Isa followed. Grant threw his arms out around us and acted like a human shield. I couldn't really see what else was going on, though I saw purple sparks erupt from Lucas's hands.

Screams filled the foyer, and footsteps pounded above us on the stairs as students scattered. I heard the sound of glass breaking and people screaming. The sound of cats screeching and hissing came from all angles. Isa crouched in front of me, like she was standing guard. Her tail stood on end, and a low growl came from her throat.

A figure ran from the fight and ducked beneath the stairs with us. I didn't realize who it was at first until he spoke.

"Talia, babe. You okay?" Cody pushed past Grant and cradled Talia in his arms.

She curled into him. "I'm fine. But I need to get back out there and kick Chloe's pretty little—"

"No," Cody said sternly. "I'm not letting you go back out there."

Grant shot Cody a look of disdain. My heart hammered. I wanted to get back out there, too. I couldn't let Lucas fight by himself. I started to get up, but Grant grabbed my hand.

"Nadine, stop. You don't have magic."

"I have to do *something!*" I didn't care what it was. All I wanted was to get back at Chloe.

I ripped my arm out of Grant's grip and rushed out from beneath the stairs before he could catch me. My eyes locked on Chloe, who'd ducked into the corner. I barely noticed magic flying around me as I stomped over to her. She didn't notice me at first, as she was preoccupied by the fight, but I sure as hell got her attention when I grabbed her by the shirt and shoved her up against the wall. Isa came streaking out from under the stairs after me. She stood at my feet and hissed at Chloe.

"What the hell is your problem?" I snapped. "Come after *me.* Don't hurt my *friends.*"

Chloe shoved me, and I stumbled back a few steps. "Get off me, bitch!"

"*I'm* the bitch!?" I snapped. "I didn't start this!"

"You did!" she yelled. "The second you came to Octavia Falls."

"I didn't do anything to you," I growled.

"You didn't have to," she spat. "It started long before either of us were born."

Was she fucking serious?

"I know our grandpas had it in for each other, but that's no reason for you to act so evil," I snarled. "There's enough room in Octavia Falls for both of us."

"That's just it, Nadine!" she screamed. "There *isn't* enough room for the both of us. That's why you need to leave!"

She shoved me again, and I shoved her back harder.

"I'm not going anywhere," I promised.

"You really want to risk it?" she asked harshly. "How badly do you want to die for this?"

My eyebrows shot up. "Die for it? What, you're going to *kill* me if I don't leave?"

She glared at me. I'd never seen so much hatred in someone's eyes before. "*Someone* has to die. Don't you get it, Nadine? Once we both go through with our Evoking Ceremonies, that's it. That's all the time we have. One of us has to leave."

"Why!?" I yelled. "What has you so fucking terrified of me?"

"*We're cursed!*"

Chloe's words stopped my heart. I swayed on my feet, but I barely had a chance to process what she said before another voice boomed throughout the foyer.

"EVERYBODY STOP!!!"

Chloe and I both turned to see Professor Richards standing in the center of the room. He held up a large vial of green liquid. Everyone had gone totally still. Ryan and Lucas both had each other by the collar, and they'd stopped with their fists pulled back. Amy and Mandy were on the ground with Camille and Gwen. Mandy had a fistful of Gwen's white hair, and Amy had twisted Camille's arm around her back.

All eyes turned to Professor Richards.

"Make one more move, and I'll set off this sleeping potion on the whole room," he threatened in a stern voice.

Nobody said a thing. All I heard was the click of heels down the hall, then Headmistress Verla stepped into the foyer. She wore a look of utter disapproval. It was so intense it could cut straight through you. For a moment, she actually sort of scared me.

"Everyone back to your dorms," she commanded. "*Now.*"

People started to hurry up the stairs and scatter in either direction. Chloe stomped past me, purposely slamming her shoulder into mine on the way. I moved slowly, still trying to grasp what she'd said.

I was cursed.

Why had Grammy hidden this from me? Why had she written it off as some dead feud?

I ended up in the back of the crowd. Ahead of me, Cody was helping Talia up the stairs, while Grant glared from behind them. Amy and Mandy made faces at Gwen and Camille while they headed back to their room. Isa joined me at my feet.

Lucas found his way over to me. A bruise was forming beneath his eye, but his knuckles looked raw, like he'd gotten in a few good punches. Shit. I didn't want this for him. I didn't want him getting hurt because of me.

"You okay, Nad?" he asked softly.

I swallowed. I couldn't lie to him. Today had been one shit show after another. I was beyond exhausted.

"There's something I need to tell you," I whispered under my breath. I didn't want to tell him about the curse out in the open, though.

"Nadine?" Headmistress Verla cocked an eyebrow in my direction. She looked less than happy.

I scooped Isa into my arms, then looked to Lucas. "Come with me."

We walked over to Verla. The room had been cleared out, so no one heard us.

Verla placed her hands on her hips, like a mother disappointed in her children. "What happened here?"

Though she looked at Lucas and me with tight lips, I realized she wasn't mad at *me*. She'd asked me over because she trusted me to tell her the truth.

"It was a prank, Headmistress," I told her. "Someone used illusion magic to make it look as if there was a dead body hanging from the tree outside. People got upset, and a fight broke out."

I didn't know why I didn't tell her it'd been my body hanging from the tree. Something didn't feel right about telling her about Chloe and me. If Chloe got in trouble for it, it'd only make things worse between us, and they were bad enough already.

Verla breathed a heavy sigh, like she couldn't deal with such pettiness today. "Very well. You may return to your dorms."

Lucas and I turned, but Verla stopped us once more.

"Oh, and Nadine?"

I stopped to look at her. "Yes?"

Her shoulders fell. "I'm very sorry about earlier. We'll get this worked out, and you'll pass your Evoking Ceremony."

I nodded, though deep down in my gut, I wasn't sure. I only had a few weeks left. On top of it, there was this curse Chloe just told me about.

"You don't look well, Nad," Lucas pointed out as we climbed the stairs. "Is there anything I can do?"

"No," I told him. "But there's something *I* have to do."

"What is it?" he asked. "Let me help."

I shook my head. "I have to do this by myself. My grandmother has some explaining to do."

☽

"NADINE." Grammy sounded pleased to see me when I arrived at her house that night. "What a pleasure!"

"Cut the crap, Grammy," I snapped.

She gaped at me. "Is something wrong?"

I narrowed my eyes at her. "You could say that."

Grammy's eyes widened in concern, and she stepped aside to let me in. She gestured to the living room, but I just stood there in the hallway, my arms crossed. I felt weak on my feet, but I was too angry to sit down. Cornelius rubbed up against my leg, but I wasn't interested in his affection.

"What's wrong?" Grammy asked.

"Why didn't you tell me about the curse?" I demanded.

Grammy's features immediately darkened. She looked pissed that I'd brought it up. "I didn't tell you because there *is* no curse, Nadine."

"Then why does Chloe Olson insist there is?" I shot back. "I knew you were hiding something from me the last time I mentioned her."

Grammy sighed. "Nadine, please sit down and let me explain."

I threw my hands up. "I don't *want* to sit down. I want you to tell me everything."

"I will," Grammy promised. "Let's talk about it over a cup of tea."

Please. Like I wanted *tea* right now.

Grammy's lips tightened. "Sit *down*, Nadine."

She spoke in a tone I'd never heard her use before. I felt like I had no choice but to sit. It seemed to be the only way I was getting answers.

While I stepped into the living room, Grammy went down the hall to brew us some tea. I was fuming so badly I could hardly sit still, which was saying something considering how exhausted I was.

Assumptions raced around in my head while I waited for Grammy to return. Did Grammy *want* the curse to hurt me? Did she think I was better off dead?

Or had Chloe been lying to me?

Somehow, I doubted that.

Grammy returned to the living room with a tray. She set it on the coffee table, then pushed a cup of tea into my hands. "Drink, Nadine."

I started to sip it, and I noticed my anger begin to wane immediately. I realized what horrible things I'd just thought about Grammy, and it killed me to think them. She loved me to death. Surely she had a good reason for not telling me.

Suddenly, I felt angry for a different reason. I set my cup back on the table and glared at her. "If you're going to serve someone a potion, you should probably tell them first."

"It's nothing more than a calming tea," Grammy assured me.

My lips tightened. "Forgive me if I'm having a hard time trusting you right now."

Grammy straightened in her chair. "Look, Nadine. I'm not going to lie to you. There *was* a curse."

Well, at least she was starting to be honest with me.

"What was the curse, exactly?" I asked. "What were our grandparents fighting over?"

Grammy took a long breath before diving into the story. "Years ago, when I was pregnant with your mother, your grandfather served on the Imperium Council. He was the last Curse Breaker and the only male to ever serve. Chloe's grandfather stole a valuable item from the council, and though he denied it, the two of them fought over it. Chloe's grandfather wanted to get rid of yours, so he cast a curse upon him and his descendants. This curse would allow only one of the families from each generation to remain in Octavia Falls. The other either had to leave… or die."

"Wait…" The pieces began falling into place. "Is that how Grampy died?"

Grammy's eyes watered. "Nadine… your grandfather was murdered. Chloe's grandfather killed him."

The air left my lungs. "Mom didn't leave the coven for my dad, did she?"

Grammy shook her head regrettably. "She left to outrun the curse."

"How exactly does this curse work?" I asked.

Grammy sighed. "According to what your mother learned before she left, the curse only touches you once you're accepted into the coven. Since you haven't gone through with your Evoking Ceremony yet, it can't hurt you."

"But it has," I argued. "Grammy, it's been there my whole life. I can feel it inside me."

Grammy dropped her gaze. I'd never seen her look so guilty.

"Why didn't you tell me?" I demanded. "Why would you keep any of this from me?"

"Because the curse is over, Nadine!" Grammy cried.

"How do you know that?" I asked. Chloe sure seemed to think it was alive and well.

Grammy's breath caught. "I refuse to believe your grandfather died without breaking it. He was a Curse Breaker."

"Oh my God..." I pressed my hand to my forehead. She was seriously basing this off... nothing?

"Why would you even take this chance?" I snapped at her. "If this could cost me my life—"

"It's going to cost me my granddaughter!" she erupted. "I already lost my husband and my daughter. I'm not going to lose you, too!"

The room went dead silent.

After a few moments, I finally spoke. "It wasn't right of you to hide this from me, Grammy. You have no proof that the curse was broken."

"And you don't know it wasn't," she said softly.

"Is that something you really want to risk?" I asked. I was offended she'd play with my life like some sort of slot machine. "The curse isn't broken, Grammy. And I think deep down, you know that."

Grammy's face paled, and her voice quivered. Slowly, she rose to her feet and came over to sit beside me on the couch. Her eyes watered, and a pang of guilt hit me. I felt bad about lashing out at her.

"Nadine, I'm sorry I didn't tell you," she said softly. "It was selfish of me. All that really matters is that you're safe. Can you forgive me?"

I hesitated. "I want to, but..."

My unspoken words hung in the air. *But she broke my trust.*

Grammy reached up and pulled a chain out from beneath her shirt. An antique skeleton key I'd never seen before hung from around her neck. It looked really old, and had a pretty swirly design on the end.

"I want you to have this," she said.

I furrowed my brow. "What does it go to?"

"It's not what it goes to," she told me. "It's what it does. I've worn this key for over forty years. Your grandfather gave it to me just before he died, in the midst of his feud against Jeb Olson. He said it was enchanted to protect the owner."

"Is that true?" I asked. "Is it really enchanted?"

"It's served me thus far," Grammy answered. "I should've given it to your mother ages ago. I want it to protect you now, Nadine. I can't lose you. You're all I have left."

She pulled the necklace over her head and handed it to me. My heart warmed at the kind gesture, and I wrapped the key tightly in my hand.

"This should protect you from the curse," Grammy said, though she looked uncertain.

Silence settled between us, until I finally spoke. "What happens once I go through with my ceremony?"

"*If* the curse is still alive, you have until Chloe goes through with hers, since you two are the only descendants of your generation."

"And if we both joined the coven?" I asked. "How long would we have?"

"Your mother guessed a month, tops," Grammy said. "But she didn't stay that long. She left the night of her ceremony."

"My ceremony is before Chloe's," I pointed out. "That puts me at an advantage."

Chloe would have to forfeit her own ceremony if she wanted to stay. Otherwise she'd be submitting to a game of Russian Roulette with this curse. The only other option was to kill me and save herself, but she hadn't done it yet. To be honest, I didn't think she had it in her.

"Please don't leave me like your mother did," Grammy whispered.

"I won't," I promised. "I'm going through with my Evoking Ceremony. I'm going to pass, and I'm going to show Chloe that I belong here."

If anything, she'd be the one that would have to leave. Because I wasn't going to.

C·

THE FOLLOWING NIGHT, I couldn't sleep, even though I was really tired. After I told Lucas about the curse, all I wanted to do was be by him because he made me feel better about the whole thing. My heart yearned to be in his presence, and I couldn't stand to let my hunger for him go unchecked.

To hell with it. I was going to be spontaneous tonight.

I crawled out of bed as quietly as I could so I wouldn't wake Talia. I changed into a swimsuit, grabbed a towel, and then quietly left the room. I tiptoed down the dark, quiet hall and stopped at Lucas's door. I knocked lightly, but no answer came, so I tried again.

A few moments later, the door swung open. A sharp breath passed my lips when I saw him standing there. He wore nothing but sweats that hung off his hips in a way that made me want to drool. His abs were freaking amazing. I just wanted to reach out and touch them. His hair was tousled and looked really sexy. Just seeing him standing there shirtless did things to my body I couldn't control.

"What's this?" he teased in a low whisper so he wouldn't wake Grant. "A booty call?"

I laughed lightly. "No. Did I wake you?"

He shook his head. "Nah, couldn't sleep."

"Me either," I admitted. "I'm going swimming and wondering if you wanted to come along."

He hesitated. "The pool's closed this time of night."

I shrugged. "You think that's going to stop me?"

"Um… it should," he said, sounding equally curious and confused.

"Well, if you don't want to come, I'll just go myself," I said.

I turned from the door and started down the hall, but I was totally bluffing. I knew he wouldn't be able to resist his curiosity.

"Wait, Nad," he hissed.

I smiled brightly and turned back to him. "You're coming?"

He groaned, though he didn't sound upset. "Hold on a minute."

Lucas ducked back into the room and changed into his swim trunks, then grabbed a towel. He emerged looking hella sexy. The light from the sconces along the wall accented the hills and valleys of his abs. It took all I had not to stare.

"What?" he asked innocently.

I forced my gaze away from him, hoping he hadn't seen me blush. "Nothing. Let's go."

Lucas and I tiptoed quietly down the stairs and to the rec center. The door was locked, but all it took was one tiny incantation from Lucas, and we were in. The air was warm and thick inside, but it felt really good. The room was dark, but a light streak of moonlight came in through the tall windows that faced the forest, glistening off the water.

"Do they have some sort of magical alarm system for this?" I asked, though I didn't really care. The threat of getting caught was all part of the fun.

Lucas shrugged. "Security isn't a huge deal around here. Most people aren't brazen enough to sneak in."

"I'm *brazen*?" I teased as I dropped my towel on one of the pool chairs.

Lucas laughed and tickled me in the side. "Why do you think I like you?"

My heart fluttered at those words. I mean, I already knew he liked me, but hearing him say it got me every time.

"Don't tickle me," I snickered. I reached out and tickled his side. An electric shock traveled through my fingertips and up my arm when I touched him. I didn't think that would ever get old.

"Hey!" Lucas cried, his voice echoing throughout the pool. "Tickle me again, and I'm throwing you in."

My jaw dropped dramatically. "You wouldn't dare!"

He cocked an eyebrow. "You wanna bet?"

I shrugged and tugged at the string on my robe. The flaps fell open, revealing my black bikini. Lucas's gazed dropped and roamed across my body. His eyes lingered on me a few moments, like I wouldn't notice.

"My eyes are up here, buddy," I joked, reaching out to tickle him again.

"Hey! I said no tickling," he teased. "That's it. I'm throwing you in."

I smirked. "You'll have to catch me first."

I started running away from him. Lucas caught me around the waist, and I yelped. My voice echoed through the room, as did Lucas's laughter.

"No!" I yelled through my laughs.

I locked my arms around Lucas's neck. He tried to throw me in, but I didn't let go. Instead, we both went tumbling down into the water together.

I held my breath as my head dipped below water. My feet touched the pool floor below me, and I pushed upward. My head broke the surface, and I inhaled a large breath. Lucas came up a second later, gasping.

"That's what you get," I laughed, splashing him.

"Hey!" he splashed me back.

That turned into a full-on splashing war. Our laughter filled the entire pool. I couldn't remember the last time I'd had this much fun.

"Your splash game is *weak*," I told him.

"Is it?" he challenged.

He kicked forward and glided through the water, until he was right in front of me. I tried to splash him, but he grabbed me around the middle and tossed me upward out of the water.

I screamed playfully as I went flying, then landed safely in the water a few feet away. "Not fair!" I cried, wiping my eyes.

"Totally fair," he countered.

I raised an eyebrow. "Oh, so we're playing dirty now?"

He smirked. "That's the only way to play, isn't it?"

That sounds like a challenge!

I ducked my head below water and swam forward, until my shoulder met his knee. I wrapped one arm around his leg, then pushed off the bottom of the pool. He was light in the water, but as more of his body got out of the water, he got really heavy. I pushed with all my might, until my head broke the water. Lucas flailed as he went tumbling backward, kicking up water.

I laughed uncontrollably as he shook the water from his hair. Droplets splashed my face, but I was having so much fun I didn't care.

"Come here," Lucas growled playfully.

I splashed him lightly. "Stay away."

He grabbed my arm and dragged me through the water. My laughter instantly died when he wrapped his arms around me. Suddenly, I felt really hot—like the water might start sizzling on my skin at any moment. Our chests pressed together, though he held my arms tight at my sides.

Lucas's gaze flickered down to my lips, and he spoke softly. "Try to get me now."

I struggled out of his hold and wrapped my arms around his neck. "I've already got you," I whispered.

Lucas chuckled under his breath, but I felt like we weren't joking around anymore. Images of the night at Lake Santos flashed through my mind. It felt like we were back there—holding each other, ready to kiss.

My breaths grew shallow, making my breasts rise and fall from the water rapidly. His gaze darted downward, first to the key around my neck, then to my breasts, before landing on my eyes again. My heart pummeled against my rib cage. Being this close to him made every nerve in my body come to life. I wondered if he could feel me shaking.

"So, what's this?" I asked. I didn't mean to lean closer to him, but I felt my lips magnetize to his. "Is this a continuation of where we left off at the lake?"

Lucas leaned closer. His lips were barely an inch from mine. His sweet, warm breath brushed across my cheek. My pulse quickened.

"I-I…" Lucas stuttered.

He sighed, shattering the whole moment. My heart dropped.

"I don't know, Nad," he finally said.

I drew away. "I thought you wanted this."

"I do," he said quickly. "But do *you*?"

Truth be told, I wanted Lucas so bad it hurt. Problem was, the future scared me. Would this relationship work if the Reaper's Shadow curse kept us at a distance?

I couldn't think about that. So I resolved to enjoying every moment with Lucas that I could.

"I don't know what the future holds," I admitted. "But I know that I want you right now."

Lucas's expression softened, like my words warmed his heart. I waved my hands through the water and stepped closer to him. With each step I took, he took a step away. It wasn't like he was running from me—more like he was giving me a choice to pursue him.

"Why worry about the future when all we need to do is live in the moment?" I questioned.

Lucas stilled when his back hit the edge of the pool. His breath wavered. "Because our choices in the moment affect the future, Nad."

I shrugged, like none of that mattered, though I knew deep down that it did. "Let's pretend like there is no Reaper's Shadow curse," I suggested. "What's a witch gotta do to get you to ask me out?"

Lucas sighed and hoisted himself up out of the pool to sit on the edge.

Water dripped from his dark hair, and the moonlight accented the deep shadows of his muscled chest.

He looked down at me with those bewitching green eyes, sending my heart pummeling against my rib cage. "Are you sure you want to be with me, Nad? You deserve to be happy."

"We can be happy together," I promised.

He raised a curious eyebrow. "How do you know?"

I pressed my hands to the edge of the pool on either side of him and pushed myself upward so that only my legs were in the water. My hips rested on the edge of the pool between his legs. Heat pooled between my thighs as I came in so close we were practically touching. Energy sizzled between us, and I saw it in the way he looked at me that he felt it, too. The sexual tension was palpable.

"Why don't you kiss me and find out?" I whispered.

A moment passed where I didn't know what might happen next. We felt frozen in time, and I held my breath.

Then Lucas's hand came up to cradle the back of my neck, and he drew me to him. My whole body felt like it was melting into the water as his warm lips moved over mine. My lips parted, and he deepened the kiss.

My arms suddenly became weak, and I lowered myself back into the water. That didn't stop Lucas from kissing me deeper, though. His lips never parted from mine as he followed me into the water. He took my face in his hands and ran his tongue over my bottom lip. I moaned as I wrapped my arms and legs around him, pressing myself so close to him that it should be a sin.

Lucas's hands roamed downward, until they were cupping my ass. I gasped and pressed my hips into him, until I could feel his erection pressing up against my most sensitive areas. My fingers trembled as I ran them through his hair. He made little noises of pleasure that sent waves of heat all over my body. A glorious high filled me, like I was mere meters away from cresting the top of a mountain. This was how it should be with us. This was what it should feel like to be with the person you loved. To be denied of that was a curse... literally.

I wanted more with Lucas—as much as I could possibly get. We were two lost souls who found each other in the darkness. Somehow, we had created a spark out of nothing. When he kissed me like this, it was as if the spark could never die. The very air he breathed was mine, and as long as we were together, the fire we shared could never die.

Boldly, I reached up and tugged on the string of my bikini top. The fabric fell away, and I pressed my exposed breasts to Lucas's chest. My nipples hardened beneath the coolness of the air.

Lucas's entire body quivered. I half expected him to draw away, to tell me to cover up and remind me we couldn't touch like this, but he didn't. Instead, his hands traveled up my body, before settling on the curve of my breasts.

My heart hammered so hard I was sure he could feel it. The air around us seemed heavy with hormones so thick I could hardly breathe. Lucas's hands massaged my breasts as mine tangled in his hair. Our lips moved in perfect sync as we made out passionately. The room spun around me so fast I didn't know which way was up or down. The only thing rooting me in place was Lucas's body against mine. We could've been making out for only a minute, or it could've been hours. All I knew was that it'd never be long enough.

Bang!

A noise like the slamming of a door startled the two of us apart. I grabbed for the fabric of my bikini and pressed it over my breasts. Lucas and I shared an expression of total horror.

"We should probably go," he suggested.

I quickly agreed as I tied my bikini back on. We jumped out of the water and gathered our things, then snuck quietly out of the pool. Lucas took my hand as we ducked through the shadows in the hall. We didn't see anyone, but we made our way back to the dorms slowly and carefully. My heart pounded in exhilaration. I didn't think either of us wanted to leave the other.

My heart sank when we arrived back at my dorm. I stuck my arms through the sleeves of my robe and draped my towel around my neck.

"That was a lot of fun," I whispered to Lucas. "It helped take my mind off things."

Lucas's face fell. "You mean the curse?"

I nodded.

"Any ideas what you're going to do about it?" he asked.

"I think it's pretty obvious," I replied. "Either me or Chloe has to leave Octavia Falls. I'm staying."

"You're playing a game of chicken, Nad," he pointed out. "Chloe's not going to cave."

"She's going to have to, because I won't," I promised.

Lucas frowned, like what he was about to say pained him. "Or she'll kill you."

I rolled my eyes. "If she was going to kill me, she'd have done it already."

Lucas's eyes roamed over me, and he took my hand. "Maybe you don't have to go through with your Evoking Ceremony. If you don't do it, the curse would never activate. You could stay."

"And then I'd never be a true member of the coven," I reminded him. "That's what Chloe wants. She wants to prove I don't belong. And I do, Lucas."

"I just want you to be safe," he said.

"This isn't up for discussion," I stated firmly. "My mind's made up."

Lucas sighed.

"Let's forget about that," I suggested, before wrapping him in my arms. "I don't want to ruin the amazing night we just had together."

Lucas pressed his nose into my hair. After a long moment of silence, he spoke. "What's your secret?"

"My secret?"

"Yeah. You're so positive lately. How do you do it?"

"I don't know. It might have something to do with this." I drew away and lifted the key around my neck.

"What is it?" he asked.

I shrugged. "Something my grandma gave me. It's supposed to be enchanted."

Lucas's eyebrows shot up. "Then it must be rare. We aren't so great at enchantments in the Miriamic Coven. Can I see it?"

"Go ahead."

He reached out and lifted the key in his hand. Though it was dark in the hall, he inspected it closely. As I watched his eyes roam over it, I saw something in them. It was like *he* needed protection. What from, I wasn't sure—whether it was from himself or some darker force. All I knew was Lucas seemed to need it more than I did.

I didn't realize what I was doing until I did it. I reached up and undid the clasp on my necklace. I started to fasten it around his neck.

"What are you doing?" he asked.

"I want you to wear it," I said.

"Nad, I can't," he declined, but I'd already placed it around his neck. "It's from your grandma."

"So?" I challenged. "You want to try being more positive? Let's see if it helps. I want you to have it."

"I can't," he insisted. He reached up to start taking it off, but I placed my hands on his to stop him. My skin tingled where I touched him.

I looked him straight in the eyes. "You know I don't take no for an answer. Consider it an early birthday present. It's yours."

Lucas relaxed. He came in close and pushed a strand of wet hair behind my ear. Butterflies danced around in my stomach. "Thank you, Nad."

Lucas just hovered there, neither of us wanting to move. He was barely a foot away, just staring down at me. My mouth grew dry as I awaited another kiss. I wished I could invite him inside, but Talia was sleeping.

I licked my lips, but my voice wavered. "Thank *you* for tonight. We should do it again some time. It'd be fun."

He nodded as his eyes roamed my face, before traveling down my body. He reached out and ran his fingers down the arm of my plush robe. "You know what else would be fun?"

My whole body trembled. I could think of quite a few things. "What?"

Lucas looked like he was holding his breath. Then all at once, the question spilled out of him. "Would you like to go to the Midnight Formal with me?"

I went speechless. Instead of jumping at the chance, I spat out like an idiot, "I… I thought you didn't dance."

He smiled sweetly. "I'd dance for you, Nad."

My heart never felt as warm as it did in that moment. Lucas made my heart sing in ways no one ever had before. That was when I knew—no matter the limitations, I wanted to spend my life with Lucas. I'd walk to the ends of the earth and back for him.

I became so overwhelmed with joy that all I could do was throw my arms around his neck to keep it from bursting out of me. "Yes, Lucas," I whispered. "I'll go to the dance with you."

I drew away and took his face in my hands. He looked down at me with a blissful expression in his eye.

I smiled back. "And I'll share every dance with you after."

His eyes widened, and he went breathless. "Is that a decision?"

I nodded eagerly. "Yes. I want to be with you."

Lucas wrapped me in his arms, and I felt so warm and safe there. "I'll find a way around this curse, Nad."

"I hope we can," I whispered back. "I'd do anything to be with you."

He shivered, but I thought it was a good shiver. "Anything?"

"Yes," I said. "Wouldn't you?"

He let out a deep sigh and pulled me tighter. "Absolutely."

NINETEEN

The night at the pool was the most fun I'd ever had. Kissing her like that was beyond incredible. I'd never kissed someone like that, and no one had ever kissed me back with such passion. And her breasts... oh my Goddess. There were no words. I could hardly believe she'd let me touch them. It felt like a dream.

But it was real, and I couldn't stop playing it over and over in my mind. Nadine wanted to be with me, no matter what.

She had no idea how much it meant to me that she was willing to give up her grandmother's necklace. I didn't think she understood how valuable an enchantment like this was in the magical community. When Nadine gave me that key, it was like she gave me her heart.

It was in that moment that I realized I was done for.

As long as Nadine was staying in Octavia Falls, I was going to be with her.

One day, I flagged Samantha down after Necromancy Safety.

"Lucas?" She looked surprised to see me. "What's up?"

I glanced around the hall to make sure no one was around to hear. "I have some questions about the Reaper Moon. Mind if we talk?"

She looked a little hesitant. "I already told you everything I know."

"I just want to know how the last guy did it," I begged. "How'd he get in contact with the reapers on the Reaper Moon? I mean, did he just walk up to them and ask?"

She bit her lower lip. "I think it requires a ritual."

That's what I was afraid of.

"What kind? How?" I asked.

She shot me a look of apology. "I'm sorry, Lucas. I don't know. You're going to have to ask someone else."

And that's exactly what I was going to do until I found answers. Who better to go to than the last guy who figured it out?

I didn't tell Nadine what I was up to. I knew it wasn't right to keep secrets from her, but I didn't want her talking me out of it. I could already hear her voice in my head.

"I'm not worth risking the Abyss," she would say.

But she was. She totally was.

Friday night arrived, and I ducked out the back door of the school before Grant or anyone else could find me. It was my twentieth birthday, and I was pretty sure Grant wanted to go party or something dumb like that, but I had other plans in mind.

As I rounded the side of the school, I heard Ryan's voice. "Where's the money you owe me, Gregory?"

"I'll get it," Gregory replied, his voice shaking.

"You better," Ryan spat. "Now get out of here!"

I heard Gregory scramble off in the other direction. I spun on my heel and rounded the other side of the school. I didn't need another confrontation with Ryan. I felt bad for Gregory, but at least Ryan seemed distracted enough that he was off my back for a while.

I left campus and walked into town. It wasn't far, and I didn't have my own car. Snow fell gently from the sky, but the air actually felt nice. I stopped at a psychic shop along Main Street and went inside.

The shop was really small and had only a handful of products on display—things like tarot cards and herbs. It was dark inside, with black walls, dim lighting, and a deep red curtain separating the main room from another room in the back. There was no one there when I walked in, but I suspected the Seer who ran the place could sense my presence. She was supposed to be one of the best in town—slated to be the next on the Imperium Council. I'd never met her, but I'd heard of her. So when I decided to visit a Seer to figure some shit out, I thought she might be the best person to ask for help.

I barely waited a minute before the curtain behind the counter opened. A woman stepped into the room. She was at least twice my age and had beautiful tight curls framing her face. She wore dark clothes and a purple shawl over her shoulders.

She smiled kindly. "Lucas, I thought I'd be seeing you again."

I hesitated. "Um… I don't believe we've met."

"Right," she said, like she just remembered. "I was in costume. I'm Everly Hall."

She reached across the counter, and I shook her hand. "Nice to meet you. Were you… were you the night hag on Halloween?"

She smiled. "I was."

Creepy…

"What did the card mean?" I asked.

She gestured to the curtain. "Why don't we sit down and talk about it?"

I followed her into the next room, which was just as small as the first. There were candles lit around the perimeter. In the center of the room stood a round table covered in black cloth. A crystal ball and tarot cards sat neatly on top of it.

"Please, sit," Everly said, gesturing to one of the chairs.

I took a seat, but I shifted uncomfortably. I'd come here to get answers, but now I had no idea what to expect.

"What can I do for you, Lucas?" Everly asked as she sat across from me.

I cleared my throat. "First of all, you can tell me about Halloween."

She shook her head and wore an expression of regret. "I'm afraid I can't always make sense of the messages I receive."

"Do you know who sent you the message?" I asked. "What did they say, exactly?"

Her shoulders fell. "I don't know. I did as I was told to do. I found you, gave you the card, and…"

She trailed off and stared into the distance. After a few moments, she shook her head, like she couldn't remember. "I gave you a warning, didn't I?"

"Yeah," I told her. "You said I needed to stop… something. You don't remember?"

She looked at a loss for words. "The way my powers work, I don't always remember the messages I relay. It's automatic."

Well, that was a freaking dead end. I decided to focus on the real reason I came.

I leaned my elbows on the table. "I'm not actually here about Halloween. I'm looking for answers about my future."

"Knowledge can be a dangerous thing, Lucas," she warned.

"It's not like that," I assured her. "I just need some guidance."

She straightened in her chair. "I may be able to help with that."

My shoulders relaxed, and I felt at ease. "The thing is, there's this girl."

Everly's eyes brightened. "Ooh, tell me about her."

"Nadine is… amazing," I stated. "She's just so curious about life, so full of this amazing energy that lifts me up every time I'm around her. I want to be around her all the time. I want to be… *with* her. But…"

"But you're the Reaper's Apprentice," Everly finished for me. "Which means you can't be with her without hurting her."

"See? You understand," I said. "Apparently that's not common knowledge around school. The thing is, to be with her, I'd have to get rid of my gift."

Everly looked thoughtful. "And you're wondering whether you should or not?"

I shook my head. "No. I'm wondering *how*."

Her face fell. "Do you realize what you're saying? Rejecting your powers like that—"

"I know," I said quickly. "I'm not here for a lecture."

"It's not my job to give you one," she stated simply.

"I have to get in touch with a reaper, which I can only do on the Reaper Moon," I said. "Problem is… I don't know how to do it. I mean, it might be as easy as walking up to them, but if I have to do a ritual, I want to be prepared. I heard a story about a guy who did this years ago. Do you think we can contact him?"

Everly sighed. "I'm sorry, Lucas, but my powers don't work that way. The messages I receive are powerful, but I can't decide who gives them."

"Can we at least try?" I begged.

She narrowed her eyes. "You do realize what you're getting into, don't you?"

"Yes, and I've thought it over pretty extensively. Will you help me or not?"

Silence settled over the room for several long seconds. I held my breath.

Finally, Everly sighed. "I'm not one to refuse help when it's asked of me, so long as you understand what you're doing."

I nodded firmly. "All I want is information."

She raised an eyebrow. "You realize I can't guarantee that, don't you?"

"Yes, but I want to try," I told her.

She took a long breath. "Okay, I will help you. My fee is a hundred dollars per page."

"Page?" I asked curiously.

She reached over to a nearby shelf and pulled out a stack of paper and a pen, then placed them in front of her. "I'm an automatic writer, Lucas. It's how I receive the messages."

I shifted in my chair. I was probably going to have to borrow money for this, but to hell with it. I'd pay it back. Anything for answers.

"I'll pay whatever you charge," I finally said.

She nodded. "Then let's get started."

Everly closed her eyes and positioned her pen above the paper. She breathed in and out, barely making a sound. A creepy clock with skeleton-shaped fingers ticked on the wall. I wondered if I was supposed to do something, but Everly didn't give any instructions. I just sat there... waiting.

At least if she didn't write anything, I didn't owe her anything, right?

After two minutes that felt like two hours, the temperature in the room dropped. The hair stood on the back of my neck, and I shivered. I should've been creeped out, but I wasn't.

Without warning, Everly's eyes began to move rapidly beneath her lids. Her eyelids fluttered open and closed the tiniest bit, and it really freaked me out. She was obviously in a really deep trance.

Everly started scribbling on the paper, and the pen made chilling scratching noises against it. My heart leapt to my throat in anticipation. I jumped to my feet and rounded the table to read what she was writing. She didn't respond at all, just kept writing like she was possessed.

So you want to know about the Reaper Moon? she wrote in smooth, clear handwriting.

I glanced around the room, as if expecting to spot a ghost hovering somewhere nearby, but I didn't see a thing.

"Yes," I said aloud. I spoke quickly, like I feared the spirit may leave us at any time. "What can you tell me about contacting the reapers? Is there a ritual involved?"

Everly began scribbling on the next line. *Yes, but why would you want to do it?*

"That's private," I said.

Won't you confide in your brother, Lucas?

I gasped. My eyes went as wide as saucers. The spirit that spoke through Everly was *Eric*?

Maybe, I thought. I didn't want to get my hopes up if this was some sort of trick. I *hoped* it was him, though.

"E-Eric?" I asked, stumbling over the word. My throat closed up as I spoke his name. It'd been so long since I said it out loud.

It's me.

My heart began to hammer fiercely. I wasn't sure if I was excited to talk to him again or pissed this might be an attempt at manipulation.

"How do I know it's you?" I asked. My eyes darted around the room, even though I couldn't see anything.

We had a code word. Remember?

I furrowed my brow. Code word?

Then it hit me. Years ago, when my brother and I were just kids, we lay out under the stars one night talking about death. We decided that if one of us croaked off before the other, we'd contact the other using a code word. It was how we'd know we weren't being punked by some mischievous spirit. I couldn't believe I'd almost forgotten.

"I remember," I said.

I gripped on hard to the back of Everly's chair as she began scribbling on the next line.

Mystic and Midnight.

They were the names of the two cats we had when we were kids. My knees became weak beneath me. Before I collapsed, I dragged my chair around the table and sank into it beside Everly. She kept on writing while I tried to catch my breath and wrap my head around the fact that my brother was back in the same room as me.

Do you believe me now? she wrote on the next line.

That snapped me back to attention. I realized I may not have a lot of time left with Eric, and I wanted to get in as much conversation as I could.

I straightened in my chair. "I can't believe it's you. I mean, I do, I just…"

I couldn't find the words.

"W-what's it like where you're at?" I asked.

I held my breath, awaiting the answer. I hoped to our goddess he wasn't where I thought he was. I didn't know if I could handle that. He took his own life, but he didn't deserve an eternity in the Abyss for it.

Alora's wonderful, Eric answered.

My jaw dropped open. I never thought I'd feel such relief to hear Eric was safe and happy with our ancestors.

"You're in Alora?" I asked breathlessly. "That's great."

There's no time for small talk, the next message read.

"You're right," I said. "Do you know anything the Reaper Moon?"

I leaned over Everly's shoulder and watched carefully as she wrote out the next message.

The people here talk a lot. I've picked up a lot of information. I've come to tell you not to do it.

I gaped like a fish. "Wha—why?"

My own *brother* wasn't going to support me?

Mother Miriam gave you this gift for a reason. Don't give it up like I did.

"This isn't the same thing!" I cried. "Please, just tell me how to do it!"

Everly's pen paused above the paper, though her eyes continued to move rapidly—like she was still in the trance.

"Eric, please!" I begged.

Finally, Everly placed her pen back to the paper and wrote, *You must go to the cemetery and find the grave of Caesar Peppertrine. It is there where you'll find the scroll that tells you how to contact the reapers.*

"Caesar Peppertrine?" I asked.

Everly was already writing another message.

Be careful, Eric cautioned. *You must heed the warning from the card I gave you on Halloween. The choice is yours, Lucas.*

I swore my heart stopped for a couple seconds as I read the message. "*You're* the one who sent me the Death card? What does it mean?"

Everly's pen didn't move.

"Eric!" I shot to my feet and looked around the room, but I couldn't see him. "What does it mean!?"

Everly cleared her throat, and my stomach dropped. I looked to her to see her eyes were wide open. She swayed a little, like she was dazed.

"No!" I cried, my heart racing. "You can't be done. I have more questions!"

Everly set her pen down and spoke calmly. "I'm sorry, Lucas. I did what I could. You must recall I did not promise you *any* answers."

I slammed my hands down on the table, making the pen jump an inch into the air. "Then bring him back!"

She shook her head regrettably. "I'm afraid he's already gone."

I couldn't explain the wave of anger, disappointment, and sadness that washed through me. All three emotions hit me at once. All I wanted was a few more moments with Eric.

Like a brick to the gut, I realized how dangerous that thought could be. It was like all the other thoughts I heard, and I didn't want to be that guy.

I was going to live my life, and I was going to die happy.

And that meant going down this road so I could be with Nadine.

☾

CAESAR PEPPERTRINE DIDN'T EXIST.

At least, that was the conclusion I was coming to. His name was nowhere in the coven's records. For the last week, I'd been leaving campus between classes to search the graveyard, but it was so huge it seemed to be taking forever. I entertained the idea that Caesar Peppertrine's grave wasn't on coven grounds, but it made no sense. Eric had specifically told me to go to *the cemetery*, which could only mean ours here in town; otherwise, he would've specified.

I wondered if this was Eric's way of throwing me off—of keeping me busy until the Reaper Moon had passed. But I couldn't believe my brother would lead me astray like that. He'd given me the choice to make for myself. He wouldn't lie to me.

Which only meant one thing. Caesar Peppertrine's grave was out there —and I was going to find it.

But it was going to have to wait until after tonight. Tonight, I had other plans.

I stood in front of the mirror on Saturday night, straightening the tie on my suit. The last time I'd worn it was at Eric's funeral. I expected to feel ill putting it on, but I didn't. Instead, I felt comforted, like Eric was here with me.

Grant poked his head through the open bathroom door. "You ready?"

"Almost," I said, combing my hair back one last time.

"Wow," Grant said. "Haven't seen you clean up this nice since—"

He cut off. I could already hear what he was going to say. *Since your brother's funeral.*

"It's okay." I clapped Grant on the shoulder. "You don't have to tread lightly around me anymore."

Grant gave me this confused look. "Who are you and what have you done with Lucas?"

I got it. The *old* me would've been pissed for any reminder of Eric. But now that I knew Eric was in Alora, I felt like I could breathe at the mention of him again.

I hadn't told Grant about the night with the Seer and how Eric had given me a message. I didn't want to chance anyone trying to talk me out of the Reaper Moon. I was going through with it, and that was final.

I mean, I hadn't found the scroll, but I had a week left. I wasn't giving up.

"I haven't gone anywhere, buddy," I said. "This is the old me coming back. Should we go find our dates?"

Grant frowned. "You mean *your* date."

I furrowed my brow. "What happened to yours?"

Grant raised his eyebrows, like he was *really* starting to worry about me. "Have you listened to anything I've said at all this past week? If I can't go with Talia, it's totally not worth going out with someone else."

"But you're still going," I pointed out.

Grant shrugged. "I'll be there to swoop in when Talia realizes Cody's a total douche. Plus, I'm not missing a dance, man."

"Then let's get going." I could hardly wait to see Nadine.

Grant and I took the grand staircase down to the Main Foyer.

"You go on ahead, man," I said. "I told Nadine I'd meet her here."

He gave me a salute. "See you soon."

I felt pretty awkward just standing there. I shot a glance around the foyer to see other couples chatting or sipping drinks. I was about to go sit down when movement caught my eye.

Nadine stood at the top of the stairs, looking like a radiant goddess. It nearly knocked the wind out of me. She had her hair in long, beautiful waves around her shoulders, and wore a floor-length dress that had lots of sparkly diamonds on the bust and exposed part of her midriff. It was a deep, dark purple, like the color of my magic, and it looked really good on her.

She glanced around the foyer, until her eyes fell on me. Her face lit up. My heart started pounding, and it was as if all time had stood still. I was rooted completely in place, and the only thing that moved around me was Nadine. She reached for the banister and started down the steps. I couldn't take my eyes off her.

It wasn't until she reached the bottom of the grand staircase and cleared her throat that I snapped back to attention. She blushed. "Everything okay?"

I quickly reached my hand out and took hers. "You look… absolutely perfect."

She smiled brightly. That smile lit up my whole world. "Thank you."

After a few moments of silence, I realized it was my turn to speak again. "I'm actually really glad you picked that color. It's, um, it's my favorite. I didn't know what color you'd wear, but…"

I cupped my hands together and conjured the corsage I'd bought her. I opened my palms to reveal a velvety purple rose. "It's for you."

Nadine gazed down at it, speechless. "Lucas, it's beautiful."

She held her wrist out, and I placed the corsage over her hand. She ran her fingers over the petals.

"It's not as beautiful as you," I said.

She chuckled under her breath. "That's sweet of you. You don't look too bad yourself."

"I have my moments." I took a step back and held my elbow out to her. "May I escort you to the dance?"

She beamed and hooked her elbow through mine. "You may."

I led Nadine down the hall. We walked past the cafeteria and to the end of the hall, where a pair of double doors opened to a magnificent ballroom.

Nadine's jaw dropped when we stepped inside. The ballroom walls were a midnight blue, and the carpet was a deep black. The room was cast in moonlight streaming in through the tall, arched windows. Candles hovered above our heads. They weren't attached to anything, but they bobbed up and down with ease, like one of the professors was using their Mentalist powers to set the ambiance. Tarot cards spun between the candles. I looked up and noticed they were all Major Arcana cards that spoke of good fortune and abundance. The Death card was nowhere to be seen, thank the Goddess.

A live band played at the opposite end of the room, filling the space with a punk-rock melody. On stage, two skeletons jived to the beat in a coordinated dance. It was obviously the work of a talented necromancer. Grant was already on the dancefloor busting his moves. Amy and Mandy danced alongside him in black and white gothic gowns.

"Would you like something to drink?" I asked Nadine.

"Sure," she answered with a shrug.

I led her over to the refreshments table. A sweet scent emanated from a bubbling cauldron.

"Two, please," I said to the Alchemist behind the table.

As he started serving us drinks, Nadine hesitated at my side. "What's in it?" she asked.

I could tell by the way she eyed it she worried it might flare her symptoms.

"It should be okay," I said. "It's just a hydration potion. Helps you go longer on the dancefloor."

"Oh," she said brightly, sounding intrigued. "I'll have to try it then."

We sipped our potion, which tasted fruity and sweet, with a hint of carbonation. My gaze roamed over the ballroom and stopped on the doors as Talia entered on Cody's arm.

"Uh oh," I said under my breath.

"What?" Nadine followed my gaze, and she realized what I was talking about. "What's wrong with Cody?"

I almost snorted. "Grant wants to kick his ass."

Nadine sighed, but she smiled in amusement. "Okay, he can't be *that* bad. Talia really likes him. What harm is there in letting her enjoy his company?"

The question was rhetorical, but it made me think of my mom. *She* claimed she enjoyed my dad's company. Sure, there were times when he could be fun, but they were few and far between. Not that Cody was anything like my dad, but still.

I took another sip of punch. "Depends. Want to get out there?"

She beamed. "You're really going to dance with me this time?"

I tossed my empty cup in the trash nearby, then took her hand. "I told you I would, didn't I?"

Nadine threw her cup away before she'd finished, then followed me onto the dancefloor. The song had changed since we came in, but it was the same punk-rock type of music. Nadine started swaying her hips right away, but I just sort of stood back awkwardly. I was *not* a good dancer.

"Woohoo!" Grant cupped his hands around his mouth and shouted. "Nadine is on the floor! Let's get this party *started*!"

"Get in here, girl!" Amy cried, gesturing her forward.

"Shake it!" Mandy added. She spun around and started twerking in Nadine's direction.

Nadine giggled as Grant swirled an imaginary lasso above his head. He threw it over her and reeled her to the center of the dancefloor.

"Hey there, buddy," I cut in, stepping between them. "I'm gonna have to take that from you. She's mine tonight."

Grant shrugged and stepped aside, then pretended to place the invisible lasso rope in my hands. "Go wild."

Nadine threw her head back in laughter as I pretended to reel her in. She ended up so close to me that I grabbed her around the waist. She kept dancing, so I just went along with it, moving my body to the beat. I probably looked like a total fool, but I didn't care. I had Nadine Evers in my arms. My attention was so laser-focused on her that we could've been the only two people in the room for all I knew. When she laughed and danced, it was like my whole dark world lit up, but there was only one thing to see—*her*.

"You're *dancing*!" she exclaimed.

"Don't go teasing me, now," I warned. "I might stop."

"I'm not teasing," she countered. "I'm enjoying it."

"Well, enjoy it while it lasts," I said, though something told me Nadine and I would be sharing many dances in years to come.

"Heeey!" Talia shouted as she came onto the dancefloor, dragging Cody behind her.

"Talia!" Mandy squealed. She reached out for Talia's hand, then spun her around.

Talia giggled, then returned to Cody's side. The two started grinding like they were animals. Good Goddess, I did *not* expect that out of Talia.

Nadine noticed me watching them, but she must not have noticed the look of disgust on my face. "You want to dance like that?" she teased.

I shot a glance around the crowded dancefloor. "With all these people around?"

She shrugged. "Yeah, what could it hurt? All you have to do is stand there."

I liked the sound of that. Nadine started to demonstrate. She turned around and pressed her backside against my front, then dipped down a little before coming back up.

I gasped. If she kept this up any longer, it was going to be pretty obvious to everyone just how much I liked it. But I didn't want her to stop, either.

"You okay back there?" she asked as she continued rubbing herself against me.

"Peachy," I said. I wanted to slap myself. Was that really the best I could come up with?

"Good," she teased. "Because there's more where that came from."

To my surprise, Nadine bent at the waist, pressing her ass against my dick. And no, that *wasn't* a roll of quarters in my pocket. I was *very* happy to see her. Damn, I just wanted to reach out and grab her ass, but I couldn't with all the people around. She flipped her hair, then shoved her hands into it, letting it flip around in a really sexy way.

"Woo!" Talia cheered. "Nadine's got *moves.*"

Nadine turned back toward me, blushing. She placed her arms around my neck and continued swaying her hips to the music. "I should maybe save that for when we're alone, huh?"

My eyebrows shot up. "Are you offering me a lap dance?"

Her lips twitched at the corners. "Depends. Are you accepting?"

Once this fucking curse was gone, she could give me all the lap dances she wanted. Nadine and I started dancing like normal again, and my eyes scanned the crowd. I realized for the first time that Grant had practically stopped dancing. His eyes were locked on Talia and Cody. He looked about ready to bare his teeth and growl.

I cocked my head to Nadine, and we danced a few paces over toward Grant. He didn't notice us until I nudged him with my elbow. Finally, he snapped back to reality.

"What?" he asked.

"Chill," I warned. "No one wants to see a fist fight tonight."

Grant scoffed. "Then let's pray he doesn't give me a reason."

Just then, Cody reached down and squeezed Talia's ass. It wasn't cute and sweet, either. It was a very obvious, full-on ass grab for the whole dancefloor to see.

Talia squealed and jumped away from him. She looked shocked at first, but a smile came across her face. "Cody, what'd we talk about?"

She made it sound like she was joking, but the whole thing made me uneasy. It definitely riled up Grant, because he stomped over to them.

"What the hell do you think you're doing, man?" Grant snapped.

Cody scowled. "Me? I don't even know who the fuck you are. Get out of here."

"You get out of here!" Grant countered. He shoved Cody in the shoulders, and he stumbled back into another couple.

"Grant, don't!" Talia shouted.

Cody's nostrils flared, and he looked ready to punch Grant in the face.

Talia threw herself between them. "Cody, forget about Grant. He's just a friend. Grant, it's fine. It was harmless."

"Didn't look that way to me," Grant sneered without taking his eyes off Cody.

"The girl says she's fine," Cody snapped. "Now back off."

Nadine went to Talia's side. "You okay?"

The two exchanged a few words in whispers.

Grant looked to Talia, as if expecting her to call Cody out. "Tal, come on. Don't tell me you're okay with that."

"I'm fine," she insisted. "Let's not ruin the night with a fight, okay?"

Cody scoffed as Talia turned back to him. They started dancing again, though Cody dragged her further away from us. "What a loser," he said to her, though it was loud enough for us all to hear. "You're really friends with that guy?"

"Is she really okay?" I asked Nadine as she returned to my side.

She shot a glance at Talia. "She says she is. She thinks Grant's over-reacting."

"Do *you* think he is?" I asked.

"I don't know." She frowned in contemplation. "She looks okay now."

Talia twirled on the dancefloor in Cody's arms, beaming up at him. Grant still hadn't backed down. He stood there, his hands curled into fists.

Mandy stepped in front of him and raised an eyebrow. "Are Amy and I going to have to drag you off the dancefloor? Let Talia have fun with her date."

Grant narrowed his eyes at Cody. "Do I have to?"

"Yes," she insisted.

Grant groaned, and Mandy shot him a pointed look. "Do you want Amy and me to dance around you and try to make her jealous?" she suggested.

Grant's eyes lit up at that. "Mandy, I think you just became my new best friend."

Nadine gasped dramatically. "I lost top spot?"

"Don't worry," Grant played along. "You're top five for sure."

She laughed as Grant turned to dance with Mandy and Amy. Just as they were getting into it, the song changed to a slow melody. Now this, I could do.

I stepped back and offered Nadine my hand. "May I have this dance?"

She curtsied. "Why yes, kind sir."

I couldn't help but beam as Nadine took my hand and I wrapped my arms around her waist. We swayed on the dancefloor, and my heart swelled. I loved holding her in my arms.

"I'm glad we still get dances in college," Nadine said. "I'm having lots of fun."

"Good," I replied. "I am, too."

"Even though you're dancing?" she asked playfully.

I nodded. "I mean, you basically twisted my arm, but it'll heal."

She snickered, but she went quiet a few moments later and rested her head on my chest. This moment was incredible. I wanted a million more like it, and then some.

My eyes roamed the ballroom again. Across the room, I noticed Chloe dancing with Finn, one of the Treacherous Tarantulas. She kept throwing glances toward Ryan, who sat slumped in one of the chairs and looked out at the crowd like he was too good to be there. His bowtie was already undone, like he was totally wasted already.

Fucking loser.

At least all Chloe's attention was on him and not on my precious Nadine. If she ever tried hurting her again, she was going to have to deal with me. The consequences be damned, I'd curse that bitch's ass to protect my girl.

I continued to look around the room and noticed Lena dancing with Gregory. She really had to be desperate for a date if she'd come with him. The poor guy looked at her like he was a lost puppy, but she kept pulling her head away, like she couldn't stand him breathing on her.

She shot a glance my way, but I ignored her. If she was trying to make me jealous or something, it wasn't going to work.

Finally, my eyes landed on Professor Warren and Headmistress Verla standing in the corner. We didn't need chaperones, but they were there no doubt to make sure no one spiked the punch bowl or started any fights. It wouldn't be the first time.

Verla sipped her drink slowly while Professor Warren talked to her. Whatever he was saying must've been pissing her off, because she didn't look him in the eyes. She kept her gaze on the students and pursed her lips. I couldn't tell what he was saying, but he looked somewhat annoyed with her. I hadn't realized the two were on less than friendly terms.

"What's wrong?" Nadine asked.

"Nothing," I said, turning my gaze back to her. "Professor Warren and Headmistress Verla look mad at each other."

She looked toward them and frowned. "It definitely looks like something's going on. I saw her twice this week for make-up sessions, and she seemed fine then."

I spun Nadine around, then pulled her back into my arms. "What day is your ceremony again?"

She gasped playfully. "You don't remember my birthday?"

"I don't think you ever told me," I pointed out. "I know it's next week."

She snickered lightly. "It's the thirteenth. You're coming to my Evoking Ceremony, right?"

My whole body stilled. I must've looked like a statue as it hit me. That would make the eve of her birthday, and her ceremony... the same night as the Reaper Moon.

"I know what you're thinking," she said, pushing her hair behind her ear. "Friday the thirteenth is really not the best time for a ceremony."

She chuckled nervously, but I didn't respond.

"Lucas?" Nadine asked.

I snapped out of it. I couldn't miss the Reaper Moon, but I couldn't ditch her ceremony, either.

"I'll be there," I promised.

I had to be. As for the Reaper Moon, I'd be in, out, and done before the witching hour. I'd make it to her ceremony...

I hoped.

After the slow song ended, Nadine announced that she was going to sit out the next song. I started to follow her, before Grant grabbed me by the elbow and dragged me away from her.

"Sorry," Grant said to Nadine. "I've got to steal him for a second."

"Dude, what the hell—?" I started.

Grant dragged me out the doors and turned on me as soon as we were in the hallway. He pointed a finger in my direction. "I saw that look!"

"What? What look?"

"Nadine told you the night of her ceremony, and you totally froze up," he accused. "You ditched us the night of your birthday, too. And don't think I haven't noticed you sneaking off campus. What's up with you lately?"

"Nothing," I lied, but my voice rose several pitches.

Grant gave me a stern look. "Don't lie to me. We've lived together long enough that I know your tells."

"My *tells*?" I asked.

"Your eyes narrow when you lie," Grant pointed out.

"They do not!" I defended, but I suddenly realized they *were* narrowed just a bit. I consciously widened them.

"Don't tell me you've gotten wrapped up in something bad," Grant said.

"Goddess, no," I hissed. "It's not like that at all."

He crossed his arms. "Then tell me what's up."

"Nothing," I lied again. "I swear."

Grant tapped his foot. "I'm not letting you go back in there until you tell me."

I rolled my eyes. "Then you're going to be waiting here a while."

He shrugged. "I don't have a date waiting for me. I've got all night."

I groaned. He had me there. I couldn't let Nadine think I ditched her.

"What is this? Some sort of blackmail?" I asked.

Grant pursed his lips. "It's a threat for sure."

"Come on, Grant," I complained. "Is this for real?"

"You're hiding something," he accused. "Am I going to have to save you from yourself?"

"No," I promised. "I have it handled."

He sighed and dropped his arms. "Then let me help."

I shook my head. "I don't think you're going to want to help on this one."

Grant frowned. "That's what friends do, Lucas."

I pressed my lips together. They were officially sealed. If I said any more, he'd know what I was up to.

But I didn't have to say any more. Apparently, my silence was enough.

Grant's eyes widened. "That's the night of the Reaper Moon, isn't it? You're going to do it."

"Yes," I snapped. "And you're not going to talk me out of it."

Grant gaped at me. "You're talking about the Abyss. If you give up your powers, you'll be condemned by the Goddess forever. You'll never be able to enter Alora."

I shrugged like it wasn't a big deal, but to be honest, the thought of going to hell scared me.

But not as much as being with Nadine for the rest of my life thrilled me.

Not to mention getting rid of all these thoughts—ditching the responsibility of the Reaper's Apprentice. Carrying these thoughts around was too much. I'd risk the Abyss if it meant I didn't have to carry around these secrets anymore.

"You said I had to make a decision," I reminded him. "I decided."

"Well, you're deciding wrong!" Grant exploded.

A few people at the ballroom entrance looked our way. I grabbed Grant by the shoulder and dragged him further down the hall, where we couldn't be heard.

"In all fairness, this isn't your decision to make," I snapped at him. "As soon as I figure out how to do the ritual, I'm doing this. All I need is to find the grave of some guy named Caesar Peppertrine—where there's supposed to be scroll waiting for me."

Grant raked his fingers through his hair. "Are you shitting me, Lucas? You're doing this all for… what? A girl."

His words were like a slap to the face.

"Nadine's not just *any* girl," I growled. "She's *the* girl."

"Then shouldn't you want to spend the rest of eternity with her?" he argued. "You're trading your soul to… to get laid!"

Was he fucking kidding me?

"That's not what this is about," I argued. "I hate my gift, and you know that. This is my one chance to get rid of it."

"So that's the real reason?" he mocked, crossing his arms. "You're not just upset about this sex curse?"

"It's not a *sex curse*," I shot back, fuming.

"It sure sounds like your dick's making the decisions right now," Grant snapped.

A couple walked by just then and shot us an odd look.

My teeth gritted as I exploded on Grant. "This curse isn't about my dick! It's the whole fucking package! As long as I'm the Reaper's Apprentice, I don't get to be in a relationship. I never get married; I never have kids. Nadine deserves all that."

Grant looked disgusted with me. "That's noble and all, but you're talking about eternity. Our lives here are just a blip on the map."

"Then what are we doing here?" I countered. "Our lives matter, Grant. I'm going to make mine count. Nadine actually wants to be with me. She deserves the fucking world. So yeah, I'd gladly trade my soul to give her that. You wouldn't know what that feels like because the girl you're pining for doesn't want you back!"

Grant's jaw dropped. He stood there for a moment in total silence. To be honest, I was pretty pissed at him. I didn't care.

Finally, he found his voice again. "Fine," he snapped, opening his arms wide. "You want to do this, be my guest. Just don't expect me to supply the sledgehammer when you're fucking up this asshole's grave marker."

I rolled my eyes. "Very mature."

Grant started to walk away, but he paused and turned back to me. He got up in my face and pointed a finger at me. "You know what? I hope the mausoleum *is* haunted! Maybe the spirits will make you think twice about stealing that scroll."

With that, Grant stormed off. I paced back and forth, raking my fingers through my hair. What the fuck just happened?

I ran the conversation back in my mind, wondering where everything turned to shit. Then something Grant said hit me.

The mausoleum.

He *knew* where Caesar Peppertrine's grave was. And he had no idea he'd just helped me find it.

☾·

IT MUST'VE BEEN three in the morning before Nadine and I finally left the dance. I walked her back to her room, since she looked exhausted. I wanted to make sure she got back all right.

When I made it back to my room, Grant still wasn't back yet. He was probably off somewhere being pissed at me for what I said. I changed back into my street clothes and left campus. It didn't matter how late it was; I wasn't going to sleep anyway until I found that scroll.

I had an eerie sense of déjà vu as I broke into the cemetery using my magic. I formed an orb in my hand and used it to light my path. I must've passed a thousand headstones before I reached the trees at the back of the property. Snow coated the ground, and it was really chilly out, but I barely noticed. My heart was pounding so hard at the thought of being so close.

I entered the trees and pushed through the brush until I came upon the abandoned mausoleum where I'd had my Evoking Ceremony. I climbed over broken bricks and stepped inside. Nothing had changed since the last time I'd been here, except there was a light dusting of snow covering the ground.

I glanced around at the grave markers, though there were few that were still in-tact. My eyes fell upon one that read *Caesar Peppertrine*.

"I'll be damned," I whispered as I approached. Grant must've noticed the name the night of my Evoking Ceremony.

I knelt beside the marker and ran my fingers over the engraved letters.

Something about the name seemed… off. According to coven records, this grave shouldn't even be here. In fact, there were no Peppertrines listed *anywhere* within the coven records. So where had this guy come from?

"Who are you, and what are you doing with a Reaper's Apprentice scroll?" I said under my breath.

That's when it hit me. As my eyes roamed over the letters, my brain started to notice a pattern. I quickly conjured one of my notebooks and scribbled his name down on the paper, then started crossing off letters. When I finished, it became very clear.

Caesar Peppertrine wasn't a man at all.

It was an anagram for *Reaper's Apprentice.*

This grave marker was nothing more than a message. A message for *me.*

Heart pounding, I got to my feet.

Well, there's only one way to find out what that message is.

I conjured the sledgehammer I'd brought along and started smashing it into the stone. I expected the stone to resist, but it cracked on the first swing. I put all my strength behind the hammer and swung as hard as I could.

Smash!

The stone gave way just a little more.

Smash, smash, smash!

With every swing, a little more of the marker crumbled away. Even though it was cold out, I started to sweat.

Smash!

I swung again.

Finally, I broke through. My heart lurched, and I stepped back and set my hammer aside. I stared into an open hole in the wall, trying to catch my breath.

There was no casket inside like there should have been—just utter darkness.

I stepped forward and knelt down next to the opening. An orb formed in my hand lighting the cavity in the wall. Utter relief flooded through me when my light touched an ancient scroll sitting in the center. It looked as if it'd gone untouched for years.

"It's here…" I whispered.

I reached into the cavity and pulled out the scroll. It felt really old and fragile. My pulse quickened as I unrolled the scroll, but my stomach dropped the further I read.

I was naïve to think this was going to be simple.

I'd be lucky if I managed to pull this off at all.

nadine

TWENTY

I couldn't believe my Evoking Ceremony had arrived so quickly. I shook as I thought of what the night would bring. After tonight, I would either be welcomed into the coven, or banished. I would cement my life here with Grammy, Lucas, and my friends, or I would be forced to leave.

Part of me worried that Chloe had won—that she'd sabotaged enough of my lessons that I wasn't prepared enough.

I forcefully pushed the thought from my mind. She hadn't won yet. I couldn't start getting down on myself before I even began.

"Where's Lucas?" I demanded of Grant. "Why isn't he here yet?"

I sat in Grammy's living room, with Isa purring softly on my lap. The coffee table had been removed, and in its place were five candles set in a circle on the floor. I was surrounded by three of the people I loved most in the world—Grammy, Talia, and Grant.

But the one person I really wanted to be here wasn't. I was really worried about him, because I didn't think he'd bail on me. I brought his number up on my phone again, but before I could call him, Grant reached out and took my hand.

"It's not going to help," he said with a frown.

"We should check on him," I insisted.

"Yeah, it's really weird he's not here yet," Talia agreed.

"There's no time," Grammy argued. "The witching hour is approaching. This is Nadine's one chance to contact Mother Miriam. We must go through with the ceremony, no matter what."

"What about Chloe?" I asked, my guts twisting.

Grammy cocked an eyebrow. "What about her?"

"She sabotaged all my training lessons," I pointed out. "I wouldn't put it past her to sabotage this as well."

Grammy shook her head. "She can't touch you tonight, Nadine."

"What do you mean?" I asked.

"Mother Miriam protects you on the night of your ceremony, so you can go through with it in peace," Grammy explained. "That's why Chloe tried to hurt you during your training—because she knew she couldn't get to you tonight."

I dropped my gaze and muttered, "Well, she might've had the right idea."

I wasn't ready for this.

"Don't say that," Grammy demanded. "You must not let Chloe get to you, especially tonight."

She was right. I had to go into this with a clear head.

"Maybe I need more of that calming tea," I suggested.

I set Isa aside and started to get up, but Grammy stood at the same time. "Let me get it for you, Nadine."

She was coddling me again, which was unnecessary. I'd napped most of the day so I'd have enough energy for tonight. I could get my own tea.

She started for the kitchen, but I didn't sit back down. I followed behind her. Grant and Talia immediately started whispering, and I didn't miss the look of concern in their eyes before I left the room. It was almost like one of them knew something was up.

Grammy poured me a cup of tea. When she turned, she looked surprised to see me there. "Here you go."

She handed me the cup, and I began sipping on it. Neither of us moved from where we stood.

"How's that feel?" Grammy asked.

I didn't feel any change, to be honest. "Getting better," I said, mostly because I wanted it to be true.

Grammy sighed. "Whatever happens tonight, Nadine, you will complete your Evoking Ceremony."

I furrowed my brow. What was she getting at? "I know."

She tilted her head to the side. "Then why are you letting yourself get so nervous about it?"

"Um… because it's nerve-racking?"

Grammy reached out and placed a hand on my shoulder. "Tonight is a special night. You only get one chance at this. Embrace it."

A lump formed in my throat, and even the tea didn't help wash it down. "Grammy, I don't know how," I admitted.

"I'll show you," she said kindly. She reached out for my tea and set it on the counter beside her, then she wrapped her arms around me. I melted into the hug. "See? Embraced."

I chuckled lightly under my breath, but I didn't move to pull away. Her hug was so comforting, and it instantly helped wash away some of my worry. "What do you think is going to happen?"

"I don't know," she said quietly. "It's different for everyone."

I finally drew away, but as soon as I did, a knot in my chest tightened. "I know. How do you think Mother Miriam will test me?"

Grammy's features softened. "Well, Nadine… you're very curious. Why don't we wait and find out?"

I frowned, but a smile twitched at the corners of my lips. "Grammy, that's not helpful."

She smiled back. "The truth is, there is no magic formula, Nadine. Sometimes, people who seem to be the best among us end up banished, and others are accepted. It's not the actions you let others see that makes you a part of the Miriamic family. It's the intention that's in your heart."

The knot in my chest eased ever so slightly. I'd said something similar to Lucas at the abandoned house in the woods. He'd acted like such a jerk to me when all he wanted to do was protect me. Were my own intentions enough to get me into the coven?

"Headmistress Verla seems to think Mother Miriam will try to address my grief," I told Grammy. "I don't know if I'm ready for that."

Grammy's gaze dropped, like she was really contemplating what I said. Finally, she sighed. "Nadine, do you think Mother Miriam only accepts perfect souls into her family?"

I hesitated. Of course not. There were people like Ryan and Gwen who'd already gotten their powers. Obviously Mother Miriam chose them for a purpose.

"No," I admitted.

"She will not banish you for the grief that's in your heart," Grammy promised. "She's there to *help* you with that."

I swallowed. "How did you get over Grampy's death?"

Grammy took a few breaths before answering. "That's not something you get over."

"Oh," I said flatly. That wasn't at all the answer I expected.

Grammy reached out and guided my chin upward to look her in the eye. "It's something you *accept*, but not forget."

"I don't understand," I admitted.

"Death is not an end for us, Nadine," Grammy reminded me.

"I know," I said. "We go on to live in Alora."

She shook her head, like that wasn't what she meant. "Your parents live on in your heart. Every hug, every kiss, every moment they supported you—it filled your heart with love, Nadine. And every action you've had from the moment they died has been a chance to spread that love they showed you. Your parents left you with a gift. You must not wrap it up and try to give it back. You must open it and let your love pour out to the world."

I got so choked up I could hardly get the words out. "Thank you, Grammy."

She smiled. "Anytime. The witching hour is almost here. Shall we get started?"

"But what about Lucas?" I asked. "He's coming. He promised me he'd be here."

Grammy frowned. "I'm afraid we'll have to start without him."

I couldn't do that. Lucas would make it. He'd be at my side while I went through my trials. He had to be.

I narrowed my eyes at Grammy. "Is this one of my tests? To see what I'd do without him?"

Grammy threw her head back and laughed. "This is not a test, Nadine. This is real."

"Well, how am I supposed to know that?" I asked.

"You can't," she admitted. "But here's what you need to remember..."

Grammy got a really serious look on her face. "Don't live your life like it's a test, Nadine. Live your *test* like it's your life."

Grammy started back toward the living room, but I just stood there, contemplating what she said. It took me repeating it several times in my mind to realize what she meant.

This test wasn't about doing the right things to get into the coven. It was about showing Mother Miriam who I was on a deeply spiritual level. All I could do was strive to make her proud.

"Nadine?" Grammy called from the living room.

"Coming," I called back.

I took another sip of calming tea, before leaving it on the counter and returning to the living room. I was disappointed to see that Lucas still wasn't there.

Grant must've noticed my unease, because he quickly stood and grabbed my shoulders. He looked me straight in the eye and said, "It's going to be okay, Nadine. Focus on the ceremony."

I searched his eyes. "You know something, don't you?"

Grant pressed his lips together. "I know that if Lucas can't make it, he has a good reason."

"Or something bad happened to him," I pointed out.

"Worry about your ceremony," he insisted, "then we'll worry about Lucas."

I sighed. I didn't have any other choice, did I?

Grant stepped aside, and Talia stood to pull me into a hug. "You're going to do great, Nadine," she encouraged. "You've got this."

I squeezed her back. "Thanks, Tal. I'm really glad you're here."

She smiled brightly. "I wouldn't miss it for the world."

At my feet, Isa purred and rubbed herself against my leg. I bent to pick her up, then pressed my nose into her fur.

"I'll be all right," I whispered to her. "I'm ready, Mom."

Deep down, I didn't feel like it was true, but I couldn't back out now.

"It's time, Nadine," Grammy said.

I handed Isa to Talia, then stepped into the middle of the room. The candles weren't even lit yet, but I swore I could feel a heightened sense of energy inside the circle. I lay on my back on the carpet and closed my eyes. No sooner had I laid my head down did I hear the sound of Grammy's clock striking midnight from the hall.

"The witching hour has arrived," Grammy said in a grave tone. "We can begin."

I heard the sound of Grant striking a lighter, but I kept my eyes closed. My whole body quaked in anticipation. Isa meowed from Talia's lap, but I shut out all external stimuli and focused on keeping my body relaxed.

Grammy began to recite an incantation. *"The clock has struck the witching hour. It's time to wake this witch's power."*

A shiver traveled down my spine. Grammy spoke in a voice I'd never heard her use before. It was so full of finite clarity. At first, it was strange, but her voice began to soothe me the longer she spoke.

"We call our goddess down to earth. To bear witness to this new rebirth," she continued. *"A series of tests she shall partake. And join the coven before day breaks."*

I felt my body begin to rise from the floor, and then—

Darkness enveloped me. I didn't know where I was or how I'd gotten there. I lay on a warm, hard surface. When I tried to move, I went nowhere. I was paralyzed.

"Hello?" I called, my voice wavering. "Is anyone there?"

As I spoke, I realized the weight of a blindfold around my eyes. I started to struggle even more, and I found that I could move my feet, but my arms were bound to my sides. I began to panic.

"Help!" I cried. "Somebody help me!"

A million questions raced through my head all at once. Where was I? What had happened to me? Who had done this?

The sound of echoing voices met my ears. Three girls giggled in unison, and a knot in my stomach twisted so tight I could swear the ropes around my arms tightened as well.

The Lucky Three.

"Chloe!?" I demanded. "Let me go! This isn't funny anymore."

I heard the sound of footsteps approach. They were soft, as if she walked on the carpet.

"Oh, Nadine," Chloe scoffed. "But it *is* funny."

"Chloe!" I screamed as I listened to the sound of her footsteps retreat. "What did you do to me? Let me go!"

She chuckled again. "I didn't do this to you, Nadine. *You* did this."

Suddenly, I stopped struggling. I tried flipping back through my memory to figure out how I'd gotten here, but I couldn't remember. Though I had every reason to believe Chloe had done this to me—given her track record and complete and utter disdain for me—I had no proof. I couldn't say with certainty that she was wrong, either. But how could I tie myself up and blindfold myself?

I racked my brain, trying to come up with an answer. What bothered me more than being tied up was that I couldn't recall the events leading up to it.

"Hello?" I cried. "Can anyone hear me?"

Chloe cleared her throat. I gave a start—as I hadn't realized she was still there.

"No one's coming to your rescue," Chloe said.

"You could help," I bit at her.

"Why would I do that when you can just untie yourself?" she asked.

I scoffed. "Untie myself? How am I supposed to do that?"

"I don't know," Chloe said, like she didn't care one way or another. "Get creative."

It was in that moment that I realized I didn't have a single idea. I'd been here for several minutes already, and all I could do was question how I got here. I needed to look for the solution. Once this blindfold was off, maybe then I'd find my answer.

I began to struggle more, but the more I struggled, the tighter the rope held on me. My whole body ached, and I thought the circulation in my arms might stop dead at any moment.

"I can't move," I sobbed. "Please, somebody help."

Chloe chuckled. "Stop playing the victim, Nadine."

My whole body stilled. I'd heard Chloe say that before. It was in Introduction to Tarot, when I drew the Eight of Swords card.

"Her feet are unbound. She has the ability to go in any direction she chooses. The woman in this card is bound by her own doing. All she has to do is stop playing the victim," I recalled Chloe saying.

And that's the moment it became clear to me. My feet *were* unbound. I could go anywhere I wanted.

"I. Am. Not. A. Victim," I stated with every ounce of conviction I had in me.

Once I realized that, the solution was simple. I pulled my knees to my chest and rolled over. All I had to do was get to my knees, then stand on my own two feet. The moment I stood upright, the rope that bound me loosened and fell away. I reached up and tugged the blindfold off my eyes.

I glanced around to see that I was standing in the middle of the Main

Foyer. It was really dark, except for a small fire that burned in the fireplace. I looked around for Chloe, but she was gone.

Before I could take another breath, an earth-shattering scream tore through the night. I whirled around and saw that the front doors of the school were wide open. A strong breeze swept past the doors, blowing leaves all over the place. I could barely see anything through the darkness of the night.

I ran outside in the direction of the scream, but I stopped dead when the scene came into view.

I stared up at a tall oak tree. Chloe's feet hovered just above the ground, kicking frantically and searching for a foothold to save herself. Her hands grasped her neck, where a tight noose had been slung around her throat.

For a moment, a pang of satisfaction hit me. I didn't dare admit to anyone, but watching Chloe hang like that made me feel a bit... triumphant.

I knew immediately it was the devil on my shoulder talking, because I felt the sudden urge to punch that sucker out. I didn't care what Chloe had done to me in the past. She didn't deserve a death like this.

Chloe clawed at the rope around her neck. "Help!" she gasped, though I could barely understand the word.

Screw the dark side of me that enjoyed watching her hang. The real Nadine found it sickening.

I raced over to her and got beneath her, my heart racing in panic. I lifted her onto my shoulders, though it took every ounce of my strength to keep my aching knees from collapsing beneath me.

"I've got you, Chloe!" I called up to her.

Her center of gravity shifted from side to side. I assumed it was because she was struggling to get the noose off her neck.

"Are you okay?" I asked, since I couldn't see anything. "Can you—?"

Chloe's weight gave way, and we both went tumbling to the ground, screaming. She pressed her hand to her bruised neck and gasped for breath.

"W-why did you save me, Nadine?" she managed to choke out.

Our eyes connected, and for the first time since I met her, I saw a look of pure gratitude in her eyes.

"I had to," I told her.

"No, you didn't," she argued, like she couldn't understand me at all. "I've been awful to you. You should've enjoyed watching me hang."

I shook my head. "Not like that. We're part of the same coven. We help each other, even if you're my enemy."

Chloe opened her mouth to say something, but she never got the chance. The sound of a woman's maniacal laughter reached us. I gave a start, and both of us looked in the direction of the voice. It was coming from somewhere inside the school.

"What's going—?" I started to ask, but I cut off when I looked back to Chloe.

Except she wasn't there. I glanced around frantically, wondering where she'd disappeared to. She couldn't have run off that fast.

My heart started pounding fiercely as the laughter continued. Something about it sounded chillingly familiar, though I couldn't put my finger on it. Curiously, I rose to my feet and stepped toward the school. I followed the sound of laughter through the dark hallways of Miriam Mansion. Light flickered from the sconces on the wall, and the hair on the back of my neck stood.

"Hello?" I called down the hall.

No answer came.

Cautiously, I stepped forward until I came to the double door entrance to the school's ballroom. I peeked inside to see a woman sitting cross-legged on the ground, her back to me. She wore all leather and had long brown hair flowing down her back. The room was almost entirely black, except for the light coming from five candles set around the girl. Each candle was connected by a line of salt that created a pentagram. Another salt line surrounded that, enclosing everything into a circle. The woman looked like she was doing something with her hands, but I couldn't see what it was.

"Are you going to stand there all day, Nadine?" she asked bluntly.

I hesitated. How'd she know I was here?

"I know you're out there," she called without turning her head. "Come see what I've made for you... for *us*."

Her voice sounded so familiar. Something told me I knew this woman, but I couldn't place her.

Carefully, I took a step forward. "Do I know you?"

She chuckled, like the question amused her. "Oh, Nadine. Don't you recognize yourself?"

Finally, she turned toward me, and my heart lurched into my throat. My own face stared back at me.

But at the same time, it wasn't *me*. She was more like my evil twin—with dark makeup around the eyes and a smirk of unadulterated pride I'd never be caught dead wearing. I had more self-respect and humility than that.

"What the hell is going on?" I demanded. This had to be another one of Chloe's illusions.

She gave me a sinister smile. "Come look."

I hesitated, but I was too curious to see what she was holding. I stepped around her and saw that she had a small stuffed doll in her hand.

A voodoo doll.

My knees shook as I stared down at the doll. The coven didn't practice voodoo. Hell, I didn't even know if voodoo was *real*.

Two other dolls lay on the ground in front of my doppelganger. Each was faceless and dressed only in black fabric, except they each had a different color of yarn sewn onto their heads. The one on the left depicted a girl with short brown hair. The one on the right had long white-blonde hair. And the one she held had black hair.

"Are those the Lucky Three?" I asked, but my voice came out scratchy and dry.

She smirked proudly. "What do you think of them? I made them for you."

"Well, I don't want them," I snapped. No good could come of this.

She tilted her head. "I thought this was what we *both* wanted, Nadine. *Revenge.*"

"I just want them to stop tormenting me," I stated. "I don't want to hurt anyone."

She smirked. "But it'd be *so* fun."

She set the Chloe doll between the other two and picked up a dagger that lay at her side. I hadn't seen it before. She brought the blade to the pad of her thumb and pressed until thick red liquid began to drip down the blade.

"For Gwen, I was thinking poison." She pressed her bloody finger to the Gwen doll's mouth and wiped the blood across it. "Killed by her own Cast."

She set the blade aside and picked up a pin. "For Camille, a heart attack."

She stabbed the pin into the brunette doll's heart. Her eyes widened in pleasure. "It should go undetected. Finally, for Chloe, I've saved something special."

An evil smile spread across her face as she picked up a red string of yarn and began to tie it around the Chloe doll's neck. She held the doll up by the string and smiled down at it with crazy eyes.

"Hanging," she chuckled.

My guts twisted, and I took a step back. "This isn't what I want."

"No?" My doppelganger tilted her head. "But it's the only way to save ourselves, Nadine."

"I'm no killer," I spat.

"But you are," she reminded me. "You let Rocky outside without his leash."

Rocky had been our neighbor's dog. They'd hired me as a kid to dog sit when they went on vacation. One day, I accidentally left the door open, and he slipped outside and was hit by a car. It'd been so long ago that I barely remembered Rocky.

"How do you know about that?" I demanded.

Her lips curled into a sneer. "Because *I'm* the one who left the door open! That dog was a fucking nightmare! We did it on purpose."

"No!" I cried. "It was an accident."

She got to her feet, and I backed up another step. She stared at me under dark lashes as she stepped out of the pentagram. "Tell yourself that all you want, Nadine. It doesn't change what you did."

"I'm not like you!" I cried. "Killing people isn't how I handle things. It'll only get me banished from the coven."

"But you *want* to," she accused, taking another step toward me. "You *want* to get rid of Chloe. We both do."

"Not like this," I insisted. "There has to be another way."

"There *is* no other way!" she exploded. "Let me out to play, and I'll do my worst."

I took another step back. "No."

I hadn't realized how far we'd moved across the ballroom until my heel touched the wall. I ended up pressed flat against it.

Dark Nadine got so close to me that I could feel her breath on my face. "Admit it, Nadine. You're *weak*."

"That's not true," I said.

"It is," she growled. "You're so weak even your body's rejected you. It hates you so much it's trying to kill itself just to get rid of you."

"You're wrong," I stated. My hands shook and curled into fists. Who the hell did this bitch think she was?

She narrowed her eyes. "How do you expect Lucas to love you if he has to take care of you all the time? You're *weak*, Nadine. Let me take over, and I'll make you strong."

Strong. I'd do anything to be strong again—to live a life where the constant joint pain and debilitating fatigue didn't drag me down.

She reached out and lifted a strand of my hair. She spoke in a smooth, alluring voice. "You're a burden, Nadine. I can change that."

The more she spoke, the more I became entranced by her.

"And our parents?" she continued. "I can make you forget all about them."

I swallowed. "I don't want to forget about them."

"Yes, you do," she snapped, her eyes suddenly darkening again. "You want to forget the pain! You want to get rid of the memories and forget they ever existed! You don't want them anymore! Why do you think they died? They couldn't stand being your parents. They left because of *you*, and you want to leave, too. Don't you, Nadine!?"

"No!" I screamed. "I want them back! But I can't! So I'll live with the pain, because it reminds me that they were there to begin with. I loved my parents, and they loved me. I. Am. Not. Their. *Burden!*"

I shoved Dark Nadine as hard as I could, and she went stumbling backward. I made a run for it, but I barely made it a few steps before something hard slammed into my back.

The air left my lungs, and I went tumbling down. I threw my hands outward to catch myself, but I saw stars. I quickly rolled over to see her coming at me. Dark black magic crackled in her hands.

She threw her head back and laughed as she approached. "Try to run, Nadine. I will *always* be with you. You and I are one in the same."

"We're not!" I screamed.

She came close enough to touch. I kicked my heel into her gut. She stumbled back, and the magic in her hand fizzled out. She gasped for breath as I scrambled to my feet and ran across the ballroom.

But Dark Nadine moved faster than me. She sprinted in front of me and cut me off on my way to the door. With a single wave of her hand, the doors swung shut, slamming so hard against the frame it shook the room.

"There's nowhere to go," she mocked. "You can't outrun me."

My gaze darted to my left, toward the pentagram circle. The dagger still lay in the middle of it next to the dolls.

"I can try," I spat.

I jumped away from her and sprinted toward the dagger. I heard her footsteps behind me and dove for the knife. She caught me by the legs and landed on top of me. I was barely six inches from the dagger and couldn't reach it.

"Get off me!" I cried, struggling out of her hold.

I managed to yank one of my feet away, then slammed it into her face. Her head snapped backward, but she grabbed tighter to my leg, until I thought it was going to bruise. Her eyebrows slammed together, and her nostrils flared.

"Bitch!" she snarled.

She pulled me backward with all her strength, dragging me through the salt circle and away from the dagger. I clawed at the carpet, but it was no use. There was nothing to hang on to.

Then my hands found something—one of the candles. I curled my fingers around it and swung my arm toward her. I shoved the flame up into her face. Her shrill cry echoed off the walls of the empty ballroom.

As her hands came up to cradle her burnt skin, I took my chance and dove for the dagger again. My fingers touched the cool handle. I was just about to use it against her when a black heel stomped on my wrist.

"Gah!" I screamed as my bones crushed into the ground. I heard a horrifying *snap*, and pain shot up through my arm and down to my fingertips. And still, she didn't let up.

Dark Nadine bent down, her chest heaving with shallow breaths. A burn red with blisters marred the side of her face. "I told you that you can't outrun me."

She reached over and picked up the Chloe doll, then ripped the hair from its head. I tried to struggle away from her, but each time I moved, an ungodly pain rippled up and down my arm. She placed all her weight on my wrist and laughed maniacally.

"See this doll, Nadine?" She held it in front of my face and smiled proudly. "That's *you*."

She held the doll over one of the candle flames.

"No!" I cried, horror twisting deep within my gut. My toes started to heat, like there was a fire burning beneath me. "Don't!"

She chuckled, as if she enjoyed the sound of me begging. "Too late."

She lowered the doll, and the fabric caught fire. A shriek so loud it could wake the dead erupted out of my lungs. Though there was no fire at my feet, I felt the flames licking up my legs. It was like my skin was searing straight off my bones.

Dark Nadine rose to her feet and took a step back. I wished I could say it was a relief when she released my wrist, but I barely felt the pain of broken bones anymore. All I could feel was the fire consuming my body. I writhed on the ground, as if I could outrun the red-hot pain consuming me. It was as if a million heated pins had pricked my body all at once. My vision started to blur as the invisible flames licked up my body and began to sear the skin from my face.

"I was right about you, Nadine!" Dark Nadine mocked. "You're weak! Always have been. You can push me down. You can try to control me. But I will *always* win."

I gritted my teeth. Pushing past the fiery inferno, I lifted my arm. "Not this time."

I took the dagger in my good hand and forced all of the strength I had through my arm. I lifted the dagger and plunged it downward… straight into Dark Nadine's foot. It sliced through her boot, into her skin, and out the bottom of her sole. It embedded so far that the blade didn't even show —it had stuck straight into the floor and rooted her in place.

She screamed a chilling cry and dropped the doll. It fell within my reach, and I grabbed it, stomping out the fire with my hand. Relief washed over me as the pain stopped spreading. I could've sworn if I looked at myself, skin would be hanging off my bones, but I pushed past it and scrambled to my feet. I backed up several paces.

Dark Nadine tried to come for me, but the dagger kept her in place. She screamed in frustration and pain as her foot tugged on the dagger, ripping into more flesh as she tried to come after me.

"I'm not weak!" I yelled at her.

I whirled around and ran for the doors.

"You're nothing without me!" she shouted from behind me.

I flung the doors open and stumbled out into the hall. As quickly as I could, I closed them again. My heart slammed against my rib cage as I glanced around. My eyes landed on a branched candlestick sitting on a table in a nearby alcove. I ran for it and snatched it up, then returned to the doors, where I shoved the candlestick through the handles to trap my darkness inside.

She screamed again, louder this time. Her shriek echoed down the hall, and I guessed she must've ripped the dagger from her foot.

"I'll come for you, Nadine!" she raged through the closed doors. "I'll come for you!"

My heart raced as I whirled around and sprinted away from the ballroom and the evil woman locked inside. I glanced back to make sure she wasn't coming for me, but the hall was empty. As I turned forward again, my toes caught on the hallway rug, and I stumbled forward. I threw my hands out to catch myself…

But instead of landing on carpet, my hands sank into the earth. One second I was running away from my darkness in the halls of Miriam Mansion, and the next, I was lying in the grass, the daylit sky overcast above me.

Dark Nadine completely fell from my mind, as if the moment with her had never happened. The pain of a broken wrist vanished. My attention became completely wrapped in the scene before me.

The first thing I saw was a stone—a smooth, polished stone. I lifted my head to see that it was a gravestone, one of many throughout the graveyard. My eyes drifted over the two names etched into the grave marker.

Nathan Evers. Faith Evers. Loving father and mother.

Somehow, I'd ended up at my parents' graves.

LUCAS

TWENTY-ONE

The setting sun lit the sky in a bright orange hue as I approached the gates to the cemetery. The Reaper Moon would rise soon, and then I could begin the ritual. I was excited by the idea—to get rid of the voices, to ditch the curse. It would be a dream come true.

And yet another part of me feared I might not have what it takes. This was my one and only shot, and if I couldn't summon the reapers by night's end, Nadine and I would always be kept at arm's length.

I steeled my shaking nerves and stepped into the cemetery. I trudged through the snow until I came upon a tall statue at the center of the cemetery. It depicted a reaper at least ten feet tall, clothed in a dark, flowing robe. Where his face should be was nothing but a dark hole. His fingers were only bone. One of his hands reached outward, as if inviting me closer. The other held on to a tall scythe.

At the base of the statue was a name carved into the stone. *Edgar Nowak. Reaper's Apprentice.*

He'd been the one before me.

Beneath his name were his birth and death dates. The rumors were true. The poor bastard had lived to be over a hundred. I didn't want to do the math to figure out how many thoughts he'd carried with him to the afterlife.

I took a deep breath as the sun dipped below the horizon. "Almost time…"

I knelt at the head of Edgar's grave and waited. As I waited, I tried to calm myself, to push all doubt out of my mind.

I can do this, I told myself. *I will summon a reaper.*

I didn't know if I meant it, or if it was just wishful thinking.

Darkness continued to fall over the night, until finally the last few rays of sunshine disappeared. Above me, the full moon shone. I liked to think the clear skies were a beacon of hope, as if opening me to Alora above. But somehow, the stars seemed dimmer than they should, like there was a darkness cutting me off.

My gaze darted around the cemetery. The shadows of the gravestones were ominous. A shiver ran down my spine, but I knew my unease was all in my head. Tonight, there were no zombies that were going to jump out of the bushes. Tonight, the only enemy was myself. Though I was on my knees, my legs shook beneath me.

I summoned the scroll I'd stolen from the mausoleum and read over it again for the hundredth time. It shook in my hands. I had to get this right. It had to be perfect.

Give up your blood to a reaper's grave. Shed doubt, fear not, stand firm and brave. Face the thoughts that you've neglected. Accept and let go of all you've collected.

The interpretation was clear. I had to revisit all the thoughts that'd been given to me as the Reaper's Apprentice before handing them over.

This was going to be a long fucking night.

"Well," I sighed to myself. "It's now or never."

I summoned a knife and pressed the blade to my opposite palm. I winced as the knife sliced into my skin, but after the initial shock, I didn't mind. The stinging pain was sort of welcome.

Blood dripped out of my palm and stained the snow below me. I reached out and smeared the blood across the base of the reaper's statue, straight across his name. Then I shoved my hand into the snow to numb the sting. It eased it, until my hand became so numb I couldn't feel anything at all.

With my good hand, I summoned the leather-bound spell book where I recorded all the thoughts I'd heard. I didn't have to open it to recall the exact wording of the first thought I'd ever collected.

"I made a mistake," I repeated Eric's last thought, though it barely came out. I'd never spoken his words out loud, and I knew why. The words cut

deep into my chest, tearing deep, sharp holes in my heart. I hated that he'd died with this last thought on his mind. He should've died happy.

But it was done now. He'd moved on. It was time I did, too.

I swallowed the lump in my throat and continued. *"I don't want to die."*

Tears pricked at my eyes. Fuck, I was only on the first one. How was I going to make it through hundreds?

The hard part is over, I told myself. *You've faced Eric's last thought. You can handle a handful of strangers' thoughts. Let's get this over with.*

I opened my book and began to read the words I'd recorded. Some thoughts were easier than others. Some didn't make sense at all. Every now and then, there were those that tore me to the very core. I couldn't help but wonder if these people had crossed over all right. Had I done right by holding on to their thoughts so they could make it to the other side? Or had their dark past behind those thoughts held them back?

"I hope she got what she deserved," I read.

The thoughts just kept going like that—revenge, regret, anger, sadness.

I'm not ready to go.

I should've stopped him from hurting her.

I'll get my revenge in the afterlife.

I tried not to think about how much time had passed. The coldness of the night brushed across the back of my neck and seeped through my jacket. My fingers became numb, and I curled my arms around myself to try to keep warm. It barely helped though. I shivered, and my breath turned to fog each time I breathed out.

I'll miss you.

I hope you keep your promise.

Is it playtime?

Page after page, it kept going. Hundreds of thoughts piling up. The more I read, the harder it became. It was like each thought I read added another ten-pound weight to my chest.

Finally, after an eternity of reviewing each and every thought in my journal, I reached the last page I'd filled in. I read out the last thought and breathed a sigh of relief. I'd done it. I reached the end!

I glanced around the cemetery, waiting for the reapers to appear, but I saw nothing.

"Hello?" I called out to the darkness. "Anyone there? I did like the spell said. I faced the thoughts! Where are you!?"

No answer came.

My guts sank. Frantically, I flipped back to the front of the journal and read the thoughts over again.

Still nothing.

"This is what I'm supposed to do, isn't it?" I shouted. I was a fool if I actually thought someone was going to answer.

"I must be doing something wrong," I muttered to myself. I turned back to the scroll and unrolled it all the way. I flipped it over once, then twice, to make sure I hadn't missed anything. "This is it… that's all I have to do. What am I doing wrong?"

That was my only explanation. I wasn't doing it right.

Face the thoughts…

Maybe reading them wasn't enough. Maybe it was about *feeling* them.

I took a deep breath and started at the beginning again for the third time. This time, I didn't just read the words on the page. I took a breath for each thought and allowed the messages to seep deep into my soul. I gave each of them the time and consideration they deserved.

By the time I was done, hours must've passed. Fuck, if this took me much longer, I was going to miss Nadine's ceremony.

I held my breath and looked around the cemetery again. I could swear I felt a presence there, but it must've been wishful thinking, because there were no reapers. No… anything.

"Come on…" I gritted my teeth and muttered under my breath. I reread the ritual again, and something jumped out at me.

"I have to let the thoughts go," I realized.

It was so simple.

I conjured a lighter and held the edge of my journal above the flame. The pages caught fire instantly, and the flames eagerly ate away at the paper. Once the flames came too close to my hands, I tossed the journal to the snow in front of me. I watched as the flames ate away at the words on the page. Pieces of burnt paper broke off and drifted away in the wind, tumbling across the surface of the snow.

I wish I could say I felt something, but I didn't. It should've been a relief, but the weight on my chest only became heavier.

Nothing within the cemetery changed. It was just shadows, just cold, just emptiness!

"Fuck the reapers!" I shouted to the skies. Frustration curled its evil arms around me, squeezing me so tight it was the only thing I could feel. My eyebrows knitted tightly together, and my lips pressed into a firm line.

Was this some kind of sick joke they were playing on me? Was this fucking ritual even real?

I got to my feet. "Where are you!?" I screamed, my voice echoing over the cemetery. "You're supposed to be here! I summoned you! Come and take this curse from me!"

I reacted without thinking about it. I curled my hand into a fist and slammed my knuckles against the base of the reaper statue. A sharp, unbearable pain shot across my hand.

"Fuuuck!" I cried. I sucked air through my teeth and tried to catch my breath. "Is this what you wanted? Is this what the ritual needs? Blood and broken bones? Have them. I don't fucking care anymore."

Heavy, shallow breaths racked my chest, and my arms quaked. I held my hand tight to my abdomen, but the pain started to ease quickly. I flexed my hand to find it wasn't broken. Hurt like a son of a bitch, though.

"Face the thoughts you've neglected. Accept and let go of all you've collected," I spat. "You want to know the truth of what I've neglected? You want to know!?"

I was raging like a mad man at nothing but a lifeless statue, but I didn't care.

"I fucking *hate* myself!" I screamed. "Is that what you want to hear? Let's see… what have I collected? Shame! Guilt! Depression! You need a longer list? *I* didn't see the signs that my brother was at the edge of his life. *I* could have stopped it if I just took a second to understand what he was going through—to listen to his cries for help. I should've known when he didn't show up for my ceremony that something was wrong. I should've helped!"

I barely took a breath before I continued raging. "And guess what else? I made a promise to the highest power of all the coven, and I broke it. I said I'd accept whatever Mother Miriam had in store, but I rejected it the night she gave it to me. I *should* feel guilty about that. You want to know why I'm doing this? Because I'm damned to the Abyss anyway! Might as well try to enjoy the one chance at happiness I'll ever get. But I don't deserve even that! We all know it. That's why you're not here, isn't it? I'm not worthy! You think so, too; otherwise you'd be here!"

I plopped my ass on the ground and leaned my back against the base of the reaper statue. I pulled my knees to my chest and buried my face in my arms. My whole body shook, but I'd be damned if it didn't feel good to get all that out in the open.

"Lucas."

My gaze snapped upward at the sound of the voice. The blood drained from my face when I saw a cloaked man standing there. He was as solid as I was. I could hardly believe what I was seeing.

It worked!?

My heart began to pitter-patter against my rib cage. "You're a reaper?" I questioned cautiously. Part of me worried this might be some sort of joke. My eyes roamed over him, looking for signs of death, but his hands were covered in dark gloves, and I couldn't see his face.

"I'm Edgar Nowak, the newest member of the Reaper Order," he stated. "I take it you've summoned me to remove your power."

"So it's true?" I asked hopefully. "You can do it?"

"Yes," he said, but a grave warning lurked in his tone. "You understand what this means, don't you?"

"I know," I said desperately. "Refusing Mother Miriam's gift will damn me to the Abyss. But I want it gone."

"The Abyss is not a damnation to be taken lightly. Abandoning Mother Miriam is a sin that can never be forgiven," he warned. "You will burn for all eternity. The flesh will be seared from your bones, regrown, and burned off again and again. Splinters will be shoved beneath your finger-nails, before each fingernail is ripped from your nail bed one by one. Red-hot rods will be shoved into your eyes. You will not feel a moment of relief, young reaper. You will be faced with a nightmare most cannot even begin to imagine. You will suffer in ways men have never suffered before. Are you sure you want to do this?"

Nothing he said scared me. The real hell was never getting a chance to live a full life with Nadine.

I stood and planted my feet firmly beneath me. All the shaking that had rocked my body moments ago had vanished. I held my head high as I answered. "I'm sure. Tell me what to do."

nadine
TWENTY-TWO

My heart jumped into my throat, and I scurried backward until my back hit the gravestone behind me. My stomach felt as if a gaping hole were about to erupt open. I pulled my knees to my chest and curled myself into a ball. I buried my face into my knees, because I couldn't stand to look at my parents' graves.

I shouldn't be here, I thought. Why had I come? I knew I'd never be able to handle it—seeing their names on the headstone, knowing their bodies had been placed into the ground at that very spot.

Your parents are dead.

I didn't know where the voice had come from, but it must've been my own. It was a dark, cruel reminder of everything I'd been through after losing them. I wanted them back. I wanted them back more than anything. And I never would...

"Nadine," a woman's voice said.

I must've been hallucinating, because she sounded just like my mother. I lifted my gaze. I nearly dropped dead right then and there. Two figures stood above me, but it was like looking at ghosts.

"Nadine?" Dad asked, reaching out his hand.

Nothing about him had changed. He had brown hair, electric blue eyes, and a graying beard. Yet something felt... off.

Of course it does! He's dead! I reminded myself.

"It's okay, Nadine," Mom encouraged. Her voice sounded like a song. She was so pretty. Why hadn't I ever realized how pretty she was before?

My parents held their hands out to me, waiting for me to accept them.

"Is it really you?" I asked, my voice cracking.

Dad nodded. "It's us, baby girl."

Sobs began to rock my shoulders. I reached out and took each of their hands, and they helped me to my feet. I wrapped an arm around each of them, until the three of us were locked into an embrace. They felt so real —so solid. I didn't know how, but they were here with me. Hot, heavy tears streamed down my face, but the hole in my belly started to close. I felt like I could breathe for the first time in months.

"How are you here?" I asked. I wished I could keep them here forever. "This is impossible."

Mom drew away from me and tilted her head. "Impossible how, sweetheart?"

I sniffled and wiped the tears from my eyes. "You know."

Mom and Dad exchanged a shocked expression. They *didn't* know.

"We know what?" Dad asked. "What's going on?"

A weight settled on my chest. How could they pretend like they didn't know what happened? Tears fell down my cheeks. I wrapped my arms around myself because it was all I could do to hold myself together.

"You don't remember?" I asked.

Mom tilted her head to the side. "Remember what?"

"You're really going to make me say it, aren't you?" I sobbed.

"We don't understand," Dad insisted. "Tell us what's wrong, Nadine."

My bottom lip trembled. I wanted to tell them, but I couldn't get the words out. I just totally froze up.

Mom stepped forward and took my arm. I couldn't believe how warm and real she felt. All I wanted to do was wrap her in my arms again.

But I couldn't. Because no matter how much I wanted my parents with me, it couldn't happen. I didn't know how it was happening now, but it wasn't real.

"Let's go home," Mom suggested. "We'll get this all sorted out."

I jerked away from her, but my voice came out really small. "I can't go home with you."

"Of course you can," Dad said, like this was any old day. "We had plans to work on the car this afternoon."

"And you and I were going to make cookies," Mom reminded me.

My stomach dropped. I wanted to do all of that so badly. I'd love to drop everything and go home with them. But instead, I took a step back.

"I'm sorry, but I can't," I told them. "You don't belong here. I have to go back home to Octavia Falls."

Mom's brow furrowed. "You don't live in Octavia Falls, Nadine. You've never been there. Are you having an episode?"

"No, I'm not having an episode," I snapped. Why couldn't they see? How could I make them understand?

"Then tell us what's wrong," Dad demanded.

"You're *dead*!" I burst.

The world seemed to stop spinning. The entire cemetery went silent, though my voice continued to echo in the distance.

Dead. My parents were dead.

I'd said it aloud so many times before, but I never *felt* it like I did in that moment. They were truly, honestly, one-hundred-percent gone from this earth. And nothing I could do—no amount of praying, séances, necromancy, or potions—could bring them back.

Dad looked at me. His eyebrows knit together, creating deep lines of concern on his forehead. "What do you mean, baby girl? Your mother and I are fine."

"No, you're not!" I cried. "You died last summer. I planned your funeral. I watched your caskets be placed into the ground right—"

I cut off. As I gestured to their grave plot, I realized their names had been removed. There was nothing but smooth stone where their names had been carved.

"Nadine?" Mom asked, worry lacing her tone. "Are you okay?"

"No!" I cried, rounding the gravestone to inspect it from every angle. "No, I'm not okay. This is where I buried you. You're not real! You're ghosts!"

And that's when it truly hit me. This was it for us. The next time I'd meet them would be in Alora.

"You're ghosts," I repeated in a low whisper. As I said it—as I felt it deep down within my soul—the names on the gravestone began to appear again. Bits of stone sank inward in the shape of letters, until it showed my parents' names again.

Warmth spread throughout my heart when I realized what this meant.

I'd been given a second chance to speak to them. I could say all the things I didn't get the chance to say!

"Nadine—" Mom started, but I cut her off.

"We might not have much time," I said quickly. "Please let me get this out before you leave."

I walked over to my father and pulled him into a tight hug. "Dad, I should have said thank you more. You supported me in *everything*. Do you remember when I was eight and snuck DVDs to my room to watch those homicide detective shows you and Mom thought I was too young for? You caught me one day, and I thought I would be grounded for life. But instead, you came into my room, sat next to me on the bed, and started watching with me. You didn't say a thing, just held me in your arms and kept watching."

Sobs bubbled up in my throat, but I continued. "When I was ten and told you I wanted to be a homicide detective, you didn't think that was too off-the-wall. You bought me my first *Clue* game for my birthday, and you played every Sunday since. You taught me more about cars than most girls will ever know, and you made me fight when I thought there was no fight left in me."

I drew away and wiped at my nose. Dad stared down at me with the softest, kindest expression. That was one of the things I missed most about him—the kindness.

"You taught me how to be good to other people," I told him. "And I'm never going to forget that."

Tears welled in my father's eyes. "I love you, baby girl."

"I love you, too."

Dad and I shared another embrace. I didn't want to pull away, but I had more to say to my mother.

I turned to her. "Mom, I wish I'd listened to you more. You are *so* wise. Especially about boys."

Mom chuckled, but she couldn't hide the tears. "I *do* have some experience in that area."

"I miss everything about you," I said. "The smell of your hair, and the way you'd dance when you were doing dishes. I miss coming home to the smell of freshly baked bread and cookies on the counter. Sometimes, I want to crawl into your bed like I did when I was a kid—because when I lost you, it was just one huge nightmare. But I know everything is going to be okay, because you taught me how to be independent in ways I didn't realize."

Mom pulled me into a hug before I was done telling her how much I missed her. I hugged her back so hard that it made my arms hurt.

Finally, we drew away from each other, and I looked to both of my parents. "You have both been wonderful to me. You had to put up with me when I acted out, and stood by me with unwavering faith when I was in and out of the hospital. You two have just been amazing. I couldn't have asked for better parents. I'm so lucky to be your daughter. And just because you're gone doesn't change that. You'll always be my parents, and you'll always be with me… right here."

I placed my finger to my heart, and Mom and Dad totally lost it. The three of us started sobbing together. But they were beautiful, wonderful tears. A huge weight lifted off my shoulders, and I felt so light I could float to the stars.

I wiped my eyes. "I have to admit. This is probably the hardest thing I've ever had to do—and that's saying a lot."

I took a deep, wavering breath. For a moment, I worried that the words wouldn't come out. And then they just… did. And it was the most freeing, beautiful moment of my life.

"Goodbye," I said.

Mom and Dad shared a smile. "Goodbye, Nadine. We love you."

Peace washed over me as my parents faded from view. I should've run after them. I should've sobbed and begged them to come back. But I didn't, because somehow, I was finally okay with letting go. It didn't mean I didn't love them. It didn't mean I didn't care that they were gone.

It just meant… everything was going to be okay.

"You've done well, my child."

I whirled around at the sound of an unfamiliar voice. The cemetery had transformed around me. Instead of being day, it had instantly transformed into night. I wasn't standing near the same plot as I was before. In fact, I wasn't even sure I was standing in the same cemetery. The air was cold, and snow covered the ground. The full moon glowed above us.

A woman stood several feet away from me, cloaked in a velvet hood. I tilted my head to try to get a better look, but the hood fell so far over her eyes that even the moonlight didn't touch her face.

"Excuse me?" I asked.

She reached up and lowered her hood. My heart stalled in my chest when I saw her. I'd seen those high cheekbones, full lips, and beautiful eyes before—in the painting that hung above the mantle at school. It was Mother Miriam.

I found myself rooted in place as I took her in. Positive energy radiated off of her in waves, and she seemed to glow slightly in the moonlight. The cool air around us warmed, and I truly felt like I was standing in the presence of a goddess.

"Mother Miriam?" I asked breathlessly, just to see if it was real.

She nodded lightly, then stretched out her hand. "Come with me, child."

I hesitated a moment. Was I worthy enough to take her hand?

I wanted to be. And she was offering. So I took it.

All the pain in my muscles and joints washed away. When I touched her, it was like taking the hand of someone I'd known forever. All my hesitation fell away, and I felt totally at ease in her presence.

"What's going on?" I asked as she led me through the cemetery.

Mother Miriam spoke slowly, like we were in no rush. "There's something you must see, Nadine."

Though I'd never heard her speak my name before, something about it seemed so familiar. It was like I'd known her my whole life.

We passed by gravestone after gravestone, until I spotted a shadowed figure in the distance. He sat in the snow, his back pressed against the base of a tall reaper statue. His knees were curled to his chest, and he shook in the cold.

"Who is that?" I asked Mother Miriam.

"I think you already know," she said kindly.

My pulse quickened as we came closer. I began to make out the shape of his shoulders.

"Lucas?" I realized, before raising my voice so he could hear me. "Lucas!?"

He didn't respond.

"He can't hear you," Mother Miriam told me.

I looked to her as we came to a stop several gravestones away from him. "What is this, then? A vision?"

"Of sorts," she said with a nod.

"Is it real?" I asked.

She gestured around us. "Everything you see here is happening, Nadine."

She was like the Ghost of Christmas Present.

I furrowed my brow. "What are we here for? What's Lucas doing?"

Mother Miriam's breath wavered, and my stomach dropped. Though she hadn't answered, I sensed that it was something dark and dangerous. I gazed closer at Lucas, and that was when I noticed the pool of blood in the snow beneath him.

"Lucas is summoning the reapers," Mother Miriam said solemnly.

"Summoning them… why?"

"Because their power can take his away," she explained.

"He's not going to be the Reaper's Apprentice anymore?" I asked.

I wanted to be excited about it. It meant the Reaper's Shadow curse couldn't touch us. We could be together.

But I sensed something deeper in the way Mother Miriam spoke. She obviously cared very deeply for Lucas.

"If he completes the ritual, he will be washed of his gift," she explained.

"Why's that bad, though?" I asked. "He doesn't want it."

She turned her gaze back to Lucas. She got this faraway look in her eyes—like she was recalling a special memory. "Because he made a promise to me, Nadine. When I offered him his power, he agreed to accept whatever gift I gave him. And now he is refusing that gift. He went back on his word. I can't accept him into Alora if he does that."

The air in the cemetery seemed heavy as a rock. I couldn't breathe it in. I just stood there, completely frozen and trying to wrap my head around her meaning.

"You're saying if he goes through with this, he'll be cast out of the coven?" I asked. "He'll be damned to the Abyss?"

Deep, unsettling worry twisted around my heart. Mother Miriam nodded solemnly.

"Then we have to stop him!" I insisted. "Lucas!"

Mother Miriam placed a gentle hand on my shoulder to stop me. "I'm afraid we can't stop it, my child."

A thick lump rose to my throat. "You don't have to send him to the Abyss. I-I thought the coven granted second chances."

"I *am* offering him a second chance… through you."

"W-what do you mean?" I asked, but my throat closed so tightly around my words that it barely came out.

"Lucas is doing this for you," she stated. "As long as you're around, he will give up his gift to be with you. Once his magic is gone, he's condemned himself, and his soul can't enter into Alora… not without a trade."

My knees grew weak as I realized what she was offering. "I can trade my soul for his?"

"These last few months, your souls have intertwined," she explained. "I can take one, but not the other."

"We'll be apart," I realized with sinking clarity. "No matter what, we'll never be together."

"Yes," Mother Miriam confirmed. "There are only two outcomes, Nadine. If he gives up his gift for you and you live out your lives together, he'll end up in the Abyss. Or you can trade your soul for his. I will take away his gift, and he will live his life without the voices, but I will accept him into Alora with open arms. Yet you will be condemned to the Abyss in his place, forever."

The fact that those were our only two options burned me to the very core. All I wanted was to be with Lucas.

But we couldn't have that.

If I did this for him, it meant giving up my life and my magic. It meant leaving Grammy behind and never seeing my parents again in Alora. I'd be banished to hell. I'd have to give up absolutely *everything* for him.

"Time is running out, Nadine," Mother Miriam stated. "Will you give up your soul to take Lucas's place?"

TWENTY-THREE

"Take my hand."

That's all the reaper said. I couldn't believe it was that simple.

"That's it?" I asked.

Edgar's robes billowed in the wind. "That's all. I will take the thoughts you've collected with me. You will be relieved of your duties. Your power will be taken from you, and you will be sentenced to the Abyss."

I took a step forward and reached for him. My hand just barely grazed his before he jerked away. His head snapped to the side, like he heard a noise in the distance that had caught his full attention.

I looked in the same direction, but I didn't see anything. "What is it?"

Edgar turned to me, though I still couldn't see his features beneath his hood. "I'm sorry. I must go. I have a soul to collect."

"Wait!" I cried, but he was already backing away from me.

The reaper whirled around. His body glided above the snow and left no prints. I started sprinting after him, but he moved so fast I couldn't keep up.

"Come back!" I screamed.

The air seemed to suck out of the cemetery the faster I ran. It was only moments before he had vanished from sight.

Panic swept through me. Had I lost my chance? Had he totally abandoned me? Was he coming back?

I slowed and stared after the reaper where he'd disappeared into the trees. A feeling of hopelessness settled over me. I'd missed my chance, hadn't I?

"I thought we had an agreement!" I shouted.

A leaf tumbled in the wind and caught on my shoe. I kicked it off, but the wind swirled around me, sending the leaf back into my leg. I tried twice more to shake it off, but each time, it came back. Frustrated, I bent to grab it, ready to tear the freaking thing to shreds—

But it wasn't a leaf at all. I took it in my hands and lifted it. My stomach dropped out of my abdomen. It was a tarot card, the *Death* card —perhaps the very one I'd thrown into the wind on Halloween. Somehow, it'd come back for me.

It had to be a message. My eyes went wide. I glanced around, like I expected to see someone standing there willing to explain.

"Eric?" I called out to the darkness. "Is this yours? What does it mean? What do you want me to do?"

The voice that answered was the last one I'd ever expected to hear.

"I did it to save you, Lucas. I will always love you."

I whirled around, expecting *her* to be standing there, but there was nothing but tombstones beside me.

I'd heard her last thought.

The heart-wrenching realization hit me like the weight of a thousand stunning spells. For a moment, I couldn't move, couldn't think. All I could do was stand there as my entire world stopped spinning.

Not my Nadine.

The second her name passed through my mind, I snapped back to attention. *No one* was taking my Nadine from me!

I started sprinting. I'd never run so hard and fast in my life. The only time that came close was the night of my Evoking Ceremony when I'd rushed home to Eric. It struck me how frightening similar this was. Hurdling over grave stones and sprinting out of the cemetery was a sick form of déjà vu.

I just hoped this time I wasn't too late…

My sliced palm stung as I pumped my arms. My legs protested as I pushed them harder than I'd ever pushed before. My chest burned with the need for air. But none of that mattered right now, because the thought of losing Nadine hurt more than any other pain I could imagine. I'd gladly welcome a thousand eternities of flesh-burning torture for her.

Houses blurred past me as I ran through town. I sprinted down her grandmother's street—and stopped in my tracks when I caught sight of the scene in Helena's living room. I had a mere split second to take it in.

Through the window, I saw Helena, Grant, and Talia seated around Nadine's body. She hovered in the air as if she was lying on an invisible table. Everyone watched on silently, oblivious to the fact that there was a fucking *reaper* standing over her! He stood beside her like he was hungry for his next meal.

The only one who seemed to notice something was amiss was Isa. She stood on Talia's lap, her hair on end, hissing.

The reaper reached out for Nadine and scooped her up. Suddenly, I was seeing double. Nadine's body remained hovered in the air, but a transparent figure identical to her lay cradled in Edgar's arms. I didn't know how I was seeing her soul, but I sensed it was because the reaper had touched both of us tonight.

"Stop!" I screamed.

But no one heard me. Nadine's body dropped out of the air, slamming to the ground beneath her. All at once, Helena, Grant, and Talia leapt to their feet. Sheer and utter worry marred each of their faces.

I barely had a chance to process it before the reaper was on the move. He stepped through the wall and onto the porch like a ghost. My precious Nadine's spirit lay lifeless in his arms.

"You can't do this!" I demanded.

He looked toward me, but he must've decided I meant nothing, because he turned away and started toward the trees at the side of Helena's house. I didn't know how far I'd already run, but I knew one thing for certain: I'd race to the ends of the earth for Nadine.

I followed the reaper as fast as my legs could carry me. I trampled over dead plants in Helena's garden and crunched down snow as I raced over the lawn. I followed the reaper into the forest, where the snow was minimal and a clear dirt path paved the way.

"Come back!" I shouted.

Edgar didn't slow, but somehow, I was catching up.

I heard him mumble something under his breath, and then something frightening happened. I could barely believe my eyes.

In the middle of the forest, a portal opened. One moment, all I saw was shadows of trees in the moonlight. The next, a wide, swirling archway grew from nothing. It expanded until it was large enough to step through. At first, all I saw was blackness around the edges. Then came the distorted image of the horrifying landscape beyond. In the flickering of the portal, I could make out fires that went for miles across a dark, desolate landscape.

The Abyss.

He was taking my Nadine to the Abyss! This was either a sick joke, or a horrible mistake. I had to stop this!

I didn't know if it was sheer willpower or by the fate of the Goddess, but I finally reached him. My hands shot upward, and my fingers wrapped around the dark fabric of his hood.

I yanked downward, and his hood fell away. He whirled around and thrust his arm outward. A blast of red magic shot out of his hand and slammed into my chest. I went flying backward but hardly made it three feet before slamming into a tree. I slumped to the ground, gasping for air.

It barely fazed me, because what I saw next shook me to my very core. The reaper turned, and I caught sight of his face—his true, deadly form. The legends of the reapers were true. They walked the earth as a shadow of death. His face was nothing but a skull. There were no muscles, no skin —just pure white bone. His eyes were completely hollow—a deep, dark black that seemed to suck my life energy just looking at them. He was the very embodiment of death.

"You can't save her," he snarled. "She's *my* assignment."

His jaw moved, but he had no lips to form his words. Somehow, they came out sounding clear.

"I'd be damned if I didn't try," I growled.

I raised my hands, and purple magic shot out of my palms. A stunning spell slammed into his chest. His feet swept out from under him, and he went tumbling backward. Nadine's spirit fell from his arms, and she hovered in the air limply.

I jumped to my feet. At the same time, the reaper sliced his hand through the air, and I felt a sharp pain on my face, as if an invisible dagger had cut my skin open. The warmth of blood trickled down my face, but I didn't stop to assess the damage. I hurdled over the reaper and reached out for Nadine. I nearly touched her soul, but I didn't get there before a cold hand grasped my ankle.

"Let me go!" I shouted.

I drew my foot back and slammed my heel into his face. A satisfying *crunch* met my ears, though it didn't seem to slow him down. He squeezed my ankle tighter and yanked me backward, dragging me through the snowy dirt. My hands clawed desperately outward, but I couldn't find a handhold.

"You can't stop this," he warned, before drawing his arm back and slamming it into my cheek to slow me down.

Ever been punched by a reaper? Turns out, their swing is fucking *strong*. He had the punch of a freaking heavyweight champion, yet he didn't have a single muscle on him. Pain radiated across my face, and a blast of red flashed across my vision. The world spun around me. I was half surprised he hadn't knocked me out right then and there.

The reaper left my side to go to Nadine, but there was no way I was giving up now. I jumped to my feet, though it felt as if the earth was rocking beneath me. I forced my eyes open, but only my right one followed my command. The left was completely swollen shut.

He reached out for Nadine. I couldn't stand the excruciating thought of death touching her. Not today.

I totally and one-hundred percent lost it.

"You're gonna have to try harder than that," I growled.

Fury swept through me, and I threw all of my anger into my magic. A sizzling ball of magic swelled in my palms. As the magic came too much to hold on to, it shot from my hands and went spinning toward the reaper. My battle magic landed at his feet and exploded, sending him blasting away from the portal and my Nadine.

It disoriented him enough that I gained the upper hand. I threw all my weight at him and grabbed him by the back of the robes. I gritted my teeth and screamed as I spun him around. I intended to use his moment to smash his head into a tree, but I guess I forgot we were fighting on different planes. My magic worked against him, but other weapons didn't. His skull went through the damn tree. I swung him to the ground and threw myself between him and Nadine.

"You can't have her!" I cried.

He pushed himself up, like he hadn't felt a thing. How the hell was I supposed to fight a freaking *skeleton*? He didn't feel pain. He couldn't be choked or bruised or knocked out. Plus, he was fucking strong. I was at a total disadvantage, but I'd still do anything to defeat him.

Just as I was about to speak another incantation, the reaper reacted. Red magic slammed into my ribs. It was so heavy and strong that it knocked me on my ass in no time flat. My vision blurred. I tried to push myself up, but a sharp, searing pain like a sword in my side shot through my ribs.

Broken.

"Shit," I growled beneath my breath as I pushed myself to my feet.

Edgar yanked his glove from his hand and thrust his palm out in my direction. Suddenly, excruciating pain assaulted me from all angles. Every muscle in my body seemed to twist at his command, and my skin felt like it was separating from my body. The pain permeated deep into my bones.

It was battle magic like I'd never seen before.

"Gah!" I screamed as blinding pain overtook every nerve ending.

My knees buckled beneath me, and my back arched as I cried out. I tried to move my hands, to force defensive magic out through them, but they stayed curled into fists at my side. My scream echoed through the forest, laced with the chilling overtone of torture.

"You don't know what you're doing, Lucas," Edgar warned. His boney fingers twisted, like he intended to crush me by sheer will. "She's dead. You can't bring her back. It's against the rules."

"Screw the rules!" I spat. It took all my energy to push past his magic and speak. "Let her stay."

"It doesn't work that way," he insisted. "I need a soul."

"Then take me instead!" I begged through gritted teeth. "I've got a soul. I haven't been damned yet."

"And you won't be," he stated coolly.

The pain intensified as the realization hit me. "She did this for me. Didn't she?"

At this point, the reaper's spell might as well have been a mere tickle across my skin. The excruciating pain was nothing compared to the heartbreak that crushed my very soul in that moment. Nadine gave herself up for me, and that's something I would eternally blame myself for. I would never forgive myself for being the reason she was damned.

Edgar nodded. "She gave up her life to stop the ritual. She gave her soul in place of yours. She is sentenced to the Abyss. I must take her and leave now."

Pure fury rocked my body. I'd do anything to save Nadine from damnation. She was the sun my earth moved around, the gravity that kept me grounded, and the force that kept my world from spinning off its axis. She was the air in my lungs and the magic that flowed through me. I loved her like the night sky loved the stars. She was mine, and I was hers. Forever.

"You're not going *anywhere* with her," I growled.

"Only a reaper has control over the life and death of a soul!" he yelled furiously. "If you restore this soul, you accept your reaper magic, and it will bind itself to you once and for all. After that, I can't take that magic away. If you wish to continue with our agreement from earlier, you must let me take her soul to the Abyss."

So I either give up my gift, or save her life?

The answer was simple. Her soul was staying.

Magic like I'd never felt before ignited deep within my belly. I gathered it tight within my chest and pushed outward with all my might. Darkness clouded my vision as the magic passed through me. Then…

Boom!

My magic exploded, whipping through me like a tidal wave. By some miracle, my magic overpowered his, counteracting his spell. The pain washed away, and I fell onto my hands and knees, gasping. One hand clutched my broken ribs as I waited for my vision to return.

When it finally did, I looked up to see an empty forest. I immediately whirled around toward the portal to see Edgar hovering over Nadine's spirit. He bent beside her and touched her.

Not today, motherfucker!

I scrambled to my feet and ran forward. My foot swung outward like I was about to kick the field goal of the century. I kicked as hard as I possibly could, and my foot connected perfectly with his skull.

Edgar's vertebrae snapped, and his head flew off his skeleton. It went soaring forward straight toward the portal, his scream echoing through the forest. And then…

Silence.

His head was gone, lost to the Abyss. I could hardly believe what I'd done.

But we weren't finished. Edgar's body whirled toward me. It was kind of creepy to see a headless guy moving through the forest. His arms raised, and his shoulders heaved as a spell formed in his hands.

On instinct, I threw my hands upward. I had no intention, no clue what I was doing. All I knew in that split second was I had to protect myself.

A battle orb shot out of Edgar's hands...

But it never reached me. The magic bounced off an invisible shield and ricocheted back at him.

The battle orb slammed into his chest and exploded. His headless body blasted backward. His heel teetered on the edge of the portal, and his arms desperately reached out for something to grab on to—but they found nothing. He went tumbling backward, and the portal swallowed him up.

The reaper was gone.

I gasped, utterly shocked by what just happened. Did I just send the reaper to the Abyss? Had I just used *shield* magic?

I barely had time to question it before the ground began to shake. The earth rumbled around me, and I could barely stay on my feet.

Oh, fuck.

Lightning crackled out of the portal, and thunder boomed through the forest. My stomach twisted into tight knots. I didn't know how much more I could handle. For a second, I thought I was going to have to deal with this damn reaper clawing his way out of the depths of hell.

Then suddenly, the portal slammed closed.

Utter silence settled over the forest, and the image of the trees became clear again. It was as if the portal had never been there in the first place.

Relief washed over me. It was over. I'd defeated the reaper. I'd saved Nadine.

I rushed over to her floating spirit, my heart racing. I reached out and touched the side of her face. My fingers didn't move through her spirit like I expected them to. They touched solid skin—I guess for the same reason I could see her.

I scooped Nadine in my arms. She was as light as air, but she was warm and solid in my arms. I could feel the life inside of her as I cradled her to my chest.

I pressed my lips to her forehead and wept as I lifted her. "Hang on, Nad. We're going to get you home."

Carrying Nadine's spirit back to the house was like stepping out of a fire a hero. I had a sliced hand, at least two broken ribs, and one hell of a black eye. But most of all, I had Nadine.

I didn't take my eyes off her as I carried her limp spirit back to the house. I could've sworn we moved in slow motion. The relief I felt made my heart sing. Nadine was so perfect it was enough to stop time just looking at her.

I climbed the stairs to Helena's front door. It was only when I opened it and heard the panicked shouts inside that time seemed to speed up again.

"She's still not breathing!" Grant cried.

"I'm working as fast as I can!" Helena shouted back.

"How could this happen?" Talia sobbed.

I stepped into the living room, my heart hammering like a bass drum. I hoped I wasn't too late. Grant knelt over Nadine's lifeless body, performing CPR, while Helena clutched a mortar and pestle—an ancient herb crusher. She ground herbs into powder that I assumed were meant to heal. Talia was pacing back and forth, stroking Isa's fur.

I cleared my throat, and all eyes turned toward me. Grant's eyes grew as wide as saucers, and Talia's jaw dropped. Helena was so shocked she dropped the mortar and pestle, and the herbs spilled all over the carpet.

It was clear as day—they could see Nadine's spirit in my arms. It must've had something to do with me touching her after I'd touched a reaper.

I felt death in the room. It was like a dark hole that nothing could enter and escape. It was just... nothing. And that feeling centered over Nadine's heart. Her body wasn't going to last much longer without her soul in it.

"W-wha... How did you...?" Helena stuttered.

"I'll explain later," I said. My knees quaked as I rushed to Nadine's side. Grant scurried out of the way.

"*What* am I seeing?" Talia asked breathlessly.

"I could ask the same thing," Grant said in astonishment.

"You saved her?" Helena breathed.

I swallowed. "Not yet."

I pressed my lips to the side of Nadine's spirit cheek, then positioned her spirit over her body. A single tear ran down my face and dripped onto her chest.

"I love you, Nad," I whispered. "Now and forever."

I gently lay her spirit back into her body... and waited...

Lucas Taylor couldn't see the light within himself, but I could. Though dark cloud after dark cloud had swept into his life to block out the light, it continued to burn bright. The world would be a much better place with him in it. *My* world had been made better with him in it.

He didn't deserve an eternity in the Abyss. He deserved to be with his brother and the rest of the coven in Alora, where he would be happy.

I loved him. I loved him more than the grass beneath my feet, more than the stars in the sky, more than the very air I breathed. My heart beat for him, and my world moved with him. I didn't know how much I truly cared about him until that moment. I was unconditionally and undeniably in love with him.

I turned my gaze from the nearby gravestones to look at Mother Miriam. "I'll do it."

The scary part was, giving myself up for Lucas didn't scare me at all.

A proud smile crossed Mother Miriam's face. "Then it is time."

She formed a ball of magic in her hand. It was the whitest, most pure magic I'd ever seen. A mesmerizing rainbow of colors swirled within it. She threw the magic upward, and it exploded into a million tiny little stars above my head that rained down on me like snowflakes. The flakes of magic touched my skin, and my whole body started to glow.

"Wait, this is it?" I asked. "I don't get to say goodbye?"

"You have one chance," she reminded me.

Right. Lucas would hear my last thought.

"*I did it to save you, Lucas. I will always love you,*" I thought.

The glow of my skin brightened, until a blinding white light completely consumed my vision. Even as I squeezed my eyes shut, it was all I could see.

The last thing I heard was Mother Miriam's soft, calming voice. "Just remember, Nadine. You are not defined by what happens to you. You are defined by how you react to it."

The light became too bright to bear, and then… nothing.

I saw nothing. I felt nothing. There was no light or dark, no pain or comfort, no sense of time or space. Just… nothing. I could've been stuck in this state for eternity and never known it.

Then something happened. A voice called out to me like a beacon in the darkness.

"Nad!"

It took me a few moments to make sense of my name. I couldn't remember what had happened to me or why I was here. Then it all came rushing back.

The Abyss!

My heart lurched to life in my chest. My eyes shot open, and I sprang upward. A high-pitched scream pierced my ears. It took me a moment to realize it was my own voice.

"Nad, it's okay!" Lucas's soothing voice came from beside me.

As my vision focused, I saw his beautiful face in front of me. His left eye was black and swollen, but he was incredibly beautiful nonetheless.

"Lucas, you're hurt," I said breathlessly.

He shrugged. "Totally worth it."

My heart raced, and my whole body quivered. Frantically, I glanced around the room to see I was sitting on the floor in Grammy's living room. The candles that had surrounded me had been burnt out. Grammy, Grant, and Talia all looked down on me with wide-eyed expressions of disbelief. Isa jumped out of Talia's arms and purred as she rubbed against my side.

It was all a test, I realized. *None of it was real.*

I placed my hand to my thumping heart as it started to slow. "Oh my God. I thought I died!"

Lucas's features fell. "Nad… you did."

"W-what?" I nearly choked on the word.

Grammy knelt beside me and swept me into her arms. She kissed me on the cheek over and over, and squeezed me so tight I thought she might suffocate me. Tears streamed down her face.

"I'm so relieved that you're okay, Nadine," she whispered. "I thought I'd lost you."

As Grammy drew away, Grant and Talia threw themselves at me. They both curled me into a tight group hug.

"We're not losing you, you hear me?" Grant said pointedly.

Talia swatted me on the shoulder. "Don't *ever* do that to us again."

"Do what?" I asked. "What happened?"

Everyone stared back at me like they didn't know where to start. The only one who looked remotely understanding was Lucas. I looked to him for an explanation.

Grammy cleared her throat. "We'll just… give you two a moment."

Grant and Talia nodded in agreement, and the three of them quietly left the room.

Tears welled in Lucas's eyes as he stared at me like I was the only girl in the world. He took my face in his hands. They were so warm and comforting.

"You gave up yourself for me," he reminded me. "I had to fight a reaper to get you back."

My breath caught in my chest. Lucas had saved my life?

His eyes sparkled in a mix of pain and relief. "Why'd you do it?"

I placed my hand over my mouth to keep the sobs from spilling out. My eyes searched his. After taking a moment to breathe, I dropped my shaking hand.

"Don't you get it, Lucas?" I asked. "I love you."

"I know," he said. "But—"

"No," I cut him off. "I really, *really* love you… Enough to go to hell in your place."

Tears spilled over Lucas's lids, and my heart swelled. "I love you, too, Nad."

Lucas swept me into his arms, and we kissed with a passion like never before. His love poured into me like pure, warm water filling my soul, and mine poured back.

The roller coaster ride we'd been on slowed in that moment, reaching its peak at the highest point of the track. My heart lifted in anticipation of the freefall.

I parted my lips, and Lucas kissed me deeper. I went spiraling downward, my stomach flipping in my abdomen.

But it didn't feel like we were on a roller coaster anymore. The safety harness had given way, and I'd grown wings. I was safe here with Lucas, because he was my wings, and he would never let me fall.

Lucas drew away from me and pressed his forehead to mine. Desperation filled his tone. "I never want to lose you, Nad."

Tears rolled down my cheeks, and a sob broke in my chest. "I never want to lose you, either."

"I don't care about the Reaper's Shadow curse," Lucas said. "I'll tip-toe around it for eternity just to be with you every single day for the rest of my life. I'll do everything in my power to protect you from it."

I wiped the tears from my cheeks. "I agree. If we can't be together fully, we'll take what we can get."

Lucas's gaze dropped, and his fingers ran over my arm. His voice trembled when he spoke. "Can I have *you*?"

My heart pitter-pattered against my rib cage. "For as long as I can have you," I whispered.

His lips pressed to mine again, and we shared an amazing kiss that made my head spin.

I didn't know how long we were kissing, but we were interrupted by the sound of Grant clearing his throat. We drew away and glanced toward the entrance to the living room. Grant stood there holding an ice pack.

He smiled. "You two make me want to cry."

"Spying on us?" Lucas teased.

Grant chuckled. "No. Just wondering when we can come back in to see what Cast Nadine got."

I gasped. I'd nearly forgotten!

"Yes!" I cried. "Everyone, come in."

My heart pounded fiercely as I got to my feet. Grant handed Lucas the ice pack, and he pressed it to his swollen eye. Grammy and Talia entered the room behind him.

"Well, come on," Grant encouraged, nudging me in the side. "What's your Cast?"

"I don't know. Let's see."

I stretched my arms out and flipped them over, looking for any signs of a tattoo. Grammy started spinning me around so we could look at all angles. Isa rubbed against my leg, so I took off my shoes and checked my feet, then lifted my pants legs to check my calves.

"Lucas might have to strip you down to check," Grant teased.

Talia and Grammy both chuckled under their breath, but Lucas looked thoroughly unamused. He'd taken a seat on the couch and clutched his side with one arm, holding the ice pack to his eye with the other. I noticed for the first time he was sweating a little.

"Will you be okay?" I asked him.

"Fine," he said, waving a hand. "Find your mark."

I lifted the hem of my shirt to check my stomach, and that's when I saw it. Just above the inside of my hip lay a black mark.

My whole body gave a start. I gasped and dropped my shirt.

"What is it?" Talia asked, looking intrigued.

"Come on, Nadine. Let us see," Grammy begged.

Grant eyed me curiously. "Judging by your reaction, I'm guessing Mortana."

I felt the blood drain from my face. I swallowed and lifted my shirt to show everyone the tattoo. "I got... Curse Breaker."

I let out a wavered breath. All eyes locked on the crescent-moon tattoo on my hip.

Grammy's hand shook as she brought it to her mouth. I wasn't sure if she was terrified or delighted by the news. Talia and Grant shared a confused expression. Lucas had gone totally still. The room was dead silent.

"How is this possible?" I asked. "The Curse Breakers died out."

Grammy finally found her voice. "Yes, but Mother Miriam can assign you *any* Cast she sees fit. She must think you're worthy, Nadine."

I gaped at her. "Me?"

"What'd she test you on?" Grant asked eagerly.

"I started out tied up in the Main Foyer," I told them, before diving into an explanation of everything else that happened.

By the time I was finished, we'd all taken a seat. I was sitting beside Lucas, and Isa was purring in my lap.

Grammy leaned forward in her chair and rested her elbow on her knee. "It sounds like you impressed Mother Miriam. You showed her you're willing to take responsibility."

"And you showed some serious integrity saving Chloe's life," Talia added.

"Also strength and resilience," Grant said.

"Yeah," Talia agreed. "You fought the darkness inside of you instead of giving into it. You didn't let it consume you, which means you'll be able to fight the darkness of any curse you break."

My heart melted.

"And then you traded your soul for mine," Lucas pointed out. "You're pure of heart, Nad. Something no other witch has been since the Curse Breakers died out."

"Wow," I said breathlessly. "I guess I didn't realize what I was capable of."

"You're capable of anything you put your mind to," Grammy encouraged. "But you must be careful, Nadine."

I tilted my head to the side. "What do you mean?"

"You're the only Curse Breaker of your generation," she pointed out. "Just as your grandfather was. People will try to use you."

I shot a nervous glance around the room. "To break curses?"

Grammy dropped her gaze and shook her head. "For much more than that, I'm afraid. Recall that when a member of each of the five Casts comes together, they can create elaborate spells."

"Like the space-bending spell that expands the school," I stated, remembering how she explained it to me on my first day at Miriam College.

She nodded. "I'll be honest, Nadine. If your grandfather were here, he'd tell you this is as much a curse as it is a blessing."

I looked to Lucas, then to my friends, as if expecting one of them to counter her claim. Everyone wore the same uncertain expression. I suddenly felt worry knot deep within my belly.

"So I pose a threat," I realized.

"Or people will threaten *you*," Lucas added, looking terrified for me. "They're going to want a piece of your magic."

My stomach dropped. How could I get this wonderful gift, only for it to put me in the line of fire? Octavia Falls was my home. I should be safe here, but I wasn't. I hadn't been since the moment I stepped foot in town. Something told me Chloe was just the least of my coming threats.

But I'd be damned if I didn't fight for my right to stay.

"Then I'll hide it," I stated, my mind made up.

Talia tilted her head to the side. "Hide your powers? How?"

"I don't know," I admitted. "We could tell people I didn't go through with the ceremony."

"But you need to stay in classes to learn how to control your magic," Grant pointed out.

I sighed. "True."

Lucas looked deeply contemplative, then his eyes lit up. "I know how to hide it."

"You do?" I asked.

He smirked. "You can pose as an Alchemist."

I frowned. "But I don't have Alchemy powers."

Grant's jaw dropped. "That could actually work."

"What?" I asked. "How can I possibly pull that off?"

"It's a good theory," Grammy agreed. "Curse Breakers' powers work by transferring magic from one place to another. You can use Alchemy crystals to brew potions."

"Alchemy crystals?" I asked.

"It's like this," Grammy explained. "I transfer my Alchemy magic into a crystal. You take that magic and transfer it into a potion."

"Couldn't anyone do that?" I asked.

She shook her head. "Only a member of each Cast can access the crystal magic of that cast. Alchemists can use Alchemy crystals, Seers use Seer crystals. But as Curse Breaker, you can move magic from one place to another."

"So I could use crystals to pose as any Cast?" I asked.

Grammy shook her head. "Not quite. It gives you no powers. A Seer crystal wouldn't allow you to see or hear spirits. You couldn't control a corpse with a necromancy crystal. Your power lies in the *transfer* of magic. And that's the beauty of Alchemy. Brewing potions is a simple transfer of Alchemy magic. We're actually not the only race who can do it."

"So... as long as I had Alchemy magic to draw from, I could fool everyone," I realized.

"It's our best shot," Talia said.

"It could be the only way to protect you," Lucas added.

"Then I'll do it," I said. "I'll let everyone believe I'm an Alchemist."

"What about your tattoo?" Talia questioned.

"I'll get a fake one," I decided. "I'll put it somewhere that's easily noticeable, so no one will question it."

"You'll have to practice your Curse Breaker powers in private," Lucas pointed out.

"I will," I agreed. "For as long as I can manage, I'll remain a secret."

"One of the coven's greatest secrets of all," Lucas whispered ominously.

I nodded, accepting my new title. "I'll be the coven's secret."

☾

I HAD SO much to process from that night that I didn't even know where to start. Since it was really late and everyone was tired, Grammy invited all of us to stay the night at her house. I was relieved, because I could hardly keep my eyes open anymore.

I stood from the couch and tugged on Lucas's arm. "Let's go to bed."

"In a minute," he argued.

I tugged him a little harder, and he winced. I immediately dropped his arm. "What's wrong?"

"Nothing," he said, but I heard the lie in his voice.

I gazed down at him sternly. "Don't lie to me. Let me see."

"I'll be fine, Nad," he said.

"If that's true, let me see it," I demanded. "No secrets, Lucas."

He sighed and stood. Everyone else was already moving out of the living room, but when he lifted his shirt, we all stopped dead. A huge purple bruise marred the side of his torso.

My stomach plummeted to my toes. "Why didn't you say something!?"

Lucas dropped his gaze. "I didn't want you to worry."

"You need help," I stated. "We're going to the hospital. No objections."

Lucas sighed. "Nad, come on. It's way too late for that."

"It's never too late to get you help," I replied.

"The doctors aren't going to do anything but tell me to rest," he argued. "Besides, you're too tired for an emergency room visit."

Yes and no. I was exhausted, but I wanted to be with him.

Grant quickly stepped in. "I'll take you, bro."

Lucas frowned.

"Lucas, you're going," I repeated. "You're not burdening anyone by getting medical treatment. Please accept that."

He sighed. "Okay. But you need to rest. I'll see you tomorrow."

I protested a while longer, but Lucas insisted he was only going to the ER if I went to bed. As long as he was getting medical attention, that was good enough for me. Talia went to the guest room upstairs, while I took the guest room next to the bathroom. My moving boxes were still piled in the corner. I found some pajamas in one of them and changed. I tossed my dirty clothes into one of the open boxes on the top, but they caught on the corner and knocked it over.

Isa meowed from where she lay on the bed.

Sighing, I bent to clean up the contents. As I reached for the last item that had spilled out, my breath caught. It was a small wooden box I hadn't opened since my parents died. I took a deep breath and reached out for it. When I held it, I was surprised to realize I no longer felt a deep black hole within my gut when I thought of them.

I took the box and crawled under the covers with it. The lamp beside my bed illuminated the soft curves of the box and the glossy finish. I reached up and lightly touched my silver star necklace.

Isa walked across the bed and curled up next to me.

I took a deep breath. "I'm not scared anymore, Mom."

I opened the box, and my heart warmed. A pile of envelopes sat inside, each one of them a different color from the last. My name had been scrawled on each one in my mother's smooth handwriting.

I swallowed and pulled the first envelope from the top. I flipped open the card to read the letter my parents had written me.

Happy eighteenth birthday, Nadine!

This year has been crazy. Remember the escape room, when we almost lost because of your dad but you turned it around and got us out in the last minute? We'll never forget the trip we took to Washington D.C. this summer. We got lost for three hours looking for the Washington Monument. How's that even possible? Don't forget when your mom tried skiing on that spontaneous trip we took this

winter. Miserable failure! We hope this year will bring many bright beginnings.
Never stop enjoying the mystery in life.

We love you, Nadine.

- Mom and Dad

Tears welled in my eyes. The past year brought the worst of the worst endings.

I set the birthday card aside and pulled out the next one.

Happy seventeenth birthday, Nadine!

They all started out like that, each one sharing memories from the previous year and wishes for the year to come. It hurt that it was my birthday and I wouldn't be getting a card from them this year.

I finished reading through all the letters and was placing them back in the box when a knock came at my door. I cleared my throat. "Come in."

Grammy opened the door. "You're still up."

I nodded. "Just looking over some old keepsakes."

She eyed the box I held in my lap. "Are those your birthday letters?"

I nodded.

She held up a finger. "Give me a minute."

I furrowed my brow as Grammy left the room. She came back in a minute later holding a piece of paper in her hand. She crossed the room and sat at the edge of my bed.

"I found this while we were cleaning out the old house," she admitted. "I was saving it for your birthday. And since it's your birthday now…"

Grammy handed over the piece of paper, and I realized it was an envelope like all the others. My name was written across the front in my mother's handwriting.

I froze in place, unable to breathe. "Grammy, what is this?"

She shrugged. "I didn't read it. It's for you."

I swallowed and took the letter from her hand, then opened it. My quiet tears turned into full-on sobs as I began to read the letter.

Nadine,

We know we usually save these cards for your birthday, but we have so much to say. We know you're upset about the police academy. We know it's all you ever wanted. But there's a saying we want you to remember. You've heard us say it many times before. 'When one door closes, another one opens.' We know that's not what you want to hear right now, but you'll realize one day when all of this is over that it's true. Everything happens for a reason. We believe that bigger and better things are in store for you. All you have to do is look for the blessing and be willing to receive it.

We will always be here for you and love you no matter what.

-Mom and Dad

A beautiful swelling of joy grew in my heart. I didn't feel sad when I thought about them. I felt *joy*. I had eighteen wonderful years with them. I was the luckiest girl in the world to be their daughter. I couldn't ask for anything more than that.

It was true this year had been rough, but wonderful things had happened, too. My parents' death had led me to Octavia Falls, and I couldn't imagine being anywhere else.

I sniffled and closed the card, then added it to my box. "Thank you for saving that for me, Grammy."

"What's it say?" she asked curiously.

I smiled. "It says everything is going to be okay."

In that moment, I truly meant it.

But I never would've said it, had I known the types of dark and sinister trials awaiting me next semester.

TWENTY-FIVE

I lay on the bed in my hospital room. It was still dark outside, but the sun would rise soon. It'd been a really long night, but I didn't sleep. I lay there thinking of Nadine, how she was alive against all odds. I was the luckiest guy in the world.

"I was wrong," I admitted quietly without turning my gaze from the window.

Grant sat in the chair next to my bed. I was surprised he hadn't gone home yet.

"Wrong about what?" he asked.

I sighed and finally turned to look at him. "I was wrong about trying to give my gift back. You were right. I never should've risked it."

Grant eyed me solemnly, and his shoulders fell. "I'm just glad you didn't trade your soul. I was really looking forward to fucking shit up with you in Alora."

A half-smile crept across my face. "Well, we still have our chance. Bring it in, man."

Grant stood from his chair and leaned over my bed to give me a hug.

I clapped him on the back. "I'm sorry for what I said to you."

"I'm sorry, too," he said. "Friends?"

"Always."

Just then, a knock came at the door. Grant turned as an older man stepped into the room.

"What's the verdict, doc?" Grant asked.

The doctor adjusted his glasses and looked down to the clipboard in his hands. "I'm afraid it's not good. We're looking at two broken ribs and a fractured occipital bone."

Grant cocked an eyebrow at me. "You're lucky that's all you walked away with."

I smirked. "Still totally worth it."

The doctor furrowed his brow. "If you don't mind me asking, what were you boys doing to cause this?"

Grant and I shared a look, but I answered. "I beat the shit out of a reaper."

The doctor laughed lightly. He thought I was joking. "Okay, well, let's talk treatment. Unfortunately, there's not much we can do but send you home with pain meds and advise you to get plenty of rest. No sports until you heal. It should take about six weeks until you're good as new."

"Thanks, doc," I said.

"I'll have the nurse get your discharge papers," the doctor said. "Have a good night, boys."

He left the room, and I looked sideways at Grant. "Told you they wouldn't do anything."

He shrugged. "You get pain meds."

I chuckled. "I'm sure you could brew me something better."

Grant yawned really wide, then stood. "I'm gonna take a piss."

"Thanks for announcing it," I joked.

Grant walked off, and I turned back to the window. I really hoped Nadine was resting right now. She needed it after everything she'd been through tonight. I missed her so much already.

Part of me was disappointed that the night hadn't gone as planned. Another part of me was glad Nadine had saved me from the Abyss. I was stupid to try to contact the reapers in the first place. I mean, how could I think the Abyss was preferable to any sort of life with her—and an eternity thereafter?

It was the voices, the thoughts I carried. The weight of the coven's secrets had pushed me to do the unthinkable. But the weird thing was, after burning the journal where I wrote them all down, I didn't feel their weight as heavily anymore. It was like holding on to those thoughts in the journal was the real thing that was weighing me down.

A thought struck. I conjured my positivity journal and a pen. I opened up to the next page and started scribbling down the greatest perk my gift had ever given me:

I saved Nadine's life.

Once I started writing, I couldn't stop. For the first time since Professor Warren gave me this notebook, the positivity just flowed out of me. I pictured all the wonderful things that saving her life meant. She'd live on and would bring beauty into the world everywhere she went.

But it wasn't just about her, either. Suddenly, all these other things started rushing through my mind.

I help others cross over.

I serve the coven.

I'm ready to start doing better.

I felt totally at peace as I closed the journal and subconjured it. That last thought stuck in my mind. I'd admitted my faults tonight. I realized things about myself that I never knew before. For the first time in a year, I could finally face myself, instead of shoving everything down and ignoring it. I wasn't *there* yet, but I was ready to try.

I closed my eyes and relaxed into the pillow as Grant came out of the bathroom.

"You okay, man?" Grant asked.

A smile touched the corners of my lips. "Nadine's alive. We're together now."

"I would hope so, after tonight."

My eyes shot open and darted to the doorway. Nadine stood there, twisting her purse strap around in her fingers.

"Nad," I said breathlessly. "I thought you were at home resting."

"I couldn't sleep," she admitted.

That was so unlike her.

Grant cleared his throat. "I'm gonna go see what I can find in the vending machine."

He left the room, leaving Nadine and me in private. The door swung shut behind him, and Nadine stepped forward. She pulled a chair to the side of my bed and sat down, then took my gauze-wrapped hand in hers.

"Tonight was… crazy," she breathed.

"I know," I whispered, unable to take my eyes off her. "But we made it."

Silence settled over the room for a few moments, until she finally spoke. "I can't believe you'd go to hell just to spend your life with me."

I placed my good hand over hers. "Nad, you know I'd do anything for you."

"And I for you," she whispered. "Which is why—"

"Hang on," I said, suddenly realizing something.

She tilted her head curiously as I raised my hand and curled it into a fist.

"It's your birthday," I pointed out. "I got you something."

I conjured her present and unfurled my fingers. It was a brass key, but it wasn't like the antique one she'd given me. This was old, but still modern.

She reached out and took it. "What does it go to?"

A smile spread across my face. "The abandoned mansion behind the school."

She stared down at it, gaping like she couldn't believe it.

"I went back after that night," I admitted. "I found it upstairs in one of the bedrooms. It works on all the doors."

She blinked a few times. "I don't get it, Lucas. Why are you giving me this?"

"Because that place is ours, Nad," I said. "It's our special place, and this is me promising you we'll be making lots of memories there."

Her eyes sparkled, and she curled her fingers around the key.

"I love it!" she cried, before throwing herself over me. I winced as her weight pressed into my broken ribs.

Nadine kissed me gently, and my stomach flipped in my abdomen. Kissing her was never going to get old.

"This is amazing, Lucas," she said as she drew away.

I smiled. "I'm glad you like it."

Nadine sat back down and took a deep breath. "Look, there's a reason I couldn't sleep—a reason I came to visit you."

"Uh, oh," I said, my guts sinking.

"It's not bad," she said quickly, and I relaxed. "It's… complicated, I guess. I was lying there in bed, thinking about being a Curse Breaker, when it hit me."

"What hit you?" I asked when she paused.

Her eyes brightened. "Lucas... we could break the Reaper's Shadow curse."

Her words thrilled me. What a blessing that would be!

But my thrill only lasted a split second. This curse was one of the darkest I'd ever known. She couldn't break it on her own—especially as a novice. Breaking this curse... well, it could consume her before she managed it. The magic was so strong and so dark, it could overpower her. She could die in the attempt, and I'd lose her all over again.

That wasn't a risk I was willing to take.

"Nad, I don't think that's possible," I said solemnly.

"Why not?" she argued. "I'm a Curse Breaker."

"Yes, but you're the *only* one," I pointed out. "A curse this big could hurt you. I don't want you getting mixed up in magic you can't handle."

"I'll practice," she promised.

"I don't want to lose you," I replied firmly. "I thought I was going to lose you tonight, and I don't want either of us to go through with that again. Magic like this... it could be too much for you. You could get your-self killed."

"I was willing to go to the Abyss for you," she reminded me. "I'll risk this, too."

"But you don't have to," I assured her. "We agreed we'd live with the curse, to work around it."

"That was before we knew I was a Curse Breaker," she said. "The least we can do is *try*."

My heart sank. The last thing I wanted to do was risk losing my Nadine again. She didn't know how much magic she could handle or what breaking this curse could do to her.

"Curse breaking is a complicated process, Nad," I said.

She tilted her head to the side. "Don't you want to get rid of it?"

"Of course I do," I insisted. "I just don't want you to get hurt."

"I won't," she promised, but I wasn't sure I believed her. "I'm going to figure out this curse, and I'm going to break it. I don't care how long it takes me."

My lips tightened. "You're going to do it with or without my help?"

"I *hope* you'll help me," she said quietly. "I want this for both of us."

"I do, too," I replied. "I just... I can't watch you put yourself in danger."

She stared at me under long lashes and spoke softly. "You know me, Lucas. I don't run from danger."

"And that's why I'm here—to drag you away from it," I teased.

Nadine dropped her gaze. Apparently, she didn't find that funny. "Maybe we should take some time to think about it."

"Agreed," I stated, though I wasn't planning on changing my mind. I just hoped *she* would.

"I don't think I'll be around for winter break," she announced, finally lifting her gaze to meet mine.

"What?" I gasped. The thought of being away from her killed me. "Why not?"

"I need to go home," she said.

"Octavia Falls *is* your home," I reminded her.

"I know. But I want to visit my parents' graves." Before I could suggest coming along, she added, "It's something I need to do by myself."

"Are you sure?" I asked. I didn't want her going *anywhere* alone, but I couldn't force her to take me with her.

She nodded. "I'll be fine. I'll stay with a friend from high school. When I get back, we can figure out this curse and what to do about it."

"Okay," I heard myself agree, though I was thoroughly against all of this. "I'm going to miss you."

"I'm going to miss you, too," she said, choking up.

I couldn't stand to see her like this. All I wanted was to make her happy.

I reached an arm out. "Come here, Nad."

She leaned onto the bed and curled into me. Her head rested on my shoulder, and though her weight put pressure on my ribs, I didn't care. Because I had my Nadine with me. We could handle this curse later. Right now, all I could do was be grateful that Nadine and I had both survived the night. All was good in the world.

Or it would've been—if I hadn't been hit by the most debilitating nausea in the next moment. A brick slammed into my guts, and bile shot up my throat. I sprang upright in bed, throwing Nadine off of me. I leaned over and heaved. A sharp, searing pain radiated across my side.

Nadine gasped. "Lucas!"

I was pretty sure she said something else, but I didn't hear her over the high-pitched ringing in my ears. I'd never felt anything like it in all the time I'd been a Reaper's Apprentice.

A child's voice played in my mind as if he was sitting at my side.

"Playtime is over. No child in the coven is safe."

The air sucked out of the room. This thought was shockingly similar to another I'd heard months ago—the one that left me curled on the bathroom floor between classes. *Is it playtime?*

But this new one came with a warning.

A dark, ominous cloud seemed to swirl around me as realization hit. These two kids' deaths were connected. The warning was clear: someone had murdered these kids.

And there was no telling who they'd come for next.

END OF BOOK ONE

Flip the page to read a special excerpt from book two: *The Reaper's Shadow*!

Hidden Legends

Read more from the Hidden Legends universe! Each Hidden Legends series takes place within the same world, but in separate and unique societies. Every series stands on its own, and they can be read in any order.

☽

ELEMENTALS, DRAGONS, & MORE

Academy of Magical Creatures by Megan Linski & Alicia Rades

☽

SHIFTERS, FAE, & SORCERESSES

University of Sorcery by Megan Linski

☽

SUPERNATURAL PRISON

Prison for Supernatural Offenders by Megan Linski & Alicia Rades

☽

Never miss a new release! Join our newsletter at www.hiddenlegendsbooks.com/fanclub

THE REAPER'S SHADOW
CHAPTER ONE

Lucas

A Year Ago

The coven had lost a child.

Two days ago, a six-year-old boy named Caleb Thomas had gone missing from his bed in the middle of the night. There was no evidence left behind—just an open window he'd been snatched through. He came from a prominent Alchemy family, so the chances he'd run away were slim to none.

But that was all anyone knew. That, and no magic could track him.

We had Seers on every corner, and not one of them had a vision of the missing boy. The coven must've had dozens of psychometrists—people who got visions through touch. They were experts at finding things.

And yet the child was still missing.

I didn't know that was possible.

The dark skies outside the school crackled with lightning, and thunder shook the walls. The Main Foyer was deserted, except for Grant and me. We sat in front of the empty fireplace, balking at the absurdity of it all.

"I don't get it," Grant remarked. He lounged across one of the plush red chairs, his legs hanging over the armrest. He flipped through the school newspaper.

"I know. It's crazy," I agreed. "Maybe you'll get Seer at your Evoking Ceremony this weekend. Maybe we can find him."

"That's not what I meant." Grant shifted in his chair to sit up straight. His eyes darkened as he waved the school paper in the air. "I don't get how the coven can be in an uproar about this whole thing and there's not *one* mention of it in the school paper."

"What?" I balked.

Grant tossed the paper onto the coffee table between us, and it made a hard *smacking* noise as it landed.

I scrambled forward and snatched it up. The paper's name, *The Epitaph*, was scrawled across the top in big, bold letters. Below that was a headline highlighting this year's top fashion for the Midnight Formal.

What the hell? The Formal was two months away. Little Caleb Thomas was missing *now*!

I started flipping through the newspaper, but there was no mention of the boy at all. I crumpled the paper in my fists.

I must've got a look on my face, because Grant narrowed his eyes at me. "What are you thinking?"

I took a couple of shallow breaths, my nostrils flaring. "I think I'm going to have a chat with the head of the paper."

I shot up out of my seat and stomped past the grand staircase.

"Lucas, wait!" Grant called, but I ignored him.

I clutched my copy of *The Epitaph* tight in my fist and stormed down the hall to Professor Carlisle's office. He was my conjuring professor and the faculty advisor for the paper. Rumor had it, he spent twenty years as a journalist at the *Miriamic Messenger* before becoming a professor, and that's how he landed the role as the school paper advisor.

I passed through his classroom and stomped straight through the open door of his office. He sat at his desk, scribbling away at something.

"Your paper is garbage!" I raged, slamming it down on his desk.

The ancient gray cat lounging nearby jumped so high it fell off the edge of the desk. Professor Carlisle gave a start. He looked up to me and adjusted his glasses. His bushy gray eyebrows shot up, nearly touching his hairline.

"Mister Taylor, how may I help you?" He looked delighted to see me, but I was more than a little ticked off.

"I want to know why you're letting the school paper publish this garbage," I demanded. "Why isn't there *one* mention of Caleb Thomas in here?"

"The missing boy?" he asked, looking surprised. "I believe the *Miriamic Messenger* has that topic covered."

"The town paper has shared the facts—which isn't much, to be frank," I pointed out. "Why isn't the school paper doing a feature? Talk about the implications this has on the coven. Analyze what this means for our magic—or run a study on what types of magic might be able to cover this up. Discuss what we can do as students to contribute to the search for the child. The possibilities are endless!"

Professor Carlisle's eyes brightened. He leaned back in his chair, looking intrigued. "Those are all good ideas, Mister Taylor. If you want to submit a piece for consideration, I'm more than happy to look at it."

My stomach dropped. That wasn't my intention for coming to him at all.

"I'm not a journalist," I stated bluntly.

"Well, why not?" Professor Carlisle asked brightly, spreading his arms wide. For a guy pushing eighty, he had a lot of energy. "You seem to have a lot of ideas. The paper could use an opinionated view like yours."

"What the paper *needs* is an investigative journalist," I said. "Someone has to figure out how this boy went missing without a trace."

"That's what the Imperium's for," he reminded me. "Unfortunately, the newspaper club is very small, and I encourage all my students to report on the topics that matter most to them."

My eyebrows shot up. What kind of idiots were in the newspaper club if they thought some stupid dance was more important than a child's life?

"If you're going to go digging on this, I'd love to bring you on board," Professor Carlisle offered.

"That's not what I was suggesting," I told him, rather harshly. "Like I said, I'm not a reporter."

Professor Carlisle shrugged, like there was nothing more he could do about it. "Well, then, I'm afraid we're going to have to leave this matter to the professionals."

"I thought *you* were a professional," I growled before turning on my heel and storming out of the room.

As I walked down the hall, I couldn't get this single thought out of my mind: *Protect the coven.*

I wanted to find this little boy. I wanted to help.

Problem was, I didn't know how.

☾

Present Day

Another child had gone missing. Same story, different kid.

One moment, ten-year-old Isaac Miller was at home in his bed, sleeping soundlessly. The next he just… vanished. Nothing but an open window beside his bed remained. His family was high-profile like the last, though they were Mentalists instead of Alchemists. Like last time, no magic in the coven could trace him.

After Caleb Thomas went missing, the coven sort of gave up on him. There were no leads, nothing we could do. His case was a total dead end, and we didn't know if he was dead or alive. How could you search for a missing person when the only evidence left behind was their absence?

But this time, I knew something. I was the *only* one who knew *anything.* It wasn't much, but I knew one thing.

Those children were dead.

And whoever killed them was going to strike again.

I'd heard them die. They used the same word, like it was some sort of code.

Caleb's last thought echoed in my mind. It was the child's voice I heard last semester… the one I couldn't match to an obituary.

Is it playtime?

No, it wasn't, and Isaac knew it.

Playtime is over. No child in the coven is safe.

The similarities frightened me to my very core.

I didn't have proof these voices were those of the missing children, but deep down in my gut, I felt it.

At the time I heard the second voice, no one knew Isaac was even missing. It wasn't until morning that word got out about his disappear-

408

ance. He was older than Caleb by a few years, but the similarities between the disappearances were too coincidental to dismiss.

The one thing that didn't seem to fit—and the thing that frightened me most—was that little Caleb died a *year* after his disappearance. Isaac Miller was killed the same night he was taken.

Don't ask how I knew it was murder. It wasn't like the kids had told me.

But I could feel it in their thoughts—the way my guts twisted when I heard their voices, the way I heaved and shook and felt hot and cold at the same time. It was dark. It was sinister. And it *wasn't* an accident.

As soon as I was discharged from the hospital after my encounter with a reaper, I marched straight up to the Imperium's doors. They met on the top floor of Octavia Hall. I pounded on the heavy door, and it swung open under my weight.

Their meeting quarters looked more like an attic than anything—with a vaulted ceiling, fireplace, and huge window overlooking the town—but it was really big and clean. There were books stacked neatly along all the walls, along with potion vials, crystals, and endless decks of tarot cards. A large round table sat in the center of the room.

The four priestesses were crowded around the table. Each one spoke over each other so loudly that their voices spilled out into the hall. I couldn't make out what they were saying. They stopped abruptly when they heard the door creak open.

"The missing children are dead," I said bluntly.

A woman with a cauldron tattoo on the back of her neck whirled around, eyes wide. Technically, all priestesses held the same power, but she was the oldest of all of them and looked like she naturally took on the role of leader.

I recognized her as Priestess Margaret. She had long silver hair tied into a braid that hung over her shoulder to show off her tattoo, and she wore a gray shawl around her shoulders. Like all the priestesses, she was very pretty.

"Lucas Taylor," she said breathlessly, recognition crossing her features. "The Reaper's Apprentice."

I nodded firmly.

She reached out a hand to invite me inside. "You have heard the child pass?"

"Not just one," I said as I entered the room, my heart racing. "Remember Caleb Thomas, the boy who went missing last year?"

The four priestesses exchanged a terrified glance.

"I think I heard him, too," I admitted.

Priestess Margaret took my hand and dragged me to the table. "Sit. Tell us everything you know."

It wasn't much—and I could tell the priestesses were disappointed by that as I explained to them what I'd heard.

"This makes no sense," one of them protested. She had a wild mane of dark curls and a tree tattooed on her shoulder. I recognized her as Priestess Lilian, Chloe's grandmother. "Why would somebody wait a year to harm one child, only to hurt the other the day they're taken?"

"I wondered the same thing," I told them. "The M.O. doesn't match up. But I know what I heard."

Priestess Charlotte spoke up. She was as old as the others, but her long red hair hadn't started to gray. I noticed the skull tattoo on her wrist. "Perhaps we need to consider the possibility of a third missing child. It could explain the timeline of the deaths. Perhaps Caleb wasn't the child you heard, but it was another one."

"But no others have been reported missing," the fourth and final priestess stated. Priestess Stella was the youngest of the four, but she had this look about her that suggested she was very wise. I couldn't see her tattoo, but I knew she was a Seer.

"Then let's assume it's just the two for now," Priestess Margaret replied. "The first thing we must do is enact safety measures to ensure the children of the coven are safe."

"What about catching the perpetrator?" I demanded.

Margaret shot me a look of sympathy. "With all due respect, we don't know what we're dealing with yet. Our number one priority is keeping the children who *are* alive safe."

"Doesn't that start with explaining what happened to the others?" I demanded. It frustrated me that they weren't launching a murder investigation immediately.

"We will absolutely investigate," Margaret promised me. "The Miriamic Police Department will be informed of what you've told us as soon as we're done here."

"Is there any way I can help?" I asked.

Margaret frowned. "I'm afraid not—not unless you know anything else."

"That's all I know," I replied, regret twisting in my gut. I wished I knew more to help them. I didn't want anyone else getting hurt. I didn't want to listen to another child die. That was something I was determined to prevent.

"There must be *something* I can do," I insisted.

"I'm sorry, Lucas," Margaret said. "Unless you're a police officer or an investigative journalist, I don't think there's anything you can do."

An idea struck, and I shot to my feet. "Well, maybe there *is* something I can do. Thank you for your time, priestesses."

I left the Imperium headquarters and rushed back to school, inspiration sizzling in my bones. If the Imperium Council thought there was only one way to help, then I was taking it. I wasn't here just to sit around and wait for people to die. I could do better to serve the coven.

And I would.

I marched down the hall, through one of the classrooms, and straight to Professor Carlisle's office. He was hunched over his desk, catching up on grades, when I entered the room.

"I'll do it," I announced.

Professor Carlisle looked up from his paperwork, a delightful smile on his face. "Mister Taylor. It's a pleasure to see you. What, may I ask, is it you want to do?"

"I'll take that position on the school paper you offered me last year," I stated.

His face fell. I'd never seen him look so pale before. "I'm sorry, but *The Epitaph* is no longer in print. No one joined the newspaper club this semester."

"Then we'll bring it back," I said confidently.

Professor Carlisle laughed, like he thought I was joking. "And what? You'll write the whole paper? You'll be the only club member?"

I shrugged. "If I have to be."

He kept on laughing, like the idea was hilarious. "It would never work. We'd never have enough content."

"Then I'll start my own publication," I said simply. I hadn't even realized I came up with the idea until I said it. "I guess I won't need an advisor."

I turned around and started to leave, but Professor Carlisle stopped me. "Mister Taylor, wait!"

His laughter had completely died. I turned to face him.

He eyed me curiously. "What exactly is it you'd like to report on?"

"I want to investigate the missing children," I told him.

He adjusted his glasses. "Well, that is quite a heavy topic. Are you sure?"

"Absolutely," I said.

He cocked an eyebrow. "And you'd do this on your own?"

"Yes," I said, my mind made up.

He sighed. "That won't be necessary. The school already has printing resources available, and I must say I've missed advising on the paper. Let's bring *The Epitaph* back."

"Really?" I asked, hope surging in my chest.

Professor Carlisle nodded. "Really. Let me know as soon as you have something worth printing."

I nodded. "I will."

I left the room feeling like I'd seized some sort of power back from the perp who did this. Two kids were gone, and nothing was going to change that. But we could stop it from happening again.

Whoever murdered those kids better watch out...

Because I was coming for them.

Continue The Reaper's Shadow to solve the mystery!

BONUS OFFERS

Find coloring pages, games, quizzes, and bonus content at hiddenlegendsbooks.com.

Join the *Orenda Academy: Hidden Legends Fan Group* on Facebook for all things Hidden Legends!

Check out the *College of Witchcraft Official Playlist* on Spotify!

Never miss a new release! Join Alicia's email list at aliciaradesauthor.com/newsletter.

About the Author

Alicia Rades is a USA Today bestselling author of young adult and new adult paranormal fiction. When she's not dreaming up magical stories, she's either binge-watching Netflix, meditating, or spending time with her family. She has an unhealthy obsession with psychic characters and writes with a deck of tarot cards next to her computer.

www.ingramcontent.com/pod-product-compliance
Lightning Source LLC
Chambersburg PA
CBHW060946190726
48286CB00005B/1442